LOVE LETTERS IN THE SAND

Liverpool, 1958: Nursery nurse Irene Miller falls for her friend Peggy's handsome older brother, Marty. But he is trapped in an unhappy marriage. Meanwhile, Irene's friend Peggy is desperate to marry her long-term boyfriend Pete, but Peggy's staunchly Catholic parents would never accept a Protestant son-in-law. When her mother decides to remarry, her brother heads off to sea, and she loses her job, Irene feels utterly alone in the world. An unexpected job offer from America offers her a lifeline. But it would mean never seeing Marty again. Will Irene and Peggy ever solve their problems by running away – or should they follow their hearts back home to Liverpool?

LOVE LETTERS IN THE SAND

by

June Francis

Magna Large Print Books
Long Preston, North Yorkshire,
BD23 4ND, England.

British Library Cataloguing in Publication Data.

Francis, June
    Love letters in the sand.

    A catalogue record of this book is
    available from the British Library

    ISBN   978-0-7505-4291-3

First published in Great Britain in 2015 by
Severn House Publishers Ltd.

Copyright © June Francis 2015

Cover illustration © Patricia Turner by arrangement with
Arcangel Images

The moral right of the author has been asserted.

Published in Large Print 2016 by arrangement with
Severn House Publishers Ltd.

Magna Large Print is an imprint of Library Magna Books Ltd.

Printed and bound in Great Britain by
T.J. (International) Ltd., Cornwall, PL28 8RW

Prologue

July 1957

She was going to die! Panic threatened to choke her and her head felt as if it were about to explode. If she tried to take a breath, her lungs would fill with water. A voice in her head cried, 'Don't give up! Keep going!'

But it was such a struggle and her arms felt like chunks of lead as she fought to raise her upper body above the surface of the water. At last she managed to gasp some air, only to choke on seawater. Her head went under again and strands of sodden hair clung to her face like ribbons of seaweed.

Frantically she attempted to claw it away and break the surface once more. The saltiness of the water stung her eyes so she could hardly see. She had lost all sense of direction. Where was the beach? The horizon? The sandbank? Was she imagining her mother's voice yelling, *'You stupid bloody fool, this isn't the time to play the hero!'*

Irene went under again and this time her terror was so paralysing that she could not move her arms or legs. Then she felt a tug on the back of her bathing costume and hope soared inside her. But almost straightaway, it struck her that the someone who had come to her rescue was having difficulty lifting her. Was that because her swim-

7

suit just soaked up water? Why couldn't her mother have bought her one of those new bikinis instead of this old thing? It was going to drag them both down!

Then with a mighty heave and a noise like a plunger in a blocked sink, she was sucked up and her head broke the surface. She recognized the face of her stepfather, although she could not see him clearly. Then his expression altered and his normally cheerful fat face convulsed and it was obvious he was having trouble breathing. She cried out to him and it was now her turn to try to keep him afloat.

Oh my God, St Jude and Our Lord, she prayed as he began to sink, dragging her down with him. She wanted to believe it was only a dream. Then she felt a stinging tug at her scalp and she was being hauled to the surface once more. Frantically she tried to hold on to her stepfather but to her horror he slipped from her grip.

She could breathe again. She was flipped over on to her back and she felt herself being towed. 'Make an effort, love,' an unfamiliar Scouse voice panted. She wanted to say *I'm trying!* but speaking was too difficult.

At last they reached the shallows and her feet scrabbled to get a grip. Waves lapped her goose-pimpled thighs and her curling toes gripped the wet sand. She collapsed on top of him. For several moments they just lay there, panting. Then he pushed her off him and she rolled on to the sand. It took an effort for her to turn her head but she had to see this man who had saved her life. Her eyes were sore from the seawater and his face was blurry and indistinct, but she could tell he was staring straight at her.

Then abruptly he heaved himself on to all fours and water trickled from his half-naked body into the sand. 'Think twice before you do anything so stupid again,' he rasped. 'You don't take risks with the currents and tide here!'

'But I saw a child with a dog on the sandbank and I knew there were patches of soft black sand between the channels and the tide had turned.' In her head the words had sounded loud but in reality they were slurred and barely above a whisper. And her rescuer seemed to vanish from sight.

Then, from a long way off, she heard her mother's voice ringing out. 'Where's Terence?'

Irene could only shake her head and weep.

'Yer bloody fool, do you realize what yer stupidity has cost us? Yer should have kept yer eye on the tide,' her mother screamed.

It was true. The tide had washed away the castle Irene had been helping the orphan children to build the day before, and gone too were the love letters written in the sand by her friends Pete Marshall and Peggy McGrath. The tide was also to wash up her stepfather's body further along the Lancashire coast the next day and Irene's life was never to be the same again.

One

'Are you deaf, girl?' cried an exasperated voice, shaking Irene's shoulder. 'Time yer were up! I've got to go out and I want yer to do something for me while yer still here.'

Irene Miller lifted her head from the pillow and blinked up at her mother. For a moment she could only stare at her and then she groaned. 'I dreamed I was drowning again.'

Maisie's lips tightened. 'It's God's punishment on yer. Yer could have been responsible for that young man's death as well as my Terence's because of yer daftness. Although who he was we'll probably never know. He didn't stop around to be thanked.'

Irene flinched, thinking how many times she had heard those words before. Her mother's accusations were the last thing she needed. Her guilt was punishment enough. 'I wish I could have thanked that young man. But you're not being fair, Mam. I'm a good swimmer and I'd always been told it was safe swimming in the sea when the tide was coming in. Besides, there really was a child on that sandbank playing with a dog.'

'Well, if yer were telling the truth, girl, then yer should have mentioned it to one of the lads and let them go.'

10

'I was already in the sea and thought it would be quicker if I went to warn her of the danger.' Irene flung back the bedclothes and climbed out of bed.

'There were no reports of a missing child, so someone must have been keeping their eye on her or she had the sense to head for shore,' said Maisie. 'If you'd done the same thing, Terence would still be here.'

'I've said before dozens of times and I'll say it again,' said Irene emphatically, 'I'm really, really sorry Uncle Terence died. He was a lovely man and a real hero. If it hadn't been for him keeping me afloat that bit longer, that bloke would never have been able to save me.'

Maisie sat abruptly on the pink candlewick bedspread. 'But it was all too much for Terence at his age! My husband gave his life for you!' Her mother's tone, once again, indicated she did not believe her daughter worthy of such a gift, though had her brother Jimmy been in her position she wondered if her mother would have felt differently. Jimmy had always been their mother's favourite.

Irene removed and folded her flower-sprigged flannelette pyjama top before popping it under her pillow. 'Do we have to go over this again?' she said wearily. 'Although he'd retired, Uncle Terence was a policeman to his very core and still saw it as his duty to rescue people. That it happened to be me in difficulty that time was just one of those things.'

'You should have thought twice before behaving like you were that girl who went to the rescue of those people who were shipwrecked years ago.'

'You mean Grace Darling,' muttered Irene, who had not thought anything of the sort at the time.

'The last thing I wanted was to be widowed again. It was bad enough losing yer dad in the war.' Maisie rose to her feet and went over to the dressing table to gaze at her reflection in the oval mirror. 'I like a man about the place,' she chunnered on. 'And I can't see our Jimmy staying around much longer. I suspect he's got a girl but is keeping quiet about her.'

Irene froze. 'What makes you say that?'

Maisie whirled round and stared at her only daughter. 'I'm not daft! Our Jimmy never used to bother with Brylcreem until recently.'

Irene swallowed a laugh. 'That's not much to go on! The group are being asked to play at more functions these days and he doesn't want his hair flopping about. They'll be playing at the Gianellis' New Year's Eve party tomorrow. You're still going, aren't you?' She reached for her flesh-coloured brassiere.

'I don't know. I mightn't be in the mood,' Maisie muttered.

Irene stared at her and suddenly noticed something that she should have been aware of earlier. 'You've put off your blacks!'

'And what if I have?' Maisie snapped. 'Black really isn't me colour. It leeches the roses from me cheeks. Besides, it's time I saw a bit of life again. I'm only thirty-nine. I need to start making the best of meself. Terence wouldn't have expected me to mourn forever.'

Forever! Irene thought cynically that it wasn't even six months since Terence had drowned and, despite the fact that theirs had been a marriage of convenience, her mother had certainly played the part of the grieving widow for all it was worth. Yet suddenly now here she was talking about moving on and starting over.

Irene felt uneasy as she fastened her bra and put on her vest. Was her mother thinking of marrying again? She considered Maisie to be a good-looking woman for her age – she had more or less kept her figure and she had no grey in her hair. It was only when she opened her mouth that the first impression was spoilt.

'So what are you going to do?' asked Irene. 'What bit of life d'you want to see?'

Maisie did not reply but headed for the door. 'Don't forget to wash the back kitchen floor for me.'

'I won't forget, but I was planning on going into town early,' said Irene, taking a clean pair of knickers from a drawer. 'I've only got two days in lieu.'

'I'm not asking much of yer,' snapped Maisie. 'I am yer mother and since I brought yer up almost single-handed, you ought to show a bit of gratitude, girl.' She hurried from the bedroom.

Irene pulled on a jumper and went after her. 'When will you be back?' she called down the stairs. 'Where are you going so early?'

'Ask no questions and yer'll get told no lies,' retorted Maisie from the lobby as she shrugged on a maroon, fur-collared coat.

'I'd never get to know anything if I didn't ask,' said Irene. 'I don't know why you have to be so secretive all of a sudden, Mam.'

13

'You'll find out soon enough,' Maisie muttered. 'And don't forget I want the back kitchen floor scrubbed on yer hands and knees! Don't yer be just wiping the tiles over with the mop.'

Irene sighed and gazed after her mother's retreating figure as she slammed the front door behind her.

Jimmy appeared in the kitchen doorway, wearing navy blue trousers and a thick navy blue sweater. 'Will you be long?' he called upstairs.

'No! That was Mam going out. Did she mention to you where she was going?'

'No. Didn't ask. Will you hurry up? I don't want to be late,' Jimmy replied.

Irene returned to her bedroom and finished getting ready. She combed her blonde hair and tied it in a ponytail before hurrying downstairs. As she passed through the kitchen, she asked Jimmy to pour her a cup of tea. He opened his mouth to speak but changed his mind as she whizzed into the back kitchen.

She ran the cold tap and reached for the block of Lux toilet soap and washed her face, neck and hands. She wished they had a bathroom like the one in her stepbrother Billy's modern house in Formby, but chance would be a fine thing.

She dried herself on a clean towel before returning to the kitchen. 'Have you noticed Mam's stopped wearing black? She said she wanted to see a bit of life and make the best of herself. I think it's because she'll be forty next birthday.'

Jimmy grinned. 'Who does she think she's kidding? She was thirty-nine three years ago. What is it with women and reaching forty?'

14

'The same as with men, I suppose,' said Irene moodily, sitting down at the table and reaching for the bread knife. She cut herself a slice from the loaf. 'Anyway, are you almost ready to leave?'

'Of course I am, you ninny, otherwise I wouldn't be wanting you to get a move on. Are you sure you want to go into town this early?'

'Yes!' said Irene firmly. 'I don't want to miss out on getting tickets for the pantomime at the Empire next week. "Cinderella" was great last year.'

'OK, as long as you're ready to leave in ten minutes,' said Jimmy, taking a comb from his pocket and reaching for the jar of Brylcreem in the sideboard cupboard. 'Remember this time last year we could ride on the "Ovee"? Alderman Braddock never did manage to save the Overhead Railway despite his determination to keep it open.' He placed a dab of hair cream on the palm of his hand and moved to the fireplace, gazing at his reflection in the mirror above the mantelpiece. He spread the Brylcreem into his light brown hair before combing the front into a quiff and the sides back into a DA.

Irene watched him as she reached for the cup of cooling tea he had poured. She took a mouthful, grimaced and reached for the sugar. 'It's going to take them ages to dismantle it,' she said, sugaring her tea before spreading plum jam on her bread. 'By the way, Mam thinks you've got a girl.'

Jimmy whirled round. 'What makes her think that? You haven't been saying anything, have you?'

'There's no way I'd mention Tony Gianelli's cousin Lucia having a crush on you. She's far too young and we both know it.'

15

'I wouldn't argue. But she's a good kid and has an old head on her shoulders. Still, I'm no cradle snatcher.'

Irene changed the subject. 'I'd like to know where Mam's gone and how long she'll be. She'll have a face on her if that floor's not scrubbed when she gets back.'

'You worry too much about her. Daft, when you're hardly here.'

Irene knew he was right but it was a habit from back when she did live permanently at home. She ate the last of the bread and jam and drained her teacup before going into the back kitchen and cleaning her teeth at the sink. Then she ran upstairs for her handbag, reappearing shortly after to find Jimmy wearing a donkey jacket and sailor's cap.

Irene dragged a woolly Fair Isle hat from the pocket of her green tent coat and pulled it over her hair. She drew a couple of blonde curls from beneath her hat so that they dangled in front of her ears. 'I wonder if I should get my ears pierced,' she murmured. 'Although Matron probably wouldn't approve.'

Jimmy rolled his eyes. 'Stop titivating and let's get going.'

'You're one to talk with your Tony Curtis quiff,' she teased. 'If only you had his good looks.'

'Watch your tongue, kid,' he said, elbowing her out of the way as they both attempted to get through the doorway at the same time.

The house was situated not far from the library and sausage factory where Maisie worked, as well as being only a short walk to Seaforth and Litherland railway station that had once been linked to the Overhead Railway at Seaforth Sands.

'So are you going to give it a few years and see if Lucia still fancies you when she's grown up?' asked Irene mischievously, hurrying along Bridge Road with its mixture of shops, some with mock Tudor designs fronting the living areas above, as well as terraced housing on the other side of the road.

Jimmy glanced at his sister. 'I'm not making plans. I just want to drift for the moment and enjoy myself.'

Irene nodded. 'She's not bad looking, but Maggie Gregory is better.'

'I thought you had no time for Maggie.'

'I don't. She likes herself enough for both of us. Besides, she used to be a real sneak and was horrible to her cousin Betty.'

'Well that's families for you, a mix of good and bad.'

Irene agreed. 'Remember the time Mam frightened the life out of you when she got that letter from her brother saying he'd met a girl and was getting married, so he wouldn't be coming home?'

Irene certainly had never forgotten it. The war had ended and their uncle had just been demobbed. The news had come as a terrible shock because Maisie had got it fixed in her head that she and her brother would live together as they had done since they were orphaned in early adolescence. She had been depending on him to help support his niece and nephew.

'I was lucky she only managed to hit me with a couple of potatoes instead of the saucepan,' said

17

Jimmy, grinning.

'She might have knocked you unconscious if you hadn't got out of there on the double.'

Fortunately, Irene had been on her way home from nursery school and had just crossed the Leeds and Liverpool canal when she and her teacher caught sight of Jimmy tearing towards them through the falling snow. He had blurted out that his Mam had gone mad and he did not know what to do. Nellie Lachlan had dealt with the situation, just as Irene knew she would. From that moment on Irene decided that when she grew up she wanted to be just like her.

Nellie had been widowed during the war and, after miscarrying her baby, she had helped out at the private nursery which Jimmy and Irene had attended until it closed down. After the war Nellie had married Michelangelo Gianelli, a half-English, half-Italian former POW, a widower with a small son. They and their children lived on the other side of the canal. They were a musical family and it was that interest in music which had led to Irene getting to know Betty Booth, who had become her best friend.

Irene sighed, thinking about Betty and how much she missed her. She had married an American, Stuart Anderson, and now lived in California.

'Are you listening to me, our kid?' Jimmy asked, pausing outside the entrance to the railway station.

Irene bit her lip. 'Sorry, I was thinking of Betty thousands of miles away in San Jose.'

'You should save up and go and visit her,' said Jimmy, turning into the entrance and heading up

18

the incline that led to the ticket office and railway platforms.

Irene slanted him a look of disbelief. 'How much d'you think I get paid? Even though I passed my exams and I'm a qualified nursery nurse now I still don't get paid enough to save that much.'

'OK! Keep your hair on! It's you that wanted to train as a nursery nurse.'

Irene dug her hands deep into her pockets and said quietly, 'I love working with children.' She increased her pace in order to keep up with her brother. 'The kids at Fair Haven are so rewarding, especially those who have disabilities that might make them unattractive to prospective adoptive parents. They'll have tougher lives than we ever had, despite us losing our dad when we were only little.'

Jimmy said seriously, 'I remember when you were a toddler. You wanted a doll, one whose eyes opened and shut.'

'I didn't get it though,' said Irene wryly.

'I didn't get the train set I asked for either,' said Jimmy, reaching into a pocket for money. 'If I ever have a son, the first thing I'll buy him will be a train set.'

Irene delved into her handbag. 'You might have all daughters who'll demand a walking, talking doll.'

'They'll have a train set and like it,' laughed Jimmy, handing over money for their tickets.

'Even Meccano won't have a miniature Overhead Railway if that's what you had in mind,' she said with amusement in her voice.

'More's the pity,' said a man behind them. 'Me

19

and hundreds of others working along the dock road really miss it. You do realize it used to run the whole seven miles of the dock road from the Dingle to Seaforth Sands, girl?'

Jimmy glanced at the elderly man with the moustache. 'Hello, Mr Murphy.'

'Hello, Jimmy.' He gazed in the direction of Gladstone Dock half a mile or so away. 'This time last year we boarded it for the last time together.'

'It wouldn't surprise me if they come to regret dismantling it,' said Jimmy, handing a railway ticket to his sister.

Her eyes lit up and she thanked him and put her money back in her purse. 'Brothers have some use after all,' she said.

'So this is your sister,' said Mr Murphy, eyeing Irene up and down.

'Aye,' said Jimmy, strolling towards the platform for the Liverpool train.

'I remember her being born,' said Mr Murphy, hobbling after him. 'She's grown into a good-looking lass. Your dad would have been proud of her.'

'You knew my dad!' Irene exclaimed.

'Aye. If I hadn't been sick that night during the Blitz, most likely I'd have been killed alongside him,' said the elderly man. 'He was a good worker and a brave man. I remember when we were both working at Gladstone Dock, just after it was built. The old king was on the throne then.'

'You mean the Queen's father?' said Irene.

'Naw! His father! Of course, before Gladstone Dock was built, Seaforth Sands was a popular place for day trippers, although yer had to be

20

careful where yer walked.' Mr Murphy stroked his moustache. 'I remember my old mother having a nasty experience when she got stuck in a patch of sinking sand. I was only a kid at the time and was terrified we wouldn't be able to get her out. She ruined a brand-new pair of white kid sandals and seemed more upset about that than the fact that she might have been sucked under.'

'My Mam would be the same,' said Jimmy. 'She likes to wear nice things. Still, she's not really one for going near the water. Can't swim.'

'My mother didn't swim either. It wasn't considered the done thing in her day, taking off your clothes in public. As for the bathing suits they wear today...' His bushy grey eyebrows shot up. 'Me mam would have had a fit if she'd known what giving women the vote would lead to! Have you seen that picture in the newspaper of Diana Dors wearing a mink bikini?'

Irene had seen it and wished she had the money to afford a mink bikini, instead of the ugly all-in-one woollen swimming costume that was no longer in her possession. She had chucked it in the bin after that fateful day.

Jimmy touched her shoulder. 'You OK?'

'Just thinking.'

'You think too much,' he said frankly. 'Does you no good. Anyway, here comes the train.'

She followed him and Mr Murphy and several other passengers into a carriage, hoping to get a window seat because she enjoyed watching the scenery going past. It wasn't as good as being on the Ovee with its view of the docks and the Mersey. Fortunately, because she was small and reasonably slender, she managed to squeeze in between two women who made room for her.

Her thoughts drifted, even as she half-listened to Jimmy and Mr Murphy discussing the money that must be getting spent dismantling the Ovee – money that they felt should have been used to repair and renovate the cast iron structure of that most unique railway, which had opened in 1893 and soon earned itself the nickname of the Dockers' Umbrella. It had been an ideal place for dock workers to shelter from the rain and some Liverpudlians had also attempted to shield themselves from falling bombs during the war, with varying success.

'Everything is changing,' she heard a woman say.

'And not always for the better,' said another.

Irene thought about change. The trams were no more, and even the Punch and Judy show that had been a feature of Lime Street for years was no longer the attraction it had once been. Her mother blamed the television, which did not make sense to Irene because there were scarcely any children's programmes on telly, although some of the three- and four-year-olds at the children's home enjoyed *Andy Pandy* or *Bill and Ben, the Flower Pot Men*. On Fridays there was also *The Woodentops*.

She wondered if she would ever have children of her own, although she was in no rush to get married and settle down. She wanted to have some fun, travel maybe. She would do what her brother suggested and try to save up and go to America and visit Betty. She thought of what she had seen of the States at the cinema and what Betty had written in letters about her new home in California.

Irene was roused from her thoughts as the train drew up at Orrell Road station and a number of passengers departed, while others entered their carriage. To her surprise she heard a familiar voice greet her brother. She glanced up and smiled at the dark-haired Pete Marshall. He was the same age as Jimmy, although he looked older due to the lines that pain had etched on his face.

'I didn't know you used the train,' she said.

'I don't normally,' replied Pete, limping over to where she and Jimmy were seated. 'I felt like a change. I'm surprised to see you here.'

Neither made an effort to stand and offer him their seat, knowing he was touchy about being a cripple. 'I've a couple of days off, so I'm going into town to book tickets for the pantomime,' said Irene, smiling.

'Don't you wish you had a car, Pete?' said Jimmy.

'Not half,' said Pete with a wry smile.

He and Jimmy began to discuss the merits of various cars, although no doubt the most either could afford would be an old banger and, as neither knew much about the innards of cars, would cost them all their spare cash in repairs when it broke down.

Pete was a clerk in a shipping office at King's Dock. Before the accident that had crippled him, he'd had other ambitions. Irene thought of his twin brother, Norman, who was training to be a marine engineer. She could not help but feel sorry for Pete, who had once been a real dare-devil, but it was that recklessness that had led to

23

him falling from a first-floor window.

The men's conversation moved on to the subject of football and she stopped listening.

The train pulled in at Sandhills and some passengers left while others climbed aboard. Irene glanced at one of the young men who entered and their eyes met. She would have looked away, only he was staring at her as if he could not believe his eyes. Her heart began to pound. She had the strangest feeling that they had met before, although she could not think where. Then an older man standing beside him spoke to him and he looked away. Irene now became aware that she was being stared at by someone else and realized it was Peggy McGrath. Irene smiled, expecting Peggy to speak before shifting her attention to Pete. The two had been seeing each other off and on for a long time. Their friends wondered if they would ever get married. To her surprise Peggy didn't say a word and neither she nor Pete made any sign of knowing the other.

Irene sighed, realizing that they must have broken up again. It was time they made up their minds one way or another about the future, she thought, willing Peggy to say something – anything – to Pete, whom she regarded as extremely vulnerable beneath his generally taciturn exterior.

Then Irene realized that the younger of the two men who had got on the train with Peggy was staring at her again. He raised an eyebrow. To her annoyance she blushed. Hurriedly she turned to her brother and said the first thing that came into her head. He looked at her as if she had lost the plot.

'What are you asking me that for? You know I'm going to be there. I'm playing guitar for the group,' he said.

'Sorry,' she muttered, wishing she could sink through the floor. 'I don't know what I was thinking. I meant to ask Pete if he was going to the party.'

Pete nodded.

She pinned on a smile. 'I'm looking forward to it, aren't you?'

He shrugged.

'We could shuffle around the floor,' she suggested. 'Soft-shoe shuffle as they danced it in the old days?'

That brought a smile to his good-looking face. 'Can't wait.'

'It's Irene, isn't it?' Peggy broke in.

The question caused Irene to stare at her as if she had now run mad.

'Surely you don't normally take the train into town for work?' Peggy went on.

Irene was aware of her brother grinning. 'No, I work in the opposite direction,' she said, deciding to play Peggy's game. 'I've a couple of days off from work in lieu of working Christmas and Boxing Day.' She paused. 'Didn't you used to work with Jeanette?'

'That's right.' Peggy smiled. 'I haven't seen much of her since she got married. What about you?'

'Had a word with her the other Saturday when I was going up to Lenny's place on Hope Street,' said Irene. 'Apparently she's back working in the milk bar on Leece Street, part-time. I suppose once she starts with a baby she'll give it up.'

At that moment, the older man who had climbed into the carriage at the same time as the other two stood up. 'See you tonight, Peggy,' he said, and left.

He was followed by several other passengers but the younger man who had been staring at Irene unfurled his newspaper and began to read the sports page on the back.

'That was me dad,' whispered Peggy, bringing her head down close to Irene's. 'I didn't want him knowing I knew you three. He'd only demand to know all the ins and outs about how we met, where we met, what colour you are...' She glanced at Pete and frowned before returning her attention to Irene. 'So what's this about a party?'

'It's at the Gianellis' tomorrow evening,' she replied.

'I suppose Tony'll be singing,' said Peggy. 'Fabulous voice! And Jimmy...' She turned to him. 'You'll be playing the guitar, you said?'

He nodded.

Peggy smiled. 'You remind me of Elvis with that quiff,' she said.

'He only copied it from Tony Curtis,' said Irene who, unlike her brother, was not an Elvis fan. 'I prefer Pat Boone and his "Love Letters in the Sand".'

'I used to like that,' said Peggy, casting another glance at Pete.

'Have you heard "Jailhouse Rock"?' asked Jimmy enthusiastically.

'No, but I've heard it's a hit in America,' countered Peggy. 'Along with the film which will probably arrive here next year. I've a feeling I'll probably prefer Elvis singing "Let Me Be Your Teddy Bear" that was out this summer.'

'Well, you're a girl, you would,' said Jimmy. 'A mate on one of the liners brought me the record of *Jailhouse*.'

Irene glanced at her brother. 'But you've the sheet music of "Teddy Bear", haven't you?'

Jimmy nodded. 'We're going to have a go at it tomorrow evening.'

'I'd like to hear you play,' said Peggy, darting a look first at the man next to her, who seemed absorbed by the sports page, and then at Pete before giving Jimmy and Irene all her attention once more.

'I'm sure Mr and Mrs Gianelli won't mind you coming along,' said Irene helpfully.

'I'll be there then,' whispered Peggy. 'What time does it start?'

Irene told her.

Peggy nudged the arm of the man standing next to her, almost causing him to drop the newspaper. 'No saying anything to Mam and Dad, Marty!'

Marty! Irene squeezed her eyes shut and then opened them and stared at him. *Peggy's brother!* 'You're going to have to tell them something, our kid,' he was saying. 'They'll be expecting you home when the clock strikes midnight.'

Peggy scowled. 'Why should I have to be in by then? I'm not bloody Cinderella.'

'Don't swear,' he chided. 'I hate hearing a woman swear.'

Peggy sighed heavily. 'You swear! And you wouldn't think the way Dad behaves that I'm over twenty-one. You're not going to be at ours at

27

that time, are you?'

'No, but only because I've got to be somewhere else,' said Marty, a shadow crossing his face. 'It's no secret.'

'But with our Tommy having been gone for nearly four years now, Mam'll want you to let the new year in,' said Peggy. 'You know he's broken her heart. The swine.'

'I'm no tall, dark stranger!' Marty frowned. 'I suppose Tommy could be dead. Bernie thinks he's dead. Anyway, Mam's got you girls and I can't get out of the big family reunion on New Year's Eve. The cousin is coming over from Ireland. He's going to let the new year in. I could suggest he lets new year in at Mam and Dad's, as well, if you like? That might let you off the leash.'

Peggy's face brightened. 'That's all right then. You getting off at Central?' He nodded. 'I'll get off at Moorfields with Jimmy and change trains to St James Street,' she said.

Jimmy and Marty nodded at each other. Pete glanced at them but remained silent. Irene looked at him, wondering if he had caught this train hoping to see Peggy and straighten matters out between them. If so it didn't appear that his plan was going to work.

Jimmy and Peggy left the carriage as arranged and they'd hardly vanished from sight when Pete followed in their wake. Irene felt sorry for him but guessed there was nothing she could do to make things right for him and Peggy.

She was suddenly conscious of the brother, Marty, staring at her again. For a moment she boldly stared back before lowering her gaze. She

28

had seen enough to conclude that he was not what you'd call handsome but had nice blue eyes.

At last the train arrived at Central Station and she wasted no time getting off and hurrying out of the station. Once on the pavement she hesitated before walking up Ranelagh Street towards Lewis's, planning to gaze in the shop windows. Despite having no money to spare, she enjoyed window-shopping. The January sales would be starting soon and there were already mannequins dressed for the onslaught. She paused a moment and gazed at a powder-blue jersey wool dress and matching long cardigan on a dummy.

'That's an outfit the Queen Mother would wear,' said a voice behind her.

Irene whirled round to find herself staring at Marty. 'I wasn't intending to buy it,' she said, collecting herself.

'I thought you might have been fancying a new outfit for the party you mentioned on the train.'

'No, but there's no harm in looking.'

She carried on walking and he fell into step beside her. 'D'you work in town?' he asked.

'If you were listening to what I said to your sister earlier, you'll have heard me say I work in the opposite direction. I've only come in to get tickets for the Empire. I thought of taking my Mam for her birthday.'

He smiled. 'It's "Babes in the Wood" with Jimmy Jewel and Ben Warriss. They make me laugh but I doubt they'll be as good as last year's star of the show.'

She nodded. 'I remember how funny Ken Dodd was – and the Beverley Sisters were good as well.

Mam had seen him in a show in Blackpool the other year and she really liked him.'

'Apparently he started performing when he was just a kid, gave shows in his backyard,' said Marty.

'Dorothy Wilson, the Liverpool actress, used to do the same,' said Irene. 'It must make a difference starting so early to become a big star.'

He nodded and changed the subject. 'The bloke with the limp...'

She stiffened. 'What about him?'

'He knows our Peg, doesn't he?'

'Why ask me?' she said bluntly. 'You're her brother! Ask her!'

'Yeah, and that's why it'd be a waste of time me asking her,' he said grimly. 'Is he a Proddy?'

She stopped and stared at him. 'I've just realized, you're the brother that Jeanette went to the wrestling with when she was attacked outside the Stadium a few years back.'

'It was a terrible thing to happen.' Marty's expression was unhappy. 'She was lucky to get away without being injured. If she'd been prepared to wait for me, I could have saved her from being frightened out of her wits. Anyway, they got the bloke and he was put away.' He paused. 'So, this bloke with the limp...'

'Why are you so interested in him?' she burst out. 'Anyway, if you wanted to know more about him, why didn't you speak to him? Now, I've no more time to waste, so I'll be saying tarrah!' Irene crossed the road into Lime Street, thinking about what she had heard from Jeanette about Peggy's brother having once beaten up a bloke for being

30

too familiar with his sister. She certainly didn't want Marty having a go at Pete Marshall who might have trouble defending himself.

Two

Irene let herself into the house and stood with her back to the front door, listening. She thought she could hear someone moaning but decided it must only be the wind. She hurried up the lobby, stuffing her woolly hat and gloves in the pockets of her coat before hanging it on a hook on the wall at the foot of the stairs. She could still hear the moaning and it seemed to be coming from the kitchen. She opened the door cautiously, only to freeze when she saw her mother, still wearing her hat and coat, huddled on the sofa which had been moved closer to the fire.

Irene's heart began to thud and she hurried over to the sofa and knelt beside it. 'Mam, what's wrong?' she asked, placing a hand on her shoulder.

Maisie lifted her head, holding a bloodstained handkerchief to her mouth. Irene gasped. 'What have you done to your face? Did you walk into a lamp post?'

'No, I've had me bloody teeth out,' Maisie mumbled through the handkerchief.

'You mean ... all of them?' cried Irene, flabbergasted.

Maisie nodded.

Irene sat back on her heels, scarcely able to believe that her mother had visited the dentist, never mind had the guts to have all her teeth taken out. 'Why didn't you say that you were going? I would have gone with you!' Irene cried.

'I didn't want yer with me,' Maisie mumbled, wincing as she dabbed at her swollen upper lip. 'I asked Gertie Marshall instead because I had to have someone with me.'

'You mean the twins' mam?'

'I didn't know we knew any other Marshalls,' said Maisie sarcastically, leaning her head back against the cushion.

'Sorry, didn't think,' said Irene, glancing towards the closed door to the back kitchen. 'Is she still here?' she asked, dropping her voice.

'No, she had to go. She's looking after her granddaughter this afternoon. I wish yer'd stop asking me bloody questions,' she added fretfully. 'I'm suffering here.'

'Sorry, Mam.' Irene would have liked answers to several more questions but she made do with asking, 'Would you like a cup of tea and for me to put more coal on the fire?'

'That would be good of yer, girl.' Maisie gazed at her daughter from beneath drooping eyelids. 'I don't want anything to eat yet but if yer could cook yours and our Jimmy's tea this evening that would save me getting up from this sofa.' She closed her eyes. 'Anyway, they're out now and soon I'll have a mouthful of teeth just like a Maclean toothpaste advert.'

An image of a shark flashed into Irene's mind but she kept quiet about it and went to put the kettle on. She could not help wondering why her mother had decided to have all her teeth out today of all days. It wasn't as if she had been complaining of toothache recently, although she did have a mouthful of discoloured teeth due to her bad smoking habit. Suddenly it occurred to Irene that it might have had something to do with Maisie's New Year's resolution to make the best of herself. She would have been better giving up smoking.

While she was waiting for the kettle to boil she put plenty of milk in her mother's cup as well as two sugars, and then she built up the fire.

'How about filling me a hot water bottle, love?' Maisie murmured from the sofa, without opening her eyes.

Irene returned to the back kitchen and, after making a pot of tea, put the kettle on once more and made herself a brawn butty, having dropped in at the cooked meat shop on Bridge Road on her way home. She gazed down at the red and navy tiles and then placed the two cups of tea and a plate with her sandwich on a tray, thinking that her mother's suffering had driven all thought of the floor being scrubbed from her mind.

She helped Maisie to sit up against a couple of cushions and handed her a cup of tea. 'I don't suppose you'll be fit to go to the Gianellis' New Year party tomorrow night?' she said.

Maisie stared at her in disbelief. 'Too bloody right, I won't,' she mumbled. 'At least there's a silver lining to every dark cloud.' She took a cautious sip of tea. 'I'm glad yer had the sense to think I wouldn't be able to drink it hot,' she added.

'What d'you mean "dark cloud", Mam? What have you got against Nellie Gianelli?' Irene bit

33

into her brawn butty.

'Why should I have anything against her? It's this rock'n'roll music I can't stand but don't yer go telling our Jimmy that.'

Irene did not quite believe her mother. 'It wouldn't be all rock'n'roll. There's bound to be some waltzes and foxtrots and people doing the hokey-cokey and the Conga. But I can understand you not feeling up to going if you're suffering.'

'It's not only that I'm suffering; it's that I won't be wanting to open me mouth when I haven't a tooth in me head, yer dafty.' Maisie eyed Irene's half-eaten brawn butty in frustration. 'I'm hungry.'

Irene almost offered the sandwich to her mother but thought better of it. 'I'd make you one, Mam, but you'd have difficulty eating it.'

'I suppose yer right.' Maisie sipped her tea. 'Good cup of tea this, and not too hot.'

'Thanks.' Praise was not often forthcoming from her mother so Irene was pleased to hear it. 'Could you manage something to eat a bit later? I could do you some Heinz cream of chicken soup?'

Maisie nodded. 'Thanks, love. I'll see how I am in an hour.' She drained the cup and placed it in its saucer and put both on the floor. Then she leaned back and closed her eyes. 'And don't be forgetting to scrub that kitchen floor,' she muttered.

Irene went into the back kitchen. She opened a can and put the soup in a pan to heat up later. While she scrubbed the tiles on her hands and knees, her thoughts were of the party tomorrow evening. She came to the conclusion it would be selfish of her to leave her mother alone and in pain at home. Shame! She would have liked to see how Peggy and Pete were with each other away from the watchful eyes of her father and brother.

Her thoughts drifted to the conversation she'd had with Marty McGrath. She had remembered more of the story surrounding Jeanette's evening out with him at the Stadium. Jeanette had only agreed to go in exchange for a favour he'd done for her. Marty had, apparently, fallen out with his girlfriend and decided to try and get her back by making her jealous. It was a few years ago now but as far as Irene knew the plan had worked.

But had he married the girlfriend?

Irene realized that she really would like to know. It should be easy to find out. She might not be going to the party but Jimmy would and he could ask Peggy.

'You look like death warmed up, Mam,' said Jimmy, after recovering from the initial shock of finding his mother lying on the sofa, hugging a hot water bottle.

'Thanks,' she mumbled, closing her eyes.

He hesitated and went out again, to return not long after with a bowl containing three hyacinths in bud. 'By the time these flower, Mam, you'll have your new teeth and be flashing dazzling smiles, just like a film star,' he said.

Maisie's expression was pleased. 'You're a good lad! Put them where I can see them. And Irene, could you get me two Aspro and another cup of tea? I could be a reasonably happy woman if you also reheated this hot water bottle and put it in my bed. I'll go up early and read my *Red Letter* magazine there.'

Once Maisie had disappeared upstairs, Irene and Jimmy sat down to plates of home-made chips, fried egg and beans. Over the meal, she told him about her conversation with Peggy's brother.

'Perhaps I'm making more of it than I should,' she said, dipping a chip in a beautifully golden egg yolk. 'What d'you think? Could Marty have caught sight of Peggy and Pete together in the past?'

'How should I know? Anyway, it's none of our business,' said Jimmy, making a chip butty.

'But they're our friends,' said Irene, frowning.

Jimmy shrugged and bit into his butty. 'So what? I'm not interfering,' he said with his mouth full. 'Especially knowing Peggy's a Catholic and Pete isn't! If her father's dead set against her marrying a Proddy, then it can only mean trouble all round. You keep out of it.'

Irene had decided that she did not want to keep out of it but knew it was pointless saying so to her brother. Only when the pair of them had finished their meal and were drinking a second cup of tea did she say, 'Mam married Uncle Terence and he was a Proddy!'

'He wasn't religious – and you can bet it was she who stipulated they married at English Martyrs.'

'But Mam allowed me to go with my friends to the state school at Litherland High, and she's best mates with Gertie who's a Proddy,' she countered.

'That's because she doesn't consider a girl's education as important as a boy's. I bet if Dad hadn't been killed in the war, he would have insisted on you going to a convent school. From what I've

36

heard, he was strict Irish Catholic. I bet it's the same with Peggy's father.'

Irene sighed, drained her teacup to the dregs and stood up. 'It's not right. We're supposed to love each other, even our enemies.'

He shrugged. 'Some hope! Anyway, you'll find a lot of the oldies saying you're better sticking with your own kind.'

'But times are changing!' Irene insisted. 'You can't tell me that two wars and the Labour party haven't made a difference to how people view religion, the class system and a woman's place in the scheme of things.'

Jimmy yawned and stretched. 'You're not going to start banging on about women's rights, are you?'

She felt her temper rising. 'What's wrong with women wanting equal wages with men for the same job? Besides, they don't want to be stuck at home all day with kids. These days a lot of wives don't want to give up their jobs once they're married. Some want to carry on working even when a baby comes along.'

'OK! Don't lose your rag! I wasn't looking for an argument. I'm all for women getting their due. Although what this has to do with Peggy and Pete, I don't know.'

'She shouldn't care about having her father's permission when it comes to marrying the person she loves,' said Irene, her hands gripping the edge of the table. 'Especially when she's already over twenty-one. It's too, *too* old-fashioned! We're not living in Victorian times any more! Parents don't own their children, so fathers shouldn't be giving away their daughters as if they were parcels for husbands to unwrap once they're married!'

Jimmy looked shocked. 'What a thing to say! I wish you'd stop going on. Go and do something useful, like wash the dishes.'

She gasped. 'I hope that's a joke! Anyway, I'll only wash them if you dry!'

Jimmy grinned unexpectedly. 'Anything for a bit of peace.' He stood up. 'I don't know why you go on the way you do when you have a job that only women do.'

'Because I'm not just thinking about myself, that's why!' she snapped.

'OK! I hope there's nothing more you're going to nag about,' he groaned, picking up his plate and cutlery.

Irene hesitated. 'Well, actually there is. Could you ask Peggy whether her brother, Marty, married that girl who went for Jeanette at the Stadium?'

'What for?' He fixed her with a stare. 'You're not fancying him, are you? The way you were looking at him on the train I thought it might have been love at first sight with you.'

She let out a tinkle of laughter. 'You are joking? Forget I asked! I was just being nosy. I don't suppose it's important. It's not as if it's going to change my life, is it?'

Three

Peggy drew the skirts of the scarlet tent coat, which had been a Christmas present to herself, tightly about her legs. The last thing she wanted was to get flakes of grimy whitewash emulsion on the material. Carefully, she drew back the bolt on the backyard door, glad that at least her father was handy with the oilcan. The other bolt lower down made scarcely a sound and neither did the latch when she lifted it, enabling her to slip through the gap between door and frame like a shadow.

She closed the door and released the breath she had been holding in. Then she walked as swiftly as possible in the black patent-leather high heels along the entry, lit only at the far end by a street lamp on a yard wall. She came to a shorter entry that ran between the end house on their street and the pub on the corner that faced on to the main road.

The din from the customers talking and singing and that of a piano being played was ear-splitting. A young man, hanging about outside the pub with some others, wolf-whistled as she click-clacked past the group. A faint smile curved her painted lips as she stood waiting to cross Scotland Road to the bus stop on the other side.

A hand suddenly clapped her on the shoulder, causing her to almost jump out of her skin. 'Where d'you think you're going?' growled her father.

39

Peggy had her answer ready before he spun her round to face him. She presumed Marty had made no mention of her plans to their parents. 'I've a message for Bernie!' she blurted out.

'Who's this message from?' demanded her father.

Peggy moistened her lips. 'You can't expect me to tell you that, Dad. It's private!'

He prodded her with his forefinger. 'You shouldn't be delivering private messages to her. What's she up to? I've never trusted her. Blowsy, big-mouthed, she tricked my son into marriage.' William McGrath's heavy-lidded eyes were like slits. 'As for you, daughter, you not only seem to think I'm half-blind, believing you can sneak out the back way, but you're a fool if you think I'll fall for that tale! I want to see this message.'

Despite her shaking knees and the sick feeling in her stomach, Peggy managed to say in a trembling voice, 'It's by word of mouth, Dad. And I can't tell you because I crossed my heart and hoped to die when asked.'

'Don't you dare to defy me, girl!' His fingers tightened on her shoulder. 'You'll tell me now or you'll be sorry. Besides, I'm not having a daughter of mine walking the streets alone on New Year's Eve, all dressed up to the nines and with a painted face. People will think you're a tart!'

The insult angered her. 'I'm no tart! And it's an important message!'

His eyes narrowed. 'The pair of you are meeting someone, aren't you? And her a married woman!'

Before she could say another word, a familiar voice said, 'What's going on?'

40

Peggy experienced a flood of relief and smiled at Marty. He was accompanied by the cousin from Ireland. They were carrying a crate of beer between them and she guessed they were taking it to Bernie's mother's house where the whole family would be celebrating the arrival of 1958.

'This one says she's got a message for Bernie,' said William. 'She won't tell me what it says. I'd have it out with that wife of yours, if I were you, lad! Wives shouldn't be having secrets from their husbands.'

Marty's eyes flicked over his sister's face. 'It's probably just some women's thing and nothing to get worked up about, Dad.'

Growing up with a mother and two sisters and then living with Bernie, her mother, a widowed sister and her daughter under the same roof for near enough four years, he had long come to the conclusion that a man was best turning a blind eye to women's shenanigans.

William scowled. 'You're not going to do anything?'

'What d'you expect me to do, Dad? Use thumbscrews on our Peg? She can come along with me and Dougal and give the message to Bernie.' He jerked his head in his sister's direction. 'Let's be having you then!'

Peggy felt the pressure on her shoulder slacken as her father removed his hand. 'You'd better not be late getting back, girl,' he warned. 'As for you, Martin, make sure she gets home safe. Now promise me, the pair of you.'

They both promised, knowing it was easier than arguing. Then they watched their father go

41

straight into the pub.

Peggy glanced at Marty. 'Thanks! I'll be seeing you.' She made to cross the road.

'Not so fast,' he said, grabbing her arm before lowering his side of the beer crate to the ground with his other hand. 'Where d'you think you're going?'

'As if you didn't know,' she said. 'Let me go! If you're not careful, you'll be turning into Dad!'

Marty's well-formed mouth tightened. 'Dougal, you hold on to the crate. I need to sort our Peg out.'

'I'll leave you to it,' said Bernie's cousin from Ireland, and headed off along the pavement dragging the crate with one end lifted off the ground.

'I hope you're not going to try and stop me having some fun?' said Peggy, tapping her foot on the ground. 'Living with Mam and Dad now you and Tommy are no longer at home isn't a barrel of laughs.'

'It's never been a barrel of laughs,' said Marty, keeping a tight grip on her arm. 'But I don't like the idea of you travelling about on your own on New Year's Eve. Too many drunks and mad drivers.'

'I'll be fine!' she said, attempting to prise his fingers from her arm. 'I'll get Jimmy to see me home.'

'Jimmy! You mean the guitarist on the train?'

'That's him. He's a nice Catholic boy,' she said with an edge to her voice.

Marty stared at her unblinking. 'He's not the one you've been seeing, though, is he?'

Her eyes widened. 'I don't know what you mean.'

Marty's eyes narrowed. 'This message you have for Bernie doesn't exist, does it?'

'It does!' she said indignantly. 'It's from an old workmate of hers. She wants to meet up in town and have a coffee and a chat. You can give the message to Bernie for me, save me the effort. Her name's Marie Gallagher, and the meeting place, if Bernie can make it, is Lyon's cafe on Lime Street at eleven o'clock on Friday. Now can I go? I've already missed one bus, I don't want to miss another.'

'I'll see you across the road.'

'I'm not a little kid! I can look after myself,' she said, exasperated, not putting it past her brother to accompany her all the way to the Gianellis' house. He could be so bossy at times!

Fortunately there wasn't much of a queue at the bus stop and he released her.

'I want the address, just in case,' he said.

Just in case of what? she wondered. *Does he think I'm going to vanish off the face of the earth like our Tommy?* She knew from that stubborn expression on Marty's face that she was going to have to tell him. Brothers! They could be a real pain in the neck.

As she sat on the bus, her mood changed and she was conscious of a bubbly feeling inside her. Despite their latest quarrel, she was looking forward to seeing Pete. If only he'd been Catholic, how simple her life would be. They wanted to get married but religion always got in the way of them deciding to go ahead and tie the knot. They were forever going over the same old ground and both of them ended up hurt, angry and frustrated.

43

Last time they quarrelled, Pete had the nerve to call her a coward, saying that she enjoyed leading him on and then calling a halt as she didn't want to get into trouble. He'd shocked her when he'd said that perhaps the best way out of their situation was for her to get pregnant. *Never!* She hadn't forgotten the names her father had called Bernie and Marty for 'jumping the gun' as William had put it. The worst of it was that she wanted Pete as much as he wanted her, he just didn't understand how important having a white wedding in her own church was to her. He had no time for religion, although that did not stop him from going to church at Christmas with his mother. She had yet to meet widow Gertie Marshall and the thought of doing so had her all on edge because she had the feeling that no girl was going to be good enough for her Pete. The accident that caused him to spend months in hospital had forged a special bond between mother and son. She might not have been so loving if she had known what he'd been up to at the time.

Pete thought it was well past time that Peggy met his mother and he confronted her parents. She had refused point-blank. The very thought of him coming face to face with her parents filled her with dread. She did not need to be told that her fear was out of all proportion because Pete had already half-promised to marry in her church. Even so, once her father discovered that Pete was not a Catholic, she just knew an encounter between the two men would be fraught with unpleasantness. It would take a miracle for Pete to get over the threshold once he admitted to being a Proddy.

Even if Pete was allowed inside the house there was the matter of his gammy leg. Her father was bound to comment on it. If he did, Pete would just walk out because he was so touchy about being what he called a cripple.

The whole situation was hopeless, she thought miserably. She was wasting her time even being on this bus. It would be more sensible to get off at the next stop and catch a bus into town and go to the cinema. How she wished she was Irene Miller, who had no father, just a mother who didn't care who you married, as long as you didn't end up a spinster looking after someone else's kids.

Four

Irene watched her mother remove a pipe cleaner from a lock of hair that sprang back into a curl. 'You're not going out tonight after all, are you, Mam?'

'Don't be daft, girl, but I don't need yer here,' Maisie mumbled. 'Gertie's coming round, and a couple of other friends, so you can go to the Gianellis' party with a clear conscience.'

Irene felt a lift of her heart and then just as quickly came a sinking feeling. 'If you're thinking you're going to spoil my evening because I decided to stay home and keep you company, forget it, Mam! I don't mind seeing the New Year in with you.'

'Are yer calling me a liar, daughter?'

45

'No, but I didn't think you'd be up to having friends in.'

'I'm telling yer the truth! I really have got the girls coming round.' Maisie sighed heavily. 'Cross me bloody heart!'

'Well, even if you have, they're going to need food and drink and I can help you prepare that.'

'They're bringing the food and drink, so you can scoot,' said Maisie, sounding exasperated as she picked up a hairbrush.

That's a relief, thought Irene. 'Who's coming besides Gertie?'

'Doris from up the street and Aline, who works with us. They're both widows. Aline is originally from Glasgow and she's promised to bring some Scottish dancing records and a bottle of whisky.' Maisie gave a gummy grin. 'That'll deaden me pain. We might even have a go at the Highland Fling.' She eyed the tartan trews that Irene was wearing. 'If I thought I'd fit into those, I'd borrow them.'

Irene rolled her eyes. 'I have to admire your guts, Mam.'

Maisie tilted her head to one side. 'I'm determined to enjoy meself this evening as much as I can. Anyway, go and get changed and I'll let yer know whether yer pass muster. It's time you found yerself a fella. I suppose there might be some good ones at the party.'

Irene wished her mother wouldn't go on about fellas. She left Maisie titivating in front of the mirror and almost danced upstairs. As she opened her wardrobe door, she hummed to herself, searching through the garments she had left hang-

46

ing there when she moved out to accommodation at Fair Haven. She wondered why she was bothering when she knew that she had only one decent outfit to wear for a party – the circular red and green cotton skirt Maisie had bought for her last birthday. She could match it with a lemon, lacy patterned, three-quarter-sleeve top with an opening at the neck fastened with tiny pearl buttons. She had knitted it herself and, despite a couple of slipped stitches, it didn't look half bad.

She took out both garments, plus a cardigan and a pair of black ballerina pumps from the bottom of the wardrobe. Then she went over to the chest of drawers and removed a suspender belt, stockings, a net underskirt and the black waspie belt she had bought with the Christmas money Jimmy had given her. She wondered if the day would ever come when she could afford a whole pile of fashionable clothes that would result in her attracting the Prince Charming her mother was hoping would one day claim her only daughter.

As she changed into her party clothes, Irene prayed that she would not bump into any drunks outside the Red Lion pub up by the canal. Jimmy had gone on ahead to the Gianellis' to rehearse with the group beforehand, so she would have to walk there alone.

Once dressed, Irene loosened her hair and gave it a good brush before tying it up in a pony tail with a black velvet ribbon. Then she took a coral lipstick from her handbag and went into her mother's bedroom where there was a full-length mirror. She applied lipstick and then inspected herself from head to toe.

Not bad! she thought, smiling to herself and performing a twirl. She straightened a stocking seam before loosening a couple of strands of hair and twisting them into kiss curls either side of her face. Once she had been straw blonde but gradually her hair had turned a darker shade of fair. What she needed was some summer sunshine to lighten it. She could not afford to visit the hairdresser's and have it bleached.

Her eyes narrowed as she inspected her face more closely. Was that a spot? She groaned inwardly, hoping it wouldn't develop into a full-blown pimple during the evening. She went over to her mother's dressing table and picked up the Max Factor pan stick lying there and put a dab on the spot and rubbed it in.

Suddenly she thought she heard her mother's voice but could not make out what she was saying, so she hurried downstairs. 'What did you say, Mam?'

'I said what's taking yer so long up there, girl? Let's be having a look at yer.'

Irene rotated slowly. 'Well?' she asked, gazing at her mother.

Maisie nodded approvingly. 'That was a good buy, that skirt, and yer made a decent job of the jumper. I hope yer going to be warm enough.'

'I have my cardigan and I'll soon get hot dancing.' She fetched her coat and scarf. 'When are Gertie and the others coming?'

'Soon! Now stop fussing and get going. I'll see yer in the New Year.'

Irene left the house and walked up the street towards the library. As she approached the build-

48

ing, a bus drew up at the bus stop and several people got off. She recognized Pete and his mother and, smiling, she waved and danced towards them. 'Hi Pete! Hallo, Mrs Marshall! Mam's expecting you. I really appreciated you going to the dentist with her. I would have gone if only she'd asked, but you know what she's like.'

Gertie beamed at her. 'I was glad to be of help, love. That's what friends are for. You off to the party now? Our Pete will keep yer company. You can't be too careful on New Year's Eve when there's lots of people about, drinking and acting the goat.'

'Will you be all right, Mam, going the rest of the way yourself?' asked Pete.

'I'll be fine, son. Nobody's going to take a fancy to a scrawny bird like me. You go and enjoy yourself.'

He squeezed her shoulder. 'I'll see you later, Mam.'

She nodded and, with a wave of her hand, scuttled off.

Irene and Pete headed for the lift bridge. 'I thought I wasn't going to make the party,' said Irene happily. 'Volunteered to stay in with Mam but she had her own plans. I hope Peggy makes it,' she added, slanting him a sidelong glance. 'When I saw you yesterday I wondered if the pair of you had split up again. I know it's none of my business—'

'No, it isn't,' he said roughly, pausing on the bridge and staring down at the water which appeared silky in the lights from the pub.

'Sorry,' she muttered, thinking he must be in

one of his touchy moods.

'I just don't want to talk about it!' he burst out. 'I'm fed up with the whole situation!'

'OK! You don't have to talk about it,' she murmured, thinking how much easier life would be if people didn't fall in love. She hesitated before adding, 'Her brother asked me about you, you know.'

Pete started walking again, dragging his damaged leg. 'What did you tell him?'

'I didn't tell him anything.'

'Good! Peggy used to complain about Marty always coming the over-protective older brother. That's what me and our Norm used to say about our Dougie but I know now he was only trying to do his best after our dad was killed in the war. He wanted to make things easier for Ma. Me and our Norm were right scallywags when we were kids.' He glanced at Irene. 'What about your Jimmy? Does he come the big brother?'

'Too right he does! He had a twin once, you know? I don't remember him at all because he was run over when he was only a toddler.'

'So Jimmy never got used to having him around growing up together,' said Pete. 'Me and our Norm always had each other to play with and go places. He followed my lead because I was the elder by half an hour.'

'You must really miss him now he's working away.'

'We both would have joined the merchant navy if it wasn't for the accident,' said Pete moodily.

'I'm sure your mother's glad to have one of you at home.'

His expression clouded. 'I'm not sure how

50

she'd cope living on her own.'

'What about when you do get married?' asked Irene, without thinking. 'She'll be on her own then.'

Pete gave a mirthless laugh. 'Can't see that happening right now. Anyway, if it does happen, my wife and I could live with Ma. Thousands of young couples live with their parents these days. I know people say it's not the best way to start married life, but there just aren't enough houses getting built to replace those destroyed during the war.'

She agreed, having read about that herself in the *Echo*. They walked on in silence until they arrived in Litherland Park, a crescent where the Gianellis lived in a five-bedroomed house called The Chestnuts. The sound of music could be heard coming from the dwelling as they made their way up the drive to the front door. The lights were on in the downstairs rooms, as well as in the lobby and one of the first-floor bedrooms.

Pete rang the bell.

They heard hurrying footsteps and the door was opened by Nellie's niece, Lucia, who was wearing a pink jumper and maroon skirt and strapped brown shoes. Her brown hair was twisted in a knot on top of her head and the style made her look older than her age. 'Hi, glad you could both make it.' She smiled broadly at Pete and Irene.

'Are all the family here?' asked Irene, stepping over the threshold.

Lucia's eyes gleamed. 'I wouldn't be here if the kids weren't here. Let's be having your coats!'

Irene handed over hers. 'Are you all staying the night?'

51

'Yes, we'll bunk down somewhere. The two younger ones are already asleep upstairs. If you want a word with Aunt Nellie, you'll find her and Mam in the kitchen. You know the way.'

'Is Peggy McGrath here?' asked Irene.

Lucia frowned. 'Is she the dark-haired, buxom one who was a workmate of Jeanette?'

'That's her.'

'No, but someone who has turned up unexpectedly is Maggie Gregory. You want to see what she's wearing! It's fabulous!' Lucia turned to Pete. 'Can I take your overcoat, Mr Marshall?'

He rested his walking stick against the wall before removing the tweed garment and handing it over to her with an unexpected smile. Watching him, Irene thought how the smile completely altered his face. He was really good looking when he stopped being moody and miserable.

'You can call me Pete,' he said.

Lucia mumbled something, blushed and hurried upstairs.

Irene turned to him. 'Did you hear what she said? Maggie's here.'

Pete frowned. 'I thought she was still living in London.'

'Last I heard she was supposed to be coming up for Christmas to see the family but called off at the last minute.'

'Perhaps she had a modelling assignment.'

'No idea.' Irene changed the subject. 'I'd better say hello to Mrs Gianelli. I'll see you later, Pete.'

He picked up his stick and limped over to a door on the left. The sound of Tony Gianelli singing the catchy 'Why Do Fools Fall in Love' flooded out, only to be cut off as the door closed behind Pete.

Irene turned away and headed for the kitchen, wondering if Peggy might yet turn up for the party.

Peggy was not far away, standing within a stone's throw of a telephone box outside Litherland library. No sooner had she got off the bus than she had caught sight of a crowd outside the Red Lion. It was obvious that some were already worse for drink if their performance of 'Knees Up Mother Brown' was anything to go by. Then she had spotted someone she recognized on the edge of the merrymakers and it gave her such a shock that she thought she would pass out.

Her first instinct was to go up there and demand to know where Tommy had been since he went missing but then her common sense had asserted itself. She knew him well enough to know that she wouldn't get a straight answer. This brother of hers was not only devious but a thief, a born liar and a selfish sod. What would it have cost him to write a letter to their mother all the years he'd been away? Had he been here in Litherland at all during that time? Mary McGrath had been in desperate need of assurance that Tommy was still alive, although he'd rarely been anything but trouble.

What was he doing here in Litherland? Who did he know who lived in this neighbourhood? Perhaps she should stay put and keep an eye on him and see where he went when he left. The only fault with that idea was that she might be hanging around for ages and it was freezing. She supposed if Tommy went inside the pub, she could slip in after him. Although her parents had always told her that respectable girls didn't go into pubs, unless accompanied by a family member or close friend.

As she watched her brother, she noticed a packet changing hands. She groaned inwardly. What was Tommy up to now? She could not help but be suspicious after the trouble he'd been in before he disappeared. It occurred to her that the sensible thing to do would be to get in touch with Marty, because if she attempted to follow Tommy when he left, it wouldn't be easy to keep up with him in her high heels.

She felt inside her pocket for change and then opened the door of the telephone box. She dialled Bernie's mother's number and asked to speak to her brother.

After she had finished talking to Marty, she checked whether Tommy was still outside the pub before going back inside the telephone box to keep out of the cold. Every few minutes she popped outside to see if he was still hanging around. It was just as well that she did because otherwise she would have missed him going inside the Red Lion. Should she follow him or stay right where she was until Marty turned up? She decided she must be bloody mad to do what she was doing. Her father had said that he wouldn't allow Tommy inside the house if he ever dared show his face there again. This despite all their mother's pleas for him to be lenient with their second son if the prodigal were to return.

The longer she stood in the telephone box, the more Peggy wished she had not spotted her brother. She could have been at the party right

54

now, saying sorry to Pete for ignoring him on the train. Surely he'd forgive her and they could have a slow, smoochy dance. Hopefully it wouldn't be long before Marty turned up and she could dash off before the old year ended.

Perhaps if Pete had been aware that Peggy was not far away and thinking of him, then he might have joined her in the telephone box. There had been dancing but the musicians were now taking a break. As it was, he was eyeing up Maggie who had certainly matured since she had left Liverpool for London to pursue a modelling course and career.

He was trying to remember how old she was. Certainly younger than she looked but she must be eighteen at least. When he had entered the room, she had been talking to Jimmy in that carrying voice of hers about her favourite songs. One was 'Why Do Fools Fall in Love?' which had been a hit a year or so ago. He thought how apt the words were when he considered his love life. Why hadn't Peggy come to the party after saying she was planning to be here? Could she have had an accident? He felt as if a cold hand clutched his heart.

'Is anyone sitting here, Pete?' Maggie asked.

He realized his thoughts had drifted, so he had not noticed her making a move. 'Not that I've noticed,' he said.

'You seemed miles away.' Maggie sat beside him, folding her legs elegantly so that her knees were together and her ankles displayed to an advantage. She was wearing sheer nylons and red patent-leather high-heeled court shoes. 'I wondered what you were thinking,' she added.

'Did you have a good Christmas?' he asked, having no intention of unburdening himself to her.

She wrinkled her dainty nose. 'I was supposed to be staying with Jared and family in Formby but I couldn't make it here in time, so I spent it with some friends in London. How was your Christmas?'

'Ma would have liked it better if our Norm could have been with us, but that's–'

'I saw your Norm not so long ago,' she interrupted. 'He came into London from the Isle of Grain. Apparently there's an oil refinery there.'

Pete had known his twin had visited the British Petroleum refinery in December but Norm had made no mention of seeing Maggie. 'So how did he look?' he asked.

'Fit! Healthy! We had a coffee and caught up on news, nattering about family and friends back home in Liverpool.' She glanced about her. 'I thought Peggy might be here. Aren't you two...?'

'No,' he said curtly. 'So how come you heard about the party?'

Maggie smiled and reached into her handbag and took out a posh-looking cigarette case and lighter. 'I didn't! Nobody was home when I arrived in Formby. Fortunately one of the neighbours had a key to our Jared's house, so I was able to let myself in. Apparently my relatives have all gone north to Whalley.'

She opened the cigarette case and offered it to him. He refused and so she took one herself and

56

lit up. He watched her puff contentedly for a minute or so, thinking she still had not answered his question and wondering why Norm had made no mention of seeing her in his letter.

'I remembered dear cousin Betty saying the New Year's Eve party was a regular event at the Gianellis' house,' Maggie continued. 'I found the phone number in a note pad by the telephone and so phoned up and explained I was all on my tod. I was told I was welcome to come and join in the fun. So far it's been quite tame by London's standards.' She sounded bored.

Pete's only knowledge of the London scene came from what he had seen on the cinema screen and the television and he would admit he and Norm hadn't been inclined to go haring off to the Big Smoke. It seemed his twin thought differently these days, however. Was Maggie the attraction? There was no getting away from it – she had grown into a beauty, even if she was a bit too skinny for his liking.

'So when will you be going back to London?' he asked.

'Not for a few days. I've some modelling work in Chester. I like Chester, don't you?' She flicked him a glance from beneath luxuriously thick black eyelashes which seemed at odds with her fine blonde hair.

'It's not a place I visit,' said Pete. 'Too many steps to negotiate by train. I used to like the ferry but again it's bus, boat, bus.'

She looked at his outstretched leg. 'You should buy a car. It would be easier for you to get about.'

'Thanks for the advice,' he said tersely.

57

'No need to get touchy!' She patted his thigh. 'I was only trying to be helpful. Your Norm fancied the idea of a car.'

What am I supposed to say to that? His twin would be earning a good screw when he worked his way up to being a chief marine engineer. Pete tried not to be envious as he struggled with the anger and depression that was always there in the background, threatening to overwhelm him, since the fall that changed his life.

At that moment Lucia approached them. 'The buffet will be served in the dining room in a quarter of an hour,' she announced before hurrying over to where Jimmy, Tony and the three other musicians were talking in low voices in a corner of the room. She stayed for several minutes before sitting down close to them as Tony launched into 'Love Me Tender'.

'Did you see that film with Peter Egan and Elvis Presley playing brothers who are in love with the same girl?' asked Maggie. 'It's a cowboy film! I *love* cowboy films. I'd love to be in one. It's set just after the American Civil War, but Elvis sings in it. I think he's fab but your Norm doesn't. I told him he's a real square.'

'Shush!' hissed Irene, who had come over and was now perching on the arm of the sofa next to Pete with a glass in her hand.

Maggie scowled at her. 'Oh, it's you, Irene!'

Irene said, 'Who else? Now quiet, I want to listen to this and so does everyone else.'

Maggie opened her mouth but she never got to say what she wanted because Pete put his hand across it, silencing her. She looked over his hand, her eyes wide with astonishment. He removed his hand and mouthed, 'Not a word.'

She remained silent but was obviously annoyed. When the song finished, she got up and went over to where Jimmy was talking to Lucia.

'She'll tell your Norm on you for shutting her up,' joked Irene, placing her empty glass on a coffee table.

'She met our Norm in London,' said Pete.

'So I believe. She mentioned it to our Jimmy,' said Irene. 'D'you think anything will come of them seeing each other? I'd have thought she'd have bigger fish to fry these days. No insult intended to your Norm,' she added.

Pete said bitterly, 'He's out in the world now and will be making his own decisions, not discussing them with me.'

At that moment the buffet was announced. 'I see Peggy hasn't turned up.' Irene sighed. 'Would you like me to bring you something to eat when I get mine?'

'Thanks, kid.' He forced a smile. 'Sorry to sound such a grump.'

'And shall we have that dance you promised me afterwards?' she asked with a smile.

He nodded and watched her go over to the table, thinking he could do worse than date Irene. It was obvious that Peggy had decided it would be a mistake to come to the party if he was going to be there. It seemed that their relationship could be over for good this time.

Marty roared up on a motorbike with a sidecar, much to Peggy's amazement, and came to a skidding halt. She was huddled inside her coat, standing on the corner outside the library because someone had wanted to use the public telephone and the tips of her ears and her toes were freezing.

'What are you doing on that?' she asked. 'And why haven't you got a crash helmet on?'

'I came in a rush and Dougal couldn't put his hand on his crash helmet right away. Would you believe he and his mother, sister and brother came over from Ireland all packed in this?' Marty paused. 'Are you absolutely sure it's our Tommy?'

'Of course! I wouldn't have brought you out here on a wild goose chase. He's still in the pub as far as I know.' She jerked her head in the direction of the Red Lion. 'It's that way.'

'All right, you skedaddle off to the party and I'll go and take a look.'

'OK, but if you're going to park up there, then you might as well give me a lift that short distance.'

'Hop on then.'

She managed to perch on the pillion sideways, hooking a hand through the belt of the heavy gabardine coat he wore. She presumed this too belonged to Dougal. A minute later she was dismounting, wishing him luck with Tommy before heading towards the footbridge over the canal. Once she got walking, her ears and feet warmed up and it was not long before she arrived at the house.

The door was opened by Nellie. 'Sorry I'm late, Mrs Gianelli,' said Peggy, smiling. 'I hope it's OK for me to arrive at this hour?'

'Of course,' said Nellie warmly. 'Come on in.

You look cold.'

'I'm not as cold as I was,' said Peggy, stepping over the threshold. 'I've been hanging around by the library waiting for my brother to turn up.'

Nellie looked at her questioningly.

'It's a long story' said Peggy.

'Well, there's a good fire in the dining room and there's still some of the buffet left. Let me take your coat?'

'I'd rather keep it on for a while if you don't mind,' said Peggy, following Nellie into a back room which was deserted. She could hear the song 'Chicka Boom' coming from the parlour. Immediately she remembered it being a hit for American pop singer Guy Mitchell. 'That's an oldie. Tony's in good voice.'

'My niece requested it,' said Nellie.

'It's still a catchy number,' said Peggy.

'I won't argue with that. Would you like a Babycham?'

Peggy thanked her and asked whether Pete was there.

Nellie nodded. 'I'll tell him you've arrived, shall I?'

'No, I can wait.' Peggy would much rather surprise him. That way she'd know from his expression whether he was pleased to see her or not.

She went over to the glowing fire and opened her coat, closing her eyes in sheer bliss as the heat began to penetrate her chilled body. It must be terrible to be homeless and have to sleep in doorways or park benches, she thought. One of her mother's fears concerning Tommy was that he had ended up sleeping rough and died of exposure – that was if he hadn't been stabbed in the back by some villain.

Peggy and Marty had tried to reassure her that nobody was going to kill their brother. Tommy with his baby face and cherubic smile would manage to fool people into believing he was as angelic as he looked. Someone, most probably a woman, would take him in and feed him. Strangely that thought didn't always reassure Mary McGrath.

Now Peggy was warmer, she removed her coat and hung it on the back of a chair. She went over to the remains of the buffet and helped herself to some food. As she bit into a ham sandwich, Nellie brought in a glass of Babycham. They spoke for a few minutes about the weather and Peggy's job with a shipping warehouse company and then Nellie excused herself and left the room.

Peggy sat over by the fire, eating and drinking and thinking about her brothers, wondering what Marty was saying to Tommy right now. The door opened and in came a girl who Peggy vaguely recognized. 'Aren't you Maggie?' she asked.

'That's right. You're Peggy, aren't you? Well, I tell you now if you've still got any interest in Pete Marshall you'd better get in there. He's shuffling around the floor with Irene Miller.' Maggie's eyes hardened. 'That girl! She'd steal anyone's boyfriend if you ask me.'

Peggy was taken aback. 'I didn't ask you!'

'No, but you know what I mean.'

'I'm not sure I do,' said Peggy. 'Irene's always seemed a decent sort to me.'

'I don't understand you! You must be blind!' said Maggie, and flounced out.

Peggy shook her head, remembering that Maggie was the one who had fancied herself as a model and she had to admit she was good looking with a slender figure. She ate the last mouthful of Dundee cake, drained her glass and hurried from the room.

In the lobby there were several people putting on hats and coats. She wondered what was happening because surely it wasn't almost midnight yet. The music had stopped and the door to the other room was ajar. She crossed the lobby and pushed the door wide and peered inside.

Irene was talking with Jimmy and Tony, and Pete was sitting on a sofa with his dark head resting against the back of it, with his eyes closed. All the tension, pain and anger was smoothed from his face. She felt a catch at her heart and wanted to go over and kiss him.

As if sensing someone was watching him, he opened his eyes. In that moment she swore that his expression was one of relief and pleasure.

'Bit late, aren't you?' he said.

They were not the most welcoming words she had ever heard but at least the pair of them were on speaking terms. She crossed the room and sat next to him.

'I would have been here earlier, only I spotted our Tommy outside the Red Lion, so I phoned our Marty from a telephone box.'

Pete looked astounded. 'After all this time! Are you sure it was him?'

'Yes! I know my own brother! I kept a watch out until Marty arrived. Would you believe he was on a motorbike with a sidecar?'

63

'Who does it belong to?'

'Bernie's cousin, Dougal. I just hope Marty doesn't go and hit a wall on the way home because he has no crash helmet.'

'Has he ridden a motorbike before?'

'When he was eighteen he bought a second-hand one but he came off it several times, so Mam nagged him into getting rid of it. He could be a bit of a daredevil at times but never did anything criminal, not like our Tommy.' She darted him a sidelong look. 'You won't go mentioning him to your policeman brother, will you?'

'What d'you think I am, a snout?' Pete shifted uncomfortably on the sofa.

Watching him, Peggy realized he was in pain and remembered what Maggie had told her. 'Have you been dancing with Irene? I wish it had been with me,' she said, slipping her arm through his. 'Still, I think now you'd be better off at home. I'll come with you, if you like? I can help you getting on and off the bus.'

'But you've only just got here,' Pete said.

'I know but I'm really late for the party, aren't I? I thought you could introduce me to your mother.'

His expression softened. 'Thanks for the offer, Peg, but I've to pick up Ma from Irene's mam's on the way. We might just get a taxi.'

'Did I hear my name mentioned?' asked Irene.

Peggy looked up at her and experienced a moment of doubt. 'Oh, it's you,' she said in a flat voice.

'You don't have to sound so pleased to see me,' said Irene mildly. 'I'm glad you made it.'

'Really?' Peggy continued to stare up at her with a doubtful look in her eyes.

Irene frowned. 'Honest to God! I'm glad you're here to keep Pete company. I just came to say hello and tarrah! Some of the party are going outside, either to first-foot or so they can join the celebrations in the road. I want to hear the ships on the river sounding their hooters. I love that sound, as well as that of church bells. Then I'm nipping off home. I want to check that Mam's all right.'

'What's wrong with your mam?' asked Peggy. 'Pete said his mother was with her.'

'She's had all her teeth out,' Irene replied.

Peggy shuddered. 'Bloody hell!'

Irene agreed that it was bloody hell, according to Maisie.

Pete looked at the two girls and then said, 'Let's go!' He reached for his stick.

Irene offered her hand to help him to his feet but he shook his head. Peggy's hand was still through Pete's arm and she intended it staying there. She was going to stick close to him. This was the night she was going to meet his mother and she felt the need to hang on to him.

Their progress along the pavement was not as fast as she would have liked and they only managed to reach the other side of the canal when church bells and ships' hooters on the Mersey began to fill the air with sound, along with cheers and people singing 'Auld Lang Syne'.

'Happy New Year!' Irene cried, turning to the other two.

'Happy 1958!' said Pete, pecking her cheek.

'Do I get a kiss?' asked Peggy, wishing the other girl to Timbuktu.

Pete brushed her cheek with his lips. 'Happy New Year.'

'Couldn't I have a proper kiss?' she murmured, gazing up into his eyes. 'That was only a peck.'

'Don't you remember the song "A Bushel and a Peck"?' he said in a low voice. 'It's an oldie but the tune's very catchy.'

She sang the first few lines softly and then leaned into him, putting her arm around his neck and kissing him on the lips.

Irene looked away, feeling slightly envious of the couple despite being in no rush to be tied down.

There came the sound of a motorcycle engine and she glanced in its direction. The vehicle drew up alongside her and she stared at Marty in disbelief, vaguely aware that Pete and Peggy had drawn apart.

'What a way to spend New Year's Eve,' complained Marty, rubbing his eyes and blinking at the three of them. 'I was just coming to find you, Peg.'

'What happened?' she asked. 'Did you get to speak to Tommy?'

'Like hell I did! I bloody lost him in Blundell Sands!'

'What's he doing there?' cried Peggy.

'Who's Tommy?' asked Irene.

'The black sheep of the family,' said Peggy grimly. 'He had a big row with Dad a few years ago and he stormed out of the house and disappeared off the face of the earth.' That was only half the

66

story but she was too ashamed to tell Irene the whole of it. 'Anyway, I spotted him this evening outside the Red Lion, so I phoned our Marty.' She turned to her brother. 'So, what happened?'

'I was lucky enough to see him catch the bus and I managed to follow it as far as Blundell Sands,' said Marty.

'And...?' Peggy prompted.

'He got off and I hung back because I didn't want him to get suspicious. I didn't have too much of a problem following him because the roads weren't too badly lit, wide and straight, then suddenly he just vanished.'

'People don't just vanish,' put in Irene.

'Don't you believe it!' said Marty.

She said, 'He could have suspected he was being followed because of the noise of the motor-cycle engine. He might have even noticed you when he was on the bus. It's not as if that vehicle is just any ordinary motor bike – it has a sidecar. Most likely he nipped up a drive to one of the houses. He could have hidden behind a tree by a gate and watched you go past.'

Marty had been staring at Irene the whole time she had been talking. 'Quite the little detective, aren't you?' he said, an edge to his voice.

Irene's eyes glinted with annoyance. 'I was only trying to help. I work in Blundell Sands, so I know the neighbourhood. Some of the houses are really large. They have quite a bit of ground. Some have even been turned into flats. Where you lost him, was it far from the shore?'

He hesitated. 'I couldn't say for sure. But I did notice that some of the houses had been turned

67

into flats like you said. I even got off the motorbike and went up one of the drives. The house had little name plates with numbers and doorbells next to them.'

'I don't suppose you had time to read any of the names?' asked Peggy.

'No, and besides I didn't want to rouse suspicion at that time of night by lingering.' He paused. 'Anyway, what are you doing with *him?*' Marty jerked his head in Pete's direction. 'You acted like you didn't know him when we were on the train.'

Pete met Marty's gaze squarely. 'The name's Pete Marshall ... and yes, Peggy and I have been going out with each other off and on for some time.'

'Off and on? Why's that? Can't make up your mind whether she's worth the hassle?' said Marty.

Irene gasped.

Colour flooded Peggy's face. 'Marty, how can you say that?' she cried. 'I wish I hadn't phoned you about our Tommy now! Why don't you just go home, seeing as how you lost him, and leave us alone!'

Marty's hands curled into fists. 'If I'm going home, you're coming with me, Peg. I promised Dad, remember?'

'Don't you bully her!' said Pete, his fingers tightening on his stick.

'Yeah, don't you bully her,' put in Irene.

Marty stared at her. 'Who's bullying her? You don't know our father. I'm protecting her.'

Peggy sighed. 'He's right. You don't know our dad.'

'He could be combing the streets for you,' said Marty. 'Or he just might be that drunk he's passed out on the sofa.'

Peggy glanced at Pete. 'I'd better go.'

'OK! I suppose that's the sensible thing to do.' She looked relieved. 'But I'll see you again, won't I?'

Pete's eyes flickered in Marty's direction. 'Yes, I'll be in touch,' he said.

Irene also glanced at Marty. 'I hope you're not going to tell your father about any of this?'

He stared at her in astonishment. 'It's none of your business, love.'

She flushed and tilted her chin and gazed up into his shadowy features. 'Peggy and Pete are my friends, so of course it's my business,' she said firmly.

Marty brought his head closer to hers. 'You know your problem, love, it's that you need to step back sometimes. You could land yourself in trouble again if you don't start thinking twice before making a move. You know the old proverb "look before you leap"?'

'I don't know what you mean by *again!*' she said, exasperated.

'You obviously don't remember getting yourself in a right fix a few months back.' He smiled unexpectedly. 'I'll say this for you – at least you care about others.'

Irene was still puzzled by that word *again*. As for his smile, it made her feel slightly marshmallowy inside. Before she could change her mind, she said, 'Do you remember passing a school or seeing a sign for Fair Haven Children's Home when you

69

were in Blundell Sands?'

His brow furrowed. 'Why d'you ask?'

'I work at the children's home. If your brother is living in a flat nearby I could keep an eye open for him. D'you have a photo of him?'

'I don't carry one round with me, love! I'm not that fond of him.'

Irene raised her eyebrows. 'I don't know why I'm even bothering trying to trace him for you if that's the way you feel! But I'm still willing to help Peggy if she wants him found.'

'I do,' said Peggy. 'For Mam's sake.'

Irene nodded. 'OK. It's even possible I could catch sight of him when I come here to visit my Mam and Jimmy, if your brother frequents the Red Lion.'

'Peggy can get a photo from Mam and pass it on to you,' said Marty. 'Thanks, I do appreciate your help.' He hesitated before saying, 'Did you get your tickets for the pantomime, by the way?'

Irene had almost forgotten that she had mentioned that to him. 'Yes. Anyway, I'd better be going.' She hesitated before adding, 'Happy New Year.'

'Thanks, kid.' Marty bent his head and, to her amazement, kissed her. 'Hope it's a good one for you.' He turned to his sister. 'Come on, Peg. Time we were off.'

Irene could only stare after him as he helped Peggy on to the pillion seat. Then she gave herself a little shake and slipped her hand through Pete's arm.

'Goodnight, Peg,' said Pete.

'Goodnight,' Peggy called, waving a hand. 'I'll

70

be in touch, Irene.'

As Irene and Pete walked away and the motor-bike roared into life, Marty asked, 'What's he done to his leg?'

'Never mind that! You kissed Irene,' Peggy burst out.

He shrugged. 'So what? It's New Year. Every-body kisses everybody at New Year. Although I draw the line at kissing your friend Pete.'

'Very funny! D'you find her attractive?'

'Wildly, but you don't have to remind me I'm a married man,' he drawled.

'You're being sarcastic,' said Peggy. 'But honestly, do you think she's attractive to men?'

'You worried that your friend Pete might kiss her, too?'

'I wish you'd stop calling him "my friend Pete"!'

'Well, shut up then, and let me concentrate on getting us home,' Marty shouted above the roar of the engine. 'And you'd better decide whether you're going to mention having seen Tommy to Mam or not.'

Peggy nodded and decided to play it by ear.

'So what is wrong with his leg?' asked Marty a short while later.

'He fell from a window sill.'

Marty decided that perhaps it was best not to ask any further questions. There was probably some daft story behind the accident.

As they drew up outside their parents' house, Peggy whispered, 'You won't mention Pete to Mam and Dad, will you?'

'It's up to you to do that,' said Marty. 'I'm not coming in. I'd best get home. By the way, I think it's best if we don't mention having seen our Tommy to anyone. I'd like to find him first.'

'OK. Does Bernie know what you've been doing all this time?'

'Of course not! I just told Dougal to tell her that I've borrowed his motorbike because you wanted to see me urgently.'

'I bet she's working herself up into a state because of the time you've been. I'd better not mention you kissing Irene to her,' she added mischievously.

'It was no big deal,' Marty murmured. 'Bernie thinks nothing of kissing all her male cousins who come to the house.' He watched as the front door opened, proving that their mother had probably been watching out for Peggy through the parlour window. 'See you!'

He roared off before his mother could delay him. From what he knew of his wife, Bernie would definitely have a face on her by the time he arrived home. Unless by some miracle he was fortunate enough to find her fast asleep.

His luck was out.

Bernie was lying on the bed with a burning cigarette dangling from her fingers. She was wearing a primrose brushed-nylon nightie with a yellow quilted housecoat over it and looked paler than usual. She had smudged bright blue eye shadow and mascara on the pillow case and her hair was an untidy mess.

'About time, too,' she said. 'What did your Peggy want?'

'She was worried about drunks, so wanted me to pick her up.'

Bernie's eyes narrowed. 'I don't know if I believe you.'

Marty did not immediately respond but removed his jacket and tie before going over to the cot in the corner of the room. He did not trust Bernie not to mention Tommy to one of her sisters. Then she might mention it to her mother who'd never had anything good to say about his brother. His expression softened as he gazed down at his daughter, sleeping top and tail with Jerry who was almost a year older.

'Well?' Bernie snapped.

He frowned. 'Keep your voice down or you'll wake the kids.'

'The last trumpet's not going to do that,' she said. 'Answer my question.'

He was silent, thinking of his brother stealing flowers in the park to give to their mother when they were kids. But as soon as the parky had appeared, Tommy had thrust them into Marty's hand and made a run for it. His brother had always had a strong sense of self-preservation. Another time Tommy had stolen sweets from a box on the counter while the old lady who owned the sweet shop had her back turned to them. A few years later Tommy had tried to break into their gas meter but their dad had caught him. He would have had a worse walloping if Tommy hadn't clung to their mother, saying that he had wanted to buy her a birthday present but had no money. She had hung on to her husband's arm, so preventing him from beating the daylights out of her blue-eyed boy.

'You've gone off in a trance,' Bernie hissed.

'I'm just thinking.' Marty tucked the blankets more securely about his daughter. He noticed that one of Jerry's feet was sticking out of the bedcovers so he covered it. Then he turned to face Bernie and saw that she was smoking again. 'Put that ciggie out!' he ordered. 'You'll set fire to the bed one of these days and I don't want the children going up in smoke.'

Bernie stubbed out the cigarette on a saucer. 'What about me going up in smoke? Would you care, Marty?'

'What a daft question!' He dragged his shirt over his head.

Bernie stifled a yawn and removed her housecoat before pulling the bedcovers up to her chin. 'You still haven't answered my question.'

'I wasn't chasing after some imaginary woman if that's what you're hinting at,' said Marty softly.

'Keep yer hair on! I suppose I have to take your word for it that you don't have a fancy woman.'

He felt like saying 'just like I took yours that the baby you were expecting was mine'. He had no doubt about Josie being his daughter and he loved the bones of her but he knew that he had not been Bernie's first lover. Inexplicably to him now, he had been besotted with her when he was younger, finding her exciting and sexy. When she had started coming on to him, he was never sure just who had seduced who that evening after he had taken Jeanette to the Stadium. It was the only time he and Bernie had sex.

He switched off the light and got into bed and lay on his back with the bedcovers up to his shoulders, thinking now of the names of the boyfriends she had supposedly had before him. She must have had sex with at least one of them because she had been no virgin when he'd gone with her.

'Yer haven't even wished me a Happy New Year and kissed me,' said Bernie, rousing him from his reverie.

Marty thought about Irene Miller and the kiss he had landed on her mouth. *What the hell had made me do that?* He wondered how she would have reacted if he had told her he had wanted to kiss her the moment she had collapsed on top of him on the beach after he had saved her from drowning. At the time he'd had no idea that she was a friend of Peggy's.

'I sometimes think yer must have a double out there,' muttered Bernie. 'You're not a bit like yer used to be when we were courting.'

Courting! They had never been a courting couple. She had homed in on him and he had been hooked. He recalled his father tearing into him when he had told his parents that Bernie was having a baby. Even now he could go hot all over, remembering the emotion in his voice when he said that he was going to marry her. His father had accused him of having his brain in his pants. He winced, ashamed of his naivety even at twenty-two. Once married to Bernie, it had not taken him long to realize they had little in common.

As for Bernie's widowed mother, Carmel, she had told Marty to his face from the beginning that she didn't think much of either of the McGrath boys. Apparently she remembered them attending the same junior school as her boys and even then had considered Tommy, in particular, a right tearaway and a criminal in the making despite his angelic looks. This was due to Tommy having tricked her youngest son, Patrick, out of his bag of marbles in the school playground. She had gone up to the school and confronted the headmaster and Tommy had suffered six of the best for that misdemeanour.

On another occasion Tommy had punched Patrick on the nose when they were boxing at the church boys' club. His nose had bled copiously and Carmel had been informed. Then there had been the fight outside the Grafton dance hall in their late teens one New Year's Eve.

Bernie had been there and she had hurried home to tell her mother that her brother had been arrested along with a gang of Teddy Boys. The gang had included Tommy. Patrick and Tommy had both appeared in court but fortunately only the ring leaders had been fined; the rest had got off with a warning.

But these happenings paled into insignificance when the police had turned up on the McGraths' doorstep wanting to speak to Tommy.

'Wouldn't you like another baby?' asked Bernie, rubbing her head against the curve of his shoulder, catching him unawares.

He had almost forgotten she was there. His stomach tensed and he felt trapped. He couldn't make sense of Bernie's behaviour. When they were first married, she had blown hot and cold if he went near her. He had accepted her excuse that she was worried about damaging the baby.

She had almost blown a gasket when she had got pregnant so soon after Jerry was born. He soon realized that she wasn't that fussy on kids, and often didn't want sex, so why should she suddenly decide she wanted another baby now? Being the youngest of ten, six girls and four boys, she was forever complaining about the way her older sisters treated her. Yet she wasn't slow in coming forward and accepting their offers of help with the kids, as well as gifts of clothing for them.

Marty liked children but he didn't want the responsibility of a whole string of them to feed and clothe. He wanted out of his mother-in-law's house and didn't plan on waiting until he went out feet first in a box. If he had learnt anything, it was that the only reliable way for a good Catholic husband to limit the size of his family was by abstinence from intercourse. He told her to go to sleep and turned his back on her, thinking of Irene. 'Goodnight, Bernie, and Happy New Year.'

Five

'*Georgie Porgie, pudding and pie, kissed the girls and made them cry,*' chanted the little girls and boys in the charge of Irene and the other nursery nurse.

'I didn't kiss you,' piped up a boy who was lumbering along as best he could, having been born with a club foot.

'Take no notice of them, George,' said Irene, who had the two youngest children by the hand. 'You just remember you were named after a king of England.'

'But did he kiss the girls, Miss?' asked Caroline, holding up her chubby face framed by a red pixie hood. Her cheeks were pinched and rosy with the cold. She had a hare lip and Irene had heard another member of staff saying she would have been a pretty little thing if it hadn't been for that disfigurement.

'I'm sure he wasn't the George referred to in the nursery rhyme,' replied Irene. 'Our Queen's father was a good king who led us through the war.'

'What's a war, Miss?' asked May, wisps of carrot-coloured hair escaping from beneath her blue pixie hood.

Irene gazed down into her heart-shaped freckled face, thinking May's skin would be smothered in freckles in the summer. Hopefully they wouldn't be the bane of her life when she grew up and her complexion became almost as important as clothes.

'Should we change the subject?' suggested Deirdre. 'I think they're too young to learn about war. Let's have another nursery rhyme instead.'

'Can I choose, Miss?' asked George. 'Can we have "One, Two, Buckle My Shoe"?'

'I'd like "Baa, Baa, Black Sheep",' chimed in one of the girls.

'What about me? Can I choose one?' chorused two of the other children.

'Shush, all of you!' Irene ordered. 'Or we'll go back right now instead of going to the beach.'

The children fell silent.

Irene glanced at Deirdre and said mischievously, 'Shall we teach them "She Sells Seashells on the Seashore"?'

78

Deirdre's lips twitched. 'You've got a wicked sense of humour. Imagine the noise out of them if we attempted that! Let's have "Little Miss Muffet".'

'You're asking for trouble,' said Irene *sotto voce*. 'One of them is bound to ask what a tuffet is or what curds are.'

'It's obvious that a tuffet is something you sit on and as for curds, they have something to do with milk.' Deirdre stopped abruptly. 'Which reminds me...'

Irene gazed at her expectantly. 'Are you going to suggest that we heat up their milk?'

Deirdre nodded. 'The wind off the sea will have a real edge to it and I think they'll need a warm drink. I know these children have to learn that life isn't going to do them any favours as they grow up, but even so...'

Irene agreed. She couldn't see any harm in heating up the milk that the Government provided free. Matron might think differently, however. Her mind drifted. She was aware of the children chanting 'Little Miss Muffet' while at the same time she wondered how best to approach Miss Molyneux, who was in charge of the under-sevens, to suggest taking some of the children to see a pantomime.

Thinking of pantomimes she was reminded of Marty McGrath. Why had he kissed her after the party? One moment he had appeared to disapprove of her and the next he had turned all friendly-like. She had decided he had done it just to see her reaction. Perhaps she should have slapped his face; that would have made him think twice. Probably she was making too much of it.

After all it had been New Year's Eve, a time when people often kiss perfect strangers. More puzzling was what he had meant by that *again?* Had Peggy told him that she had a habit of interfering in her life? She could not remember doing so. Jeanette might have done, so perhaps he'd mixed the pair of them up.

She was roused from her thoughts by one of the children saying, 'You're not singing, Miss.'

'Yes, come on, Nurse Miller, you pick the next one,' said Deirdre heartily.

Irene was aware of George's big brown eyes on her face and remembered his request. 'We'll have "One, Two, Buckle My Shoe".' It was a good counting rhyme and would help the children learn their numbers.

By the time they had sung it three times, they had arrived at the shore. The tide was on its way in, but there was still enough sand for them to walk on and the children were able to watch the waves rolling in with a faint hiss.

'There's a ship, Miss!' shouted one of the boys.

Irene pointed out that there was in fact more than one vessel and counted them aloud and had the children repeat the numbers after her. She was enjoying their company and the outing, with the feel of the breeze on her face and the smell of the sea and talking to them about the driftwood, seaweed and the variety of shells that littered the high tide line. There was even a short length of frayed rope and a mermaid's purse.

She suggested the children collect some of the shells, a length of seaweed and the empty case of fish eggs and she put them in a hessian bag, thinking they could go on the nature table.

'Do you think it's cold enough for snow, Miss?' asked May, sidling up to Irene and slipping her hand into hers.

At that moment a snowflake landed on Irene's cheek and then another and another. She looked round for Deirdre and saw her hurrying towards her with her group of children. 'I think it's time we were getting back,' she said.

They wasted no time hurrying from the beach and making their way back to Fair Haven, thinking how much more pleasant it would be for the little ones once spring arrived. But first things first, she must have a word with Miss Molyneux about that pantomime trip. Even if she could not go with the children herself, one of the nursery teachers and Deirdre could accompany them.

Of course, this extra expenditure on the children meant that Miss Molyneux would need to consult their patron, a spinster lady called Miss Talbot, from one of the old land-owning Lancashire families. During the war, she had given over two of the houses she owned for the provision of orphaned children. The work had continued after the war. In particular, she favoured those with some kind of disfigurement or handicap, although not all of the children were visibly damaged. It was said that the lady herself had been born with a cleft palate.

As it happened, a visit to a pantomime had already been arranged for the children. A performance of *Aladdin* was to be put on by an amateur dramatic society at a local church hall. Irene was pleased that someone else had thought of the idea as well. Which meant she could just fix her thoughts on going to the pantomime in town with her mother – as long as Maisie was feeling up to a night out.

Irene stared at her mother and said, 'Smile again!'

Maisie bared her new dentures. 'So what d'you think? Wasn't I right getting all my old teeth out?'

'Definitely – and you'll never have toothache again, Mam.'

'And that can only be a good thing,' said Maisie, looking pleased with herself. 'What I need now is a new hairdo.'

'You mean have a perm?'

'Not just a perm. I thought of getting my hair dyed.'

'There's nothing wrong with the colour of your hair.'

'I thought auburn,' said Maisie, preening herself in front of the mirror. 'I've always fancied being a redhead like Maureen O'Hara in *The Quiet Man*.'

'Mam, aren't you a bit older than her? Besides, I think she's a natural redhead and has the right skin tone to go with the hair.'

Maisie placed her hands on her hips and glared at her daughter. 'Don't you criticize me, girl! I'm not too bloody old to make the best of meself.'

Irene took a step back. 'I'm not saying you are, but it'll cost a bit!'

Maisie sniffed. 'It's my money! Terence left it to me. I might as well spend some of the little I have, rather than leave it to you and our Jimmy to squander.'

Irene was annoyed. 'I'm not after your money! You can dye your hair sky blue and pink with a finny-haddy border for all I care.'

'Don't be daft!' Maisie jutted her chin. 'I want to look nice for my birthday, so I'm meeting Gertie at the hairdresser's and we're going into town together afterwards because I want to buy a new dress.'

'But I've bought tickets for the pantomime at the Empire for you and me on your birthday,' Irene blurted out.

'Pantomime! I don't want to go to any ol' panto-mime on my birthday! I want to go dancing!' cried Maisie.

Irene's mouth fell open. 'Dancing! With Gertie? But, Mam, I've paid out good money for these tickets. It's Jimmy Jewel and Ben Warriss in "Babes in the Wood". Joan Regan is in it, as well. You like her singing.'

'So I do, but I don't want to spend my birthday sitting in a theatre with you, watching a pair of comedians and a singer. I want to go dancing. You can take someone else! And you don't have to buy me a present, seeing as how you've already forked out money.' Maisie continued to bare her teeth at herself in the mirror.

'I can't not give you a present,' said Irene, upset. 'Why d'you have to be so awkward, Mam? You could go dancing with Gertie another evening.'

Maisie's face turned puce and she raised a hand. 'I'll choose when I go dancing. Now get out of my sight before I clout you one.'

Irene turned on her heel and stormed out of the kitchen. She put on her coat and hat and left the house. She would go to the box office at the Empire and see if she could exchange the tickets for another time. Then she would visit Wilson's, her favourite bookshop on Renshaw Street, as it was on the way to the milk bar in Leece Street and she wanted to see Jeanette. She would treat herself to an espresso and a sausage roll for lunch and hopefully have a chat with her friend.

She met with little luck at the box office in getting tickets for another evening. The show was fully booked every single night and the only seats available were for a matinee in a fortnight's time, so she changed the tickets for that afternoon, hoping Deirdre would be willing to help her out by changing shifts with her. She wasted no time heading along Lime Street, past the Adelphi Hotel and up Renshaw Street towards the bookshop.

The last person Irene expected to see there was Marty McGrath. She was browsing the shelves on the ground floor and had just decided to buy a cut-price calendar for her mother's birthday, when to her surprise she saw him coming downstairs from the children's department. She had not considered him the type to go in bookshops, thinking he'd probably go to Blackler's basement where one could find bargains. In his hand he carried a small parcel which presumably contained a book. Suddenly he caught sight of her and she knew she had surprised him. She could feel herself going hot in the face and was annoyed with herself.

'Seen anything interesting?' he asked.

Her mind went blank and then she remembered the calendar. 'I've bought this for my mam. It's her birthday.'

'I thought you were taking her to the pantomime.'

She had forgotten that she had mentioned that to him. 'She decided that she didn't want to go.' Irene's voice cracked, to her embarrassment, not having realized just how hurt she had been by her mother's refusal.

'Shame! So what are you going to do?' His blue eyes were sympathetic as they gazed down into hers.

'Ask someone else to go with me.' She cleared her throat. 'What have you been buying?'

'A book.'

She felt embarrassed. 'Of course, stupid me!'

'It's called *Harry the Dirty Dog.*' He smiled. 'It's for Josie's birthday. Have you heard of it?'

Irene could not resist that smile. 'It's really popular with the children.'

'The woman upstairs told me it was a best seller. I'm hoping my daughter will like it.'

Irene felt shock go through her but she made a quick recovery. 'How old is she?'

'She'll be two. She's a bright kid, though. Talking already.' He shrugged. 'Probably down to there being so many women in the house, all nattering at once.'

'You ... you mean you don't just ... live with your wife and daughter?' He did not immediately answer. 'Sorry, I shouldn't have asked. None of my business,' said Irene hastily.

He gave a twisted smile. 'It was me that mentioned it. It's my mother-in-law's place. My sister-in-law and niece live there as well and her other sisters visit with their kids.'

'I see,' said Irene carefully, thinking it mustn't be easy for him living in such a household.

85

'This book!' He waggled the parcel. 'You said you worked with kids…'

She nodded. 'It only came out the other year but the kids at the nursery nearly all love Harry.'

'But not all of them?'

He's quick, thought Irene. 'No, some children don't get on with dogs. Big dogs especially can be terrifying if they come bounding up to the children when we take them for a walk on the beach.'

He frowned. 'I take it that you're not alone and keep the children away from the water, especially at this time of year?'

She stared at him in astonishment. 'I'm no fool! There are rules. I couldn't handle ten small children on my own. We look for shells and the like. They won't go near the water until summer and then they'll just paddle.' She took a deep breath. 'Satisfied?'

He nodded. 'I presume you keep an eye on the tide. We used to go to New Brighton on the ferry. I loved it when I was a kid. Ma always used to make a bit of a fuss over us getting sand in our hair, between our toes and in our clothes.'

'I hated getting it in my—' she stopped abruptly.

He grinned. 'You don't have to say it.'

She smiled. 'Have you taken your daughter to New Brighton yet?'

'Not yet.' He changed the subject. 'I was thinking of getting her a paint box as well. If I put some newspaper down, she can enjoy herself messing about.'

'We use poster paint at Fair Haven. I used to love filling in paint books at home. Mam would go mad when I sucked the paintbrush. My tongue would go a funny colour and she'd say that if I wasn't careful, I'd poison myself.'

'Mine told me the same. Remember magic painting books?'

'Yeah, and they're best when it comes to painting books for toddlers. At that age they don't have the dexterity to paint inside the lines of ordinary ones,' said Irene.

'Thanks for the tip.'

There was a pause and they smiled at each other.

'I suppose I'd better go and pay for this calendar,' said Irene.

He nodded. 'I've got to go, too. I'm on my lunch hour and have to get back to work. See you again sometime, Irene.'

She watched him leave the shop and it was only afterwards, when she was paying for the calendar, that she thought about asking about that photo of his brother she had suggested at New Year.

She hurried from the building and stood outside, looking up and down Renshaw Street, but she could see no sign of him. She wondered where he worked. With a shrug, she set off up the street, paying no attention to the businesses and shops, feeling disappointed that Marty McGrath was married with a daughter. He was easy to talk to and she had enjoyed their conversation – although he had been a bit sharp with her when she had talked about taking the children to the beach.

She sighed and put him to the back of her mind as she turned the corner into Leece Street and stopped outside the milk bar opposite the bombed remains of St Luke's church. She peered through the window and saw that several of the tables were occupied by teenagers, but a couple were vacant. She was pleased to see Jeanette behind the counter, so she went inside and wished her a happy New Year.

'Same to you,' said Jeanette, a smile lighting her pretty dainty features. 'It's great to see you.'

'Same here. So how are things with you and Davy?'

'There's plans afoot for us to share a house with Mam and Dad.'

Irene could not conceal her surprise. 'I thought they lived in a country cottage in Wirral!'

'They do! But Dad's finding it too quiet since he retired and Mam's friend, Beryl, who looked after her, has met someone and is getting married. I think it'll be too much for Dad seeing to Mam's special needs all on his own.'

'Where are you planning on living?' asked Irene.

'New Brighton. Dad thinks it'll be ideal. He'll be able to take her for walks in her wheelchair along the prom and she'll have lots of lovely sea air and in the summer there'll be plenty going on. She'll enjoy watching the children playing on the beach and splashing in the sea.'

Irene smiled. 'It sounds great. I met Peggy's brother, Marty, in the bookshop and we were talking about New Brighton.'

'I didn't know you knew Marty,' said Jeanette, looking surprised.

Irene attempted to sound casual. 'We've only met briefly a couple of times when I was with Peggy and Pete.'

'Now you really surprise me. I thought Peggy was trying to keep Pete a secret from her family.'

Irene made to speak but Jeanette held up a hand. 'No, wait, I can't just stand here chatting or the boss will have something to say. Did you plan on having something to drink or eat?'

Irene gave her order and went over to a vacant table in a corner next to a rubber plant. As she sat down, she remembered coming here with Jimmy and meeting Jeanette for the first time. The jukebox had been brand new then, and Jimmy had played a Rosemary Clooney record. Soon after, Pete, Norm and Maggie had turned up. That evening some of them had met again at the Grafton dance hall and Jeanette had brought Peggy with her. It was only later that Peggy had met Pete and they'd started dating.

Someone put a coin in the jukebox and a record dropped into place. It was Buddy Holly's 'Oh, Boy!' Her fingers tapped on the table in time to the music and she thought about the lyrics. It was fast moving and she thought the words were romantic.

Jeanette placed a tray down on the table with a steaming cup and plate of sausage roll and baked beans.

Irene sipped her espresso. 'Pete and Peggy had split up but they might just be back together again.'

'But where does Marty come in to it?' asked Jeanette.

Irene hesitated and told her about meeting him on New Year's Eve.

Jeanette hesitated. 'You do know that Marty's married?'

'He mentioned his wife and daughter earlier. I

presume the wife is the girl at the Stadium who tried to scratch your eyes out.'

'The very same! I think he was mad to marry her.'

'You don't believe they were in love?'

'Lust more than love, I'd say.'

Irene sighed. 'I'd love to see what she looks like.'

'Tarty! Bosom half hanging out of her blouse. Although maybe she doesn't always dress like she did that evening. She has a bust as good as Diana Dors.' She stared at Irene. 'You're not fancying Marty, are you?'

Irene felt the colour rush to her cheeks, reminded of Jimmy asking her the same question. 'He's a married man with a daughter. What kind of girl d'you think I am?'

'He has a son, too.'

Irene was surprised. 'He didn't mention him but maybe that's because we were talking about his daughter's birthday.'

'Well, don't take offence at my warning! Girls have fallen in love with married men before,' said Jeanette. 'I only asked because, although Marty's not what I'd call handsome, he does have a nice way with him and he knows how to look after a girl. In an odd way he's what I'd call a bit of a gentleman. Peggy used to say he was over-protective and it got on her nerves.'

'It would probably get on my nerves, too. I can look after myself,' muttered Irene, taking a bite out of the sausage roll.

'Mmmm! We all think that.' Jeanette met her gaze squarely. 'There are some right swines out there and we women need protecting sometimes.'

Irene nodded and sighed. 'I wonder what will happen with Pete and Peggy. I'm glad I'm not ready to be tied down yet. I'd like to go and see Betty in America. She's asked me to visit her.'

'Good luck to you,' said Jeanette. 'I'd best get back to work.'

'Before you go,' said Irene. 'Where does Marty work?'

'In Quiggins, the architectural ironmongers on Renshaw Street. They specialize in locks and doorknobs and the like. You'll have passed it on the way here.'

'That figures,' said Irene, taking another sip of her coffee.

Jeanette cocked an eye at her but asked no more questions.

Irene dipped chunks of sausage roll into the baked beans and thought about what Jeanette had said about Marty and his wife Bernie. Had sex been the only reason they married or had there been some love there, too? Whatever it was, Irene realized she was best keeping her distance from him.

Perhaps she would get in touch with Peggy and ask if she would like to go to the pantomime with her. That is if Maisie did not change her mind and decide to go with Irene once she knew that she had the tickets for another day. She would pop home and leave a message for her mother and then catch the train to Blundell Sands.

The words of the song 'Why Do Fools Fall in Love' was going over and over in Irene's head as she entered the house and she began singing it as she pushed open the door to the kitchen.

'I wish yer'd shut that racket!' shouted Maisie.

'I didn't expect you to be here,' said Irene.

Her mother's head popped up above the back of the sofa and Irene's mouth fell open.

'Don't you dare say anything!' Maisie warned.

Irene slowly moved forward so that she was facing her mother and could see that on an occasional table was a bottle of gin, one of tonic and a bowl with a couple of half-eaten pigs' trotters in it. 'Holy Mary, mother of God,' she whispered. 'What happened, Mam?'

'What did I say to you?' said Maisie, taking a swig of gin and tonic from a tall glass.

Irene swallowed a giggle. 'I only asked!'

'Stupid bloody girl,' said Maisie slightly breathlessly. 'I should have gone to my old hairdresser instead of somewhere new.'

'I don't know, though,' said Irene, a tremor in her voice. 'I like the short curls. It's just that your hair seems to have gone a funny colour.'

'That's because it *is* a funny colour, eejit! And I didn't want my hair short!' Maisie wailed.

'So what happened? I take it you had it permed?'

'Yeah, but me hair broke when the girl was taking out the rollers. Apparently she shouldn't have dyed it at the same time.'

Irene thought about that. 'It'll be the chemicals! They must have clashed.'

Maisie sniffed. 'I've a good mind to sue.'

'And are you going to?'

'Maybe! But I'd need a lawyer and they cost money.'

'Didn't she warn you that your hair might break?'

92

'She told me that I shouldn't have it dyed and permed at the same time.'

'So why did you do it?' cried Irene, as if she didn't know. Once her mother made up her mind to do something, there was no stopping her.

'I wanted to look like Maureen O'Hara!' cried Maisie, striking the back of the sofa with her fist. 'And I didn't want to wait because I'm not getting any younger. I want to find meself a fella to take me out.' She took another swig of gin and tonic. 'Now look at me!'

Irene's heart sank. Why did her mother have to keep going on about finding herself a fella? She'd had two husbands, why couldn't that be enough? It wasn't as if she was living alone.

She gave Maisie a long, penetrating stare. 'You'll certainly be noticed. Your hair seems to have a bluey-green sheen to it. Maybe you'll start a new fashion.' She struggled with another giggle. 'And the short curls suit you better than the way you had it when it was longer.'

'Maureen O'Hara's hair is long,' said Maisie stubbornly.

'But she's a film star, Mam! Be yourself – and if that means being a woman with greenish-blue hair, then what's wrong with that?' This time Irene could not prevent the giggle from escaping.

'That's what's wrong!' said her mother, shooting out an accusing finger. 'If you dare laugh again,' she said breathlessly, 'you'll be laughing on the other side of your face!'

Irene took herself in hand. 'I wish I could be here when our Jimmy comes in but I've got to get back to Fair Haven. I'd love to see his face when he sees your hair.'

'He'd better keep his mouth zipped or there'll be trouble,' muttered Maisie, downing the rest of her drink in one go.

'I'm sure he'll be tactful,' said Irene, who didn't believe anything of the sort. 'By the way, Mam, I bought you a calendar and I changed the pantomime tickets to a matinee in a fortnight's time. I thought you might like to go with me then.'

Maisie shook her head. 'You take someone else. I'm in no mood for pantomimes.'

'OK!' Irene made up her mind to drop Peggy a line as soon as she had a free moment.

Six

A gull keened overhead as Peggy left the Cunard Building the following Monday evening. She wished she had not promised to accompany her mother to a birthday tea for Josie. No doubt Bernie's family would be there in force. Her in-laws were bound to ask Peggy when she was going to find herself a fella and settle down. She would make some excuse as usual and then they'd ignore her and talk to each other about their husbands and kids. She pictured those self-same kids screaming and yelling, food getting thrown and little boys scrapping. Perhaps she should tell her mother that she had one of her blinding headaches, but she'd had too many of them lately. Her mother would look worried and say she should see

94

the doctor. So far she had not told her mother that she had seen Tommy on New Year's Eve.

Sometimes she felt that she spent too much time worrying about upsetting her parents. At least her father wouldn't be at the birthday tea and maybe it would be different this time. Marty might have mentioned Pete to Bernie without telling her that he was a Proddy. She would tell her mother and sisters and it would be questions, questions. She didn't know which was worse, having a boyfriend or not. Anyway, she hadn't seen or heard anything from Pete since New Year, which was now more than a fortnight ago.

Then, almost as if she had conjured him up, she spotted him on the other side of the road as she approached the bus stop. Her heart seemed to somersault as she drew almost level with him, but he didn't appear to have seen her. Should she let on to him? What if he chose to ignore her? Why should he? They had sort of made up their quarrel. This was stupid!

She began walking again, watching Pete out of the corner of her eye. He crossed the road and it was then that he saw her. She waved to him and he waved back. She felt a rush of warmth and affection and hurried to catch up with him.

'Hello you!' he said, gazing into her eyes and reaching out for her hand.

'Hi!' She squeezed his hand and smiled up at him.

They kissed and it was lovely.

'What are you doing this evening?' he asked.

'Josie's two today and I have to go to her birthday tea with Mam.' She pulled a face. 'I've been dreading it.'

'Why?'

'Because Bernie's sisters will go on about my not having a serious boyfriend and it being time I settled down. I've never dared mention you.'

'Mightn't Marty have mentioned meeting me?' asked Pete.

'I don't know. Somehow I don't think so. I know he definitely hasn't mentioned you to Mam and Dad. Otherwise they'd have said something.'

He hesitated for barely a second before saying, 'I think it's time I met them.'

For a moment she could only stare at him, her heart thudding. 'I-I ... don't ... what, all of them? If you meet Bernie's family, it means you'll meet Mam as well.'

'I'm prepared for that. It's time, Peggy. We can't go on the way we are, putting it off, breaking up, making up. We have to make a decision.'

'You don't have to sound so belligerent,' said Peggy.

'I don't mean to, but it's time I met your parents and you met Ma.' His jaw was set firm.

Peggy moistened her lips and cleared her throat. 'Dad won't be home. It'll only be Mam you have to face. But you can bet that both she and Bernie's lot will want to know how we met, where you live, what you do for a job. Her sisters will probably ask which school you went to and what church. I've never known such a nosy family as theirs.'

He lifted her hand to his mouth and kissed the back of it. 'Stop worrying. Trust me!'

She was about to say, 'I do trust you but...' Then she saw a familiar pained expression come

96

into his eyes and the words remained unspoken.

'What's the worst that can happen?' he demanded.

'Dad could turn up!'

'Sod your dad,' Pete said roughly. 'Everything is going to be fine. Now here comes the bus.'

He helped her aboard and once they were seated, he changed the subject and talked about music, work and a film he'd like to see. She couldn't get a word in and maybe that was just as well because she didn't want to tell him that this was a mistake and things were bound to go wrong. She just knew he would hate Bernie's family staring at him as he limped into the room. It might not be cruelly meant if they asked what was wrong with his leg, but he was so sensitive about the accident and his disability that he was bound to react badly to being questioned.

They were a few doors from her parents' house when Peggy could bear it no longer and blurted out, 'I don't think this is a good idea!'

His mouth tightened. 'We've come this far, it would be a mistake not to knock at the front door and see what kind of welcome I get from your mother. We'd be back to square one. Is that what you want?'

'You must know it isn't!'

'All I know is that I wouldn't even have to be here if you'd agree to get married in a registry office,' he said savagely.

'We've gone through all this!' She wrung her hands. 'I wouldn't feel properly married if I wasn't married in my own church with my family there.'

'Then let's knock at the door,' Pete muttered.

97

Not waiting for her agreement, he lifted the knocker and banged it hard. The door opened almost immediately as if the woman standing there had been watching out for visitors. She was wearing a wraparound floral pinny and her hair was in metal curlers beneath a scarf tied up in a turban.

Pete thrust out his hand. 'Good evening, Mrs McGrath. I'm Peter Marshall, Peggy's boyfriend.'

Mary blinked at him in astonishment and then slowly took his hand. 'How d'you do?'

'Not bad. I hope you're well?' said Pete, shaking her hand firmly and then dropping it.

Mary glanced at her daughter as she came out from behind Pete. 'Well!' she said. 'How long has this been going on, Peggy? I felt sure there was someone but didn't know if that someone was the one or not.'

Peggy looked at Pete, wondering what he made of that sentence, but he was not looking her way. 'Is Dad in?' she asked.

'No! You'd best come in,' said Mary, moving to one side. 'It's a nice name, Peter. The same as the apostle who holds the keys to the kingdom. Don't forget to wipe your feet on the mat, Peter.'

Pete winked at Peggy and did as he was told, following mother and daughter along a narrow lobby and into a room at the rear of the house. Mrs McGrath invited him to sit down by the fire and warm himself.

'Would you like a cup of tea, Peter, before I get myself ready? I presume our Peg has told you we're going to a party. I'm sure you'll be welcome to go with us.' He thanked her and she said, 'You

98

go and make the tea, Peggy love, while I talk to Peter.'

Peggy hesitated but Pete looked at her and said, 'Go on, Peggy. I'm dying for a cup of tea.'

Hoping that he would not say anything out of place to her mother, Peggy went into the back kitchen. As she put on the kettle, she heard her mother say, 'So, where do you live, Peter?'

'Bootle,' he replied.

'And whose parish would that be in?'

Peggy froze.

'I don't actually attend the parish church,' said Pete. 'After my father was killed in the war, Mam stopped going to church, so I go with a mate of mine who attends Our Lady, Star of the Sea. Do you know it, Mrs McGrath? It's in Seaforth.'

Peggy breathed easier. She had to admire Pete's quick thinking.

'I've heard of it,' answered Mary. 'I remember some members of our congregation moving to that parish after their house was bombed. They had family in the area.'

Peggy almost dropped the milk jug.

'Maybe your friend will know them?' Mary mentioned a name. Pete said that he'd ask his friend Jimmy.

'So your mother's a widow, poor woman,' said Mary. 'Do you have any brothers and sisters?'

'I have a twin brother and an older brother.'

'No sisters. That must be a sadness for your mother.'

'She's often said she'd have liked a daughter but that you have to take what comes,' said Pete.

'How true that is,' said Mary. 'I was blessed

99

with two sons and two daughters. Our Lillian is soon to be engaged to be married. So what work do you do, Peter? You don't mind me calling you Peter, do you?'

'Of course not, Mrs McGrath. I've been called worse.'

'And why is that?' she asked, sounding taken aback.

'None of us are perfect, Mrs McGrath. Aren't we all sinners and fall short of the glory of God?'

'That's so true, Peter, but few people would admit to it.'

Peggy wasted no time carrying in a tray of crockery. 'Has Pete told you that he's a shipping clerk, Mam?'

'That sounds a nice, steady job,' said her mother.

'I'd have liked to have a more exciting life and gone to sea,' said Pete, 'but my accident put paid to that.'

'What accident was that?' asked Mary

'You didn't notice my limp?' Pete could not conceal his surprise.

'Yes, but it would have been rude to mention it.'

Pete was silent and a muscle twitched in his neck. He cleared his throat. 'I fell from a window sill.'

'You poor boy. I bet you were cleaning windows for your mother,' said Mary.

Pete hesitated but Peggy, who was standing behind her mother, nodded vigorously at him. 'Yes, Mrs McGrath,' he said. 'I think cleaning the outsides isn't a job for a woman.'

'I suppose you ended up in hospital?'

100

'Longer than I care to think about now,' he said in a low voice.

Peggy decided the conversation was going along nicely and it was safe for her to make the tea. When she returned with the pot, Pete was alone. 'Your mother's gone to get ready,' he said. 'I like her. She's considerate of others.'

Peggy was so pleased by that remark that she put down the teapot and kissed him. 'I didn't like telling fibs, though,' he murmured against her lips.

'You have to tell little white lies sometimes,' she said, kissing Pete again before freeing herself and pouring the tea.

He rose and came up behind her and slid his arms about her waist. 'I want us to get married soon,' he murmured, nuzzling her neck.

'I want it, too. Mam's bound to tell Dad about you and maybe she'll be able to persuade him that you're the right one for me.'

'Let's hope so.'

They heard Mary coming downstairs and reluctantly drew apart. He sat down with his cup of tea. Mary entered the room, wearing a powder-blue twin set and dark blue pleated skirt.

Peggy handed a cup of tea to her mother and said, 'You look nice, Mam. I'll just pop upstairs and change out of my working clothes.'

When she came back downstairs Pete was admiring the birthday cake that Mary had made for Josie. 'I wish Ma could make one that looks as good as that,' he said. 'I'm not telling tales out of school, but she'd be the first to admit that she can't bake for toffee.'

Mary looked gratified. 'My mother taught me

101

but Peggy's never shown any real interest in baking.'

'It's a gift, Mam,' said Peggy. 'And when you make them so good, I always felt it wasn't worth me bothering. Our Marty says Bernie can't make a decent cake either. He'll be dead chuffed when he sees yours on the table.'

But in the end Marty did not arrive home in time for the party and so he never did see the cake his mother had made and Josie blowing out two pink candles in one gusty go.

Where could he be? Peggy wondered, thinking that otherwise everything had gone off brilliantly. Of course, Bernie had a face on her because of Marty's absence and she could not blame her. Yet surely he must have a very good reason for missing Josie's birthday.

Despite knowing he would get the back of Bernie's tongue when he arrived home, Marty could not have ignored the brief telephone call that he had received from his brother shortly before he left work. Tommy wanted to meet up with him and had suggested the Red Lion pub by the canal in Litherland in an hour. Before Marty could ask where the hell he had been all this time and why hadn't he been in touch – as well as why that pub – his brother had put down the phone.

Marty knew that he had no time to spare phoning Bernie if he was to arrive at the meeting place on time. It was rush hour and there would be long queues for trains and buses. As he sat on the L3 bus, heading along Stanley Road, Marty was thinking about the day the police had turned up at his parents' house, looking for his brother.

They had wanted to speak to Tommy about a stolen car. It came as no surprise to Marty when told about his mother's encounter with the police that she had immediately sprung to her younger son's defence, saying that he would never steal anything. She had suggested that they speak to him at the garage where he was a mechanic. As it turned out they had already been there and also visited the address where he had been staying, but Tommy was not to be found at either place. He had vanished along with the customer's car he had been working on the previous day.

The news soon got out that the police had called at the McGraths' house and a mechanic at the garage spoke to the press and within no time the story appeared in the Liverpool *Echo* about how Tommy had been borrowing cars he had been repairing to use as getaway vehicles, working with thieves who broke into jewellers' and pawn-brokers' shops. It seemed that in the past he had always returned the vehicles to the garage before the customers picked them up the following day, so they had never been reported as stolen. This time the thieves had been unlucky. The pawn-broker whom they intended to rob had managed to press an alarm bell before being coshed and a bobby on the beat had been nearby and come running and put in a call for assistance. Tommy must have spotted him and had driven off but one of the thieves had managed to jump on to the running board and escaped with Tommy. The car was never traced and neither were the proceeds from a robbery earlier that evening that had been left in the boot.

It was still three minutes to seven when Marty pushed open the door of the Red Lion and went inside. The interior was fuggy with cigarette smoke but not as crowded as no doubt it would be later on in the evening. He spotted Tommy almost immediately and was glad to see he was alone with a pint in front of him. From the way he was puffing on a cigarette and glancing furtively about him, he was obviously a little on edge.

Marty knew the moment his brother caught sight of him because he grinned in his direction. Marty felt like hitting him but instead raised a hand and pointed to the bar and mimed drinking before ordering a pint of Bass. After paying for it, he made his way to where his brother was sitting in a corner and sat opposite him.

'Where the hell have you been?' Marty asked without preamble. 'Mam's had you dead and buried.'

Tommy frowned. 'Don't be like that, Marty, or I'll regret getting in touch with you.'

'I bet you only did so because you knew that you'd been spotted.'

Tommy flicked ash from his cigarette. 'I won't lie to you. You've hit the nail on the head. I spotted you from the bus. Now if you'd worn a crash helmet and goggles I wouldn't have done. You've got to watch out for the little things, Marty, if you want to play detective.'

'Don't be giving me advice,' said Marty, dropping his voice. 'If you had a brain in your head you wouldn't have got involved with criminals. You'd managed to finish your apprenticeship and had a good job and were in a position of trust. What do you do? Ruin everything because sufficient has never been enough for you! You've always wanted more and so you break Mam's heart into the bargain to satisfy your own greed.'

'I didn't phone you so you could lay into me,' said Tommy sullenly. 'I guessed you'd still be working there.'

'You should be glad I'm so dependable and you could phone me without Mam and Dad knowing,' said Marty.

'Actually, I thought I was bloody clever.' He smirked. 'I doubt I'd have ever been found out if it hadn't been for that alarm going off when it did. I never actually stole a car until the last time.'

'Lower your voice!' muttered Marty. 'Where've you been these past few years?'

'That would be telling.' Tommy took a swig of his beer.

Marty swore beneath his breath. 'You are the most selfish sod I've ever met. You could have sent her a letter.'

'Letters have postmarks and you can bet she'd have shown it to Dad.' Tommy's expression darkened and he picked up his glass. 'Anyway, was it pure luck you spotted me?'

'Peggy saw you outside here. She has friends in this area, so she phoned me at Bernie's mother's.'

'Bernie's mother's!' The glass slipped in Tommy's hand and he only just managed to save it. 'What were you doing at her house? That old bitch hates me because she thinks the sun shines out of Patrick's arse!'

'I'm married to Bernie and we live there,' said

Marty tersely.

Tommy's mouth fell open and for several moments he seemed unable to speak. Then he gulped and said, 'Bloody hell, how did that happen? She's not your type.'

'I know that now, but she got pregnant. We've two kids. A boy and a girl.' Marty took a deep draught of his beer and changed the subject. 'Have you mates in the neighbourhood?'

Tommy took a deep breath. 'Have you told Bernie you saw me?'

'No, and neither have I told Mam and Dad yet. I plan on telling Mam, just so she knows you're still alive, although she'd be happier if she could see you.'

Tommy's mouth tightened. 'There's no way I'll set foot in our house while Dad's alive. I'm not like you,' he said, stubbing out his cigarette. 'He gets me goat. He always has. He's so bleedin' holier than thou! He's a hypocrite! We both know he likes a drink or two and it's Mam who's the saint for putting up with him. It's a bloody miracle that I stayed living at home as long as I did, but I didn't really have any choice, not having much money. That's why I did what I did. I was always broke.' He took out a fresh packet of cigarettes and removed one, lit up and inhaled a lungful of smoke. 'Women don't think anything of you if you don't have money to spend on them.'

'So presumably you have money now?' said Marty, noticing that it was a packet of Kensitos, not his brother's usual cheaper Woodbines. He fought the urge to ask Tommy for a cigarette. Marty had given them up when Josie was born to

106

save money but there were still times when he longed for a smoke.

'Some!' Tommy's eyes did not quite meet Marty's.

'Have you got a girl?'

Tommy hesitated. 'Not at the moment. The money from the robbery is all spent. I left the country and it costs to live.'

'What happened to the crook that managed to escape with you?'

'Dead two months ago,' said Tommy succinctly. 'Would you believe a snake bit him?'

'A snake? Where the hell have you been? And why have you come back? Do you think you're safe because the other crooks are still in jail? The police won't have closed the case yet, you know? Not until they find you and your thieving mate.'

Tommy smiled. 'They won't be looking for me, though, will they? Not after the time I've been away.'

'Maybe not,' murmured Marty, draining his glass. 'So where are you living now? What are your plans or shouldn't I ask?'

Tommy hesitated. 'I'd rather not answer either of those questions.'

Marty nodded. 'Please yourself. I suppose if anything was to happen to either Mam or Dad, and I needed to get in touch with you, I could put a notice in the *Echo*.'

Tommy blinked rapidly. 'Yer mean them dropping dead and you putting them in the Deaths!'

'Naw, I'd never presume you'd read the Deaths,' said Marty, getting to his feet. 'Well, if you've told me all you're going to tell me, I'll be on my way.

It's Josie's birthday and Bernie's doing her a special tea and I'm late.'

Tommy sighed heavily. 'I suppose you've got to keep her sweet. She's a one is Bernie. What did she have to say when I had to disappear?'

'She's like Mam and has you dead.'

Tommy looked taken aback and then said, 'I suppose that makes sense. How old is your little girl?'

'Two,' said Marty.

'And the boy?'

'Three and a bit.'

Tommy hesitated. 'Are you going to tell Bernie we've spoken?'

'No! You can bet she'd let it slip to one of her sisters and she'd tell her mother. Anyway, Mam was going to the party. She was making Josie a birthday cake. I hope they've saved a slice for me.'

Tommy dug a hand into a coat pocket and took out a couple of florins. 'Buy them some sweets from me.'

Marty hesitated.

'I earned it honestly,' said Tommy, scowling.

Marty pocketed the money, thinking the less he saw of his brother the better. 'See you around.'

It was on the way out of the Red Lion that Marty collided with a bloke. 'Sorry,' both said, glancing at each other as they made space to allow the other to pass.

Only when he was outside did Marty realize that he had seen him before. He went back inside the pub to have another look and noticed Irene's brother standing at the bar. Even as Marty gazed in Jimmy's direction, he saw Tommy approach him and exchange a few words.

It could be just small talk with a stranger, thought Marty. Should he go over there and have a word? Then he reminded himself that he was going to be late enough getting home as it was and he wanted to see Josie before she was put to bed.

Marty climbed the steps to the front door of Bernie's mother's house as one of his wife's sisters was leaving with her two children. He held the front door open for her, so she could manoeuvre the pushchair out and helped her down the steps.

'Yer in trouble, Marty,' she whispered when they reached the bottom. 'And yer missed seeing your Peggy's boyfriend. Lovely manners! Pity that he's a cripple but I believe he's got a good job. Goes to Our Lady, Star of the Sea in Seaforth, I believe. See yer, love!'

She went off down the street, pausing to wave when she hadn't gone far. Marty returned her wave, for he was still standing at the top of the steps, mulling over what she had told him. Then he went inside the house. He closed the front door gently and stood in the lobby, listening, before stepping on to the new maroon carpet runner that Bernie's mother had bought in time for Christmas.

He paused outside the kitchen door, thinking there was no need for him to put his ear to the panel because he could clearly hear Bernie's voice. 'I'll have him when he gets home,' she said. 'No phone call and he said he'd definitely be here in time to see everyone.'

'He must have a good reason for being late,' said Monica, who was Bernie's sixteen-year-old niece.

109

'You're as bad as Peggy, making excuses for him,' said Bernie.

'His mother was put out,' said her widowed sister, Cissie. 'She makes a decent cake. Nice icing, not too hard, not too soft. And that was a nice little frock she bought Josie and it was good of her to buy Jerry a present, too.'

'But the overalls for Jerry are too big for him,' Bernie complained. 'Did you hear what she said? Plenty of room for him to grow into them.'

'Nothing wrong with that,' said Cissie. 'Our Mam was the same with us when we were growing up. You being the youngest, you don't remember the time when money was really tight.'

'Don't start going on about me being spoilt,' said Bernie. 'Castoffs, that's what I used to get all the time.'

'Oh, stop moaning,' said Cissie. 'Besides, that wasn't always the case.'

'Often enough to get on my wick,' said Bernie.

'What's that supposed to mean?' asked Monica.

'Never you mind,' said her mother.

'You haven't said what you thought about Peggy's fella yet, Auntie Bernie,' said Monica.

'I never thought Peggy would bring a cripple home. I'll admit Peter is good looking, but Mr McGrath's not going to like it,' said Bernie. 'He's a bugger for perfection.'

'And he speaks nice,' said Cissie. 'Works in an office. I just wish your Marty had been here to see him.'

'Where the hell is he?' muttered Bernie. 'I bet he's gone for a drink. I'll have him!'

Marty had heard enough and he retraced his

110

steps to the front door, opened it and banged it shut and then strode up the lobby, whistling. He turned the door knob and flung open the door.

'Talk of the devil,' said Bernie, getting to her feet and glaring at her husband standing in the doorway. 'Where the hell have you been?'

'Not hell, that's for sure,' he said.

'Very funny! I'd started thinking you'd been run over by a bus.'

'Sorry I'm late. Did Josie enjoy her party?'

'Don't you "sorry" me,' snapped Bernie. 'It comes to something when a father misses his own daughter's birthday tea.'

'It wasn't deliberate.' Marty bent and lifted Josie from Monica's lap. 'Happy birthday to my beautiful girl,' he said, kissing the back of his daughter's soft neck.'

Josie snuggled into him. 'Where you bin, Daddy?'

'Out and about!' He blew a raspberry against her neck and she giggled. 'And because I missed your birthday tea, I'm going to take you somewhere special to make up for it.'

'You missed your Peggy's fella,' said Cissie.

Marty's fair head shot up and he stared at Bernie. 'He came here?'

'With Peggy and your mother. See! You should have come home earlier,' she said smugly. 'He's a real looker. If he wasn't crippled I could fancy him myself.'

Marty did not rise to the bait. 'What was Mam like with him?'

'I could tell she liked him,' said Cissie. 'She brought a lovely cake.'

111

'Your Lil didn't turn up, though,' sniffed Bernie. 'She fancies herself, that sister of yours. A children's tea is below her.'

'She's all right is our Lil,' said Marty, frowning. 'She probably had the chance of overtime.'

'And she's not going to turn that down when she's saving up to get married,' said Cissie.

'Is there any of Mam's cake left?' Marty asked.

Monica jumped to her feet. 'I saved you a slice, Uncle Marty. I knew it would all be gobbled if I didn't put a piece away.'

Marty thanked her and asked if there was any dinner. If not, then he knew they'd all been gorging themselves and he would have to go to the chippy.

'I'll go to the chippy for you if you like,' said Monica. 'After all, you've been working hard all day.'

'I've been putting new locks on a posh house in Woolton,' said Marty, digging into a pocket and producing some coins that he handed to her. 'I'll have chips, fish and peas, thanks.'

He sat down on the chair Monica had vacated with his daughter on his knee. 'A cup of tea wouldn't go amiss,' he said, looking at Bernie.

She made no move to make him one, but Cissie placed the sleeping Jerry on the sofa and vanished into the next room. Husband and wife stared at each other. 'Don't take that tone with me in front of Cissie and Monica again,' said Marty coldly. 'I had my reasons for being late, which I'd have told you about if you'd shown a bit of patience. Surely you can't believe I'd miss Josie's birthday tea without a good reason?'

112

Bernie's cheeks reddened and she folded her arms across her chest. 'So what was your reason for being late? I can smell from here you've been drinking.'

His eyes glinted. 'One drink!'

'So who were you drinking with?' she blurted out. 'Another woman?'

He just stared at her. 'I'm going to put Josie to bed and read to her.' He carried his daughter across the room and started upstairs.

Bernie hurried after him. 'Aren't yer going to tell me where you've been?' she shouted.

He felt Josie twist in his arms and stare down at her mother. 'Lower your voice,' said Marty. 'I don't want your mother coming out to see what's going on.'

'She's gone to the pictures.' Bernie gripped her hands tightly together. 'I suppose yer think I should say sorry, when it's you who should be sorry!'

'I said sorry when I came in.' He carried on up the stairs and into their bedroom. He picked up *Harry the Dirty Dog* from the chest of drawers and sat down in a chair with his daughter on his knee.

Bernie followed them in and glanced at the cover of the book. 'Why couldn't you have bought her a nice fairy story?'

'I was told this is a best-seller.'

'Well, it wouldn't have been my choice,' she muttered, sitting on the bed.

There was a silence.

'Anyway, I could do with a break from them,' said Bernie. 'I get fed up being home day after day with the kids.'

'You met your old workmate the other day,' said Marty. 'Stop making out you're hard done by. You're not short of babysitters. It seems to me that all you have to do is ask.'

'That isn't as easy as you might think it,' said Bernie, tossing her head. 'You were lucky being the eldest and having a brother and only two sisters.' She gave him a look and left the bedroom.

Marty hugged his daughter to him and managed to open the book with one hand. As he read the text and Josie pointed to the pictures, he was remembering with half a mind how there had been no books in their house when he was small. His father had never read to him and the stories his mother had told him had been those she remembered from her own childhood, about saints and fairy tales like *'The Three Bears'* and *'Jack and the Beanstalk'*.

His maternal grandmother had taught him his alphabet. Sadly she had passed away when he was only six. He had never known his paternal grandparents. He'd asked his father about them but he had told him only that they were dead. Pity his father took little interest in the kids, because they were now of an age when they were getting interesting and you could share stuff with them.

He decided he needed to talk to Peggy. No doubt she would be going to Mass on Sunday. He would skip going to the church that Bernie and her mother preferred, so he could tell his sister and mother about his meeting with Tommy.

Seven

It was Sunday morning and Peggy was writing a letter to Irene, agreeing to go to the pantomime with her the following Saturday afternoon. She slipped it into an envelope, addressed and stamped it and then sat on the bed, thinking.

She wished she could have persuaded Pete to go to Mass with her. All he needed to do now was enrol for instruction in the Roman Catholic faith. He had done the right thing in telling her mother that he sometimes attended Our Lady, Star of the Sea. So far her father had made no mention of him. She felt certain her mother would have told him that she had met Pete. So why hadn't he said anything about it to her?

She wished that she could stand up to her father more and be prepared to defy him. After all she was over twenty-one, earned her own living and had the vote. Sometimes she wished she had been born a man. They seemed to have the best of things. Better wages, never expected to help with the housework after doing a full day's work. No periods, no giving birth. Of course, men did have to go and fight in wars and there had been a lot of them this century. Two world wars, fighting in Korea, then Cyprus and the other year there had been the Suez crisis which could have blown up into a real bad conflict, only the Yanks had refused to support Great Britain. On second thoughts, she

115

was probably better off being a woman. She had a man she loved and who wanted to marry her.

At that moment her sister entered the bedroom. 'Dad says he wants you downstairs in five minutes.'

Peggy's heart seemed to flip over. 'I'll be there.'

Lil sat on the bed. 'Mam was telling me about your boyfriend. I heard her saying to Dad that he should speak to you about inviting him to Sunday lunch.'

Peggy froze. 'And what did Dad say?'

'He'd think about allowing him under his roof.'

'That sounds like him,' muttered Peggy, reaching for her Sunday hat which was a pull-on sage green felt with a narrow brim and a white and green spotted bow at the side.

'I wouldn't worry,' said Lil, getting to her feet. 'Mam will win Dad round if he gets awkward.'

'Only if he's decided that he wants to be won round,' said Peggy.

'So d'you think you'll be getting engaged soon?' asked Lil.

Peggy hesitated, gazing at herself in the mirror as she put on her hat and fiddled with her hair. 'Let's wait and see, shall we?' She did not want to put a jinx on things by saying she would soon have Pete's diamond sparkling on the third finger of her left hand. She pulled on her coat, picked up her gloves and led the way downstairs.

Her father was standing with his back to the fire, holding up the skirts of his overcoat, seemingly so he could warm his backside, while her mother was flitting about like a sparrow searching for crumbs in the street. 'Here she is, William!

116

Doesn't she look nice? In fact, don't both our daughters look nice?'

'Stop babbling, woman!' William ordered, staring at Peggy from beneath drooping eyelids. 'So what's this I hear from your mother about bringing a boyfriend home?'

Peggy could feel her knees begin to tremble. Earlier she had almost convinced herself that he wasn't going to mention Pete. She took a deep breath. 'That's right, Dad. I bet Mam told you all about him!'

'I don't gamble,' said William. 'Gambling is a mug's game.'

Peggy moistened her lips, thinking it was going to be one of those awkward conversations, and decided to keep her mouth shut until he spoke again. That way she was bound not to say the wrong thing.

'Nothing you'd like to add to what your mother told me?' said William, taking a handkerchief from a pocket and wiping one of his eyes.

'I don't know what Mam told you,' said Peggy.

'Don't give me cheek!' said William, shooting out a hand and slapping her lightly on the face. 'Respect the commandments and honour thy father.'

Peggy pressed her lips together to stop them from trembling. The blow had not hurt but the fact that her father should hit one of his daughters would upset her mother and she didn't want her getting all nervy.

'Isn't it time we were going, William?' asked Mary, twisting her gloves between her hands. 'We don't want to be late for Mass.'

117

William gave a sharp nod. 'Aye, it's probably time we were going. I want to have a word with Father Francis.' He moved away from the fire and, picking up his trilby from the sideboard, placed the hat on his iron-grey hair. 'Put the guard to the fire, Lil! Come on, Mary; stop wasting time,' he added.

Lil placed the fireguard into position while Peggy waited for her. Then the sisters linked arms and followed their parents out of the house.

Marty was standing at the back of the church, watching out for his parents and sisters while talking to an old school friend who helped out with the boys' club founded by Father Francis. It had kept many a lad from hanging around on street corners and causing mischief, including himself. He saw the family come in and excused himself.

Peggy dipped a finger in the holy water and crossed herself, having stood back while her parents and Lil went ahead. She saw Marty, looking smart in his Sunday suit, talk to them for several minutes and waited impatiently for him to approach her. 'I suppose Bernie told you about Pete and that's why you're here?' she blurted out as soon as he was in earshot.

Marty nodded. 'We were just talking about Pete. Dad said he was going to have a word with Father Francis about him. I wouldn't be too happy about that.'

Peggy bit on her lip. 'Wha– What d'you mean? You didn't tell Dad that Pete's a Proddy, did you?'

'No, that's your job. I'd do it as soon as possible if I were you.'

Peggy's mouth was suddenly dry. 'Why?' she asked huskily. 'What d'you think Father Francis will do?'

'One of Father Francis's parishioners moved to Seaforth and set up a boys' club at Our Lady, Star of the Sea. He's bound to ask if the family knows Pete Marshall.'

Peggy groaned. 'I don't remember them but I bet Mam and Dad will.'

'And another thing – I met our Tommy in the Red Lion in Litherland last night!'

Peggy's eyes opened wide. 'You saw our Tommy?'

He nodded. 'He phoned me. That's why I wasn't at the birthday tea.'

'What did he have to say?'

He told her. 'You can tell Mam.' He paused. 'By the way, on the way out of the pub, I bumped into Irene Miller's brother, not that either of us made any sign of recognizing each other. A few minutes later I saw him at the bar talking to Tommy.'

Peggy was surprised. 'I wonder what they were discussing.'

'Perhaps you could mention it to Irene next time you see her,' he said casually.

'I'm seeing her next Saturday. We're going the matinee at the Empire to see "Babes in the Wood".'

He looked surprised. 'Are you now! So she really isn't taking her mother.'

'Change of plan. Nothing wrong with that, is there?'

He only said, 'We'd better go and sit down. Mam's making signals to us.'

Peggy realized that the service was about to

119

start and joined the family in a pew.

After the service was over, she was hoping to speak to her brother again but he wasted no time in leaving church, so she never got the chance. Her father told his womenfolk to go on ahead without him, which suited her fine. It meant she could tell her mother and Lil about Tommy.

The news brought tears to Mary's eyes. 'I'm so relieved he's all right. If it wasn't for your father, I'm sure he'd have come to see me.'

'Of course he would, Mam,' said Lil, hugging her mother's arm.

'I'm sure he'll get in touch with Marty again,' said Peggy.

'It's nice to hear that he's safe and hopefully he'll get himself a proper job and keep out of trouble,' said Mary happily. 'Maybe our Marty will be able to arrange for me and Tommy to have a cup of tea and a cake in a cafe.'

The sisters smiled encouragingly, although Peggy had her doubts about such a cosy reunion taking place. To Peggy's relief when her father arrived home in time for Sunday lunch he made no mention of Pete or Father Francis and the meal went off smoothly. She was glad that her mother seemed to be managing to keep quiet about Tommy while their father was in the room. Peggy was impatient to see Pete and tell him about the latest developments in the McGrath family affairs.

The following evening Peggy left the Cunard Building and found Pete waiting for her. She slipped her hand through his arm and they began to walk in the direction of James Street.

'So how did things go with your father?' he asked.

'Mam told him about meeting you and he wanted to know if I had anything more to add to what she had already told him. I didn't get a chance to say anything really because it was time to go to Mass.' Peggy's hand tightened on his arm. 'What worries me is that he was going to speak to Father Francis about you. A family from our parish moved out to Seaforth and are members of Our Lady, Star of the Sea. Father Francis is still in contact with them, and Marty thinks he is bound to ask around about you.'

Pete stopped in his tracks. 'Hell!'

She gazed up at him, her eyes full of worry and doubt.

'Well, that's it, isn't it?' said Pete in a hard voice. 'Your father either knows I've lied about being a Catholic and he's playing some game of his own or he'll get to know sooner or later.'

'Marty thinks I should tell Dad the truth but I'm scared,' said Peggy with a worried frown.

'Could you do it if I was with you?' asked Pete, tracing the side of her face with a finger.

She did not reply immediately but after a minute said, 'I … I suppose so.'

'Then we'll do it,' said Pete firmly.

'But not this evening,' she said swiftly. 'It's Dad's darts night. Let's go to the pictures. I'd like to forget all this for a while.'

'All right!' He kissed her and they carried on walking. She told him about Tommy but he said little in response. No doubt Pete did not approve of her brother coming back into their lives. Then

121

she mentioned visiting the Empire with Irene on Saturday afternoon. Pete suggested that he meet her in town afterwards and they could go for a Chinese. She agreed and began to look forward to it. They went to the cinema to see a musical comedy called *Hollywood or Bust* starring Dean Martin and Jerry Lewis.

'I enjoyed that,' said Peggy as they were leaving the cinema.

'Do you know Irene wants to go to California?' said Pete.

'That'll be to visit Betty Booth,' said Peggy. 'Irene will really have to save up for that kind of holiday!'

'Or get herself a job there,' said Pete, squeezing Peggy's hand. He changed the subject. 'I was thinking that perhaps we should go and visit Ma instead of you going straight home. It's not late. What d'you think?'

Peggy hesitated and then agreed that since Pete had met her mother, it seemed only right that Peggy should meet his. With that settled they went for the bus. They did not talk much and when they did it was about the film they had just seen and what it would be like living in America.

They left the bus in Bootle and walked arm in arm to the Marshalls' house. Pete took a key from his pocket and opened the front door.

'We're being watched,' whispered Peggy. 'You've got nosy neighbours.

'Ignore them,' said Pete, drawing her into his arms as soon as the door closed behind them and bringing her against him as he kissed her.

'Stop it!' she whispered against his mouth.

122

'Your mother will have heard the door open.'

'We're only kissing,' Pete murmured.

And the rest, she thought as he caressed her breast.

The sound of footsteps caused them to spring apart, so that when the kitchen door opened, Pete was just ahead of her, leading her by the hand up the lobby.

Peggy received a shock when she saw a policeman standing in the doorway.

'What are you doing here?' asked Pete.

'Came to see Ma. I thought she'd be here. We want her to babysit tomorrow evening.'

'I'll mention it when she comes in,' said Pete.

The policeman stared at Peggy. 'Who's this? I've a feeling I've seen her before.'

'This is Peggy McGrath. We've been going out together,' said Pete. 'Peggy, this is my brother, Dougie.'

'Hello,' said Peggy nervously, thinking the brothers weren't a bit alike in appearance – but then neither were her brothers. She hoped that Pete would not mention Tommy to his elder brother.

Dougie held out his hand and she hastened to shake it. 'Nice to meet you,' he said. 'First time he's mentioned you. I presume you've come to see Ma.'

She nodded.

He released her hand and went back inside the kitchen.

Pete and Peggy exchanged glances and followed him. 'Shouldn't you be getting back to catching criminals?' said Pete.

'I will shortly.' Dougie glanced around the room. 'This place could do with a good tidy.'

'All right, fanatic,' said Pete, looking irritated. 'Ma and I don't have the time to be tidying up before we go out to work.' He glanced at Peggy. 'Sit down, love, and we'll have a cup of tea. Ma mightn't be long.' He left the room.

'Yes, sit down, Peggy, and tell me about yourself,' said Dougie, leaning against a table and eyeing her up and down.

Peggy felt as if he were looking at her as he would a suspected criminal. She thought of Tommy and her heart sank as she sat down in an armchair over the back of which hung a cardigan. She stared back at him, determined not to feel cowed.

'I'm trying to remember where I've seen you before,' said Dougie, his eyes narrowing. 'My memory's generally pretty good.'

Pete appeared briefly in the doorway to say, 'Peggy's a friend of Jeanette's; she works in the Cunard Building.'

Dougie's face lit up and he pointed a finger at Peggy. 'I've gotcha now! You had something to do with that fight in a chippy a few years back. You've a brother called Marty, who later helped us with information that led to the capture of the real nasty piece of work – a bloke who'd been involved in a fight and who nearly did for the doorman at the Stadium.'

'I didn't know our Marty helped the police,' said Peggy, taken aback.

'You can't know everything,' said Dougie, smiling. 'Some things have to remain hush-hush.'

Peggy still found it hard to believe that Marty was a snout. She was pretty certain her father was unaware of it because he hated the police, especially when they came knocking on his front door.

'Don't look like that, Peggy,' said Dougie. 'You should be proud that Marty's a good citizen. You ask Jeanette's brother about him. He'll tell you we could do with more of the public being like him.' He paused and added abruptly, 'On second thoughts, best not.'

Peggy had no intention of investigating further.

'You're Catholic, aren't you?' said Dougie out of the blue.

Peggy stiffened. 'What if I am?'

'What do your parents have to say about you going out with our Pete?' Dougie folded his arms across his broad chest and fixed her with a stare.

She did not reply and wished he would go away.

'You haven't told them, have you? That says something.' Dougie shook his head.

Peggy was beginning to really, really dislike this brother of Pete's.

'Leave her alone,' said Pete, entering the room carrying a tray with two steaming cups on it and a plate of biscuits. 'She's not on trial here!'

Dougie glanced at him. 'I'm only thinking of you, brother. I don't care what she is, myself. I'm not religious.'

Pete exchanged glances with Peggy and smiled as he handed her a cup of tea. 'He's always like this. Has to put his oar in everyone else's business. Ignore him.' Pete sat on the arm of Peggy's chair with his own cup of tea.

'He isn't easy to ignore,' said Peggy, reaching for a biscuit.

'He'll be going soon. Won't you, Dougie?' said Pete, glaring at his brother.

There came a noise at the front door and immediately Dougie left the room. Pete said, 'That'll be Mam. You stay here, Peggy. I'll be back in a mo'.' He limped out of the room, pulling the door to behind him but it did not click shut.

Peggy stood up and tiptoed over to the door.

'You should see Maisie Miller's hair!' she heard a female voice say. 'She came in this morning with it really short and the most peculiar colour! Nobody dared laugh to her face, though.'

'Never mind that, Mam,' said Dougie. 'Can you babysit for us tomorrow evening?'

'Sure I can, son,' said Gertie. 'But I was just telling you...'

'We've got a guest, Ma,' interrupted Pete.

'His girlfriend's here,' said Dougie. 'I'll be seeing you, Ma. Come about five.'

'All right,' said Gertie. 'Now who did he say was here, Pete?'

'My girlfriend, Peggy. Come and meet her.'

Peggy backed away from the door and sat back in her chair. She picked up her cup and sipped her tea. The door swung open and a middle-aged woman stood there.

'Well, you don't look too bad,' said Gertie, nodding her head several times.

Peggy was not sure what to say to that remark, so she just stood up and smiled at the little plump woman in a belted russet woollen coat and plaid headscarf and said, 'Hello, Mrs Marshall.'

'Hello, love! What did our Pete say your name was?'

'Peggy, Peggy McGrath. I'm pleased to meet you.' She held out a hand that trembled slightly.

'McGrath, McGrath,' murmured Gertie, screwing up her face. 'What are your mother and father's Christian names?'

'William and Mary,' replied Peggy.

'Hmmm! William McGrath. That sounds familiar.' She patted Peggy's hand. 'Can you cook, love?'

The question took Peggy aback. 'A bit, although Ma didn't really like us girls messing up her kitchen.'

'That's a shame,' said Gertie, blinking at her. 'I bet she's a good cook. A woman should be able to cook and feed her menfolk. My husband enjoyed cooking, that's why I never bothered. When he went off to war and I had to go out to work ... what with rationing ... I can't say we ate well.'

Pete grinned. 'You've improved since then, Ma, and there was always the chippy or Sayers and the cooked meat shop. I'll put the kettle on. You'll be ready for a cuppa.'

Gertie beamed at him. 'You're right there, son. I'm real parched. I think I'll fry meself an egg and do a bit of fried bread. I'm hungry.' She removed her coat and slung it on the back of the sofa and sat down. With a sigh of relief she eased off her shoes, wincing when she attempted to wiggle her toes.

Peggy wondered if she had a touch of rheumatics in her feet, just like her mother. 'I could fry you an egg, Mrs Marshall,' she said, smiling at Pete. 'If for

127

no other reason than to prove I'm not completely useless when it comes to cooking.'

Gertie smiled at her. 'That's the ticket, love.'

'Come on then, Peg,' said Pete, taking her hand. 'I'll show you where everything is.' He was keen to make Peggy feel at home.

After a quick glance at Gertie, who was now resting back in the chair with her eyes closed and her stockinged feet on the brass fender, Peggy followed him out. 'Your Mam looks tired,' she whispered.

'She works hard and isn't getting any younger. You know she's at the sausage factory where Irene's mother works?'

Peggy nodded, taking a frying pan from him. 'She seems easy-going.'

'I don't think Mam has a mean bone in her body. She's not a tidy person, though, and neither am I, so you'll have to forgive the mess,' said Pete, darting her an anxious look. 'I remember your mam's place was dead tidy. Things were different here before Dad went off to war and got himself killed.'

'I think I remember you telling me that she worked in the ammunition factory.'

'That's right. She was just too tired when she came home to make much of an effort in the house and with us. We ran wild until our Dougie took us in hand, as I told you.'

Peggy remembered it was around that time that Pete had gone slightly off the rails and had his accident. She realized for the first time that Tommy had gone off the rails without the excuse of having a father killed in the war and a mother having to go out to work.

She glanced around the kitchen. 'So where are the eggs?'

Pete took a bowl of eggs from the kitchen cabinet along with a packet of lard. 'Sure you don't mind doing this? I could do it instead.'

'No, you make your Mam a cup of tea and cut some bread. I can manage the frying.'

He handed her a box of matches. 'I'll take Ma's tea in and explain a few things to her.'

'About what?' asked Peggy.

'Us.'

She hesitated. 'What did you make of her seeming to recognize my dad's name? Has your Mam always lived in Bootle?'

'No, she grew up in Kirkdale. Her father was a photographer and had a shop on Stanley Road. Don't worry about it. She's probably getting the name mixed up with someone else. Anyway, I want to talk to her about us. I think you and she will get on, don't you?'

Peggy knew what he needed to hear and, wanting to make him happy, she agreed.

He kissed her and went into the other room, whistling. She recognized the tune of *'If You Were the Only Girl in the World'* and wished their love life could be less complicated. At least she had the outing with Irene to look forward to next Saturday.

Eight

The following Saturday, after spending the whole week at Fair Haven, Irene decided to drop in at her mother's on her way to meet Peggy outside the Empire.

Maisie was gazing at her reflection in the mirror. 'I'm never going to get used to looking like this,' she groaned.

'Stop worrying, Mam. It won't be that long before the dye grows out and you have your natural colour back.'

'I don't want me own colour back,' said Maisie, pursing her lips.

'I'm getting used to it,' said Jimmy, glancing up from the *Daily Mirror*. 'I like it. It's different.'

Maisie patted him on the head. 'I know yer just trying to make me feel better, son, but I won't be happy until I'm a redhead and me hair reaches me shoulders. I haven't forgotten the sniggering behind me back when I went into work with green hair for the first time.'

Jimmy grinned. 'At least they didn't dare snigger to your face.'

Maisie said, 'You might think it funny, but I don't. At least me new teeth are the gear. Well, I'm off to the shops now. See yer!' She fluttered her fingers at the pair of them and the door closed behind her.

'I'll have to be moving as well,' said Irene. 'I'm

meeting Peggy.'

Jimmy folded the newspaper. 'Mam was telling me about Peggy visiting Pete's mother's the other evening.'

Irene shot him a glance. 'That's a move in the right direction. What did Gertie have to say about Peggy? Did they get on OK?'

'You know Mrs Marshall, she's dead friendly and nice about people.' He fell silent.

'Is that it?' said Irene, raising her eyebrows. 'I can see I'll have to ask Peggy if I want to find out more.'

He caught her eye. 'I can tell you one thing – I bet Peggy won't know that Pete suggested to his mother that if he and Peggy were to get married this year, they could live with her.'

Irene reached for her handbag. 'I'm not sure how Peggy would take that suggestion, but you can see his point, can't you? There's a housing shortage and they could wait ages for a place of their own. She made no mention of religion or Peggy's father?'

'As it happens she did mention Peggy's dad,' said Jimmy. 'Apparently Gertie thinks she might have known him when she was young.'

'That's interesting,' Irene murmured, taking out a lipstick and going over to the mirror and outlining her lips in a lovely shade of coral. 'I wonder where they met. Did she say?'

'If she did, Mam didn't mention it.' Jimmy stifled a yawn. 'There's something else you might be interested in.'

'And what's that?' Irene popped the lipstick back in her handbag.

'I'm sure I saw Peggy's brother coming out of the Red Lion the other evening. The one that was on the train.'

Irene's heart seemed to perform a somersault. 'You mean Marty?'

He nodded.

'Did he say anything to you?'

'Nope! I can't say I placed him right away, but then I suddenly remembered where I'd seen him before.'

Irene nibbled the inside of her cheek. 'I wonder if his being in the Red Lion had anything to do with his brother, Tommy.'

'Funny you should say that. There's a bloke I've seen there recently a couple of times called Tommy Mac. He offered me cheap ciggies, but as you know I don't smoke.'

She frowned. 'I wonder if he's Marty's brother. I told you about Peggy having seen him outside the Red Lion on New Year's Eve, didn't I?'

'Can't say I remember.'

She was silent for a moment and then said, 'Does this Tommy Mac have a proper job that you know of?'

'Not that he's told me but I've a feeling he might work down at the docks.'

They stared at each other. 'Are you thinking what I'm thinking?' said Irene.

'Probably. According to Mam our dad was as honest as the day was long but not all dockers are like him. It's common knowledge that a certain amount of pilfering goes on when cargoes are being unloaded.'

'So what d'you think I should do?' asked Irene,

pulling on a glove.

'About what?' asked Jimmy, pouring himself another cup of tea.

'The brother! Should I tell Peggy?'

'Your choice,' said Jimmy.

Irene sighed and decided to give it some thought before saying anything to Peggy.

Peggy was standing at the bus stop on Scotland Road, glad to be out of the house and going to the Empire where she knew it was unlikely she would bump into her father. She felt he was watching her every move when they were in the same room. She wished he would say something about Pete, because then at least she would know where she was and whether Father Francis had revealed the truth about Pete's religion.

Suddenly she heard her name being called and turned to see Marty coming along the street carrying Josie and Monica skipping along with Jerry by the hand.

'Where's Bernie?' she asked as they came to a halt at the bus stop.

'Aunty Val's bleaching her hair,' said Monica.

'Bernie's going blonde!' Peggy stared at her brother. 'What did you have to say about that?'

Monica giggled. 'He just stared at her as if she'd run mad. She wasn't pleased, I can tell you.'

'Mam says Auntie Bernie fancies herself as Marilyn Monroe in *Gentlemen Prefer Blondes*,' said Monica.

'But that was on at the flicks years ago,' said Peggy.

Marty said, 'Makes no difference to Bernie.

She said she needs a change and as her sister's doing it for her, it's not going to cost as much as going to a proper hairdresser's.'

'I can't wait to see it,' said Peggy, smiling at Jerry and tickling him under the chin. He giggled and slipped his other hand into hers. 'So where are you taking the kids?' she asked.

'To see *"Babes in the Wood"*,' said Monica.

'That's where I'm going with Irene,' said Peggy, looking surprised.

'Bernie wanted the kids out of her hair and I thought they might enjoy the pantomime,' said Marty.

Before Peggy could comment that they might be a little too young to appreciate it the bus arrived. It was not long before they arrived in Lime Street to find Irene waiting outside the Empire. The tip of her nose was pink and her shoulders were hunched inside her coat.

'Have you been waiting long?' asked Peggy, her tone concerned. 'You look freezing.'

'Not too long,' said Irene, her eyes sliding away from Peggy to Marty and the toddler in his arms.

'You're just the person I wanted to see, Irene,' he said, setting his daughter on her feet.

Josie tugged on her father's trouser leg and Irene looked down at the lively little face, framed by fair curls peeping from a pink knitted bonnet trimmed with a band of white angora wool.

'Is this your daughter?' asked Irene.

He nodded. 'Josie, this is Miss Miller. Shake hands.'

Irene took the small hand offered. 'How d'you do, Josie?'

134

'Well, tank you,' chimed the little girl.

Marty introduced Monica to Irene and the two girls nodded at each other.

'Let's get inside,' said Peggy. 'People are going in and we want to get to our seats.'

They made their way into the foyer.

Marty said to Irene, 'I'm sure I saw your brother going into the Red Lion the other evening.'

Glad that he had mentioned it, she felt able to say, 'You did! He recognized you and thinks he might have met your brother.'

Marty nodded and lowered his voice. 'I thought I saw them talking at the bar. How long have they known each other?'

'I can't say that Jimmy knows him well,' she said hastily. 'I mean, he said that he'd only seen him there recently and has spoken to him once or twice.'

'Did he say what about?'

She hesitated. 'You did get to talk to your brother yourself, didn't you?'

'Yeah, not that he told me much and I'd like to know where he's staying. I brought a photo of him. If you wouldn't mind keeping an eye open for him in Litherland and Blundell Sands, I'd appreciate it.'

She flushed. 'So you still want my help?'

'If you don't mind.' He reached into his pocket and took out an envelope and handed it to her. 'You can let me know through our Peg if you find out anything.'

'Will do.'

'Come on, you two, or the lights will go down before we can get in our seats,' said Peggy. She

135

nodded at the envelope, 'I suppose it's about our Tommy?'

Irene nodded and placed the envelope in her handbag and hurried after Peggy. It was not long before the two friends were settled in their seats in the stalls. They were on the same row as Marty, Monica and the kids but on different sides of the theatre. The safety curtain had already been raised and the orchestra was tuning up. The noise from the children in the audience was tremendous but suddenly a hush fell over the auditorium as the velvet curtains parted and the musicians launched into the opening music.

Irene settled comfortably in her seat and prepared to enjoy herself, hoping that Peggy and the others would be as enthralled by the scene before them as she was. As the pantomime progressed, she thought how the cast seemed to know exactly how to pitch their performance to suit all ages. Any saucy innuendos intended for the adults' entertainment went over the heads of the younger audience. It was a very different pantomime to the one she had seen last year, which had featured three principle boys in the shape of the Beverley Sisters and, instead of two men playing the Ugly Sisters, Jewel and Warriss were comic robbers and were very funny to watch.

During the interval Peggy wasted no time telling Irene about Pete meeting her mother and his accompanying her to Josie's birthday tea, as well as her visit to Pete's mother.

'Has your Mam told your father about meeting Pete?' asked Irene.

'Yes, but he hasn't said much to me about it,'

said Peggy, offering a box of liquorice allsorts to Irene.

'So he doesn't know that Pete's a Proddy?'

'Not yet!' Peggy bit savagely into a liquorice tube. 'I feel as if a dark cloud's hanging over me. I'm just waiting for Dad to explode when he discovers Pete's not Catholic. Even Mam's not going to be pleased when she knows that Pete hasn't been completely honest with her.'

'But surely when you explain why, your mother will understand?' Irene paused. 'Anyway, what did you think of Pete's mam?'

'We got on all right. She and Mam are complete opposites, though. Mam likes her house to be tidy, everything in its place. And she loves cooking, unlike Pete's mam. Have you ever been to their house?' Peggy did not wait for Irene to reply. 'She just slung her coat over the back of the sofa when she came in.'

Irene remembered what her mother had told Jimmy about Gertie Marshall. 'There's worse things than being untidy,' she said firmly. 'I've been known to sling my coat on a chair and kick my shoes off in front of the fire.'

'OK, so we're not all alike,' said Peggy, offering the box of sweets to Irene again. 'But if Pete and I do get married, he's going to have to change his ways because his mother's not the only untidy one.'

'So d'you think you and Pete are any closer to tying the knot?'

Peggy chewed thoughtfully. 'I just don't know! I dread him and Dad meeting. There are times when I feel like running away.'

137

'I suppose you could always elope,' Irene said seriously.

'What's this about eloping?'

Irene started as she felt an arm brush her hair. She tilted her head and saw Marty gazing down at her from a standing position in the row behind them. She felt suddenly breathless and lowered her head swiftly.

'That wasn't meant for your ears,' said Peggy, glancing up at her brother.

'I didn't think it was,' said Marty, moving along slightly and resting his hands on the back of his sister's seat.

'I'd never elope,' said Peggy. 'So what did you come over for?'

'I wondered if Irene has had a chance to look at the photo of Tommy yet,' said Marty. 'And eloping might be your best option.'

'I want a white wedding in church with brides-maids and the organ playing "Here Comes the Bride",' said Peggy.

Irene reached into her handbag and removed the envelope he had given her. Peggy glanced at the photograph as Irene took it out and looked at it. 'He's not like either of you, is he?'

'No, he's always had a cherubic face,' said Peggy. 'Even during the war he was bonny.'

'That's because Mam saw to it that he never went without,' said Marty.

'He's got dimples and quite a nice smile,' murmured Irene.

'He knows how to turn on the charm, all right,' Marty drawled.

'Has the gift of the gab, too, does he?' said Irene.

'How did you guess?' said Marty.

Irene hesitated, wondering whether to tell him what else Jimmy had said about Tommy. She was saved by the bell ringing to warn people that the next act would soon be starting.

'See you later,' said Marty.

But as it turned out Irene did not see him after the pantomime ended. Everyone was in a rush to get home, so there was a bit of a crush in the foyer and it was difficult to find people. She didn't have time to hang around and wait outside as she was on duty in the nursery that evening. She explained the situation to Peggy and left to catch the train to Blundell Sands, not knowing when she would see Marty again and questioning whether it would even be wise to do so when just a smile from him caused her to catch her breath. It was probably best all round that he'd suggested she get in touch with Peggy in the event she discovered where Tommy was staying.

Nine

Peggy spooned up the last of her cornflakes and munched and swallowed them before hurrying to wash her plate and spoon. She gazed through the window into the yard that was still in need of a whitewash and looked even dirtier than it had on New Year's Eve. It was February and she would be glad when spring finally arrived.

'You'll miss your bus if you don't get a move

139

on,' said her mother, coming up behind her. 'And wrap up warm because it's icy out there. You'll need to watch your step.'

Peggy felt like saying *Don't fuss, Mam, I'm not a child!* but her father had been snappy with her mother that morning and she had seemed near to tears. Peggy was almost out of the front door when her mother said, 'I'd like you to bring Peter to lunch one Sunday. Maybe he could come early and we could all go to Mass together?'

Peggy paused with one foot on the doorstep and the other on the highly polished brass door tread. 'Have you asked Dad about it?'

'It was his idea,' said Mary hastily. 'I told him that Peter's mother was a widow and suggested that we invite her, too.'

'And what did he say to that?' asked Peggy.

'He didn't care one way or the other,' said Mary, 'so if you could ask Peter when you see him whether she'd like to come?'

'When?'

'Perhaps a week on Sunday. Hopefully the weather will be better by then.'

'I'll be seeing him this evening, so I'll mention it,' said Peggy, smiling. 'I'm going to have to go, Mam. We'll probably go to the pictures, so I'll be home about eleven.' She left the house and did not look back.

It was sleeting when Peggy came out of the Cunard Building and found Pete waiting for her. She was feeling anxious and the weather did not help to lighten her mood and neither did his grim expression.

'Did you hear about the plane crash in Munich?' he asked, taking her by surprise.

'No! I take it that all the passengers were killed,' she said, tucking her arm through his.

'The Busby Babes were on the plane and several of them have been killed but not all of them. It's tragic for Manchester United.'

Peggy was stunned. 'Was it the weather that caused it?'

'It was slushy on the runway and snowing, as well.' He sighed. 'All that talent! You never know the minute, do you?'

'No.'

'Imagine if it had been Liverpool's team? Or even Everton!' Pete shook his head dolefully.

'Their poor families,' she murmured. 'Do you feel like going to the pictures? I didn't see anything I liked in the *Echo* the other evening.'

'Then how d'you feel about going back to our house? Mam's supposed to be going out with Irene's mother this evening. We'd have the place to ourselves,' said Pete, his expression brightening. 'Nice roaring fire and we can get a couple of meat pies and chips from the chippy.'

She agreed, thinking it would be easier to bring up the subject of him and his mother coming to Mass and dinner if they were alone and comfortable.

An hour or so later they were sitting on the sofa drawn up in front of the fire with trays on their knees. Pete had bought a bottle of beer and a Babycham from the off licence. Peggy had asked for the television to be switched on while they ate, having remembered that *Calling Nurse Rob-*

erts was on.

'You're as bad as Mam,' said Pete, shaking his head. 'She likes this but it just reminds me of when I was in hospital.'

'You never talk much about that time,' said Peggy, not taking her eyes from the black and white screen.

'That's because they weren't the best days of my life,' murmured Pete, supping his beer.

She glanced at him and leaned sideways to kiss his cheek. 'I wish the doctors could do something so you weren't in pain.'

'So do I but there isn't anything much they can do. They made that clear to Mam before they sent me home. If I'd broken my leg in just one place it wouldn't have been so bad, but three...' His eyes clouded. 'It was my own bloody fault.'

'Maybe one day they will be able to do something for you. I mean, medicine has come on in leaps and bounds since the National Health Service was introduced. Just think of there being an inoculation for TB and there's talk of polio being a thing of the past soon.'

'It's brilliant! I've met kids who had polio,' said Pete. 'You've never been in hozzie, have you? If you had, it's not an experience you're likely to forget and I was there for weeks.' He cut into his steak and kidney pie. 'The experience changes you.'

'I should imagine it would,' murmured Peggy absently, her eyes straying to the screen where a doctor and nurse were in a clinch. Would they get married? Who was to say? She was reminded of her and Pete's situation and remembered her mother's invitation.

'Mam asked me to ask you if you'd like to come to Mass and lunch a week on Sunday?' she said.

Pete appeared not to have heard her. In fact he seemed miles away. She repeated what she had just said in a louder voice.

This time he looked at her. 'What did your dad have to say about it?'

'It's his idea. What d'you think? Mam thought your mother might like to come too. I know she's mot a Catholic but Irene's Mam is a friend of hers and she's a Catholic.'

'She'll go to a rummage sale at Our Lady, Star of the Sea's church hall but she's never been to Mass with her,' said Pete. 'I doubt Mam will agree. So tell your Mam no thanks,' said Pete.

Peggy was disappointed. 'Is that no to lunch as well as Mass? And what about you?' she asked, a tremor in her voice. 'Are you turning down the invitation, too?'

Before he could answer, there came the sound of a key in the front door and a few moments later Gertie entered the room. Her colour was high and her lips pressed tightly together. 'Well!' she exclaimed, staring at the pair of them. 'I didn't expect to see you two here!'

Pete set the tray aside. 'You all right, Ma? Want a cup of tea?'

'You two aren't drinking tea! I suppose there isn't anything stronger for me?' she said, squeezing past the sofa to stand in front of the fire and hold out her hands to the blaze.

'I'm sorry, Mrs Marshall,' said Peggy, standing up. 'I'll go if you like.'

'I didn't say you had to go, Peggy,' said Gertie,

her voice less strident. 'I'm just so annoyed with Maisie Miller.'

'What's she done?' asked Pete.

'What hasn't she done?' said Gertie, removing her hat and slinging it on an easy chair.

'What hasn't she done then?' asked Pete.

'Don't you be smart!' said Gertie, dropping into a chair. 'She hasn't kept to our agreement, that's what! We promised each other that we'd always get the bus home together.' Her voice trembled.

Pete glanced at the clock. 'It's only early. Is it that she wanted to go on somewhere else?'

'It's not that! I'd have stayed later at Reece's dance if she hadn't waltzed off almost as soon as we arrived there with some bloke who asked her to dance.' Gertie took out a handkerchief and blew her nose.

'You ... you mean she left the dance hall without you?' asked Peggy.

Gertie stared at her. 'You've got it in one, love. Twice she danced with him and then she comes and tells me she's going on somewhere else with him and she hoped I didn't mind!' Her eyes glistened as she tugged at the buttons on her coat.

Peggy set her plate aside, stood up and helped her off with her coat and then hung it on a peg in the lobby. Pete put the kettle on. Gertie sat on the sofa and picked up his plate and began to eat his chips. 'I'm hungry,' she said. 'We went out straight from work and I've only had a cake and a cup of tea from Lyon's cafe.'

Peggy glanced at Pete as he came into the room. 'Did you hear all that? Your mam's hungry so she's having some of your chips. You can share mine.'

'Thanks, Peg. I'll cut some bread and we can have butties,' he said.

With that done and having handed a cup of tea to his mother, Pete squeezed up on to the sofa with the two women. 'Peggy's brought you an invitation, Mam, from her mother. We're invited to lunch a week on Sunday.'

Gertie glanced at Peggy. 'That's kind of your mother.'

'She wondered if you'd like to come to Mass as well?'

'I don't think so, love,' said Gertie. 'I have my own church if I want to speak to God. I'd be pleased to go to lunch, though.'

'I'll tell Mam that,' said Peggy, relieved.

Gertie looked thoughtful. 'I'd be right in thinking your father will be there?'

'Yes,' said Peggy, 'and maybe our Lil and her boyfriend.'

'Nice family gathering,' said Gertie with a hint of satisfaction. 'I'm already looking forward to it. Me and our Pete will come together. What time? About two? Give your family a chance to get back from Mass.'

Peggy agreed. She glanced at Pete questioningly. He shrugged; whatever he might be thinking, for the moment he was keeping it to himself.

She would have liked to spend some proper time alone with him but when he suggested seeing her home, she shook her head. 'Just see me on to the bus. It's not that late that there'd be drunks around,' she said. 'I don't want you slipping on the ice when you're on your own.' His mouth tightened. 'Now don't get touchy!' Peggy added. 'I'm

145

only thinking of your safety and what you said earlier about your leg being broken in three places.'

He said no more but she guessed that he was thinking he was quite able to take care of himself. *But can you look after me if someone were to knock you off balance?* she wondered and was ashamed for thinking it.

When Pete arrived back at the house after seeing Peggy on to the bus, he found his mother at the table with a drawer on one of the chairs beside her. He recognized it as being from the sideboard in the parlour. She was in the process of removing several large bulky brown envelopes and placing them on the table. He sat down and asked her what was in them.

'Photographs,' said Gertie, slitting a flap with a knife. 'See where my father wrote the dates of when they were taken on the front of the envelope,' she pointed out. 'I should find the ones I'm looking for inside this one.'

'Who are they of?'

She slanted a glance at him. 'Now that would be telling, son, and I don't want to make a mistake. But you'll see them soon enough if I'm proved right. You want to marry Peggy and I guess her dad could be against a match between the pair of you.'

'That's what she's believed all the time we've been seeing each other,' said Pete.

'I can imagine,' said Gertie, a grim little smile playing around her mouth.

'So these photographs...?' asked Pete.

'Be patient.'

146

He knew there was no persuading her, so instead he asked her about Maisie Miller. 'Will you be speaking to her when you see her in work tomorrow?'

'Like hell I will,' said Gertie vehemently, beginning to go through a handful of photographs. 'If she wants to be friends with me then I expect an apology. It was downright bad manners what she did to me and I'm not going to forget that in a hurry.'

'That's not like you, Ma,' said Pete.

'No, but I'm hurt, son. We've been friends for years and she must have known how I felt,' said Gertie, sounding suddenly weary. 'Now, not another word about her.'

Ten

Irene was on pins as she leaned against the table, watching her mother applying lipstick. Irene had something serious she wished to discuss with Maisie but somehow she was put off from bringing up the subject while her mother titivated herself in front of the mirror. Despite the concern she felt for her own future, she could not help but marvel at the change in Maisie since she'd got her new teeth. She smiled more often and sometimes she even hummed a dance tune. Her hair might still look a bit unusual, to say the least, but she seemed a lot more content than she had been at the beginning of the year.

147

'So where are you going this evening, Mam?' she asked.

'Ask no questions and you get told no lies,' replied Maisie.

'Why so secretive? You always want to know where I'm going when I visit.'

'That's because you're my daughter and I used to feel responsible for yer, but not any more. You're old enough to take care of yourself. You and our Jimmy, both.'

Irene's smooth brow knitted. 'You've changed your tune. There was something I wanted to discuss with you.'

'Not now, love. I haven't time.'

Irene sighed. 'All right! But you do know you're supposedly still responsible for me until I'm twenty-one and I'm not nineteen until the end of March.'

'Yer not going to tell me yer getting married, are you, and need my permission?' Maisie smirked as she popped the Max Factor lipstick in her handbag.

'No!'

'Pity,' said Maisie. 'If yer must know I'm going dancing at Reece's in town. And if yer wondering where Jimmy is, he's at the Gianellis' rehearsing for some "gig" as he called it. I can't say I've ever heard the word before. Maybe you could talk to him about what's bothering yer.'

'Thanks,' said Irene drily. 'Are you going with Gertie Marshall?'

Maisie scowled. 'Don't talk to me about that woman! I've never known anyone so selfish! I suppose you won't be staying here the night?'

148

'No, I've got to be back in time for the night shift,' said Irene, wondering what had gone wrong between her mother and Gertie. 'So who are you going with? That Scottish woman you work with?'

Maisie smirked. 'Maybe I am, maybe I'm not! See yer next time, love.' She blew a kiss in Irene's direction and was about to leave when she added, 'Oh, by the way, there's a couple of letters for yer on the sideboard.' She hurried out.

Irene went over to the sideboard and picked up the envelopes. One was a blue airmail and would be from Betty, while the other had been posted locally. She read them swiftly and both gave her much pause for thought. She decided to pop along to the Gianellis' and have a word with her brother who was rehearsing there, and with Nellie, too.

She left the house in a hurry and headed towards the canal. As she passed the Red Lion, she couldn't help thinking of Marty and wondered whether he had heard anything more from his brother. So far she had seen no sign of Tommy, but that wasn't to say he wasn't living in Blundell Sands. She had shown his photo to Deirdre but she did not remember having seen him. Perhaps she should show it to a few more people.

She walked along Litherland Park until she came to The Chestnuts. She could hear the group practising as she rang the doorbell. She gazed at clumps of daffodils that were just showing the odd bud. No doubt, just like the hundreds of daffodil bulbs in the gardens of Fair Haven, they would be in bloom in a few weeks. Hopefully there would still be some in flower at Easter, which was at the beginning of April this year.

The door was opened by a slightly breathless Lucia. 'Oh, it's you, Irene! Jimmy didn't say you were coming.'

'That's because he didn't know,' said Irene promptly. 'May I come in? I won't be stopping long.'

'That's all right. Did you come to see Auntie Nellie? She was talking about you earlier, asking Jimmy when you'd be visiting your mother next.'

Irene wondered if Nellie had possibly heard the news about Miss Talbot and followed Lucia up the lobby. 'I'll have a word with our Jimmy and then speak to your aunt. Is she in the kitchen?'

Lucia nodded and led the way into the front room where all the noise was coming from. The music petered out as Jimmy spotted his sister. 'Hold on a mo'! My sister's here and I want a word with her,' he said.

'You OK?' asked Irene, going over to him.

'Fair to middling! You?'

'I've had some news that's upset me a bit,' she said. 'By the way, the music sounds great from outside. Mam mentioned you had some gig booked.'

'Yeah, that's right, and we're playing at Lenny's place a week on Saturday. Have you received your invitation to Jeanette and Davy's party?'

Irene smiled. 'Just got it. I wouldn't have known about it if Mam hadn't remembered at the last minute there was post for me. It's the same day as my birthday, too.'

'Thanks for reminding me,' he drawled. 'Did you know Jeanette and Davy were moving to New Brighton?'

150

She nodded. 'But I had no idea they were moving so soon. I presume Peggy and Pete will be invited.'

'I should think so. She and Peggy used to see a lot of each other when they were both working in the Cunard Building. I wonder who'll take over the flat?' he mused.

'It probably won't be anyone we know,' said Irene. 'Anyway, I'll let you get on with rehearsing.'

She was almost out of the door when he called her back. 'You haven't told me what's upset you? It's not Mam falling out with Gertie Marshall, is it?'

'No, it's something else. I'll tell you later. I just want a word with Mrs Gianelli.'

'There's something I meant to tell you,' said Jimmy.

'What?'

'I spotted that Tommy Mac at the Cavern Club the other Saturday. He was with a girl.'

Her eyes widened. 'The Cavern Club? I haven't heard of it.'

'It's a jazz club in a cellar in Mathew Street.'

'Where's that?'

'Off North John Street. It only opened last year.'

'I can't say I like the sound of it being in a cellar. What's it like?'

He grinned. 'You wouldn't like it. Smoky, crowded, noisy, condensation running down the walls.'

She shook her fair head. 'You must be mad going there.'

His grin widened. 'It's got atmosphere and we've been asked to fill a small slot.'

151

'I'll take your word for it,' she said. 'See you next Saturday if I can get the evening off.'

She heard the music start up again as she left the room, aware that Lucia had been listening to their conversation from her perch on the arm of a chair close by.

As Irene entered the kitchen, Nellie glanced up from the oven and smiled. She had a tray of flapjacks in her hands. 'You're just in time if you're hungry.'

'I am! I had nothing at Mam's. She was on her way out. Those smell wonderful. I remember you making flapjacks when you had the nursery here,' said Irene, her voice soft with reminiscence.

'Just let this lot cool down first or you'll burn your fingers,' said Nellie.

'I haven't forgotten the last time I did that,' said Irene, sitting at the table and resting on her elbows. 'I wouldn't mind having a go at making flapjacks with some of the kids back at Fair Haven.' She sighed.

Nellie glanced at Irene. 'I read about Miss Talbot's death in the *Crosby Herald* the other week and there was even a mention in the *Nursery Times*.'

'You still get that?'

Nellie shook her head. 'No, but I've a friend at Litherland Nursery who passes it on after she's read it. What do you know?'

'There's all kinds of rumours going round now that our beloved patron is dead. Her nephew and niece have inherited the property and there's talk that they'll have to sell because of death duties. If that's true, then it's likely the home will close down and the children will have to be moved elsewhere.'

'It's a shame. Does this mean you'll be out of a job?' Nellie asked.

Irene sighed. 'More than likely. That's the trouble – we don't know if there'd be jobs for us elsewhere. Besides it would all depend on where the children were moved to.'

'It's a pity you couldn't get a job at Litherland Nursery.'

'It's a thought.' Irene sighed again. 'I'm going to miss the kids. Our damaged ones could break your heart. My friend Deirdre thinks no one will ever want to adopt them.'

'She could be wrong,' said Nellie, putting on the kettle. 'There're lots of compassionate people around, as well as uncaring ones. That's the problem with working with such children. You have to try not to get too fond of them, but I know how difficult that is. Still, you're bound to get married one day and have to leave them.'

'I wasn't thinking so much about getting married but doing some travelling,' said Irene, straightening up and unhooking a couple of cups from a kitchen shelf and placing them on the table. 'I had a letter today from Betty.'

'How is she?'

'Fine, although still missing family and friends. She wants to know have I ever thought of being a private nanny. What d'you think of that?' asked Irene.

Nellie stared at her. 'Coming at a time like now? It almost sounds fortuitous! A nanny! Does she have an employer in mind?'

'She didn't name any names but I have a feeling she was thinking of someone.' Irene felt a stir of trepidation as well as excitement.

'There's no rush for you to make up your mind, is there?'

'I don't think so.' Irene took the milk out of the fridge. 'Besides, I wouldn't be going anywhere until Fair Haven closes down and that's unlikely to happen for a while. There's all the legal side to be settled, and then the arrangements for the children to be sorted out, too.'

Nellie agreed. 'Anyway, what other news do you have? Have you been anywhere interesting?'

Irene told her about the pantomime and then about the party Jeannette and Davy were throwing before they moved to New Brighton. Nellie knew about that because her stepson, Tony, would be singing with the group at Lenny's Place.

'Hopefully I'll be able to get the evening off. I could do with cheering up. It would be nice to see Peggy and Pete, too,' said Irene.

'I did hear that Pete and his mother have been invited to Sunday lunch at Peggy's parents' house,' said Nellie. 'You know my brother's their parish priest?'

Irene nodded, her eyes widening. 'Now that is news! I can't wait to hear how they get on. A wedding in the offing at last, d'you think?'

Eleven

'You ready, son?' asked Gertie, standing in front of the sideboard mirror, fluffing out her greying curls beneath a russet felt hat with a feather in it.

Pete nodded and inwardly braced himself for what he regarded as the ordeal ahead. He watched his mother remove a shopping bag from the back of a dining chair, knowing there was a box of chocolates inside for Peggy's mother. He could only hope that all would go well. If it did, then most likely the next step would be his asking Mr McGrath for his elder daughter's hand in marriage. He and Peggy had never got this far before and he was beginning to think that a wedding could well be on the cards for them later this year. Peggy was over twenty-one and didn't really need her father's permission but his instincts told him that Mr McGrath was a man who would expect any suitor for his daughters to seek it.

Pete had decided to dispense with his walking stick even though the weather was still wintry. Besides thinking that he should try and do without it more, it meant that maybe the McGraths would regard him as less of a cripple.

His mother glanced at him as he led the way out of the house. 'That's the ticket, son. Shoulders back, head high.' Her eyes twinkled. 'You've nothing to be ashamed of, you are as good as Billy McGrath.'

155

Pete could not help wondering just what it was his mother knew about Peggy's father. But he knew it was possible that before the day was over, he might just have found out.

A smiling Peggy opened the door to them. Despite her smile, Pete guessed that she was as keyed-up as he was but trying not to show it. She was wearing less make-up than usual and he also felt that was due to her father. She looked pale without a touch of rouge on her cheeks.

'Hello, love!' he said, reaching out and squeezing her hand. 'You all right?'

'Of course, why shouldn't I be? Come on in. Mam and Dad are looking forward to meeting you both,' said Peggy brightly. 'Let me take your coat, Mrs Marshall,' she added.

Gertie accepted her help off with her coat with a smile and handed her hat over to Peggy, but kept hold of her shopping bag. Having hung up his overcoat, Pete took a deep breath before following Peggy and his mother into the kitchen.

The room seemed much smaller than he remembered from his last visit but that could be due to the dining table having been opened up and four people already taking up the surrounding space. Pete's gaze went to the older man whom he recognized from that journey on the train at the end of December.

'Mr McGrath, it's good to meet you,' said Pete in his politest voice.

William had been sitting but now he stood up and glared at Pete. 'So you're him,' he said.

'He has a name, Dad,' said Peggy.

'I know that!' he snapped, not looking at her.

'Peter Marshall, the liar. He's no Catholic! I found that out from someone who remembers the family who went to live in Seaforth and attends the church there. I've also spoken to the priest on the telephone. Are you going to deny it, *boy?*'

'No,' said Pete, looking him straight in the eye. 'You should ask yourself why I wasn't completely honest with Mrs McGrath when she questioned me.'

William looked aghast. 'You have no time for the truth, do you?'

'Of course I do,' said Pete. 'But I have no time for bigotry and you shouldn't either if you take the Christian faith seriously'

'He's right, Dad,' said Peggy bravely.

'Yes, don't let's be having an argument, William!' said Mary, grabbing his sleeve.

He brushed her hand off and glared at her.

'Most likely I misunderstood what Peter told me. I do think I'm getting a little bit deaf as I get older. Let's all be friends?' She held out her hand to Gertie. 'It's nice to meet you.'

Gertie shook her hand. 'Same here, love. May I sit down and take the weight off my feet? Years of standing in the factory have given me terrible bunions.'

'Certainly,' said Mary, pulling out a chair. 'It's my knees that are starting to go with getting down and scrubbing floors. But I don't like using a mop; it doesn't do as good a job.'

'Stop babbling, Mary,' William snapped.

Gertie sat down and looked at him. 'I'm not one for judging people, Billy McGrath, and I don't like you judging my son before you even get to

157

know him. You'll find that Jesus has something to say about judging people and forgiveness.'

Mary took one look at her husband's face and said hastily, 'Let me introduce my other daughter, Lil, and her young man.'

'How do you do?' said Gertie, nodding at the couple.

'Now Lil has more sense than our Peggy,' said William. 'And who do you think you are, woman, to call me Billy?'

Gertie slanted him a challenging look. 'I once knew you as Billy Mac. That your lovely daughter, Peggy, should have fallen in love with my lad makes me think she must take after her mother. It's obvious she's a nice woman. But you – you're nothing but a hypocrite.'

Peggy and Lil gasped and Mary could only look open-mouthed at Gertie.

William's face had reddened and his heavy eyebrows beetled together. 'How dare you! I don't remember you at all.'

'I know it's years since we last saw each other.' Gertie eased herself back in the chair and took out the box of chocolates from the shopping bag and held it out to Mary. 'These are for you, love. Thank you for your kind invitation.'

Mary gazed at the box of chocolates but made no move to take them.

'Take it,' said Gertie, waving the box about. 'They're Black Magic!'

'Can't you see she doesn't want them, woman!' yelled William, causing his daughters and wife to jump.

Gertie placed the box of chocolates on the table

and took a large envelope from her shopping bag. 'Maybe these will jog your memory, Billy? I don't bandy around words like *hypocrite* for fun. My father owned a photographic studios not far from where you and I grew up,' she added. 'You must remember it? I used to pull tongues at you when you'd stand, looking in the window at the latest portraits. You had a sense of humour then.'

He blinked at her. 'All right! I remember the place but that doesn't give you a reason to come into my home and throw your weight around.'

'I come in peace,' said Gertie quietly, folding her shopping bag. 'Just take a look at those photographs and make up your mind to give my son the welcome he deserves for loving your daughter.'

Mary reached out for the envelope but William would have snatched it from beneath her hand if she hadn't managed to get a grip on it. 'Let go of it, Mary!' he ordered.

'Why, William? I thought we had no secrets from each other,' she said.

'There isn't anything world-shattering in there, Mrs McGrath,' said Gertie. 'I brought these photographs along, thinking they would jog your husband's memory. I have the negatives, by the way, Billy.' She glanced at William. 'My son and your daughter want to get married,' she continued. 'I'd like to see it happen before I'm in my dotage. I'd enjoy having her company about the place and a couple of grandchildren. She seems a good girl to me.'

'She is that,' said Mary swiftly. 'I've brought her up respectable.'

Gertie smiled. 'As I did my boys. My eldest son

159

is in the police force and Pete's twin is a marine engineer. When I mentioned the name of McGrath to our Dougie, he remembered it but I'll say no more about that.' She added virtuously, 'None of my business.'

William's face darkened. 'Are you saying that your policeman son had reason to arrest one of my sons?'

Before Gertie could answer, a voice spoke up. 'I'm hungry! The dinner will be spoiling if we don't eat soon.'

Mary sighed with relief. 'Our Lil's right. Let's eat. Forgive and forget, I say. Whatever we are, we all believe in the same God, don't we?'

Pete opened his mouth but a look from his mother silenced him.

'Come on, girls,' said Mary, and hurried out of the room.

Peggy gave Pete a stricken look and followed her mother and sister. Pete was wishing more than anything that he and his mother had not come but it was too late now. Where did he and Peggy go from here? He realized that Lil's boyfriend, whose name he had forgotten, was staring at him. Suddenly the boyfriend got up. 'I'm going for a smoke,' he said, hastening out of the room.

No sooner had he left than William opened the envelope and took out the photographs. He wasted no time riffling through them, pausing a couple of times. When he had finished, he replaced them in the envelope and dropped that on the table. 'Why couldn't my daughter get herself a nice Catholic boy?' he said, running his fingers through his hair.

Pete, who had been silent until then, felt his temper rising. 'I don't want to be one like you, Mr McGrath, that's for sure.'

William's eyes narrowed. 'Don't be funny with me, lad.'

'I don't find this situation the least bit funny,' said Pete harshly. 'Your attitude terrifies your daughter. D'you realize that? We could have married last year if you weren't such a bigot!'

'It's right for a girl to have a healthy fear of her father,' said William. 'He knows what's best for her.'

'Rubbish,' said Gertie. 'Possessive, controlling...'

William rounded on her. 'Keep out of this, Gertie!'

'Oh, you remember me now, all right, don't you?'

'Mam, say no more,' said Pete. 'I see now that whatever you say to Mr McGrath, he's never going to accept me, even if I did what Peggy wanted and took instruction in the Catholic faith – something that I have no intention of doing now.'

There was a sudden silence that was broken by Peggy blurting out, 'But you promised!'

Pete turned and saw her standing in the doorway, holding a tureen between her hands.

'I never promised, and anyway, I've changed my mind,' said Pete. 'Sweetheart, we don't need his permission to get married. If you love me, then marry me despite what he says.'

'Don't you be giving her orders!' shouted William. 'You're forcing her to choose between you and her family.'

161

'No, I'm not! It's you that's trying to force her to do that,' said Pete angrily. 'Well?' he snapped, turning to Peggy.

She stared back at him with a mixture of hurt and anger in eyes that were shiny with tears. 'You promised me that you'd take instruction and get married in my church! You agreed that our children could be brought up as Catholics,' she cried.

'I made no promises,' insisted Pete, his dark eyes glinting.

Peggy was so upset that she felt as though she couldn't breathe for a moment. Then she caught her breath. 'You're a liar, just as Dad said you were!' She slammed the tureen on the table. 'I hate you! Get out of this house!'

Pete could only stare at her and then he drew in his breath noisily and limped out of the room. His mother called him back but he was not listening. A few moments later the front door slammed.

Gertie got to her feet. 'Well, you made a right mess of that, Billy. But then you did come from a family who always thought they were in the right.' She snatched up the envelope containing the photographs and looked at Peggy. 'I might have enjoyed having you living with me as a daughter but after the way you spoke to my son, I reckon we've had a narrow escape! Say sorry to your mother for me! Tarrah!' She picked up the box of Black Magic and hurried from the room.

Peggy was trembling and wanted to smash something. How dare Pete's mother speak to her the way she did! She'd said no worse to Pete than he'd said to her. And what had she meant about her living with her as a daughter? Could he have

162

told her that they'd live with his mother after they were married without even mentioning it to her? He had no right! And besides, his mother was a slut! She'd be forever tidying up after her!

'Well, I'm glad to see the back of them,' said her father, interrupting the riot of thoughts running through her head

'What were those photographs of, Dad?' she asked.

'Nothing that need bother you,' he said.

She didn't believe him, thinking that he bore the blame for what had happened as much as Pete and his mother did. Without another word, she brushed past her father and went into the back kitchen.

'Have they gone?' asked Lil.

'What do you think?' said Peggy tartly, tears running unchecked down her cheeks.

'Oh, my poor little girl,' said Mary, holding her arms out to her.

'I'm not a little girl!' cried Peggy, and hurried out of the back kitchen.

Ignoring her father, who was standing in front of the hearth, staring into the fire, she went upstairs. A few moments later she could hear her mother's shrill voice from below, arguing with him.

Then he bellowed, 'Leave me alone, woman! And don't you dare go fussing over our Peggy. You've spoilt her, just like you spoilt Tommy! I'm going out,' he shouted.

Peggy heard the front door slam and then a few moments later, it slammed again. Perhaps her mother was going after him. From below came the sound of Lil and her boyfriend talking. She

163

thought if her sister came upstairs and told her what she had done wrong then she would scream. She was fed up with her family and Pete telling her what she should do. She was fed up with her job, too. In that moment she made up her mind to leave Liverpool – and the sooner the better!

Twelve

'Happy birthday to you, happy birthday to you,' sang Deirdre.

'Great way to enjoy a birthday,' said Irene, emptying another potty. There had been no cards from her brother or mother, which was disappointing. Although she thought maybe Jimmy would bring them with him to Jeanette and Davy's party.

'But you're off this evening, aren't you?' said Deirdre.

'That's true,' said Irene, smiling faintly. 'Pity you couldn't come to the party.'

'I could do with going to a party,' said Deirdre, scouring out one of the potties. 'I need cheering up. The trouble is nothing is certain at the moment. If we had a positive date when we'd be finishing I could start making plans. At least I've tomorrow afternoon off but I've nobody to go out with. I think I'll go to Southport, although it's not the same going on your own.'

Irene thought of Jimmy and how Deirdre just might suit him. She was no beauty but she had pleasant features and a nice way with her. Although Irene liked Lucia, she was too young and the way she hung around Jimmy made her feel a little uneasy. It would be much better if he had a proper girlfriend, someone who would put Lucia off.

'Once we're finished here,' said Irene, 'we'll get out in the fresh air with some of the children. The rain has stopped and it looks warmer out there now.'

But the heat of the sun shining through the windows proved deceptive because the air was cooler than Irene had thought. Probably that was due to the rain.

As they set off for the beach, Deirdre began to sing *'April Showers'*.

'It's not April until Tuesday and you'll have it raining again,' said Irene, laughing.

'So what!' said Deirdre, giggling. 'As the song goes, *It'll bring on the flowers that will bloom in May.*'

'Perhaps we should teach the children the rhyme to do with the number of days in the months,' said Irene, and launched into 'Thirty days have September, April, June and November.'

'Miss, Miss, I'm named after a month,' said May, skipping along beside her.

'You're right,' said Irene, gazing down at her and feeling a pang of sadness. At the moment the children did not know that most likely within a few months there would be no more walks to the beach.

'Are you named after anything, Miss?' asked George.

Irene nodded. 'My name means Peace.'

165

'A piece of what, Miss?' asked May.

Irene smiled. 'Not that kind of piece. It means when there's no fighting taking place and people are living as true friends.' She thought of the atom bomb and the peace march that would be taking place next Easter weekend at Aldermaston and changed the subject. 'Now let's see what wild flowers we can spot.'

It was soon obvious that the most common flower was the dandelion and there was even the odd wild daffodil to be seen. They came to the beach. The tide was out and the children were allowed to run along the sand and search for shells.

The beauty and the vastness of the sea drew her and she found herself looking out towards the horizon and thinking of Betty living thousands of miles away; not just the other side of the Atlantic, but clean across America, not far from the Pacific Ocean.

Irene was aware of a restlessness inside her. She had written to Betty telling her about what was likely to happen to Fair Haven and her job and was impatient to receive her friend's reply. 'One day soon,' Irene murmured.

'What was that you said?' asked Deirdre.

Irene threw her a smile. 'I was just daydreaming and talking to myself.'

'What about?'

'Travelling. Wouldn't you just love to take off and go somewhere far away?'

Deirdre shrugged. 'Not particularly. Although if I get offered a job, then I'll go wherever it takes me. But I'd rather it was in England.'

They stood a moment, gazing out to sea and then turned away and, gathering the children together, headed back towards Fair Haven.

It was as they neared the gates that Irene spotted a man standing on the opposite side of the road to the children's home. He was turned partly away from them but there was something familiar about him. He must have heard them approaching and turned and looked in their direction. Irene's heart seemed to bounce inside her chest and her pace quickened. She could feel herself smiling.

He crossed the road towards them. 'Hello, Irene!'

'Hello, Marty! What are you doing here?' She stopped a couple of feet away, aware of Deirdre and the children's curious glances.

Marty looked at the children. 'Hello, kids,' he said, nodding at them.

George and May said, 'Hello,' but the others either stared at him, dropped their gaze or looked up at Deirdre for guidance.

'Can I have a private word?' said Marty to Irene.

'Shall we go on, Irene?' asked Deirdre.

'If you don't mind,' said Irene, giving George and May a tiny push in Deirdre's direction. 'I won't be long.'

As soon as Deirdre and the children were a few yards away, Marty said without preamble, 'Our Peggy's gone missing.'

Irene was stunned. 'What d'you mean, gone missing?'

'She's vanished.' His expression was strained. 'I wondered if she'd been in touch with you.'

'No! I take it she didn't leave a note?'

167

'She left a note all right, but it didn't say anything more than for us not to worry and that she could look after herself.'

'What happened? People don't just leave home out of the blue! Did it have something to do with Pete Marshall? I heard that he and his mother were visiting your parents' house.'

'They did. Our Lil said there was an argument but she didn't hear everything that was said and neither did Ma. So I don't know all the ins and outs. But apparently Pete gave our Peggy an ultimatum. Her family or him!'

She did not believe it. 'You're joking!'

His expression hardened. 'Would I joke about such a serious matter?'

'No, of course not.' She flushed. 'I just meant I find it difficult to believe he'd say such a thing. What did Peggy say to that?'

'I don't know! Ma and Lil weren't there and Dad's isn't saying much. I think the last thing he expected was that our Peg would leave home.'

Irene folded her arms across her chest. 'You surprise me. The way she spoke about your father it was obvious that she was scared of him. I'm amazed she hasn't left home before now, the way she felt. Have you been to see Pete?'

'Have I hell,' he muttered savagely. 'All this is his fault.'

'How can you say that? It can't be all his fault.' Irene chewed on her lip and then asked abruptly, 'What did his mother have to say about it?'

There was a sudden arrested expression on Marty's face. 'Thanks for reminding me that she was there when all this was going on. I seemed to

168

remember Mam mentioning some photographs that she brought to show Dad.'

'What were they of?'

'Mam didn't get to see them. But I remember now our Lil saying that it appeared that Pete's mother knew Dad years ago.'

Irene looked triumphant. 'I bet it has something to do with them having known each other in the old days. Go and visit Pete and his mother. I bet your parents know more than they're letting on.' She paused. 'I'm going to have to go.'

'When d'you finish work?' asked Marty.

She hesitated.

'It doesn't matter,' he said with a grim expression. 'I doubt there's any way you can help find her. I'll see you around.'

She watched him stride off, hesitated and then ran after him, catching up with him on the corner of the road. 'Marty!' she said breathlessly. 'Have you had an invitation to Jeanette and Davy's party?'

He stared at her flushed face. 'Me and Bernie, both. You?'

She nodded. 'I don't suppose in the circumstances you'll be going?'

'I've already told Jeanette we wouldn't be there before I knew Peg had gone missing. Bernie doesn't like Jeanette.'

'I see,' said Irene, nibbling her bottom lip. 'Have you thought Peggy might have got in touch with Jeanette? They were friends long before Peggy and I got to know each other.'

He nodded slowly. 'You're right. Thanks. You'd better get back to the kids.'

169

'You won't know but Fair Haven is going to be sold and the children will be moved elsewhere,' she burst out.

He looked astonished. 'Why? What will you do for a job?'

'Our patron has died and her heirs won't be keeping it on.' Her voice was unsteady. 'Something to do with death duties.'

'Hell!' He frowned.

'I don't know yet what I'll do.' She paused. 'I hope you soon have some good news about Peggy.'

'Thanks.' He turned and strode away.

She hurried after Deirdre and the children. 'So who was that?' asked Deirdre when Irene caught up with them.

'My friend Peggy's brother. She's left home and the family don't know where she's gone.' Irene groaned. 'I've just remembered there was something our Jimmy told me that I should have told Marty. It's going to have to wait.' She sighed, nurturing the hope that he just might turn up at the party that evening.

Lenny's café was situated on Hope Street, somewhere between Liverpool's Philharmonic Hall and the Anglican Cathedral. Irene's friend Betty had worked there part-time as a waitress while she was a student at the nearby School of Art. It was a popular meeting place for young people who enjoyed good, cheap plain cooking and music. Not only did Lenny have the most up-to-date jukebox with the latest hit records, he was also licensed for live music and extended hours in the evening for the slightly older generation.

When Irene pushed open the door, it was to find that most of the party guests appeared to have arrived already. Jeanette's sister-in-law, Lynne, was there with her daughter, Roberta, who worked at Lenny's on Saturdays. It was Lynne's American stepbrother, Stuart Anderson, whom Betty had married.

Irene could see no sign of Marty and so, swallowing her disappointment and knowing it was for the best, she made her way over to Jimmy and Tony Gianelli. As per usual, Lucia was hanging around the group, but unusually she was wearing lipstick and had pencilled her eyebrows and wore eye shadow. It made her look older despite the midnight-blue taffeta dress she wore having puff sleeves and a sweetheart neckline above the swell of her small breasts.

Irene greeted her brother. 'You all right? How's Mam?'

Jimmy rolled his eyes and plucked a couple of chords on his guitar. 'Don't talk to me about Mam. She's never in.'

'Does she tell you where she's going or been?'

'Not always. I know she does go dancing and the other evening she went to the Royal Court to see a play.'

'I wouldn't have thought plays were Mam's thing,' said Irene, pulling a face. 'Does she ever mention who she goes with?'

He shook his head. 'I know it's not Gertie Marshall.'

'They're still out of friends?'

'Yeah! I did ask who she was going out with instead.' He shrugged. 'She just smirked and touched her nose. In other words "mind your own business"!'

Irene sighed. She had hoped the two old friends would have made up their quarrel and Gertie might have discussed what had happened at the McGraths' house with Maisie. But no such luck.

'D'you think Mam's got a fella?'

Jimmy frowned. 'I hope not. I don't want her getting bloody married again. The last thing I want is an older man coming to live in our house and throwing his weight around.'

She could understand how he felt. 'You haven't seen anything of Pete at all?' she asked.

Jimmy shook his head.

'So you haven't heard that Peggy's left home?'

Jimmy's eyes widened in surprise. 'Where's she gone?'

'That's the sixty-four-million-dollar question,' Irene murmured. 'Have you seen any more of Peggy's other brother, by the way?'

'Yeah, he was in the Red Lion the other evening with some woman,' replied Jimmy, frowning. 'But never mind him. What happened to make her leave home? Has Pete got anything to do with it?'

She told him the little she knew and then, noticing that Jeanette's half-sister had moved away and no one had collared Jeanette and Davy yet, Irene went over to say hello to them.

'You're both looking happy,' she said.

'We are happy,' said Jeanette, smiling. 'You know what they say – new house, new baby.'

Irene was delighted at their news. She congratulated them and Davy moved off to speak to a friend while the two women discussed babies and the house in New Brighton.

'You'll be getting plenty of visitors,' said Irene.

'That's what your Jimmy said but all will be welcome,' said Jeanette, smiling. 'I can't wait to move, although I'll miss ol' Liverpool.'

'But you won't be far away,' said Irene.

'No, just a ferry across the Mersey,' said Jeanette merrily.

'Now, drinks, you two?' said Davy, coming up to them. 'Can't run to champagne, which I don't like anyway, but Lenny has Babycham.'

Irene thanked him and as soon as he was gone she asked, 'Have you heard about Peggy?'

Jeanette's smile faded. 'Yes, I had a visit from Marty just a few hours ago.'

'Oh! I did suggest to him that she might have been in touch with you,' said Irene.

'I wish she had. It's worrying for the family. He asked me if I had any idea where she might have gone.'

'And have you?'

Jeanette sighed. 'I could only remember the times Peggy talked about enjoying going to Butlin's and her mentioning getting a summer job away from Liverpool. That was when we worked together.'

'But it's not yet summer!' said Irene.

'No, but there'll be places open at Easter and they must take on staff to prepare for the holiday season,' said Jeanette. 'It wouldn't surprise me if she decided to go and visit Pwllheli.'

'What about Pete – has he been in touch with you?'

'No, I sent the party invitation to Peggy,' said

Jeanette. 'I can only presume she never told him about it. I did suggest to Marty that he visit Pete. After all she might have gone running to him. Marty seemed doubtful.'

Irene looked thoughtfully. 'I suggested he visit Pete, too.'

'Perhaps he will if we've both suggested it,' said Jeanette.

'There's something else I should have told him when I saw him,' said Irene.

'You could drop him a note at Quiggins' shop,' Jeanette suggested.

Irene decided that was probably the best thing to do, so she wrote a note and borrowed an envelope from Lenny and popped it through Quiggins' letterbox on her way home.

Thirteen

When Marty was handed the envelope that had been put through Quiggins' letterbox, for a moment he hoped it was from his sister but he did not recognize the neat, rounded handwriting. He slit the envelope with his penknife and removed the single sheet of paper, reading swiftly. Then he read it again more slowly with a mixture of emotions before folding the sheet of paper and placing it in his overall pocket to get on with the job of gathering together the tools he would need for the job in Allerton and loading them in the company van.

174

As he worked, Marty determinedly forced the information in Irene's letter to the back of his mind, knowing he needed to concentrate on the task in hand. It was only at lunch time, when he was eating his corned beef and pickle sandwiches and drinking the coffee that the cook-cum-housekeeper handed to him, that he grudgingly decided perhaps he should heed Irene's words and make visiting Pete Marshall a priority. It was natural that Irene would be more concerned about Peggy being found than his making an effort to see Tommy again. Due to all the upset of Peggy having gone missing, he had yet to get his mother alone to remind her to keep quiet about his having met with Tommy. He knew he had to make the opportunity as soon as possible.

Marty could not help but feel warm towards Irene for taking the time to write to him with information. She obviously wanted to be of help to him as much as she could. There was only one jarring note in the letter and that was Irene's reminder that Pete Marshall was a cripple and his brother a policeman. Why had she felt the need to emphasize this? Was it because of something Peggy or Jeanette had said about him? He decided to visit Pete before going home and so he rang Bernie's mother to let his wife know he would be late that evening.

When he got to Pete's house the front door was opened by a small plump woman wearing a harassed expression. 'Yes?' she asked, frowning up at him.

'Is this Pete Marshall's home?' he asked.

She stared at him intently. 'Who wants to know?'

175

'I'm Marty McGrath. I'd like a few words with Pete if he's in.'

She pointed a finger at him. 'You're the eldest son, aren't yer? Hang on!' The door closed in his face before Marty could reply.

'That's a bloody good start,' he muttered, wondering how long he would be kept waiting on the step.

The door was yanked open and Pete stood there. 'What is it you want?' he asked without preamble. 'If you've coming looking for a fight, then you've come to the wrong house.'

'I'm not looking for an argument,' Marty snapped, feeling his temper rising. 'I just wondered if you've heard from our Peggy.'

Pete stared at him blankly and then he blurted out, 'What's happened? What's your father done to her?'

'As far as I know he didn't do anything to her,' said Marty, exasperated. 'All I know for certain is that she's left home and we don't know where she is.'

'Bloody hell!' Pete sagged against the door jamb.

'I take it from your reaction that you didn't know she'd gone. Mam's worried sick.'

'I can imagine she would be,' said Pete, running a hand through his dark hair. 'What's Peggy thinking of, running off like that?'

'Who knows the way a woman's mind works? I'm still trying to figure it out myself,' said Marty.

Pete stared at him. 'Did she leave a note?'

'Yeah, but it wasn't much help, just told us not to worry and that she could take care of herself,' said Marty. 'It was Irene who suggested I come

176

and see you. I don't know what went on at Mam and Dad's when you and your mother visited, and I'd like to know.'

Pete frowned. 'What have you heard?'

'That you wanted her to choose between her family and you. Now look here, mate, do you really think saying that would get you anywhere with my dad?'

'I'm not your mate,' said Pete in a hard voice. 'And I wouldn't have asked her to choose if your dad hadn't gone on about her marrying a nice Catholic boy. How d'you think that made me feel after she'd chunnered on about her father being so against me because I was a Protestant?'

Marty sighed heavily. 'He said the same thing to our Lily, so you shouldn't have taken it personally. He was the same with me about marrying a nice Catholic girl! According to him, if I did, life would be a bowl of cherries.' He mimicked his father's voice. 'All I can say is that he never took to Bernie and that cherries have hard stones in the middle.'

Pete smiled faintly. 'Ma says that there's no such thing as the perfect marriage. That's certainly the impression I got from your parents. Peggy was terrified of displeasing your father and she told me that your mother was scared of him too.'

'I wouldn't dispute that my dad has a temper,' said Marty. 'But if you knew that, then you should have taken it into consideration and watched what you said.'

'I did!' said Pete, scowling. 'What got me was that Peggy is over twenty-one, which means we could have got married without your dad's per-

177

mission, but would she go ahead? Would she hell! I thought he might give his blessing if I agreed to accept instruction in the Catholic faith and that our children were brought up Catholics ... but...'

Marty broke in. 'You understood how important that was to her?'

'Of course I did,' Pete retorted. 'I was half way to doing just that but then I decided I didn't want to turn into someone like your father.'

Marty stared at him. 'Has that remark got something to do with your mother having known my father in the past? There was mention of some photographs your mother brought. What did they have to do with all this?'

Pete straightened up from the door jamb. 'I didn't get to see them until Mam brought them home after I walked out. Peggy said she hated me and told me to get out.'

Marty rubbed the back of his neck which was aching and he felt overwhelmingly weary. 'I didn't know that. Did she see the photos?'

Pete shook his head. 'The only person to do that was your father. He wasn't allowing your mother or Peggy to do so and now I know why.'

'Can I see them?'

Pete hesitated. 'Don't you think it's more important that you try to find Peggy? Have you reported her missing to the police? You need to get her description circulated.' He paled. 'I hate to think she'd do something stupid,' he added hoarsely.

'Then don't think it,' said Marty. 'She wrote that we were not to worry, so I doubt she's going to kill herself. Anyway, Dad won't hear of involving the police. He's been out looking for her himself.'

Some of the colour had returned to Pete's face. 'Regretting upsetting her now, is he? He should have thought before he behaved the way he did. It's not as if he hasn't any experience of what the older ones call a "mixed marriage". He's a hypocrite is your father. He doesn't approve of mixed marriages and yet he made one himself,' Pete said.

For several moments Marty could only stare at him and then he shook his head. 'You're wrong! Mam comes from an Irish Catholic family.'

'Yeah, but your dad doesn't,' said Pete, his eyes glinting.

'That's rubbish! You don't know what you're saying.' Marty's fingers curled into the palms of his hands.

'I do! What d'you know about your father's family? Does he ever talk about them? I bet he doesn't.'

'How could you know that?'

'Do you really want to know? Think you can cope with the truth?' Pete mocked.

'You want to watch your mouth,' said Marty.

Pete stared him straight in the eye and clenched his fists. 'You gonna make me?'

For several moments their gazes did not waver and then Marty relaxed. 'This is bloody daft! I didn't come to pick a fight. For our Peggy's sake I want the truth.'

Pete relaxed his fists. 'Come on in then and I'll show you.' He held the door wide.

Marty wiped his feet on the coconut mat and followed him into the front parlour. Pete switched on the light and went over to a sideboard, opened a drawer and took out a large buff envelope. He motioned to Marty to sit down over by the window and moved a coffee table in front of his chair and pulled up another one close to it. Pete sat down and tipped a pile of photographs from the envelope on to the table.

'This might take a few minutes,' he said.

Marty leaned forward, resting his hands on his knees. He could not take his eyes from the photos as Pete began to sift through them. The ones Pete had turned over so far had a sepia tint to them. After a few minutes he paused and set aside a photo and then another and another. He shoved them across the table towards Marty.

'Have a look and see if you recognize anyone in them.'

Marty guessed he was supposed to spot his father. What he did not expect to see was a middle-aged man in uniform leading a parade. He was the spitting image of his father. But it couldn't possibly be him because the women in the crowd were wearing Edwardian clothes. He picked up the next photo, which was of a young man dressed in a sailor's uniform. There was a definite likeness to the other man in uniform. The third photograph showed two older men and one who looked to be about nineteen, and a young woman wearing bridal clothes.

'The bride, Alice, was my mother's best friend,' said Pete. 'They worked together and Mam was the bridesmaid at her wedding.' He frowned. 'Alice died of TB two years after that photograph was taken.' He sighed. 'Thank God that scourge will soon be a thing of the past here in Britain.'

'And the men?' asked Marty impatiently.

'Alice's brother, father and grandfather. My mother went out with the brother for a short while – if you look closely you might recognize him. She was asked what colour she was before she was allowed over the threshold of the family home. I take it you understand what I mean by that? If you look again at the first photograph, you might realize that it was the Loyal Orange Lodges march. Shortly afterwards she met my father and that was the end of the other relationship.'

Marty blinked and then looked again at Alice's brother. 'You're not trying to tell me that's my dad and he went out with your mother?'

Pete nodded.

Marty eased the tightness in his throat. His mind was in a whirl. The Orange and Green were sworn enemies. The sectarian fighting that had taken place between the two had often been vicious in the past and even now there could be trouble in Liverpool on the twelfth of July. 'If this is a joke, it isn't funny. Dad couldn't be Orange.' His voice sounded raw with emotion.

Pete was silent.

Marty shook his head and continued to stare at the photographs. It couldn't be true! It had to be a mistake. Someone who looked just like his father. Yet the more he looked at the photos the more he became convinced that Pete believed the truth of what he had said.

'You say that our Peggy has never seen these photographs?'

'No, I told you I never had a proper look at them until after the episode at your parents' home.'

181

Marty bit on a fingernail and was silent for several moments and then his head shot up. 'How did your mother come by these photographs? It seems odd to me that they should be in her possession.'

'Her father was a photographer and these photos are all that's left of those he managed to save when his shop caught fire during the war and nearly everything was destroyed. After he died, Ma found this envelope and she didn't like getting rid of what was inside. She told me that when she was alone she used to take the photos out and spread them on the dining table every now and again and think about the people she remembered. Most of them are dead now, including my father and your grandparents.'

Marty could find no words to say; he was still trying to get his head around what he had just seen and heard. If it really was all true, then his father was indeed a hypocrite.

'You know what they say about some converts?' said Pete abruptly. 'They're often more committed and aggressive about what they believe than the organizations they join.'

Marty felt a spurt of anger. 'My father's not a bad man!'

'You know him better than I do.'

'He believes in right and wrong.'

'So do I,' said Pete with a wry smile. 'I still want what I believe is right for Peggy and me, but when I spoke of it, she wouldn't listen because of your father's bigotry.'

Marty wished he knew where his sister was right now, so he could discuss this with her. 'I'd best be off,' he said abruptly. 'Bernie will be wondering where I am.'

'I'll see you out,' said Pete, limping behind Marty as he left the parlour.

Marty opened the front door and stepped outside. 'I'll let you know if our Peggy gets in touch.'

'Thanks, and if she gets in touch with me, I'll let you know too.' Pete hesitated. 'I know it's none of my business, but have you told your parents about Tommy getting in touch yet?'

Marty shook his head. 'I've told Mam but not Dad. Have you mentioned him to your policeman brother?'

'No, but I hope he's not going to bring more trouble to your parents' door.'

Marty made no comment and headed off down the street towards Stanley Road. He had a tremendous headache and wished what he had just heard would go away – but it was not going to do so. He had to talk to someone about it. His father was the obvious choice but he felt too churned up to control his feelings. Yet he needed to discuss it with someone. Maybe tomorrow he would go and speak to Father Francis. And on his way home he called in to see his mother and remind her to keep quiet about Tommy if she didn't want to have the police knocking on their door. He hoped his father would not be at home. As it was both his parents were out and so was his sister.

Marty was expecting to find the children asleep and Bernie downstairs with her mother or sister watching the television with a sour expression on her face when he arrived home. He did not blame her solely for what had gone wrong with their relationship. The thought of all the years that lay ahead of them caused his stomach to tie itself in a knot. They were Catholics and divorce was out of the question.

To his surprise, when he entered the kitchen, it was to find Monica knitting in front of the fire while watching television. How was it she was able to do two things at once? His mother was the same and so was Bernie's mother, except the older women actually seemed able to do three things at once.

'Hi, Marty,' Monica greeted him. 'Your tea's in the oven. D'you want me to get it out for you?'

'No, I'll see to it, kid. Where's Bernie?' he asked, hanging up his overcoat.

'You don't want to know,' said Monica, rolling her eyes. 'She's really cross with you. She wanted you to take her out this evening.'

He frowned. 'First I knew. I did phone your grandma and ask her to tell her I'd be late. So where has she gone?'

'The Grafton with that friend Marie from work. Have you been to your mam's? Any news about your Peggy?'

'No.'

He went and took his dinner out of the oven. It was near enough burnt to a crisp. But he was hungry, so he ate the lot. He felt slightly more cheerful afterwards and over a second cup of tea he decided he must speak to his father about what Pete had told him. He was not looking forward to it and needed to give some consideration to the best way to go about it.

'So where d'you think your Peggy's gone?'

184

asked Monica, putting her knitting away.

'I wish I knew.'

'What about that Pete who came here?'

'That's where I went this evening and he hasn't seen her,' said Marty. 'It came as a shock to him.'

'He seemed really fond of her.'

'I'm sure he is but I don't really want to discuss it just now, Monica.'

She flushed. 'Sorry. I know it's none of my business. Would you like me to leave you alone?'

'If you don't mind. I'm not good company.' He dug into his trouser pocket and produced a shilling. 'Here, buy yourself a treat. Thanks for looking after the kids.'

She took the money. 'Ta! They haven't been any trouble. See you.'

As Marty washed up, he thought about what Pete had said about Peggy being terrified of displeasing her father and he felt angry. He did believe himself that a healthy fear of those in authority could be a good thing but it seemed that in his sister's case there had been nothing healthy about the way she felt towards their father. It was the same with Tommy.

Marty was in bed when Bernie came home. When she stumbled into the darkness of their bedroom it was obvious that she'd had a drink or two and didn't care if she woke him or the children. She could be raring for either an argument or sex. He wasn't in the mood for either. She whispered to him when she climbed into bed but he pretended to be dead to the world and she was soon snoring beside him.

The following morning Bernie was still asleep

when the children woke up. Marty checked the clock and saw that it was nine o'clock. He hurriedly dressed before helping the children to put on their clothes and taking them downstairs. There was no sign of any other members of the household up and about despite it being Palm Sunday, so he raked out the ashes and cinders, while the children scrunched up a couple of sheets of newspaper he gave to them. He fetched wood chips and coal from the cellar. He warned them against playing with fire as he put a match to the newspaper. Then he put the fireguard into place before making the three of them bowls of puffed wheat with milk and sugar. Afterwards, he left them playing a game under the table while he took a cup of tea up to Bernie.

She appeared to be asleep but her position had changed, so he shook her shoulder until her eyelids fluttered open. 'Go away!' she groaned.

'Here's a cup of tea. It's half past nine. I've got to go out so you'll need to get up and look after the kids and take them to church,' said Marty. 'Everyone else is still in bed. I don't know what's up with everybody.'

She pushed herself up against the pillows and then winced and put a hand to her head. 'I suppose it would be too much to ask your lordship to take them with you? I've got a terrible headache – and don't you be saying it serves me right,' she warned, squinting up at him. 'It's your fault. If you'd been home at the proper time I wouldn't have gone out with Marie.'

'Where'd you get the money from to drink enough to have a hangover?'

'I borrowed it from Mam, so you'll have to give me the money to pay her back,' Bernie muttered.

'How much did you borrow?'

She named a figure.

He did not believe that she could have spent that much. 'I'll speak to your mother myself,' he said.

'No!' she muttered. 'I might have made a mistake.'

Too right you have! Marty did not always see eye to eye with his mother-in-law, but she had principles and stuck to them. He doubted she would hand over such a sum to her married daughter to go gallivanting without her husband.

'Drink your tea and get up! I want to be out in half an hour,' said Marty.

'You're real tight you are,' said Bernie, pulling the bedcovers up to her shoulders before reaching for her cup. 'Why couldn't you bring me coffee?' she muttered, gazing into it.

'Because there isn't any.' He left the bedroom and went downstairs to find the children had dragged the tablecloth down so that it reached the floor on one side of the table. He could hear them giggling on the other side of it and guessed they were sitting on the crossbar beneath and pretending they were in a tent. He smiled as he went and had a shave at the kitchen sink. He thought about the house he had fixed locks to yesterday, envying the owners their two bathrooms. *One day ...* he thought.

By the time he was ready to go out it was ten o'clock and Bernie had still not appeared downstairs, although he could hear signs of movement from his mother-in-law's bedroom. Taking the children by the hand, he took them upstairs and into the bedroom. He could see Bernie's hunched form beneath the bedcovers and the anger he had felt growing inside him now exploded.

'What the hell are you playing at? I work all bloody week to keep this family going and you can't even be bothered getting out of bed when I ask you. Now shift yourself!' He pulled down the bedcovers but she remained curled up in the foetal position.

'Have a heart, Marty! I don't feel well,' she whined. 'Can't your mother have them for once? She scarcely ever has them.'

'And whose fault is that?' said Marty, reining in his anger.

She did not answer.

Taking the children by the hand, he left the bedroom. He put on their coats and the bobble hats that Monica had knitted them last Christmas and ushered them out of the house. Having them with him might lighten the atmosphere at his parents' home. If his mother felt she couldn't cope with them, then hopefully Lil would be able to do so.

When he arrived at his parents' house the curtains were open and he guessed his mother might be getting ready for church. He opened the door with the front-door key he had been given on his twenty-first birthday. He went inside, ushering the children in first. Josie ran ahead up the lobby, followed more slowly by Jerry. The kitchen door opened and their grandmother, dressed in her outdoor clothes, gazed down at her in surprise. Without a word she scooped Josie up in her arms and hugged her close.

'I hope you don't mind me bringing them here, Mam, but I need to speak to Dad,' Marty said.

'He's not here,' his mother replied, her voice muffled against Josie's neck.

Marty had a sense of foreboding. 'Where is he?'

Mary lifted her head and looked at Marty. 'I told him about our Tommy getting in touch with you and he's gone to look for him.'

Oh no! Marty thought. 'Did he say where he was going first?'

'No, he just ... stormed out. I should have known better; should have kept my mouth shut. Most likely he's gone to that Red Lion pub in Litherland that Peggy mentioned to me,' she said.

Marty put his arm around her and helped her into a chair with Josie still clinging to her. 'Kids, you be good for your gran. She's had a shock.'

'What's a shock?' asked Josie, sitting on her grandmother's knee. 'Does it hurt?'

'Yes,' her grandmother, holding her close and reaching out a hand to her grandson.

Marty sat down opposite his mother. 'Mam, I went to see Pete Marshall yesterday.'

'Has Peggy been in touch with him?'

'No, he didn't even know she'd left home but he told me something, Mam, that knocked me for six.'

His mother stared at him. 'I don't think I want to know what it is if the look on your face is anything to go by,' she said, her voice trembling.

'You have to listen, Mam. He told me that his mother was the bridesmaid at Dad's sister's wedding and apparently she went out with him for a

189

short while. He showed me some photographs. They were Protestants!'

His mother cleared her throat. 'What is it that you want me to say?'

Marty didn't understand why it hadn't occurred to him until then that his mother had been party to the lie his father had lived for so many years. 'Dad's a hypocrite, Mam. He made our Peg's life a misery by his attitude to Protestants, when all the time his father belonged to the Orange Lodge. He kept it quiet all these years. Seldom spoke about his family.'

'It was because his family made him so angry,' said Mary in a shaky voice.

'What do you mean?'

'When he took me home, they asked me what colour I was. So he became a Catholic before he'd allow me to take him home to my parents. It was so I could say he was a good Catholic boy and they'd welcome him into the family. So you see he knew what he was talking about because my parents would have reacted the same way as his if he hadn't changed beforehand. He didn't want any of his children to suffer prejudice when it came to getting married.'

Marty ran a hand through his flaxen hair. 'But he was prejudiced against his own family! What did he say when your parents asked him about his parents?'

'He told them they were dead. They were as good as dead to him because they never spoke to him again after he converted. I know telling lies is a sin but he confessed it to the priest, so that was all right.'

190

Marty could have torn his hair out. 'Where are his parents now?'

'They really are dead now.' She gazed at him with sad eyes. 'It's all so long ago. You're not going to mention it to your dad, are you?'

'I have to, Mam. Try and get him to see that his attitude has affected all of us, especially our Peggy. It's the reason she and Pete Marshall's courtship has been an on-off one for ages and she's now left home and we don't know where she is.'

'Speaking to your father about all this won't bring her back. Why don't you leave him to me?' his mother said eagerly. 'I'll tell him you know his little secret and he's got to change his ways when our Peggy comes home.'

Marty shook his head. 'There's nothing little about his secret. I need to see him have a change of heart. You telling him about our Tommy is bound to have repercussions.' He glanced at the clock on the mantelpiece. By the time he caught a bus and it got him to Litherland, it would be gone eleven o'clock and the pubs would be open. 'I need to find both of them and fast.'

Fourteen

Marty was hoping that if he did not find his brother or father in the Red Lion, then maybe he would see Irene's brother, Jimmy. If he was not there, then perhaps the barman would be able to give him his address. As luck would have it, he

191

found Jimmy standing at the bar with a pint in front of him, talking to the barmaid.

Marty ordered half a pint from her and at the sound of his voice, Jimmy turned his head and stared at him. 'Your brother was in here not so long ago. He was in and out in no time, though.'

'Why was that?' asked Marty.

'I told him a man had been in here looking for him,' said the barmaid. 'He asked what he looked like and when I told him, he went all pale and shot out of here like a scalded cat.'

Marty's hand tightened on his glass. 'Was the man middle-aged with a V-shaped scar on his chin?'

She looked at him with interest. 'You know him?'

Marty nodded. 'He's our dad.'

'I suggested he try the Caradoc – and I didn't mean the Mission,' she added with a smile.

'It's a pub, not far from Gladstone Dock,' said Jimmy. 'You can get a bus down that way if you want to try and catch up with him.'

'Thanks!' Marty's expression was grim as he paid for his drink. 'Irene sent me a note saying you'd seen Tommy in a jazz club in Liverpool,' he said, raising his glass.

'That's right. The Cavern on Mathew Street.'

'Her note said that Tommy was with a girl.'

Jimmy nodded. 'She was more of a woman and they were talking earnestly. I saw him again in here with her.'

'I get you.' Marty downed his pint.

'In trouble with your dad, is he?' asked Jimmy.

'You could say that,' said Marty. 'Be seeing you.'

Jimmy placed a hand on his arm. 'Want company? If there was to be a fight, you might need help dragging them apart.'

A slow smile eased Marty's mouth. 'Thanks for the offer. Although won't you be expected home for Sunday lunch?'

'Mam's gadding about and our Irene is in Blundell Sands.' Jimmy finished his pint. 'Let's go!'

The two men went outside and headed for the bus stop. 'I got a shock today,' said Jimmy, scowling as he kicked an empty tin can that was lying in the gutter.

Marty, who was going over in his head what he was going to say to his brother and father if he caught up with them, shot him a glance. 'What kind of shock?'

'Mam told me she was getting married again.'

'You obviously don't think it's a good idea.'

'Is it hell! He'll be her third husband and she's moving to West Derby to live with him and his kids! She told me to my face that me and our Irene are surplus to requirements.' Jimmy paused. 'I don't know why I'm telling you this when I should be talking to our Irene about it.'

'Sometimes you feel you just have to get something off your chest or you'll explode,' said Marty.

'She expects me to tell our Irene,' said Jimmy angrily. 'She can't even be bothered to visit her own daughter to do so herself.'

'How d'you think she'll take the news?'

'She'll probably be as annoyed as I am. Especially as she's going to lose her job when the children's home closes down.'

'Surely Irene shouldn't have much difficulty finding another one,' said Marty.

193

Jimmy shrugged.

'So when is your Mam planning on getting married?'

'As soon as it can be arranged,' muttered Jimmy. 'I wouldn't mind so much but it's not that long since our stepfather died. He was a good bloke and we'd known him all our lives. I don't know anything about this one, except Mam met him at Reece's and they like dancing. Apparently he's a widower with three children. I think he wants a housekeeper, meself, and someone to look after his kids.'

Marty wondered if Jimmy had said as much to his mother but kept that thought to himself. 'I don't even know what his job is, except it's good and steady according to Mam.' Jimmy sighed. 'I don't know what to do.'

'About what?' asked Marty.

'Our house! It's rented and I don't want to live there on my own and there isn't a girl I want to marry right now.'

'If Irene's going to be out of a job, couldn't she live with you?' asked Marty.

Jimmy did not appear to have heard him because he said, 'Here's the bus.'

Once aboard the vehicle, Jimmy asked if there was any news of Peggy. Marty shook his head. 'It's a real worry.'

'She'll come back,' said Jimmy confidently. 'We all need a change at times, although it's tough luck on the family and Pete.'

'He didn't know she'd gone until I went to see him,' said Marty.

'That must have come as a shock,' said Jimmy,

fiddling with his bus ticket. 'I must go and see him. I could do with speaking to his mother. She might know something about this bloke Mam's planning on marrying. Although at the moment the pair of them aren't speaking.'

Marty could not resist asking, 'Why's that?'

Jimmy shrugged. 'You know women. You say one word out of place and they get all huffy.'

They fell silent and it was not until they were nearing the stop for the Caradoc that Jimmy, who had been twisting his bus ticket round and round his little finger, said, 'I've come to a decision. I'm going back to sea.'

Like many a Liverpool lad, Marty had once considered being a sailor. Only he had been sea-sick on a trip to the Isle of Man and that had put an end to that idea. 'So what stopped you going in the first place?' he asked.

'The ship was caught in this bloody big storm and one of the crew was washed overboard. We couldn't save him and the atmosphere afterwards was terrible. The whole crew couldn't wait to dock and get off the ship.'

'That doesn't bother you now?' asked Marty as Jimmy stood up.

Jimmy shrugged. 'Can't say it doesn't bother me but I haven't had a nightmare about it for ages now.'

Marty followed him off the bus.

'Our Irene has nightmares,' said Jimmy.

'About what?' asked Marty.

'Drowning. She nearly drowned last year but some bloke rescued her. Our stepfather had gone in to save her but he had a heart attack and died.

195

Her rescuer vanished before he could be thanked.'

'Maybe he didn't want to be thanked,' said Marty.

Jimmy nodded. 'I can understand that.'

'Some people don't like a fuss.'

Jimmy agreed.

It was only a short walk to the Caradoc and they went into the public bar which was fuggy with cigarette smoke. Almost immediately, Marty spotted his father drinking on his own at a table in the corner. He wasted no time going over to him as Jimmy headed for the bar.

William glanced up as his eldest son sat on a stool on the opposite side of the table. 'What are you doing here, Dad?' asked Marty.

'You have the nerve to ask me that?' muttered William. 'Why didn't you tell me you'd seen Tommy? My own son keeping secrets from me.'

'You know why, Dad, and you're a right one to talk about being secretive. I went to see Pete Marshall yesterday and he showed me some photographs and said that his mother had gone out with you in the old days. She'd been a bridesmaid at your sister's wedding. A Proddy wedding! What have you got to say about that?' Marty challenged.

William's face changed colour and then he put the heel of his hand to the table and pushed it so hard that it caught Marty in the stomach, knocking the breath out of him. 'You've got no right to go nosing into my past! That was then and now is now! I'm the head of this family and Peggy had no right to defy me,' William shouted.

'What's going on here?' Jimmy stood by the table, holding two glasses of beer.

196

'Keep out of this, Jimmy,' gasped Marty, managing to push the table away.

'That's your dad?' said Jimmy, placing the two pints on the table and pointing a finger at William.

'Who the bloody hell's this?' snarled William. He got to his feet and shot out his fist, catching Jimmy smack on the chin. He fell backwards on to the floor.

'What the hell d'you think you're doing, Dad?' yelled Marty, sinking to the floor beside Jimmy. 'You've bloody knocked him out.'

'Good!' said William, clenching both fists. 'He shouldn't have interfered.'

By then several men and a couple of women had drifted in their direction and a barman and the licensee were also heading towards them. Jimmy began to stir and his eyelids fluttered open.

'We'll have no fighting in here,' said the licensee. 'I don't want to lose my licence. You can get out!'

William took one look at him, sniffed and headed for the exit, shouldering his way through the crowd.

Jimmy groaned, fingering his jaw.

'Are you all right?' asked Marty.

'I'll survive,' said Jimmy. 'Where's my pint?'

'Drink up and get out of here,' said the barman.

'You do just that, Jimmy. I'll be back in a minute,' said Marty, once he had helped him into a seat.

He left the pub and stood outside, absently rubbing his belly, while gazing along the pavement both ways before glancing across the road at the defunct overhead railway and towards the gate of the mighty Gladstone Dock. It was then he caught

197

sight of a familiar figure marching along in the direction of Liverpool.

'He can't half pack a punch, your dad,' said Jimmy with reluctant admiration as he stood behind Marty.

'He had no right to punch you,' said Marty.

'No. I brought your pint,' said Jimmy, handing the glass to him.

'Thanks!' Marty took the glass from him and downed half the beer.

'Are you going to follow him?' asked Jimmy. 'I'll come with you. I owe him one.'

Marty had intended going after his father but now that Jimmy was sounding positively fool-hardy, he changed his mind. 'No, I've had enough of him for one day. I won't get any sense out of him until he sobers up and even then it's doubtful.'

Jimmy nodded. 'Gotcha! I was wondering whether to catch the train to Blundell Sands and have a word with our Irene. Let her know what Mam's planning.' He stared at Marty expectantly. 'How about it?'

There was no reason why Marty should go with Jimmy. In fact he knew it would be more sensible of him to go home. Trouble was that he was feeling all churned up inside. His mother would want to know whether he had seen his father or not and, if so, why hadn't he stuck with him and brought him home. Then there was Bernie to face and she would want to know the ins and outs of what he had been doing. If he kept silent, she would go on and on until he felt like walking out again and not going back. Anyway, Jimmy probably needed an eye kept on him after taking that punch from his father.

'All right, I'll come with you,' said Marty. 'I could do with some fresh sea air.'

So they took a train to Blundell Sands.

As they walked up the road to Fair Haven, Marty asked him what it was like inside the children's home.

'No idea,' said Jimmy, hands in pockets. 'Never been to the place before. Why?'

Marty stopped. 'I just wondered whether you were planning to go up to the front door and ask to see Irene? I mean she's one of the staff, isn't she?'

'You think I should go round the back?' Jimmy stroked his jaw which was slightly swollen and bruised.

Marty shrugged. 'It's only just struck me that the gates could be locked to keep the kids in. You should have telephoned and said that you had something important to tell her that couldn't wait.'

'Good idea!' said Jimmy. 'I thought I saw a telephone box just further back near the station. I could use that – if I knew the telephone number.'

Marty swore beneath his breath. 'There'll be a telephone book in there!'

They were about to turn back towards the station when Marty heard a gate squeak somewhere ahead and a moment later Irene appeared with another girl.

'You're in luck,' he said, his eyes lighting up.

He called out to Irene and he and Jimmy hurried to catch up with her and her companion.

'What are you both doing here?' she asked. 'And what's happened to your face, Jimmy?'

'Mam has gone off her nut,' he replied, grabbing his sister's arm. 'I persuaded Marty to come with me after his dad went off after punching me.'

Her eyes flared wide in dismay and she stared at Marty. 'Why on earth would he do that? And what has Mam to do with it?' Irene was bewildered.

'Mam doesn't have anything to do with it,' said Jimmy. 'Except if it wasn't for her telling me she was going to get married and move in with some widower and his kids in West Derby, I wouldn't have been drinking at the Red Lion earlier.'

'She's *what!*' cried Irene, turning and seizing hold of him by his lapels.

'I told you she's gone off her nut,' said Jimmy with a satisfied smile, prising Irene's fingers from his jacket.

'We have to stop her,' said Irene.

'You've got a hope,' said Jimmy. 'She's made up her mind and you know how stubborn she is.'

'Get somebody to talk sense into her,' said Irene. 'Nellie Gianelli, she's the one to do it. Mam has listened to her in the past.'

Jimmy shook his head. 'You haven't seen her as often as I have. She sees this as her last chance for love before she's too old.'

'But you said this bloke's got kids. He could be using her,' cried Irene.

'That's what I thought but I don't think she'll listen to us saying anything against him,' said Jimmy.

There was a silence.

'I'm going to carry on to the beach and leave

you three to it,' said Deirdre, who had been listening to all that had been said so far.

Jimmy glanced at her. 'Who are you?'

'This is Deirdre,' said Irene. 'Deirdre, you'll have guessed this is my brother, Jimmy. Mr Mc-Grath you've seen before.'

Deirdre said hello.

The two men nodded in her direction. 'Let's all go to the beach,' said Jimmy.

Irene looked at Marty. 'Are you all right with that or have you got to get off home? I've yet to hear why your father hit our Jimmy!'

'Jimmy just got in the way,' said Marty.

The four of them began to walk towards the sea. 'I'll tell you one thing,' said Jimmy. 'I'm not going to the wedding.'

Deirdre blurted out, 'You can't not go to your mother's wedding!'

'Of course I can,' said Jimmy firmly. 'In fact, I'm thinking of going back to sea. Mam hated it when I was away. Maybe it'll make her think twice about marrying some bloke I've never met.'

Scowling, Jimmy strode ahead. Deirdre glanced at Irene and then followed him. Marty said, 'Your mam's really upset him.'

'I know.' She frowned. 'Why didn't you stop your dad hitting him? I mean your dad's a big man and you're older and tougher than Jimmy. I'm sure you could have, if–'

'Are you calling me a coward?' he interrupted. 'Because if you are...'

'I ... I w-wasn't,' she stammered. 'I'm sure you aren't but I can't help wondering why you didn't.'

He blew out a breath. 'I wasn't expecting it to

201

happen! Just as I didn't expect Dad to wham me in the stomach with a table a couple of minutes before. I didn't realize how drunk he was.'

'Sorry!' She reached out a hand to him. 'Why did he do it?'

Marty took her hand. 'He'd found out that I'd seen Tommy and not told him about it, so he went searching for him.'

'I see.' Irene was intensely aware of the strength and warmth in Marty's fingers. 'So ... so this happened in the Red Lion?'

'No!' Marty explained where he and Jimmy had ended up after the Red Lion. By the time he finished, they had reached the beach and he was still holding her hand. As if just realizing he was doing so, he slackened his grip and she, reluctantly, freed her hand. Neither of them spoke, only gazed across the sand.

The tide was on its way out, leaving stretches of wet glistening sand. Across the water to the left could be seen the Wirral peninsula and, in the far distance, Wales. To the right was sparkling sea stretching to the horizon where several ships were visible. Jimmy and Deirdre were walking towards the water's edge. A couple of teenagers appeared to be writing with sticks in the sand which was starting to dry out in the sun.

Irene and Marty paused to see what was etched beneath two entwined hearts.

RONNIE JONES LOVES ELSIE MACINTOSH xxxxx

Irene and Marty smiled at each other and she felt her breath catch in her throat. For a moment neither spoke and then Marty broke the spell by muttering, 'Love's young dream.'

He turned and headed back towards the low-lying sandhills. She followed him and eventually caught up with him. 'You don't believe in young love, do you?' she said.

'When you're that young, you can mistake it for the real thing,' he said, not looking at her.

'I wouldn't argue. I fell in love with Richard Todd when he played Robin Hood and I still drooled over him as Rob Roy. I cried when he died in *The Hasty Heart*.'

Marty shook his head. 'That's different. You know he's only playing a part and besides, he's out of your reach and so you can fancy him from afar.'

'I know that,' she said, watching where she put her feet and avoiding a clump of marram grass. 'But he is a real hero.'

He stopped and stared at her. 'You're thinking of him playing Guy Gibson in *The Dam Busters*.'

'No, I'm not! Richard Todd fought in the Second World War. He was at the D-Day landings and later at Pegasus Bridge. I read about him in a film magazine.'

'All right! There's no need to get all worked up. I believe you but fancying a film star isn't the same as falling in love with someone you meet in real life.'

'I didn't say it was but I do believe you can take to someone when you're in your teens and they can be the one for you,' said Irene, her blue eyes serious. 'I mean I remember the other year Peggy and Pete doing what those teenagers were doing, writing love letters in the sand. I genuinely believe they still have strong feelings for each other. It's

203

just that when you've been brought up to believe your parents' way is the only way and they convince you that you're being selfish if you go ahead and defy them–'

'You don't have to say any more,' Marty interrupted. 'I know I've let my own experience sour me. I married too young and I have no one else to blame but myself if I'm regretting it now.'

He carried on trudging through the sand until he reached the road.

She followed him. 'How old are you?' she asked bluntly.

'Twenty-five going on twenty-six.'

'You weren't that young! Weren't you ever tempted to write love letters in the sand?' she said lightly.

'Can't say I was. Maybe that's because we only ever went to New Brighton beach and you'd have a job finding room to build even a sandcastle because the beach was generally jammed packed tight with day trippers from Liverpool.'

She nodded. 'We scarcely ever went to New Brighton because we lived not far from Seaforth Sands and there was also Crosby beach.' She gazed up at him. 'I nearly drowned just up the coast from here last summer.'

'Jimmy mentioned it earlier. You were lucky someone swam out and saved you.'

Irene nodded. 'I wished he'd stayed round long enough for me to thank him. I don't even know if I'd recognize him because I couldn't see him properly. My eyes were all blurry with seawater.'

'I'm sure he knew you were grateful,' said Marty softly, taking her hand and placing it against his chest. 'He knew you'd had a shock. Wasn't your mother screaming fit to burst because your step-father had tried to save you and died in the attempt? He was a true hero.'

Irene nodded and her fingers curled about his. 'I suppose Jimmy told you that. It makes me sad to think that Mam seems to have forgotten Uncle Terence already and is planning on marrying someone else whom I feel will never match up to him.'

'Would it do any good to tell her how you feel?'

Irene grimaced. 'I doubt it.'

They were silent a moment and then there came a shout from Jimmy.

'I'm going to have to make tracks.' Marty sighed and released her hand. 'I need to pick up the kids from Mam's and tell her about Dad before going home.'

'Perhaps he'll be there when you reach your mother's,' said Irene brightly. 'Do let me know if you hear anything from Peggy.'

'I will.'

She thanked him and watched him go, knowing she had to suppress her feelings for him but she had found his touch oh-so comforting. She swallowed the sudden lump in her throat and hurried to where she could see Jimmy and Deirdre waiting.

When Marty arrived at his mother's house, it was to find only a flushed-faced Lil and her boyfriend there. It was obvious to him they'd been snogging on the sofa but he didn't make a point of asking what his mother had been thinking of leaving the pair of them alone.

'Where's she gone?' he asked.

'She didn't say. Bernie turned up and she took the kids home after having some dinner here,' said Lil, smoothing her light brown hair. 'Did you have any luck finding Dad?'

'Last time I saw him he was heading along the dock road in this direction,' said Marty. 'He'd been drinking and he was on his own. Did Mam leave me any dinner?'

Lil nodded.

'I'd best be going, Lil,' said the boyfriend.

'I'll see you to the door,' she said.

Marty guessed they'd be at least five or ten minutes saying tarrah, so he went and took his dinner out of the oven. He wasted no time getting the food down him and by the time his younger sister reappeared, he was on his way out again.

Bernie pounced on Marty as soon as he came through the front door. 'So did yer find yer dad?' she asked.

'Let me get my coat off,' said Marty, wishing she wouldn't grab his arm so tightly with both hands.

'What about Tommy?' she asked, fixing him with a glistening stare.

His heart sank. 'Mam told you?'

'Lil did! Why didn't you?'

'What about a cup of tea?' he asked, trying to forestall the moment when he would have to talk about his brother.

'I want you to tell me exactly what you and Tommy said to each other.'

Marty frowned. 'Why should I? Now what about that cup of tea?'

'I'm your wife and I want to know,' she said. 'Why are you being so secretive?'

He stared at her wearily. 'Because your mother might be listening at the keyhole and you know she hates our Tommy. You don't need to know any more than Mam and Dad do. Trouble always follows in his wake, so I'd prefer it if he stayed out of our lives.'

'But he's your brother!'

'And don't I know it,' said Marty grimly.

She stared at him. 'Is he seeing anyone?'

'What makes you ask that?'

'I just wondered. I'll make you that cup of tea and then I'm going out. I've promised Mam I'll do a message for her. She's gone to visit a neighbour who's on her deathbed and everybody else is out.'

'Where are the kids?'

'Having a nap.'

Marty followed Bernie into the kitchen and washed his face and hands at the sink. He sensed her come up behind him. 'You've got sand in yer hair!' she said.

He stilled. 'I went to Seaforth in my search for Dad and the wind was blowing sand all over the place.' He picked up a towel and turned and faced her. 'We had a bit of a disagreement and he took off.'

Bernie nodded. 'I told your Mam that she should get out and forget it all for a while.'

'And she took notice of you?'

'Why shouldn't she? I told her to go to the pictures. It'll do her good.' Bernie smiled smugly. 'I'll see you later.'

'Don't be long. I might have to go out again.'

Her pencilled eyebrows shot up. 'You've been out nearly all day on your own.'

'You were out all last evening with your friend.'

'Yeah, but you were at work all day and then you came in late.' She tutted, fluttered her fingers at him and hurried out.

He went upstairs and found Josie lying with her eyes wide open, singing to herself. When she saw him, she dragged herself up on the bars of the cot and he lifted her out and kissed her cheek. 'Have you been a good girl for your granny McGrath and your mam?'

'I'm always a good girl, Daddy,' she said.

He felt love well up inside him and hugged her close. Then he gazed down at Jerry who was just stirring. He opened his eyes and looked up at him sleepily. Marty hooked him up with one arm and took them both downstairs. It was while he was telling them a story that it struck him that his mother would never go to the cinema on a Sunday – so where was she? He decided he would have to visit his parents' house again. Not wanting to take the children with him, he waited with mounting impatience for Bernie to come home.

She still had not arrived when Monica came in, dressed up to the nines and with smiling eyes. 'You look like you've been enjoying yourself,' he said.

'Would you mind looking after the kids? Bernie's gone out and I have to go and see Mam.'

When he arrived at his parents' house he was aware that he was the focus of attention from several of the neighbours who were talking outside while keeping an eye on their children playing in the street. Marty smiled at the women and gave them the time of the day, knowing it would be a mistake to ignore their questioning about Peggy.

For a moment he felt angry with his sister, thinking she must have realized how fast the news would get round that she had left home. It would not surprise him if the neighbours knew exactly why she'd gone. It never failed to amaze him how news spread so fast.

He let himself into the house with his key and found his mother sitting in the back room, staring into space. 'You all right, Mam?' he asked, putting his arm about her shoulders.

'He's not come home yet,' said his mother, resting her head against Marty's arm. 'I'm worried about him, son.'

'I know. I'll go looking for him again.'

'He gets so worked up about things,' she said, dabbing her eyes.

Marty nodded. 'You make yourself a cup of tea. I'll be back as soon as I can.'

This time, Marty visited several of his father's old haunts along Scotland Road and in Liverpool centre but without any luck. He returned to his parents' house but William had still not come home. Marty went out again and this time went to the church presbytery. The door was opened by the housekeeper, who told him that Father Francis had a visitor and unless it was really important, he should come back tomorrow.

'It's important,' said Marty firmly. 'Perhaps I could come in and wait?'

'If you must,' she said grudgingly. He was not put off by her tone but wiped his feet on the mat

209

and went inside.

Their exchange must have been overheard because a door opened and Father Francis appeared. 'Martin, I thought I recognized your voice. Perhaps you'd like to come in here.' Marty followed him into the room and stopped just inside when he saw the woman sitting there. 'Martin, this is my sister, Mrs Gianelli,' said the priest.

Nellie smiled at Marty. 'I had a flying visit a couple of hours ago from Irene Miller. It was mainly about her mother planning on getting married again, but for the rest I thought my brother might be interested in what she had to say.'

'I suppose she told you that my father hit Jimmy?' he said harshly, aware of feeling disappointed in Irene.

'No she didn't, as it happens. I knew Peggy was missing, of course, and your father must be very upset about that,' said Nellie, 'but I don't see what it has to do with Jimmy. Now, if he'd gone in search of Pete Marshall...'

'What happened with Jimmy and your father?' asked Father Francis.

'Dad was angry with me and Jimmy just got in the way. Last I saw of Dad he was heading along the dock road in this direction. He still hasn't come home.'

'You think he's found Tommy?' asked the priest.

'Mam told you about my having seen Tommy!'

Father Francis nodded. 'She was very upset when she came here. You don't have to worry, Martin. I have no intention of informing the police.'

Marty sighed heavily and twiddled his thumbs.

'Tommy knows Dad's looking for him now. It could be that he'll leave the area again and won't come back.'

'It's a great pity,' said Nellie, getting to her feet. 'I'll be going, Francis. My family will be wanting their supper. I'll see myself out.'

She patted his arm and then turned and smiled at Marty and held out a hand. 'I hope that Peggy gets in touch with you soon and that you're reunited with your father even sooner.'

He murmured something indistinct and then she was gone.

'Sit down, Martin,' said Francis. 'A cup of tea or perhaps something stronger?'

'To tell you the truth, Father, I'd enjoy a drink but I'd best not. I just wanted to know whether Mam told you about the secret Dad's kept from us for years?'

'I can't discuss that with you, Martin. I suggest that you concentrate on the here and now and tell me instead what you plan to do to find Peggy after your father turns up.'

Marty told him what Jeanette had suggested and talked of his plan to visit Butlin's holiday camp in Wales as soon as he could. If she was not there, then he would try other seaside resorts.

'You've set yourself quite a task,' said the priest.

'I know,' said Marty soberly. 'But Mam's going to continue to worry herself sick not knowing where Peggy is, but at least now she knows that Tommy is alive.'

'From her note, it was obviously not Peggy's intention to cause your mother worry. It might be worth trusting your sister. A time of solitude and

211

reflection could be just what she needs.'

Marty nodded. 'So how is your own little family, Martin?' asked Francis.

Marty's face softened. 'The children are doing fine, Father. Josie is getting to be a right chatterbox. I think Jerry is going to be the strong silent type.'

Francis smiled. 'And Bernadette?'

Marty hesitated. 'She finds the kids hard work and it's true they can be a handful. Her niece Monica is a great help.'

'It's important that young couples find time to spend together,' said Francis.

'I think the ratio with us is about right, Father,' said Marty firmly. 'Anyway, it's time I was going. I'm hoping Dad will have arrived home by now. Thanks for listening.'

'Maybe we can pray before you go, Martin,' said Francis.

Marty bowed his head, clasped his hands and gazed down at the carpet. A few minutes later he was on his way home. When he arrived at his mother's house it was to find that there was still no sign of his father but Lil was keeping their mother company.

'Where d'you think he's got to?' asked Mary, wringing her hands.

Marty wished he knew. He was feeling guilty, knowing that if he had kept his mouth shut, none of this would have happened. 'I'll go and search the dock road,' he said.

'It mightn't be safe you going off there on your own at this time of night,' said his mother.

Marty had been thinking the same thing himself

but was not about to say so. His father had to be found and he decided a bit of help wouldn't go amiss. He checked he had some coins in his pocket and, despite the rain, he headed for the nearest telephone box and phoned Jeanette's half-brother, Detective Inspector Sam Walker, with whom he'd had dealings before. He made no mention of Tommy, just said that his father had not come home and had last been seen heading towards Liverpool along the dock road after leaving the Caradoc pub in Seaforth. Then he returned to his mother and sister and waited for news.

Just before dawn William McGrath was found in the Leeds and Liverpool Canal, near Stanley Dock, by a dock gate policeman. When Marty heard the news that there was a bump the size of an egg on the back of his father's head, he feared that maybe Tommy had seen him along the dock road, followed him and struck from behind to get rid of their father for good. Marty kept his thoughts to himself. The police had decided that, being drunk, William had slipped on the wet cobbles and banged his head before staggering to his feet and then falling again, this time into the canal. Marty found himself thinking of Peggy and wished he knew where she was so he could get in touch with her and let her know the news.

Fifteen

April 1st 1958, Blackpool

Peggy paused outside the Church of the Sacred Heart on Talbot Street. It was not far from the Clarendon Hotel where she was staying in company with commercial travellers and off-season, long-stay guests. Unbidden Pete came into her mind and she wondered what he would have made of this building founded by the Jesuits. He'd probably hate it. Her father, though, would love it, being an admirer of the all-male Order of the Society of Jesus which was zealous in its mission.

Just thinking of those two men made her chest feel tight with emotion. Needing to breathe, she walked on past the church in the direction of the small hotel, annoyed with herself for getting upset. She had more important things to attend to; it was time she looked for a job.

At least her emotions were no longer as chaotic as when she had first arrived in the resort. Torn between relief at having made the break from her family and Pete, and hurt and disappointment that the man she loved had let her down. At least she no longer lay awake half the night feeling bitter towards her father for his bigotry and lack of understanding. She had kept going over and over her conversations with Pete. Perhaps he hadn't actually promised to convert to her faith but she

214

would have sworn on her mother's deathbed that he had given the impression he would if it meant they could marry at last. There were times when she still yearned to feel his arms around her and to taste his kisses; to hear him say that he loved her and would do anything to make her happy. Then she reminded herself of the times when they had broken up before and told herself that she had survived without him and was not going to die of a broken heart.

She did believe that if Marty had been at that ill-fated lunch party, things would not have turned out so badly. Her brother would have been able to handle their father far better than she or her mother had done. Then she reminded herself that it was Pete's mother who had put the cat among the pigeons, producing that envelope of photographs and calling her father a hypocrite. She wished that she had got to see the pictures but he hadn't even allowed her mother to look at them.

No doubt her mother was angry and upset with her for leaving. But at least she had left a note and so they shouldn't be worrying about her. After all she was a grown woman, able to make her own decisions and look after herself. She had savings and she could work. As for Pete and his mother – what had that woman been thinking of to behave the way she did? A right troublemaker she had turned out to be. Her words still stung every time Peggy thought of them.

Her hands curled into fists and she decided she'd had a lucky escape not having Mrs Marshall for a mother-in-law. Especially if it meant living under the same roof. Tears welled in her

215

eyes and she brushed them away fiercely, telling herself it didn't matter that she would never be Pete's wife; there were other fish in the sea.

She had reached the promenade and could feel the wind tugging at her headscarf and the shopping bag that dangled from her wrist. Angry waves were sweeping up the almost-deserted beach. Perhaps it would be busier this coming Easter weekend if the weather improved.

She had commented on it being unseasonably cold to her landlady, Mrs Henderson. Peggy had told her that most probably she would have to leave after the Easter bank holiday. Peggy had shown her the job application she planned to send off to Butlin's holiday camp in Pwllheli and asked her if she could keep an eye open for their reply.

That morning Mrs Henderson had appeared flustered and surprised Peggy by asking her would she mind going on a message for her. Apparently Clara, her dogsbody, had not turned up and she was short-handed. Peggy was to have her second surprise of the day when she entered the hotel to be greeted by her landlady with the words, 'Miss McGrath, how would you feel about working for me?'

Peggy stared at her blankly.

Two spots of bright pink appeared on Mrs Henderson's cheeks. 'You wanted a job. Why not here in Blackpool? You're not going to be overworked for the next few weeks, although when the summer season starts you'll find it hectic – but enjoyable,' she added hastily. 'You'll have time off to lie on the beach and swim. There's plenty of other entertainment; the top stars appearing in our

216

theatres, dancing at the Tower Ballroom and, of course, there's all the fun of the fair at the Pleasure Beach.'

'But what about my job at Butlin's?' Peggy blurted out.

'You haven't heard from them yet.' Mrs Henderson rested an elbow on the reception desk and placed her chin under her hand. 'You don't think that what Blackpool has to offer can match up to a holiday camp?'

'I haven't thought of comparing the two,' said Peggy.

'Well, think now! I'm sure Butlin's get thousands of applications – for would-be entertainers, for instance.' Her landlady stared at her intently. 'How good is your singing voice? Is your dancing outstanding? Can you amuse children? You wrote on your application form you're prepared to do anything but it could be that you end up as a chalet cleaner.'

'I was thinking mainly of administration work as you know, having seen the form,' said Peggy honestly. 'I put the rest down to give them the impression I'm an all-rounder.'

'Then be an all-rounder for me. Clara has given me quite a shock. She's going off and getting married. A soldier who's being posted to Germany, would you believe? I didn't plan on taking on any other staff for a few weeks, but between us and Gwen, the all-purpose maid, we could cope until then. I'm always willing to help my fellow human beings. I'm sure we could work well together.'

Perhaps they could, thought Peggy. At least here was someone who wanted and needed her right

217

now. 'Is bed and board included?' she asked.

'Of course. Although you'll have to move rooms.'

'I'd expect that,' said Peggy. 'I'd like to see the room. Is it on the top floor?'

'As you'd expect,' said Mrs Henderson, inclining her head. 'But it does have its own washbasin and a view of the sea. There's a bathroom with lavatory on the back landing on the floor below.'

As they went upstairs, Peggy determined to set about building a different life for herself altogether from the old. She would make new friends and enjoy herself and not worry too much about those back in Liverpool. Her heart might still be too sore to fall in love again but a light-hearted romance might be just the thing to cheer her up before the year was over.

Sixteen

Irene paused outside the newsagent's and stared at the display board outside. Written in large black letters were the words MAN'S BODY FOUND FLOATING IN CANAL, NEAR STANLEY DOCK. She was filled with a sense of foreboding and, fumbling in a pocket for change, she wasted no time going inside the shop and buying that evening's *Echo*.

As there were other customers waiting, she hurried outside and, slowly walking in the direction of Fair Haven, she read that a man's body had been found during the early hours of that morning. It had been identified as Mr William McGrath who was believed to have been drinking and had accidentally fallen into the water. The report went on to give a bit more information about his job and family and asked for any witnesses to the incident to contact their nearest police station.

Irene folded the newspaper and hurried back to Fair Haven. As she was on changing nappies and feeding the babies duties that evening, she waited until she had finished her shift and was getting ready for bed in the room that she shared with Deirdre before producing the newspaper and showing it to her friend.

'That family is really going through it,' said Irene. 'I feel so sorry for Mrs McGrath but I guess the burden of attending the inquest and arranging the funeral will fall on Marty's shoulders.'

'I guess you're right,' said Deirdre. 'But what about the sister who's missing and the brother he was searching for?'

Irene tapped a fingernail against her teeth. 'Maybe they'll see it in the newspaper or hear about it and get in touch with Marty.'

'D'you think your Jimmy will have read it?' asked Deirdre.

'I should think so,' said Irene absently, her thoughts still with Marty.

'Perhaps it'll make him think twice about going back to sea,' said Deirdre.

This time the other girl had Irene's full attention. 'Why d'you say that?'

'Well, you never know the minute when something might happen to those you care about.' Deirdre stared at her, wide-eyed, clutching her old tatty rag doll to her breast – something Irene had noticed her doing more often since they'd heard Fair Haven was likely to be closed down. 'It must be awful if you're thousands of miles away,' Deirdre added.

Irene agreed. 'But I don't think the news about Mr McGrath is going to change Jimmy's mind. He's really annoyed with Mam about her getting married and, as I told you, I wasn't able to talk to her on Sunday. I'm just hoping that when she reads the note I left, she'll get in touch with me.'

'When d'you think Jimmy will get a ship?'

'He'll have to serve his notice first,' said Irene. 'I'm sure he'll let me know in time to say tarrah to him.'

Deirdre sighed and climbed into bed. 'You'll go to your mother's wedding, won't you?'

'Probably,' murmured Irene, thinking if Maisie had been home when she'd visited Nellie Gianelli, then she would know exactly what her mother expected of her.

The following evening, Irene read an appeal to Peggy McGrath in that day's *Echo*, asking her to get in touch with her family as she was needed urgently at home. An appeal was also broadcast on the wireless, in the hope of the message reaching further afield, although no mention was made of her father's death.

Irene decided to do some letter writing. One to her mother, one to her friend Betty in America, bringing her up to date with all the news, and a letter of condolence to Marty and his family. She specifically added Peggy's name at the last minute, praying that they would hear from her soon.

Easter was over and the funeral took place on the Tuesday. Marty placed an arm around his mother's and Lil's shoulders as the three of them stood at his father's grave side in Ford cemetery. He could not help thinking about Peggy and how she should have been there. Tommy's absence did not surprise him.

A coroner had decided William McGrath's death had been accidental but Marty still felt uneasy about that verdict. He watched as his mother dropped a handful of soil on to the lid of the coffin, then he did the same and lastly Lil took her turn. Bernie and Lil's fiancé chose to remain in the background, as did the rest of those who had come to pay their respects to William McGrath.

One of Bernie's sisters was looking after the children. Then with Father Francis's final words ringing in their ears, they left the grave side.

As they approached the awaiting highly polished black Daimler, Marty was distracted by a sudden movement. He could have sworn he had caught sight of a man hovering behind a tree. He told his mother and sister to get into the car and that he would only keep them five minutes, then he sped towards the spot where the figure had been lurking. The man had moved and was now hurrying away along the road.

Marty went after him. 'What the hell are you playing at?' he said, grabbing hold of his brother and turning him round to face him. Immediately he saw that Tommy had a fading black eye. 'You could have come forward for a couple of minutes. You must know Mam would want to see you!'

221

'Let me go! I couldn't risk it.'

'She cares about you. Don't you care about her at all? After all she's lost Dad and is grieving for him.'

'I'm not going to weep for him if that's what you want,' said Tommy in a hard voice. 'As for Mam, I know you and Lil will take care of her.'

'Thanks for that! All you think about is number one.'

'I need to stay in the background in case anyone recognizes me and informs the police,' said Tommy.

'Is that why you went to a jazz club?' asked Marty sarcastically. 'You're a selfish sod! Where did you get the black eye from? Did you and Dad meet up accidentally in some pub on the dock road when he went in search of you?'

Tommy looked affronted. 'Don't be daft! As soon as I knew he was after me, I went into hiding. As for the black eye, I wasn't looking where I was going and walked into a lamp post.'

Marty pushed him away from him. 'I don't believe you.'

'Please yourself. So why did our Peg leave home?' said Tommy, changing the subject. 'I bet it was because of Dad.'

'She wanted to get married and her fella is a Proddy.'

Tommy nodded. 'Why do parents always have to interfere? Anyway, Dad's dead and nothing is going to bring him back. I'll see you around.' He turned and with his shoulders hunched up about his ears, he walked away.

Marty returned to the waiting Daimler and

climbed inside.

'Who was that you were talking to?' asked Lil.

'Tommy,' said Bernie, her eyes glinting. 'I bet it was Tommy.'

'Well, you'd lose your bet,' said Marty, and ordered the chauffeur to drive on. He was aware that his mother was staring at him. He guessed that later she would probably have plenty to say to him on the subject of his brother, never mind Peggy. Why couldn't Bernie have kept her mouth shut, instead of planting thoughts in his mother's head?

He was glad when Bernie left early, making the children her excuse, although he had a feeling that she was not going to let the subject of Tommy drop.

As soon as he arrived home, she pounced on him. 'It was your Tommy, wasn't it? You didn't want him at the funeral? That was why he didn't come over!'

'Don't be stupid! He's still wanted by the police. He's keeping his head down. Now let it go,' said Marty, removing his black tie.

'Your mother would have liked to have spoken to him. You could have persuaded him to arrange a meeting,' persisted Bernie. 'A fine brother you are! You're jealous of him because he's your mother's favourite.'

'Like hell I am,' muttered Marty, dropping his tie on the chest of drawers.

After changing into a pair of old corduroys and a short-sleeved shirt, he left the bedroom. He found Monica reading *Harry the Dirty Dog* to the children in the kitchen and was reminded of the

223

day he had purchased the book and talked to Irene Miller. He felt a rush of affection for her and yearned for that warmth she showed towards him. He thought of the last time he had been with her and how they had walked on the beach and talked about love after they had seen those teenagers writing in the sand. He liked her smile and her sudden seriousness. He liked the shape of her face and the blue of her eyes and that day he had so wanted to kiss her and taste the softness of her skin. To have her body close to his and feel her breasts crushed against his chest. He was aware of his arousal and hastily walked out of the room.

Josie called out to him but he knew that he could not go back just yet. He needed to calm himself and the only way to do that was not to think about Irene. Yet he had to write to her, thanking her for the message of condolence she had sent to him and his family.

He went out into the backyard and paced up and down, wishing he had a cigarette. Monica appeared. 'Are you OK?' she asked sympathetically.

'Life could be better.'

'Aunt Bernie was telling me that your Mam is going to Butlin's with a friend for Whit week.'

Marty stared at her and said softly, 'Did she now? That's news to me.'

'Apparently it was Aunt Bernie's suggestion that your Mam went with her friend. She said your Mam told her that your father had booked it already and she was going to cancel but Aunt Bernie said that she didn't see why the holiday should go to waste. It would be good for your mother to get away.'

Marty could not deny it but he was annoyed that his mother had not mentioned the holiday to him. It occurred to him that maybe his father's death was not such a tragedy to Mary as he had thought. It did make him wonder how many marriages were truly happy. His own certainly hadn't turned out the way he had expected. If only he had met Irene Miller earlier – how different things might be if Irene had been the children's mother! He sighed: daydreaming would get him nowhere.

Seventeen

The following Saturday Irene was able to visit her mother, who had still made no effort to contact her. It was late afternoon and Maisie was on her way out when her daughter turned up on her doorstep.

'Why didn't you let me know you were coming?' Maisie blurted out.

'Why didn't you answer my note?' Irene stared at her mother's vibrant red hair. 'Is that a wig you're wearing?'

'Don't be cheeky!' retorted Maisie, flushing as she lightly touched her hair.

'Well, is it?' Irene persisted.

Maisie sighed. 'You'd better come in.'

Irene stepped inside and closed the front door behind her. 'Well, is it a wig?'

'If it is, what's wrong with me ringing the changes by wearing one?' said Maisie, sounding

225

exasperated. 'I suppose you've come to ask me about the wedding. As it happens I'm off to meet Alfred to discuss the arrangements with the priest.'

'So that's the name of my future stepfather! When is the wedding?'

'Whit!'

'The bank holiday Saturday? I'm surprised it hadn't already been booked up in advance.'

'Are you going to say you can't make it, just like our Jimmy?' asked Maisie, an edge to her voice.

'No, I'll try and get the day off. Although I would have thought you would have invited us to meet your future husband before now.' She paused. 'Are you meeting him at the vestry? If so, I could come along with you and say hello,' said Irene.

Maisie fiddled with the clasp on her artificial crocodile skin handbag before opening it and taking out a packet of cigarettes. She lit up and immediately had a coughing fit.

'You should give them up,' said Irene, slapping her on the back.

When Maisie caught her breath she said hoarsely, 'I'm not getting married local. We're tying the knot at his church in West Derby.'

'Oh!' Irene could not disguise her surprise. 'Why's that?'

'I'm going to be living in his parish and it's what he wants.'

Irene was silent.

Maisie took a deep drag on her cigarette. 'Say what yer thinking, girl,' she said hoarsely.

'You don't really want to know, Mam.'

'What did our Jimmy tell you?'

'That he's a widower with three children and he doesn't want either of us living in his house. Jimmy's really upset.'

'Well, Jimmy has no need to be upset. He's a grown man for God's sake and you've pretty well left home. Alf's a widower who is looking for a loving companion, just like me, and there's no room for the pair of you. His children all have their own bedrooms.'

'Lucky them,' murmured Irene, going over to the window and staring out over the back yard. 'I'm surprised you didn't write back when I told you that the children's home is closing down and I'll be out of a job. I'll have nowhere to live.'

'You'll get another,' said Maisie.

'I could have been company here for you after Jimmy goes to sea.'

'It wouldn't be the same. I agree with Alfred that your children aren't any use when it comes to sharing memories.' Maisie placed a hand to her bosom. 'Someone who knows what it is to hurt so deep inside that you believe you're never going to come through on the other side.'

Irene was unmoved. 'Cut the cackle, Mam. This man is a stranger, so how can you have memories that you can share with him? I bet it's just that the pair of you want to go to bed together!'

Maisie gasped and raised a hand as if to strike her daughter. Irene stepped back hastily. 'I've a good mind to wash your mouth out with soap!' said her mother. 'Alfred and I have both lived through terrible times, the Depression and the last war.'

'Gertie Marshall lived through them so you could have made up your quarrel and reminisced together,' said Irene defiantly. 'You don't have to get married again.'

'I want to get married again!' shouted Maisie. 'I've told you in the past that I like a man about the place and Alfred misses having a woman around.' She began coughing again.

Irene did not waste time patting her on the back. 'So it's just a marriage of convenience?'

'You make it sound cold-blooded,' Maisie gasped. 'Of course, it won't be what it was like with your dad or even Terence, but we're not marrying merely for convenience and we don't want any know-all grown-up kids spoiling it.'

'How old are his children?' asked Irene, wishing she had not come but knowing she could not have avoided doing so.

'Daisy and Rose are ten and twelve and their brother Patrick is eight.' Maisie shook a finger at her. 'And don't say it!'

'Say what? That he's using you?' Irene's voice wobbled.

'Stop that!' said Maisie. 'I've well done my duty by you and Jimmy.'

'Duty! Is that all it was with you?'

'You just be glad that I did have a sense of duty. There were some mothers who put their children in a home during the war because they couldn't cope!'

'You don't have to tell me about the poor children who have been rejected or have no mums and dads,' said Irene, tears rolling down her cheeks.

Maisie stared at her. 'Now what's wrong with

you? If you care so much about such children, you should be glad I'm going to be a mother to Alfred's. Now come here!' Maisie dropped her handbag and stubbed out her cigarette in an ash tray on the sideboard and put her arms around her daughter. 'I want you to be my maid of honour. I'll get you a frock. I know your size and you can lead Daisy and Rose into the church after me.' She patted Irene on the back and then let her go. 'You be here on Whit Saturday morning and don't be late.'

She surprised Irene by kissing her cheek and then picked up her handbag and went out. For several moments Irene could only stare after her and then she pulled herself together and went and made herself a cup of tea.

She was about to sit down and drink it when she noticed the blue airmail envelope on the sideboard. At last, a reply from Betty to whom she had written again not so long ago. She snatched up the letter and hastily slit open the envelope.

Hello Irene,

Sorry to be so long in answering your letters, which had me spitting nails. I really felt for you. I could say things about your mother's behaviour but I won't because it wouldn't be helpful. But you know me, so you can guess what's on the tip of my tongue. I was also really interested in what you had to say about the children's home closing because I have BIG NEWS and that is the reason for my not writing back earlier. I'm going to have a baby and now the morning sickness has passed, I feel so much better and able to tell people I am pregnant. I am almost thinking sensibly –

which is unusual for me, some would say. Anyway, remember my asking you whether you'd ever thought of being a private nanny? Well, there are well-to-do families who would jump at the opportunity to hire a British nanny for their little ones over here. But I thought that perhaps to give you some idea what it might be like living in America and having such a position, you could come and stay with me and Stuart as soon as you are free to come. You can be nurse and nanny to both of us and the baby for as long as you like. (I'm serious, we're both in a quake at the thought of being parents.) Of course, we will pay you a proper wage, as well as provide you with bed and board. You will have to apply for a work permit and visa, but I doubt you'll have any difficulty with the necessary paperwork. Just write back as soon as you can and let me know what you decide. Stuart says if you can come then it could be that you might be able to have company on the journey if you can make it at the end of July. If you remember, his stepsister is Lynne Walker, the wife of Detective Inspector Sam Walker, Jeanette's half-brother. Lynne's daughter, Bobby, who you've met and works Saturdays at Lenny's place, is now sixteen and would love to come and stay the whole of the summer holidays. Lynne cannot come because she's having another baby. It's all babies at the moment in the family what with Jeanette pregnant as well. If you say yes, then hopefully we'll be able to arrange for you both to be met in New York and accompanied across country all the way to California.

Loads of love, Betty.

PS. Has Jimmy gone to sea yet? What is he going to do about the house if he's going to be away most of the time and you decide to come to America? I bet it'll soon be snapped up. From what I hear from Lynne,

230

the housing situation in Liverpool is still dire. It must be really difficult for young married couples having to live with parents. Also, is there any news of Peggy?

The letter was like an answer to a prayer, thought Irene, her spirits soaring. She could not be happier for Betty who had been through some bad times but now, married to Stuart and having a baby, she would have a proper little family of her own. She had given Irene plenty to think about, including where she could possibly get all the money needed to pay for her liner ticket to New York?

She tapped the letter against her teeth, knowing she did not have enough savings in her Post Office account. Her heart sank at the thought she might have to refuse Betty's offer of a job. It was then she heard a noise at the front door and hurried into the lobby just as Jimmy entered the house.

'What are you doing here?' he asked.

'I came to see Mam.'

'Is she in?'

'No, she's gone to meet Alfred. They're seeing the priest about the wedding arrangements. I could scarcely believe it when she told me she was getting married so soon.'

Jimmy shrugged. 'It's her funeral. I wouldn't want to be marrying someone with three kids at her age. I'm off.'

Irene's face fell. 'You mean you've got a ship?'

Jimmy nodded. 'I'm going to New Zealand.'

'That's the other side of the world!'

'Glad you know your geography,' he said, grinning.

'Very funny. When d'you leave?'

'The day after next but I'm meeting Pete and Tony and the rest of the band at the Gianellis' soon.'

'Do they know you're leaving?'

'Of course. I've suggested someone who can take my place on guitar and washboard and I'm hoping he'll be there. Tony'll be in charge, though.'

She walked into the kitchen and he followed her. She poured a cup of tea for him. 'What about the house?' she asked.

He followed her. 'What about it? Mam'll be here for a little while yet and won't you be coming back here once the children's home closes? You could try and get a job at Litherland Nursery and keep the home fires burning.'

She took a deep breath. 'I have other plans. That's if I can get the money together for a liner ticket.'

Jimmy frowned as he picked up that morning's newspaper from the sofa and sat down. 'Has this anything to do with Betty?'

Irene nodded. 'There was a letter here for me from her. She's having a baby and wants me to go out there.'

Jimmy glanced up from the sports page. 'You mean she wants you to look after it for her?'

'Yes, but she'd like me to go as soon as possible.'

He made no comment and she realized he was not listening to her properly, so snatched the newspaper out of his grasp. 'Did you hear what I said? She'd like me to go at the beginning of the school holidays, so I can accompany Bobby, who works Saturdays at Lenny's cafe, to California. I'm

232

not going to be living here, even if I were able to get a job at Litherland Nursery. I couldn't afford the rent and all my living expenses on my own. Anyway, what's the point of keeping the house on if you're going to be at sea for months on end and hopefully I'm going to be in America?'

Jimmy frowned. 'But it's home.'

'Don't be sentimental,' said Irene harshly, dropping the newspaper on the table and folding her arms across her chest. 'It hasn't been a proper home since Uncle Terence died. It's a house but it could be a home to a young family.'

Jimmy was silent as he reached for his cup of tea. 'I suppose you have a point. I wonder if Mam has given any thought to what we'd do about the house once she marries dear Alfred and moves in with him and his kids?'

'She's going to be here until Whit and that'll give me time to get things sorted out.'

'You do realize that we'll be homeless?'

She smiled. 'You'll have your ship and I'm sure I'll have a roof over my head whatever I do. We could be a lot worse off.'

Jimmy agreed, hesitated and then said, 'As it happens the lad who's going to take my place is Nick. You know him. Sam and Lynne Walker adopted him. He could be at the Gianellis' this evening. Why don't you come with me? I bet he's aware that Bobby wants to go and stay with Betty this summer. She was a big fan of Betty's artistic talent and wanted to be like her.'

Irene's face lit up. 'I don't mind having a word with him and I always enjoy a chat with Nellie.'

'Then make us a snack and we'll go round

there after I've listened to the football results,' said Jimmy.

It was Tony who opened the door to Jimmy and Irene. 'Hi,' he said. 'Haven't seen you for a while, Irene.' A smile lit up his handsome face. 'Jimmy!' He nodded in his direction. 'Everybody's here.'

'Including Nick?' asked Jimmy.

Tony nodded.

'Good,' said Jimmy.

'Is your step-mamma in?' asked Irene.

'Not at the moment but she shouldn't be long,' said Tony. 'Come on in!'

'Do you think Nick'll fit in?' asked Irene.

'Sure. He plays the banjo, as well as guitar and washboard,' said Tony, helping her off with her jacket. 'He's not as experienced as Jimmy on the last two, but he'll get there. Bobby's here as well. You know her, don't you?'

Irene could not conceal her surprise. 'Yes. What's she doing here?'

Tony grinned. 'Apparently she wouldn't mind having a go at singing.'

'Is Lucia here, too?' asked Jimmy, a slight frown on his face.

Tony nodded. 'She and Bobby seem to have taken to each other.'

'I'm glad to hear it,' murmured Jimmy. 'She hasn't asked to have a go at being a vocalist as well, has she?'

'If she could sing I'd have suggested that she had a go before now, instead of mooning over you,' said Tony bluntly. 'Come on through.'

They followed him into the kitchen where Bobby and Lucia were chatting as they did the

234

dishes, whilst Nick strummed a guitar and the two other lads in the group had their heads together over a sheet of music.

Nick glanced up at Irene in surprise before turning to Bobby. 'Hey, Bobby, look who's here.'

She broke off from what she was saying in mid-sentence and her face lit up as she saw Irene. 'It must be fate!' she blurted out. 'Has Betty been in touch with you?'

'Yes, I've just read her letter. It was at my mother's house,' said Irene.

'Are you going to go?' asked Bobby, drying her hands on a tea towel.

'To America?' said Irene.

'Where else?' cried Bobby, her eyes shining. 'Do say you are, so I can go with you!'

'I want to,' said Irene, finding the younger girl's excitement infectious. 'But there are matters I have to sort out first.'

'But we still have plenty of time,' said Bobby, 'although we can't really delay on booking our berths,' she added. 'I believe the voyage only takes about five days.'

'That'll depend on the weather,' said Jimmy.

'Then they'd better pray the ship doesn't run into a storm or bump into any icebergs,' said Lucia, putting away the last dish in a cupboard.

Irene noticed that Lucia did not look at Jimmy and wondered if she was annoyed about him going back to sea. Her thoughts turned to Marty and how, if she went to America, it could be years before she saw him again. But it would be for the best and she might meet someone else whom she could fall in love with and, if she didn't, then she could still have a fulfilling life looking after other people's children.

At that moment there was the sound of the front door opening and closing and then the tap-tap of high heels on linoleum. The kitchen door opened and Nellie stood there. She gazed around the room and then her eyes lit up as they fixed on Irene. 'Am I glad to see you! Were your ears burning? There's a vacancy coming up at Litherland Nursery for a nursery nurse in September. I mentioned your name. If you apply, there's a chance of you filling the position.'

There was a silence.

Then Bobby burst out, 'But she can't! We're going to America.'

'What?' Nellie stared at her and then looked at Irene. 'You've made up your mind to go and see Betty?'

'She's offered me a job. She's having a baby and she wants me to be the baby's nanny.'

Nellie looked disappointed and then she sighed. 'Ah well, if it's not meant to be.'

Jimmy said, 'It would be better if you applied for the job at the nursery, Irene. We could keep on the house then. I could send you money towards the rent. Don't forget you still have to find the money for your liner ticket.'

'Oh but...' Bobby cried, only to be silenced by a look from Nick.

Irene moistened her lips. 'I'm not making any decisions right now. I need to think about both jobs from every angle.'

'But you do want to see Betty, don't you?' Bobby burst out. 'We could have such fun on the

236

ship and when we get to America and spend time with Betty. She really misses us both.'

'If your mother heard you,' said Nick, sounding exasperated, 'she'd clout you one.'

'No, she wouldn't, but she'd be ashamed of me for being so selfish,' said Bobby.

'I wish I was going to America,' said Lucia. 'I never go anywhere because Mam and Dad can't afford it.'

'You've been to Italy with us,' said Tony. 'Bobby and Irene have never been out of the country as far as I'm aware.'

'But they might be going to *America*,' said Lucia. 'All the buildings in Italy are ancient and half of them are falling down.'

Nick shook his head at her. 'That's an exaggeration. Besides, them being ancient is what attracts the tourists!' He placed the guitar on the table. 'There's something important you haven't mentioned, you girls, and that's the music. If I was going to America I'd want to see Elvis Presley live singing *"Let Me Be Your Teddy Bear"*. And Little Richard performing *"Tutti Frutti"*. Then there's those new singers, the Everly Brothers. Have you heard *"Bye, Bye, Love"*? Imagine seeing them perform!'

'And what about all the blues and jazz singers! I'd like to go to New Orleans,' said Tony.

'Isn't that in the deep south?' said Bobby. 'We wouldn't be going there.'

'Hollywood is in California,' said Lucia. 'You could go and see the film stars.'

'I doubt it,' said Irene, almost regretfully. 'It's quite a journey as it is to San Jose. Thousands of

237

miles. The mind boggles.' She stood up. 'I'd best be getting back to Blundell Sands.'

'I'll see you out,' said Nellie.

She walked with Irene to the front door. As she put on her jacket, Nellie asked her whether she had spoken to her mother about the wedding.

'Yes, it's on Whit Saturday at Alfred's church. She wants me to be maid of honour and is buying me a frock.' Irene sighed. 'I do appreciate you thinking of me for the job at the nursery.'

Nellie smiled. 'Don't you be worrying about it. I'm sure you'll make the right decision. I'll pray for you.'

'Thanks,' said Irene, leaning forward and kissing her on the cheek. 'I'll see you soon.'

As she went down the drive she heard her name being called and glanced back at the house. Jimmy came racing after her. 'I forgot to say tarrah!' He gave her a bear hug. 'Take care of yourself and forget what I said about the house and the nursery. You do what's right for you.'

'Thanks! Don't forget to send me a postcard. It'll reach me eventually if you send it here after Mam's wedding.'

'Same here if you do go to America. Let me know how you get on at Mam's wedding.'

A thought struck Irene. 'I think I'll leave making up my mind what to do until after the wedding.'

They hugged again and then went their separate ways.

Eighteen

Irene stared at her reflection in her mother's bedroom mirror and pulled a face. She wished Maisie had consulted her about the frock she had bought, which she hadn't even had the opportunity to try on until now. No doubt Alfred Potts's ten- and twelve-year-old daughters wouldn't mind wearing lemon chiffon with puffed sleeves, but she did. Puffed sleeves were for kids, not nineteen-year-olds.

Soon she would meet Daisy, Rose, Patrick and their father for the first time as her mother had made no arrangements for Irene to do so earlier. She still hadn't made up her mind about going to America or applying for the job at Litherland Nursery. She had mentioned the latter to Deirdre, who had asked if Irene minded if she applied – which, of course, she hadn't.

Maisie entered the bedroom. 'Aren't you ready yet?' she asked, cigarette dangling from her lips.

'Ready as I'll ever be,' said Irene, picking up her posy and dolly bag containing lipstick, a small box of confetti and her purse.

'You do look nice,' said Maisie, her heavily made-up face relaxing. 'I wasn't sure if you'd think that style too young for you.'

'I could have done without the puffed sleeves but I'm not complaining,' said Irene, relieved that her mother had had the sense to buy an outfit suitable for a woman of mature years.

Maisie frowned at herself in the mirror. 'I wish our Jimmy hadn't been so awkward. I can imagine how it looks to people, him going off to sea the way he did.'

'Forget it, Mam. We'd best be going. We don't want to keep Uncle Martin waiting.' Even as she spoke, Irene's thoughts flew to Marty McGrath. He had sent her a thank you note for her letter of condolence and mentioned that his mother was spending Whit week at Butlin's, Pwllheli. He had hopes that Peggy might be there but had not mentioned the possibility to his mother, in case she built up her hopes, only to be disappointed.

Irene had wondered why he had not thought of writing to the holiday camp, enquiring about Peggy. Maybe his father's sudden death had put such an idea out of his head. Shock did strange things to people.

She was pleased that Pete Marshall had been in touch, although their mothers were still not speaking. Apparently he had bought a second-hand car and was taking driving lessons.

'Another of those airmail letters has come for you, by the way,' said Maisie. 'I put it on the side-board.'

Irene could not wait to read what Betty had to say and hurried downstairs. She noticed her uncle waiting at the front door, smoking a cigarette. 'Get a move on, Irene,' he said.

Irene nodded, went into the kitchen and picked up the flimsy blue envelope and placed it in her dolly bag. Then she hurried after her mother and aunt to her uncle's waiting car.

Some of the neighbours stood on their door-steps and gave Irene a cheer as she appeared. She grinned and waved before squeezing into the back seat, alongside her mother and her two younger cousins. She thought how fortunate it was that the car was a large one. How different it had been when Maisie had married Terence and the Millers had lived just a few doors away.

Those same neighbours watching them now had been invited to the do in the evening after that wedding. Unlike this one, which was immediate family only. Terence's son, Billy, had turned down Maisie's invitation. Irene did not blame him as she could understand his feelings.

Irene was oblivious to the conversation taking place in the car as she read the single flimsy pale blue sheet of paper covered in Betty's large scrawl. Her friend so wanted her to go to America and she looked forward to having a definite reply from her soon. She mentioned Bobby and had even written down the Walkers' address in Liverpool if she wanted to get in touch with Bobby's mother.

Irene felt a nudge in her ribs. 'Well, what does Betty have to say?' asked Maisie.

Irene folded the letter and replaced it in its envelope and put it in her dolly bag. 'Didn't I tell you what her last letter said?'

'Not that I remember,' said Maisie.

'Betty's having a baby. Isn't that great! She'd love me to go and help her before the birth and afterwards. I'll be getting paid, of course,' she added hastily. 'I'll be a proper nanny.'

'Who's this Betty?' asked her aunt.

'My best friend, she lives in America.'

241

'That's some distance,' said her uncle.

Irene agreed that it was a long way to California.

'It'd cost money to get there,' said her mother.

'I know,' said Irene, who had made enquiries and knew exactly how much it would cost.

'You could work your passage on a liner,' said her uncle. 'Write to Cunard and tell them what you're good at and ask if there are any jobs going.'

'That sounds good advice,' said Maisie, stifling a cough. 'If our Jimmy had been here he could have given you advice.'

'I can't understand your Jimmy going to sea and not coming to your wedding,' said Maisie's sister-in-law.

'I can,' said Irene's uncle. 'Jealousy. He doesn't want to see his Mam marrying another man.'

'I don't think it's that,' Irene blurted out.

'Then what is it?' asked Irene's aunt.

'Mam getting married again means nothing will ever be the same again,' said Irene.

'It's time our Jimmy found himself a decent girl and got married himself,' said her aunt. 'She'd make a home for him.'

Irene said, 'He's in no rush to get married – just like me. We both want to travel before we settle down.'

'I don't know what the world's coming to,' said her aunt. 'We were happy to get married and settle down and have kids in my day.'

'Things have changed since the war,' said Irene.

'You can say that again,' said her uncle.

But no more was said until the car drew up outside St Paul's, Spring Grove in West Derby and they all climbed out of the vehicle. The

242

church was a red sandstone building with a bell tower. Waiting in the porch was a small group.

'Is that them?' asked Irene's uncle.

'I can't see how it can be anyone else,' said Maisie, a tremor in her voice. She squared her shoulders. 'Come on then! Let's get on with it.'

Irene glanced at her mother and wondered if she was absolutely certain she was doing the right thing in getting married again. 'You can still change your mind, Mam,' she whispered, slipping a hand through her mother's arm.

Maisie gave her one of her looks. 'What are you saying that for, you dafty? Now smile and look like you're pleased to see them.'

Greetings were exchanged. Irene was surprised by how much older her future stepfather appeared in comparison to her mother. Obviously he must have married late the first time around and to a woman much younger than himself. He was not what she would call handsome but his Clark Gable moustache gave him a distinguished air and he looked really smart in a dark grey suit.

He shook her hand and said how pleased he was to meet her. She responded politely, saying, 'It's nice to meet you, too.'

He introduced his three children and they all shook hands with her. Daisy and Rosie were both dark-haired with sallow complexions, whereas their brother was fair-haired with a fresh complexion and much nicer looking. She suddenly felt sorry for the girls. They'd lost their mother and no doubt in their minds Maisie could never replace her, however hard she might try. Their immediate future was going to be much more difficult than her own in Irene's opinion, knowing her mother would stand no nonsense from them.

After the wedding, they went back to her step-father's semi-detached house which was bigger than the terrace in Litherland. Nicely decorated, with an upstairs bathroom, downstairs cloakroom, large back garden and three reception rooms, she could understand why her mother fancied living there. A buffet had been prepared and set out in the dining room. Irene was surprised by how good the food tasted and she said so.

'Thanks,' said Daisy, her cheeks turning pink. 'Mum did catering with a couple of friends and she began teaching us about food when we were only little. I'm going to do it for a job when I'm old enough.'

'Good for you,' said Irene warmly, thinking that at least her mother would not have to concern herself about Daisy's future.

'Keep in touch, girl,' said Maisie before they parted. 'And phone me if you decide you're definitely going to America, so I can see you before you go. Have you and Jimmy decided what you're doing about keeping on the house?'

'Not yet. I'll let you know, Mam,' said Irene.

There was to be no evening do or honeymoon, so Irene left with her uncle, aunt and cousins at about half past five, as they were giving her a lift into town. Her uncle dropped her off in Lime Street, as he and his family lived on the Wirral and were heading for the Mersey Tunnel. She had left her everyday clothes at the house in Litherland, so headed off to catch a bus in Skelhorne Street. She had just turned the corner opposite the Crown Hotel when a van pulled up at the kerb and she heard her name being called.

She glanced up at the driver and recognized Marty McGrath. 'What are you doing here all dressed up in your glad rags?' he asked. 'You look the gear.'

She blushed. 'My mother was married today and I'm just off to pick up my ordinary clothes in Litherland before catching the train to Blundell Sands.'

'No glass coach to whisk you there?' he joked.

Her eyes twinkled. 'As if there was ever a chance of that.'

'Did everything go off all right?'

She nodded. 'There was just close family – except Jimmy who's on his way to New Zealand.'

'When does the children's home close?'

'Sometime in July. Some of the children are going to a home in Formby, so not too far away.' She felt a lump in her throat, knowing she was going to miss George and May more than any of the other children.

'Are you all right?' asked Marty, sounding really concerned.

She nodded wordlessly.

'Could you get a job there or are you still thinking of going to see your friend, Betty, in America?' asked Marty.

Irene cleared her throat. 'I told her that I'd make up my mind after Mam's wedding.'

'So what's happening to your mother's house if you go?'

Irene stared at him and an idea came to her. 'Would you be interested in taking over the rent

245

book? I know you live with your mother-in-law but if you were thinking about moving out because you need more room ... and if you could afford the key money...' She paused. 'It's a nice little house, three bedrooms with a decent-sized back yard, but no indoor bathroom. Convenient for the shops, bus into town, as well as the train to Liverpool and Southport.'

He looked down at her with such warmth in his eyes that she just knew that she was not wasting her time, making such a suggestion.

'You're a good kid, thinking of us like this.' He hesitated. 'You said you were going to the house now. How about I give you a lift there and take a look at it now?'

She beamed up at him. 'Sounds fine to me.'

'Get in then and let's go,' said Marty, leaning across and opening the passenger door.

She hurried to the other side and climbed in. 'Thanks,' she said. 'This will save me the bus fare.'

'Money tight, is it?' he asked, pulling away from the kerb.

'I have to watch my pennies if I'm going to go to America.' She gazed ahead as he drove up Skelhorne Street past the side of the railway station and on to Copperas Hill before turning left towards London Road. Once they were across London Road and driving along St Anne's Street, she said, 'I think I'll regret it if I don't give America a try.'

He glanced at her. 'Would you stay forever?'

She frowned. 'I don't know about that.'

'You'll be missed here,' he said. 'And not only by the children you've cared for.'

She wondered if he would miss her.

'No doubt our Peggy will miss you too,' he murmured.

'I take it you haven't heard from her?' said Irene.

'No.' He sighed.

'If only she'd send a postcard it would be something,' said Irene.

He agreed.

They both fell silent and did not speak again until they had passed St Andrew's church on Linacre Road, but Irene was overwhelmingly aware of him, wondering what he was thinking. She tried to imagine him living in her old home with Bernie and the children. A sigh escaped her lips.

'Are you all right?' asked Marty, glancing at her. 'All this upheaval in your life must be upsetting.'

'It is,' she said, toying with her dolly bag. 'Although I haven't been home much since I went to work in Blundell Sands. D'you think your wife would be happy living here?' She did not wait for his answer but pointed through the windscreen to the sausage factory opposite the library ahead. 'That's where Mam used to work and Pete's mother still works there. Did I tell you they'd fallen out? I must try and see Pete before I go. And this is where we turn,' she added, pointing left.

Marty parked the van and got out, thinking about Pete and wondering how friendly Irene might have been with the other man if Peggy had not been on the scene, as was now the case. His expression was grim as he went to help Irene out of the van but she had beaten him to it. She had the front door open by the time he locked the van.

A couple of girls were playing top and whip in

247

the street and other children had obviously chalked numbers on the pavement for they were playing hopscotch. He was aware of several pairs of eyes on him as he stared up at the front of the house, noticing that the paintwork had probably been renewed during the past three years. He stepped back several paces and looked up at the roof and the chimney and could not see any obvious slates missing.

He nodded at a woman standing on the step a few doors away before following Irene into the house, closing the front door after him. He guessed that the news would soon spread that Irene Miller had come home from her mother's wedding with a man.

'Irene!' he called.

'In the back kitchen!' she replied.

He walked up the lobby, past a closed door on the right and into the open doorway a bit further on near the foot of the stairs. He went into a back room and his gaze took in its size, decoration and furnishings before crossing to the sash window and looking out on to the back yard.

Irene popped her head through the other doorway, holding a teapot in her hand. 'Cup of tea? The kettle's on.'

Marty nodded. 'Thanks.' He followed her into the back kitchen that was more the size of the scullery in his mother-in-law's house.

'Go and have a look in the yard,' said Irene. 'My stepfather built a little lean-to shed next to the lavatory. He loved doing bits of carpentry after he retired.'

'He was a policeman, wasn't he?' asked Marty,

unbolting the back door.

'Yes. He had some funny ways but he was a good stepfather. I was really sorry when he died. I still blame myself.' Tears welled in her eyes.

Marty turned swiftly and took a step towards her. 'You shouldn't still be feeling like that. It was his decision to try and save you. He must have thought there was no one else to do it.'

'I know. I suppose I'm feeling a bit emotional,' she said unsteadily, wiping her eyes with the edge of her mother's pinny that she had put on to protect her bridesmaid's frock.

He put his arms around her. 'It's not surprising. Your brother's gone to sea and your mother's married and taken on a new family.'

Her head drooped on to his chest. 'What about you? You've lost your dad, Peggy's missing and there's your brother to worry about. But then you're a man. You can cope with these things.' She stared up at him and saw a muscle clench in his jaw.

'I'm glad you think so,' he said. 'But I'm not really much of a hero. I might be able to swim but...' His voice trailed off.

She could feel the thud of his heart matching her own as they stared into each other's eyes. She stretched up her hand and caressed his cheek, then his chin that felt slightly bristly. She could not resist pressing her lips against the curve of his jaw and then the corner of his mouth. He turned his head ever so slightly but it was enough and their lips met in a kiss that felt as if it could go on forever.

Then he lifted his mouth and took a deep

breath and eased himself a few inches away from her but he did not let her go. She thought some people would say that she had led him on to kiss her. Did Marty think that?

'Say something,' he said.

'I was waiting for you to speak.'

'You mean because you don't know what to say?'

'We shouldn't be doing this,' she said. 'But if this was a film I'd probably say, "You are my hero!" because it would have been you who rescued me.'

'Such things don't only happen in films,' said Marty, releasing her abruptly. He took a deep breath, opened the back door and went into the yard.

At that moment the kettle began to whistle but Irene made no move to switch it off. She could still feel the pressure of his lips on hers and would like him to kiss her again. But that was wrong, wrong, wrong! He was a married man with a wife and two children and that was the reason he was here. Not for them to ... to...

Tears pricked her eyes. The only part she had a right to play in his life was to help him and his family have a home of their own. She felt like bursting into tears. Why couldn't she have met him first?

Taking several deep breaths, she turned off the gas under the kettle and poured scalding water into the teapot. Milk into cups came next and then spoons, sugar basin and there were still some biscuits in the tin.

She was about to call him when she heard footsteps outside and he appeared in the doorway. He cleared his throat. 'It's a good size yard and the shed would come in useful. Jimmy really should have brought your stepfather's tools inside though. It's a good job they were greased.'

His words were as matter-of-fact as they were unexpected but it was enough to enable her to behave almost normally. 'You know something about tools?'

He smiled.

She realized her stupidity. 'Of course you do. Sorry. I'm not thinking straight. Cup of tea?'

'Thanks!'

She carried the tray into the other room and placed it on the table, determined to carry on as if nothing untoward had happened. 'So what d'you think of the house so far?'

'I like the feel of it,' said Marty, watching her pour the tea as he pulled out a chair at the table and sat down. 'I'll drink my tea and then I'll look upstairs.'

'You haven't seen the parlour either,' she murmured, sitting down and pushing the biscuit tin across to him.

He stirred sugar into his tea. 'What about the furniture?'

'What about it?'

He lifted his head and looked at her. 'You wouldn't be taking it to America would you? Does Jimmy want it?'

'It doesn't belong to us. It's Mam's. I mean, some of it was Uncle Terence's but he left everything to her. He lived here with his first wife and we lived a few doors away.' Irene sipped her tea, marvelling that she could behave so calmly and rationally after that kiss and the thoughts that

251

were going round and round in her head. Her knees felt all wobbly.

'I didn't know that,' said Marty.

'Why should you? I don't think I've mentioned it before.' She reached for a Nice biscuit. Suddenly she remembered something Marty had said earlier about Terence. 'How did you know he'd been a policeman? Did Jimmy tell you?'

'I read it in the *Echo*. There was an article about him.'

'You've never mentioned that to me before,' she said.

'I read it because I was interested in finding out his name. He was a real hero.'

Their eyes met and Irene experienced that breathless feeling again. 'I was lucky, wasn't I?' she said abruptly. 'Two heroes coming to my rescue.'

Marty hesitated. 'D'you believe in luck?'

'You mean there's no such thing? That someone else was watching what I was doing?'

'Must have been if he got to you in time to save you. If he had been fast enough, then your stepfather might not have died either.'

She felt sad. 'I never thought of that. He told me off, you know? Then didn't even stay around for me to thank him.'

'Maybe it was because he was annoyed with himself.'

'You're saying he wasn't angry with me after all?'

Marty changed the subject. 'Shall we go upstairs?'

She hesitated. 'You don't need me to look at bedrooms. I'll just tidy up down here.'

He left her alone.

252

She relived the rescue as she finished her tea and washed up before going upstairs. She found Marty sitting on her bed. Before she could speak, he said, 'I think Josie would like this room.'

'It's mine.' She picked up her discarded clothes from a chair, liking the thought of Josie sleeping here.

'I thought so. If I get this house, would your mother sell the furniture to me?'

'I don't see why not.'

Marty stood up and came over to Irene. 'You do know how I feel about you. That's why it's probably best that you go to America.'

She looked up at him and so longed to just lean against him and feel his arms around her again. Of course she knew how he felt! Just as he must know how she felt towards him. So she nodded and left the bedroom.

Once downstairs, she wiped away the tears that had welled up in her eyes and took out the rent book from the sideboard drawer.

As he came into the room, she held it out to him. 'You'll find the address of the estate agent inside. I don't know if there's anyone else interested but if you're prepared to pay a little extra for the key money they ask, I dare say they'll rent out the house to you.'

He took it from her. 'Your children's books upstairs ... will you sell them to me for Josie?'

'I'd like her to have them. You don't have to pay me.'

'I'd rather pay for them, so don't argue with me,' said Marty firmly.

'All right, I won't argue.' She plucked a sum out

of her head and named it.

'Don't be daft,' said Marty, digging into his pocket and taking from a wallet several pound notes. He held them out to her.

'That's too much,' she said, not touching the money.

'You said you wouldn't argue with me,' said Marty, taking hold of her hand and folding her fingers over the notes.

She thanked them. 'You should take the books with you.'

He shook his head. 'If I don't get the key to the house, then I'm sure you'll see to it that Josie gets them.'

Irene nodded. 'You haven't seen the parlour yet,' she murmured.

'All right, I'll take a quick look at it,' he said.

A glance at the parlour and then he made for the front door. He touched her cheek and then outlined her lips with his thumb and kissed her lightly.

She leaned into him and said in a muffled voice against his chest. 'It *was* you that saved me, wasn't it?'

He did not answer, only holding her tightly for a moment. 'Take care of yourself, love. Be happy.'

He opened the front door and went outside. As she watched him get into the van, she realized he would need her mother's telephone number and signalled to him.

He wound down the window. 'What is it?'

It took her only moments to find the number in her dolly bag and write it on a scrap of paper and hand it to him. His fingers curled round hers.

'Thanks. I'll never forget you.'

'Thank you! I'll always remember you,' she whispered, stepping away from the van.

She eased the tightness in her throat as she watched the vehicle until it was out of sight. That evening she would write to Betty and tell her that she would be coming to America. She felt certain that with the money in her savings account and that which Marty had given to her, there would be enough for her ticket to New York. She would have to visit Lynne Walker to fix a date and make arrangements for Bobby to travel to America with her.

Nineteen

Irene stepped down from the Southport–Liverpool train at Central Station and wasted no time heading for Church Street where she had arranged to meet her mother outside Cooper's. It was the second week in July and today would be the first time Irene had seen her mother since the wedding although they had spoken on the telephone several times. It was from these conversations that Irene discovered Marty had moved into the house in Litherland and had bought most of the furniture and fittings too.

As she was early, Irene decided to pop into C & A Modes and have a wander round the women's department. It was whilst she was looking at frocks that she overheard a voice she recognized and had no trouble tracing it to her mother.

Maisie was arguing with a saleswoman. Irene listened to their conversation and soon realized that it was about part of the stitching coming undone on a blouse her mother had bought recently and now wanted to exchange. Irene had no doubt that her mother would win the dispute and only when all was sorted out did she approach Maisie and slip her hand through her arm.

'Hi, Mam! You should have been a lawyer; you'd always win your case.'

'You nosing, were you?' said Maisie, smiling grimly. 'I was in the right, girl, that's why that stuck-up cow caved in. They don't make clothes like they used to when I was a girl. Lovely hand-smocking I could do. I tell you, we were taught how to sew in my day.' She lit up a cigarette and took several puffs.

'Your day, Mam? You make yourself sound old.'

Maisie broke into a coughing fit and it was several moments before she managed to say in a throaty whisper, 'I feel old these days. Those children! I tell you, you and Jimmy were angels in comparison. Talk about answering me back! I would have had my face slapped if I'd spoken to a grown-up like that.'

'But you don't slap their faces, do you?'

'I've been sorely tempted! I don't know how I manage to keep my hands off Rose. Looks like butter wouldn't melt in her mouth but she's a right little madam.' Maisie's eyes smouldered. 'I haven't been feeling well either.'

Irene looked at her anxiously. 'In what way?'

'Oh, don't you be worrying,' said Maisie, still

sounding slightly breathless. 'It's just those children wearing me out.'

'Things will improve, Mam,' Irene coaxed. 'Don't get yourself worked up. They've lost their mother and it must be really strange having another woman taking her place.'

'They're bloody lucky to have me,' said Maisie, removing Irene's hand from her arm. 'I don't want any of that child physiology or whatever you call it from you! And Alfred's worse than useless when it comes to disciplining them. Let's get out of here,' she finished.

They left the department store and went into Cooper's next door with its tantalizing smell of freshly ground coffee. They found a table in the restaurant upstairs without much trouble.

Once settled and their order given, Irene gazed across at her mother. 'Were you satisfied with the money Peggy's brother paid you for the furniture?'

Maisie nodded. 'It was a fair price. I thought him a nice young man. He was saying that they still hadn't heard from Peggy.'

Irene sighed. 'I wonder where she is. I bet Pete's wondering the same.'

'I wouldn't know about that, although I wouldn't mind seeing ol' Gertie again and having a chat,' said Maisie, lighting a cigarette before resting an elbow on the tablecloth. 'Well, girl, I never thought you training to look after kids would result in you going to America. Will you be sailing on one of the Queens?' she asked, a dreamy expression on her face. 'I believe those ships are floating palaces. There's good food and dancing and entertainment. Who's to say you mightn't meet a dark handsome stranger and have a shipboard romance?'

'Mam, I'm not on the lookout for a man,' said Irene placidly. 'I have my ticket and although I won't be sailing on the *Queen Mary* or *Elizabeth*, it looks really comfortable in the brochure.'

Maisie darted a frowning glance at her daughter. 'Well, let's hope that you can still meet a decent bloke. You don't want to miss out on the fun of shipboard life. You need to grab every chance you get, girl, to enjoy life. You're a good-looking young woman.'

'Thanks for the compliment, Mam,' said Irene, smiling. 'You'll have me blushing.'

'All you have to do is pretend you're more than just a nanny. I mean think about that Dorothy Wilson, she's been on the telly. She only came from working-class roots and look where she is now!'

'I'm no actress, Mam,' said Irene.

'You can pretend,' insisted Maisie. 'That's all they do.'

As the waitress approached their table with a tray, Maisie added, 'You don't want to be wiping bottoms and mopping up sick all your life.'

Irene protested that her job entailed more than that but her mother was not listening, lost in a dream world of her own.

It was as they were saying tarrah that Maisie pressed some folded notes into Irene's hand.

'What's this?' asked Irene, astonished.

'I'd like my only daughter to look snazzy,' said Maisie. 'You don't have to thank me. Just don't forget to send me a postcard from America, saying you've bagged yourself a millionaire.'

Irene could hardly believe her mother was giving her money. 'Thanks, Mam! Are you sure you can afford it?'

'It's some of the furniture money,' said Maisie dismissively. 'Now don't forget, girl, if the flicks are anything to go by, the rich men don't always look like millionaires.'

Irene kissed her mother's cheek. 'I'll write, Mam. You take care of yourself.'

'I better had because I'll be the only one doing so,' said Maisie, patting her daughter's hand. 'Enjoy yourself.'

Irene watched her mother walk briskly away and hesitated before deciding to go back inside C & A's. She went to the ladies' toilets and counted the money in a booth with growing excitement. She decided that there was enough there to buy a decent cocktail dress, an evening stole and a really nice pair of high heels, as well as some sheer silk stockings. There was no way she was taking what Maisie had said about millionaires seriously, but she did like dancing and hopefully she would have no trouble finding a partner. For a moment she thought of Marty and the kiss they had shared. But it was no good: despite the ache of longing inside her, she must try and forget him.

It was after she had enjoyed her shopping spree that Irene decided now would be a good time to take up Lynne Walker's open invitation to visit them.

Almost as soon as Irene knocked on the front door, Lynne opened it. 'Hello, love,' she said. 'I was hoping you'd come and see us before the ship sails. Do come in! Sam's home and has a visitor.

You know him. Pete Marshall!'

Irene's face lit up. 'I was wondering how he was and kept meaning to visit but I just haven't had the time. I used to be kept up to date with all the Marshall news because Mam worked with Pete's mother.'

'Sam knows his brother, Dougie, with them both being in the police force. I sometimes wonder how two brothers can be so different.'

Irene knew what she meant so made no comment, only wondering why Pete had come to see Sam. At that moment, the parlour door opened and the two men appeared.

'I thought I recognized your voice,' said Pete, grinning.

'Once heard, never forgotten,' she said. 'How are tricks? Your mother all right?'

'Fine, although I think she misses yours,' said Pete.

'I met Mam in town earlier and she was saying the same thing about your mother,' said Irene. 'They should make up. I can give you Mam's phone number.'

'Shall we go into the kitchen?' Lynne interrupted. 'I've left Anna playing on her own.'

'I'll have to get off, love,' said Sam, lowering his head and kissing her. 'I'll see you when I see you.' He nodded in Irene's direction. 'Nice seeing you again.' He left the house.

The other three went into the back room. 'Sit down,' said Lynne. 'Keep your eye on Anna if you would while I go and make a cuppa.'

Irene placed her shopping at the side of a chair and gazed down at the child playing with a pull-along wooden bunny that jingled. Close to hand was a clown pyramid stacking toy with different coloured plastic rings scattered on the rug.

Irene remembered Jeanette's excitement when her niece was born. 'What a healthy looking child,' said Irene, kneeling on the rug.

'She'll be two and a half when the next one arrives,' said Lynne, patting her belly.

'You'll have your hands full,' said Irene.

'I know.' Lynne grimaced. 'But I'm not getting any younger and Sam and I wanted more than one. If you'll excuse me.' She went into the kitchen.

Pete and Irene exchanged looks. 'I believe you and Bobby are off to America soon,' he said.

'Yes.' She glanced up at him. 'Have you heard anything from Peggy?'

He shook his head. 'I've been out in the car looking for her at weekends. I've visited all the resorts along the North Wales coast without any luck. She could have been in any one of them without me seeing her. I've begun to wonder if I'm wasting my time, thinking I can go to a place and just spot her. If she wanted to be found, then she'd give us a hint to where she was.'

'Have you thought she mightn't be in Wales but somewhere like Southport or Blackpool?'

Pete frowned. 'Not really. She always said how much she liked Wales.'

'Even so, Southport and Blackpool are both very popular and she doesn't have to cross the Mersey to get to either of them,' said Irene.

Pete nodded thoughtfully and at that moment Lynne reappeared. She placed a plate of scones on the table and, nodding at the bags beside Irene, said, 'So what have you been buying, Irene? Clothes to wear during the voyage?'

'Only one outfit, in case there's dancing,' Irene replied. 'It was Mam's idea and it was she who gave me the money.' She reached for one of the bags and took out the cocktail dress. 'What d'you think?' she asked, holding up the dress which was midnight blue and had a skirt of chiffon with a sequinned bodice and shoelace straps.

'You'll look lovely in it,' said Lynne sincerely. 'Don't you think so, Pete?'

He nodded. 'I can see you having plenty of partners.'

Lynne agreed. 'Just don't go showing it to Bobby before the ship sails. She would want one too, and apart from being too young, she'd be pestering me to make it.'

Irene bit her lower lip. 'I'd forgotten you were a dressmaker.'

'Don't worry about it, love,' said Lynne, squeezing her hand. 'I just want you both to enjoy yourselves on the voyage – besides, all those sequins would take ages to sew on. I wouldn't want the job.'

Reassured, Irene folded the frock and put it back in its bag. 'Has Betty written to you about who's meeting us in New York?'

'Yes, but it was Lenny who has arranged it as he's an old friend of Dorothy Wilson. Dorothy's appearing on Broadway and then she'll be travelling across America to Hollywood. So you and Bobby can travel most of the way with her.'

Irene felt a thrill of excitement. 'You're joking!'

Lynne smiled. 'Honest to God and cross my heart!' She sketched a cross on the bodice of her maternity smock. 'You'll be met off the boat by her personal assistant. Everything is working out just fine, as I even have someone to make the journey back with Bobby.'

'Who?' asked Irene, who had been wondering about that.

'Mrs Gianelli's widowed sister who lives in America.'

Irene's mouth gaped open and then she swallowed. 'I didn't know you knew Nellie Gianelli?'

'I didn't until Nick stepped into your brother's shoes in the music group!' Lynne left the kitchen and returned with the teapot and poured the tea. 'I remember reading somewhere that "all things work together for good". I've forgotten now where I saw it but if your Jimmy hadn't decided to go to sea, then my daughter wouldn't be going to America right now. It's as if it were meant.'

Irene nodded, thinking who was she to argue with Lynne's reasoning.

'I wish I could believe that things will work together for good where me and Peggy are concerned,' said Pete.

Lynne leaned over and touched his shoulder. 'I'm sure Peggy will come back and you'll be able to sort out what went wrong. Sometimes we just need time to ourselves to think things through.'

Pete just looked at her, hoping with all his heart that it was true.

Twenty

Marty placed the key in the lock, hoping that Bernie was in a better mood this evening. She had been furious with him for coming to see the house without her and going ahead with arranging to rent it without discussing it with her first. He knew that he had made it worse by refusing to be drawn into an argument, saying that he had done so because she was always going on about her friend's house but he knew that even if he had consulted her she would have complained about moving a few miles away from family and friends.

When he told her about buying the furniture, she reacted predictably and said that she wanted new. When he answered that they could not afford it, she had responded by telling him that her friend had bought a lovely three-piece suite on hire purchase. He had told her that he had no intention of getting into debt by buying furniture on the never-never. He'd had to pay a hefty amount of key money and they had to watch what they spent for the next few months.

She had not spoken to him for two days but that didn't stop her going on at him about his selfishness in front of her mother, sister and Monica. Eventually the three of them had got fed up with her and told her to stop moaning.

His own mother had been almost as bad, saying, 'I don't know why you want to go and live in Seaforth. It's miles away. You could have come and lived here.'

He had kept quiet about that being a stupid idea, as the plan was to have a home of their own and it would hardly have gone down well with his mother-in-law, or his wife, if they'd simply decamped to his mother's place. 'But I won't be seeing as much of you,' she had said.

'You've got our Lil.' He had given her a hug. 'She and her fella won't find it easy getting a place of their own. They could move in with you.' Her face had brightened at that idea and she had suggested it to the engaged couple the next day. The wedding had then been brought forward and was now to take place in September.

To Marty's relief he heard the sound of Bernie's laughter as he walked up the lobby. Perhaps that friend of hers from her old work had come to visit? Then he heard a male voice and recognized it instantly. What the hell was Tommy doing here?

Marty opened the kitchen door and stood in the doorway, gazing at the scene before him. Jerry was running a couple of Dinky cars along the rug in front of the fire whilst Josie was undressing a celluloid doll.

'So here you are,' said Bernie brightly, glancing up from a photograph she was holding. Marty noticed that his brother had several more in his fist.

'How did you know where to find us?' asked Marty, closing the door behind him.

'Purely by accident,' said Bernie, taking another photo from Tommy. 'He's brought presents for the children, as well as some chocolates for

265

me. Isn't that nice of him?'

'Great!' said Marty drily. 'How did this accident happen?'

'I'd just left the Red Lion and was crossing the road when I spotted Bernie,' said Tommy. 'I could scarcely believe my eyes.'

Why did those words sound glib to him? Marty wondered.

'I told him we'd moved here and invited him to dinner,' said Bernie.

'What is for dinner?' asked Marty.

'You! You're always thinking of your stomach!' she said archly.

That wasn't true. But he had been working hard all day and so was bloody hungry. 'So what is there to eat?'

'Hot pot! I bought some nice breast of lamb from the butcher's in Linacre Road. I also got some pickled red cabbage and beetroot to go with it.'

'What a thoughtful wife you are!' said Tommy.

'If only your brother appreciated me,' said Bernie, handing the photographs back to Tommy and springing to her feet. 'I'll go and see if it's ready.'

Marty noticed that there were new lace-edged chair back covers on the armchairs and wondered where they had come from. Bernie had asked him about decorating the kitchen and their bedroom and he had agreed to make a start soon but if she was going to start spending the housekeeping on knick-knacks, then she would be running short of money and he would not be able to afford to do any decorating.

He sat down and began to unlace his shoes. Josie immediately scrambled to her feet and fetched his slippers. 'For Daddy?' She placed them in front of him on the rag rug that his mother had made for his old bedroom years ago. He thanked her and put them on.

'You've got her well trained,' said Tommy, pocketing the photographs. 'Pretty little girl, isn't she?'

'I'm Daddy's bestest girl,' said Josie, picking up the doll and placing it in Marty's lap. 'He bought dolly for me, Daddy.'

'She's got a look of our Peg,' said Tommy.

'I've always thought that,' said Bernie, coming in from the back kitchen with a casserole dish and placing it on a cork mat on the table. She was smiling to herself as she began to dish out the food. 'Jerry also takes after your side of the family. Marty, could you fasten Josie into her feeding chair? Tommy, could you get Jerry to leave those cars alone and sit at the table? Then if you could cut some bread?'

Tommy had trouble persuading Jerry to let go of the cars and eventually allowed him to take them with him to the table. By then Marty had cut the bread and was sitting next to his daughter.

He looked across the table at his brother. 'So what were you doing at the Red Lion?' he asked.

'Having a pint! What else should I be doing?' Tommy's expression was one of such innocence that if Marty had not already been suspicious of him, he would have been now.

'If you'd been the age you are now during the war, you'd have been a spiv selling stuff on the black market,' said Marty, reaching for his spoon.

267

Tommy shook his head dolefully. 'If you're not careful you'll grow into Dad.'

'Yes, what a thing to say about your brother, Marty,' said Bernie, shaking her head at him.

Marty continued to stare at Tommy. 'I don't want you bringing trouble to my door. Bernie might think the sun shines out of you but I don't.'

'OK!' said Tommy, frowning. 'If you'd rather I stayed away, I will. I always believed, though, what Mam taught us, that families should stick together. You know the kind of thing – help each other in times of need.'

'You're not in need,' said Marty.

Tommy agreed. 'But you might be one day and you'll be glad of my help, bruv.'

Marty raised his eyebrows but made no comment.

They ate in silence and when the men's plates were cleared, Tommy took out a packet of Players Weights. He offered one to Bernie.

'Ta,' she said. 'You don't have to offer Marty one. He's given them up.'

'You were smoking Kensitos last time. Collected all the cards, have you?' asked Marty mildly.

Tommy's hand tightened in the act of lighting Bernie's cigarette and he hesitated before saying, 'Players are a better smoke.' He flicked the lighter and lit his own cigarette. 'So where d'you think our Peg is?'

'One of her friends suggested that she might have got herself a summer job in a holiday resort,' said Bernie.

'Oh!' exclaimed Tommy. 'I suppose that's possible.'

'Apparently it was something Peggy talked about when they were both working in the Cunard building,' said Marty.

Tommy looked interested. 'I wouldn't mind a trip to the seaside.'

'Me too,' said Bernie, the cigarette dangling from the corner of her mouth jerking up and down. 'Can you ride a motorbike, Tommy?'

'Sure,' he said, grinning. 'Why d'you ask?'

'Our Dougal is over from Ireland. He's got himself a job on a building site for the summer. He has a motorbike and sidecar,' said Bernie, smiling. 'He keeps it in Mam's backyard and it would be easy enough to sneak it out. Marty's going to be busy during his coming week's holiday decorating this place. It would be great to be able to take the children to the seaside while he's busy.'

'You're not taking the kids anywhere in that sidecar, Bernie,' Marty warned. 'Especially not with our Tommy in charge of the motorbike. I'm surprised at you suggesting it.'

Tommy put on an injured expression. 'You're forgetting I was a motor mechanic once. I know about machines.'

'I haven't forgotten,' said Marty, his eyes glinting. 'You're still wanted for theft.'

Tommy and Bernie exchanged looks and she laughed nervously. 'I'm only teasing you, Marty. I knew you'd never agree. You're such an old stick in the mud.'

'Thanks,' said Marty, getting to his feet and lifting Josie out of her feeding chair. 'You were quick enough to marry me.'

Bernie's lips tightened and she rested her

269

elbows on the table. 'And you know why.'

'What's this?' asked Tommy, a wicked gleam in his eye. 'An argument between husband and wife?'

'Shut up, Tommy,' said Marty.

He suddenly noticed a postcard behind the clock on the mantelpiece and picked it up. 'Who's this from?'

Bernie glanced at it. 'Oh, it came this morning all the way from New Zealand. It's from someone called Jimmy. Going by the postmark it's taken ages to get here.'

'It'll be from Jimmy Miller,' Marty murmured.

'I know a Jimmy Miller,' said Tommy. 'He drinks in the Red Lion.'

'That's right,' said Marty. 'He used to live here but decided to go back to sea.'

'It's to a Mrs Maisie somebody,' said Bernie. 'I couldn't read the surname.'

'That'll be his mother,' said Marty. 'I've her address somewhere. She lives in West Derby now. Maybe Mrs Gianelli might have it to hand. I'll go round there. I could do with a walk.'

Both Tommy and Bernie stared at him. 'You might as well take the kids with you,' she said quickly. 'Give me a bit of peace and the walk will tire them out.'

Marty looked at his brother. 'Don't you make yourself too comfortable.'

'I'll be going soon,' said Tommy, lighting another cigarette. 'I just fancy another cup of tea first.'

Marty set off with the children over the bridge and along Sefton Road to the crescent where the Gianellis lived, knowing he might have made a mistake leaving his brother and wife alone. They had looked all chummy-chummy when he'd come in. Still, as long as Tommy didn't persuade Bernie to store any pilfered goods in their house, he was glad to get away from the pair.

Josie chattered away to him while Jerry, clutching the cars Tommy had given him, ran on ahead to where a tent could be seen in a front garden, as well as a small boy wearing an Indian feathered headdress. The front door was open and a young woman was sitting on the step, knitting while keeping her eye on the children. Music could be heard coming from inside.

Marty was surprised to see her but he recognized her. 'Aren't you Irene's friend from the children's home?'

'Deirdre,' she said, smiling. 'It's Mr McGrath, isn't it?'

He nodded.

'You're probably wondering what I'm doing here,' said Deirdre. 'I have a job at Litherland Nursery and rent a room from Mrs Gianelli during the week.'

There were footsteps from inside and Nellie appeared.

'Hello, Mrs Gianelli,' said Marty. 'I don't know if Irene mentioned to you that I was moving into her mother's old house, but a card has come for her mother from Jimmy. I was wondering if you have her address in West Derby.'

She nodded, adding, 'Are these your children?'

'Yeah, Josie and Jerry.'

'Perhaps they'd like to stay and play with the other children while I get that address,' said Nellie.

'Come on in!'

He went inside and while she was writing down Maisie's new married name and address, he asked her if she had heard from Irene yet. She told him that Irene and Bobby had only left for America three days ago, so it was too soon. She asked after Peggy, only to be told that there was no news of her either. He stayed only long enough to get the information he wanted and then left with the children.

When he arrived home it was to find Bernie alone in the house, washing dishes. 'So Tommy's gone,' murmured Marty. 'Did he say where he was staying?'

Bernie shrugged. 'You don't think he's going to tell me if he won't even tell his own brother? He just said that he'll see you around.'

Marty wondered what they had talked about but did not bother asking. She would only tell him what she wanted him to know and the rest she would keep to herself. As he lay in bed that night with Bernie fidgeting beside him, his thoughts were of Irene. He imagined her arriving in New York and making that long journey across America to California in the tracks of many an emigrant who had gone west in search of a new life. He wished she was lying beside him instead of Bernie.

Twenty-One

'It shouldn't be long now before we arrive in New York!' Bobby shouted.

'I can't wait,' said Irene, gazing across the dark blue sea. The wind was tearing the clouds apart enabling the sun to shine through at last. In the distance they could make out land. 'It's going to be really odd when we're on *terra firma* again. I remember our Jimmy saying the ground goes up and down in a really peculiar way until you get your land legs back again.'

'At least we weren't seasick,' said Bobby, glancing along the almost deserted deck. 'I reckon it's all those trips on the ferry to New Brighton that enabled us to cope,' she joked.

The voyage had not met their expectations because, despite it being summer, the weather had been far from kind. Fortunately there had been a library and a cinema on board and a few other hardy souls to keep them company walking the decks as well as attending the keep-fit classes in the gym. There had been little dancing because most of the band had been seasick as well, so Irene had not had the opportunity to wear her sequinned cocktail frock after all.

'California is a lot different to Lancashire, you know,' said Bobby seriously.

'I'd never have thought of that,' teased Irene, excited and nervous at the thought of going through customs and finding Dorothy Wilson's personal assistant in the inevitable crowds that would be there, meeting other passengers off the ship.

As it turned out it was not as difficult as Irene imagined and once through customs and having collected their luggage, they saw a young dark-haired man holding a small placard with hers and Bobby's name on it. They went over to him and introduced themselves.

He smiled as he placed the placard under his arm. 'Good day, ladies. I'm Harry. Is this all your luggage?'

'Yes,' said Irene, feeling as if she had been found wanting. No doubt his employer always travelled with loads of luggage.

'Come this way. I have a car waiting.'

Irene and Bobby glanced at each other and mouthed *Bet it's a limousine!* as they followed him. He led them to a long turquoise and white automobile, trimmed with chrome. He put down the luggage and unlocked the boot and placed their suitcases inside. 'This is called a trunk over here,' he said.

Irene nodded. 'What make of car is it?' she asked, thinking it would be something to tell Pete when she wrote to him.

'A Chevrolet,' said Harry, slamming the lid shut. 'Are you interested in cars, Miss Miller?'

'Only in so much as I have a friend who is,' she replied.

Harry unlocked the rear doors and held them open while they climbed inside and made themselves comfortable. He slid into the driving seat and glanced over his shoulder at Irene. 'Before we go any further, Miss, I need to tell you that Miss Wilson sends her apologies.'

Irene's heart sank. 'What's happened?'

'She had to fly to England, having received news that a dear friend is having an operation and she wants to be with him.'

'I bet that friend is Lenny,' said Bobby, glancing at Irene. 'I knew he'd been having some trouble. I hope he'll be OK.'

'So do I,' said Irene, although naturally her first concern was for Bobby and herself. 'So what about our planned journey to California?'

'It's to go ahead, Miss,' he replied. 'We'll set off in the morning. But, first things first. I'm to take you to the hotel where she has a suite and you're to stay there tonight. I've ordered coffee and cakes to be served in her suite an hour after we get there. I hope that meets with your approval?'

'It sure does,' murmured Bobby, who winked at Irene before leaning back against the soft leather and gazing out of the window.

'A suite,' whispered Irene. 'How much is that going to cost us?'

'Miss Wilson thought you might worry about that,' said Harry. 'I was to tell you that it's all taken care of. You're to be her guests as if she was there herself to greet you with true Liverpudlian hospitality.'

Irene had a sudden urge to giggle. When had she ever stayed in a suite in Liverpool?

A small smile played around Bobby's lips. 'You're in America now, Irene,' she murmured. 'Relax and enjoy it. Everything is going to be hunky dory.'

'Hunky dory! What's that supposed to mean?' said Irene.

'It means satisfactory, Miss,' said Harry, meeting her eyes in the mirror before smoothly setting the Chevrolet in motion.

'Miss Wilson is an old friend of Mam and Sam's, so it doesn't surprise me that she's gone out of her way to help us,' said Bobby.

'Right, I'll relax as you suggest.' Irene subsided into the luxurious soft leather and, following Bobby's example, gazed out of the window at the passing scene.

'Aren't you excited, Irene?' asked Bobby. 'The people, the buildings, I can't wait to see Broadway and the Empire State Building.'

'The great White Way,' said Harry. 'Miss Wilson was so excited when she saw her name up in lights.'

'There is no way that my name is ever going to be up in lights,' said Irene.

'Nor mine,' said Bobby. 'Although maybe one day my paintings will be displayed in an art gallery.'

'It doesn't do any harm to dream,' said Irene.

'And does Miss Miller have a dream to fulfil while she's over here?' asked Harry.

'Only seeing as much of another country as I can,' she said firmly. 'I've come over here to do a job. I'm the sensible type.'

'We can't all be dreamers,' said Harry.

'Are you a dreamer, Harry?' asked Bobby, resting her arms on the back of his seat.

'My folks would say so. I'm an aspiring screenwriter,' he said.

Irene's interest was roused. 'What have you written?'

'Several plays, had one performed on stage. Now there's an important mogul in Hollywood who's shown an interest in my latest script.'

'What do you write about? Swashbuckling historical adventures? Thrillers? Romantic comedy, the kind Cary Grant stars in, like *An Affair to Remember?*' She had seen the film last year and considered it one of the most romantic films she had ever seen.

He did not reply and she wondered if she had said too much and he thought she was mocking him. Although when she heard the blare of a horn, she realized that it could be that he had decided to concentrate on his driving instead of making conversation.

Eventually the car drew up at a kerb and Irene and Bobby got out. Irene gazed up at the frontage of an imposing building and thought that Dorothy Wilson must be doing very well for herself if she could afford to have a suite here.

Harry removed their luggage from the trunk and spoke to a doorman as he came forward. He opened the door for the two girls and they went inside. Another man in uniform came forward and took their luggage.

'He'll take your bags up to the suite while you go to reception and sign in,' said Harry. 'I'll park the car and be with you soon.'

Irene and Bobby gazed around at the sumptuous entrance and reception area, all marble and gilt, brocade satin hangings and cushions on huge sofas. 'Wow!' exclaimed the younger girl. 'I can't wait to tell Mam and Sam about this.'

'You might want to send them a postcard saying we've arrived safely,' suggested Irene.

Bobby nodded. 'You'll want to send one to your mother, won't you?' she said.

Irene nodded, thinking, if the truth were known she was feeling overwhelmed by such luxury, so getting in touch with those back home was important to keep her feet on the ground. 'I must send one to the Gianellis, Deirdre ... and Pete and his mother, as well,' she murmured, feeling in two minds as to whether she should post one off to Marty and his family. What would Bernie think if she did? Surely Marty would have mentioned her name in connection with the house, if at no other time?

'I'll send a separate one to Nick and Anna,' said Bobby.

Irene decided she would also send individual postcards to Georgie and May. It would make the two children feel special receiving one each.

The suite was luxurious, with two bedrooms, a bathroom and living room. Irene felt as if she had stepped into a movie set and, trying not to feel overwhelmed, started unpacking a few things.

By the time she had used the bathroom, unpacked her night-dress and slipped it under the pillow of one of the beds, Harry arrived. He was followed, within minutes, by coffee and cakes.

'I've never tasted such lovely cakes,' said Bobby, licking chocolate butter cream from around her mouth.

'There's lots of treats in store for you on the journey ahead. Miss Wilson said I was to take you the scenic route,' said Harry.

'To the Wild and Woolly West,' Irene murmured.

Harry smiled at her. 'You've seen the movie *Hollywood or Bust?*'

She nodded.

'I have, too,' said Bobby. 'It starred Dean Martin and Jerry Lewis.'

'Can't wait,' said Irene, feeling a thrill of excitement, thinking that at least she had some idea of what to expect from the journey. Old-fashioned showboats on the Mississippi/Missouri; cowboys, cattle and flowers in Oklahoma; oil wells in Texas; the Grand Canyon and Indians in Arizona; the Boulder Dam in Nevada and then San Jose. *California, here I come!* She imagined a postcard from each state dropping through the letterboxes back home.

Twenty-Two

Pete was fed up and more than a little angry as he parked his second-hand Ford Consul outside the house. He locked it and limped up to the front door and went inside. He found his mother in the back kitchen, stirring a pan of scouse.

'You all right, son?' she asked. 'You look tired.'

'You can say that again,' said Pete, before disappearing down the yard to the lavatory.

'A postcard has come,' she said, when he arrived back into the kitchen. 'All the way from New York.'

279

'It'll be from Irene.' He picked up the postcard and sat down at the table, glancing at the picture of the Empire State Building. He turned it over, noticing that the writing was small so Irene could cram in as much information as she could. When he finished reading it, he dropped it on the table-cloth.

'She asks about Peggy,' said Gertie, sighing as she dished out the scouse. 'That girl! I take it you've had no luck, son?'

Pete shook his head. 'You've read it then, Ma. This scouse looks good. Any pickled red cabbage?'

Gertie placed a jar of pickled red cabbage on the table and sat down. 'No doubt she'll have sent a postcard to her mother.'

'I presume you're talking about Irene now,' said Pete.

'She's Maisie's only daughter,' she murmured, staring into space. 'I wonder how she's getting on? I miss her.'

'Then do something!' exclaimed Pete. 'I gave you her phone number. It wouldn't surprise me if she was missing you, too. She's moved to the other side of Liverpool where she knows no one and her son and daughter are both out of the country and her only brother lives on the Wirral. I bet she's lonely.'

'But she's got a new husband and three step-children,' said Gertie. 'How can she be lonely?'

'It's not the same as having someone to talk to who you've known for years. Give her a ring, Mam.'

'Perhaps I will,' said Gertie, smiling at her son. 'Now get on with your scouse before it gets cold.'

Halfway through his meal, Pete looked across at his mother and said, 'I think I'll go and visit Marty. You know he's moved into Maisie's old house?'

Gertie nodded. 'Are you thinking he might have heard from Peggy?'

'Him or his mother. I did get in touch with him at his workplace a couple of weeks ago but he hadn't heard anything. She's been gone four and a half months. I really thought she would have been in touch by now.'

Gertie leaned across and patted his hand. 'You go and see her brother. It's possible he just might have news.'

An hour later, after a wash and change of clothes, Pete headed off to Marty's. The front door was open and he could hear a babble of voices coming from inside. He hesitated, thinking that perhaps now was not the right time to call after all, and was about to turn round and get back in the car and go home when a grim-faced Marty came out.

'Something wrong?' asked Pete, noticing a streak of white paint on Marty's cheek.

For a moment he appeared to stare right through Pete and then shook his head as if to clear it and stared at the car parked at the kerb. 'That yours?'

Pete nodded.

Marty took a deep breath. 'There's been an accident. I don't have the works' van because I'm on a week's holiday. I'll pay for the petrol if you let me borrow your car. I have to get to Blackpool hospital.'

281

'Blackpool!' Pete thought of it being a seaside resort and wondered if it could be Peggy who was involved in the accident and went cold inside. He asked huskily, 'Who's been hurt?'

Before Marty could answer, two other people came out of the house. Pete recognized Monica but not the man whose arm she grabbed. 'Wait until the morning, cousin Dougal! There's nothing you can do tonight about your motorbike.'

Relief trickled through Pete. 'Your motorbike was in an accident?' he said. 'For a moment I thought Peggy...'

'As it happens it was our Peg who phoned Bernie's mother,' Marty interrupted, holding out a hand. 'Give me your car keys, Pete, and let me get going.'

Pete stared at him as if he had run mad. 'You don't think I'm going to let you go on your own? I'm coming with you! You can tell me what happened on the way.' He opened the door and told Marty to get in the other side. Marty wasted no time going round and getting inside the car.

Dougal wasn't to be left out. 'I'm coming with yus. I want to see the damage that yer bleeding brother's caused, Marty, and see that he pays for it. He had no right to take me motorbike. He's a bleeding thief.'

'Please yourself, Dougal, but if you're going to go on in that tone all the way to Blackpool, I'll turf you out,' said Marty harshly. 'I'll deal with my brother, not you. Don't forget that he and Bernie are both injured.'

Monica's worried face appeared at the car window. 'You mustn't worry about Josie and Jerry,

282

Marty. I'll pick them up from Mrs Gianelli's and stay here with them until you get back.'

He thanked her.

Pete drove off. His heart was racing and several thoughts were struggling for prominence in his mind. He'd need to fill up with petrol on the way and take the road to Preston before turning off for Blackpool. And how was it that it had been Peggy who had phoned about the accident? How badly hurt were Bernie and Tommy? And was there going to be an altercation in the car between Dougal and Marty? He hoped not!

As it was nobody spoke until they had left Litherland well behind and were through Maghull and passing between fields.

'So how come Peggy telephoned?' asked Pete, his voice sounding loud in the enclosed space of the car.

'She was there when it happened,' said Marty. 'Keep your eyes on the road and don't be looking at me!' He lowered his voice. 'We don't want another accident. As it is she's blaming herself.'

'Why?' asked Pete, fixing his eyes on the road ahead and trying to ignore his aching leg and foot.

Dougal answered from the back seat. 'Bernie spotted her and shouted her name.'

'So distracting Tommy who took his eyes off the road, swerved and went into a skid and crashed into a lamp post,' said Marty.

Pete let out a whistle. 'That's bad. Peggy managed to say all that over the phone?'

'Yes! Tommy's injuries don't appear too severe,' said Marty. 'A suspected broken arm, scratches and bruises. Fortunately he was wearing a crash

283

helmet but it appears Bernie wasn't and was thrown off the pillion seat and landed on the pavement and was knocked unconscious.'

'She should have had my wife's crash helmet on,' groaned Dougal, resting his elbows on the back of Pete's seat. 'Bleedin' vanity, I bet yus. I hope she'll be all right.'

Pete fell silent. How long had Peggy been in Blackpool? When he thought of the time he had wasted visiting the resorts on the Welsh coast...

'Was Peggy on her own?' he asked.

'Yes. She gave an address in case she's no longer at the hospital when I get there. She works at a hotel on the Promenade between the South and Central Piers. My hope is that she'll be allowed to stay with Bernie in case she wakes up.'

So Bernie was still unconscious when Peggy phoned, thought Pete, remembering his own accident and how he'd had concussion, which had not been too severe, unlike his other injuries. He glanced at Marty and one look was enough to cause him to ask no more questions. Instead he thought about seeing Peggy and what he could say to her when they finally met again.

Peggy was sitting on a bench in a corridor of the Victoria hospital, trying not to think of Bernie, who had been X-rayed and was now in a side ward. A nurse was with her and, as far as Peggy knew, Bernie had stirred but drifted into unconsciousness again. As for Tommy, his arm had been X-rayed and it was now being put in plaster. She'd had little opportunity to ask him how he came to be with Bernie on a motorbike.

She could not wait for Marty to get here, although she did not doubt that sooner or later, there would be a reckoning over her leaving home and not getting in touch.

She had nearly jumped out of her skin when she had heard her name being screeched earlier that day but it had certainly attracted her attention. When a motorbike and sidecar had hit the lamp post, she had immediately run to see if she could help. She had been shocked when she recognized the woman lying on the pavement. She had knelt beside her, aware of the motorcyclist grunting with pain as he struggled to remove his helmet. When she realized it was her brother, she had almost fainted.

By then, the incident had attracted attention and someone had dashed into a shop and an ambulance had been called. The unconscious Bernie had been stretchered into the ambulance shortly after it arrived and Tommy had climbed into the back. Wordlessly he continued to stare at Peggy as if he had seen a ghost. A policeman arrived and dealt with the damaged motorcycle and asked for witnesses.

Peggy had explained who she was and what she had seen and had been allowed to go in the ambulance with her brother and sister-in-law to the hospital. She had phoned Bernie's mother's house from there and asked to speak to Marty – only to be told that he no longer lived there, which had come as another shock. So she had to tell Bernie's mother about the accident and had been almost deafened by the scream that came down the line and then came the obscenities at the mention of

Tommy's name. Fortunately Monica had snatched the phone out of her grandmother's hand and said that she would get a message to Marty.

Peggy had also phoned Mrs Henderson, to explain the situation. Although obviously put out by Peggy's inability to return to the hotel where she was needed as it was their busiest day of the week, she told her to just get there as soon as she could.

Peggy had decided to wait until she could speak to Tommy properly before going back to the hotel. Hopefully by then Bernie would be fully conscious. She sighed heavily, wondering what Marty would say to her when he eventually arrived. She did not doubt he was going to be angry. Restlessly, she stood up, only to come over all faint and realized that she had not had anything to eat or drink for ages. Everything steadied and she decided she needed some fresh air. If she went for a walk outside, she was bound to find a shop open nearby and could get something to eat. She spoke to one of the nurses and left.

It was twilight as she walked along East Park Drive not far from Stanley Park and the zoo. A car suddenly slammed on its brakes and stopped alongside her. The passenger door opened and a familiar voice said, 'Peggy?'

She stared at her brother in relief. 'Marty!'

He got out of the car and, holding the door wide, told her to get inside. 'You can direct Pete to the hospital. I'll get in the back.'

Pete! She tripped over her feet as she slipped on the edge of the kerb. Marty gave her a helping hand and she fell into the passenger seat. She did

286

not dare look up as she squirmed around in an attempt to get into a sitting position. She could hear Pete's breathing and Marty settling in the back seat.

'Are you comfortable?' asked Pete.

At the sound of the coldness in his voice, she felt the tears threaten.

He spoke again. 'Do I go straight on for the hospital?'

She cleared her throat and managed to give him directions.

After that no one asked any more questions until Pete parked the car outside the hospital. Then Marty said, 'There's no need for you to come in, Peg. I think you've done enough for today. I'm sure Pete will take you back to your hotel.'

'I'm sorry, Marty,' she blurted out.

'You could have sent a postcard,' he said.

'I'm coming in the hospital with you,' said Dougal, getting out of the car.

'Please yourself,' said Marty, and walked away.

Peggy opened the car door and made to get out and follow him.

'Where are you going?' asked Pete.

'I can find my own way,' she said. 'I don't expect you to do me any favours.'

'Don't be bloody stupid! You don't think I'm going to let you walk the streets on your own in the dark,' said Pete vehemently. 'Get back in and shut the door!'

Peggy did as she was told and Pete started up the car again.

The atmosphere felt as if it could be sliced with a knife. 'You'd best direct me,' said Pete, after

287

several minutes. 'Which end of the promenade are you?'

She told him.

He drove on in silence and she was aware of him wincing several times. 'Are you all right?' she asked eventually when they turned on to the promenade.

'What d'you think?' he said.

'That you're in pain. You're an idiot.'

'That's gratitude for you.' He did not look at her.

'Did you drive all the way here?'

'Yes, it's my car.'

'When did you buy it?'

'When I decided I needed to find you.'

'You ... you've been looking for me?'

'Rhyl, Prestatyn, Colwyn Bay, Llandudno ... today I went to Southport for a change,' said Pete. 'I was going to come here next week. Perhaps I mightn't have found you. It was purely by chance that Bernie saw you, wasn't it?'

'Yes.' Peggy moistened her lips. 'I thought you'd want nothing more to do with me. I was so angry with you when I ran away.'

'You don't think I wasn't furious with you?' he said, frowning.

'Of course!' She turned in the seat to face him. 'I just had to get away. I couldn't stand it any more, what with Dad and you giving me ultimatums. Anyway, I can't ever go back to Liverpool because it would all start up again. Even if I found myself a place of my own, Dad would come looking for me.'

Pete slowed down. 'Tommy didn't tell you?'

'Tell me what?' she asked.

He pulled over and stopped the car. 'Can you cope with another shock?' He hesitated. 'Your dad's dead.'

He heard the intake of her breath and then she was silent for so long that he reached out and shook her shoulder. 'I shouldn't have told you like that! Are you all right?'

'How did he die?' she asked in a small voice.

'He was drunk and fell in the canal near Stanley Dock.'

'You mean the one near the tobacco warehouse?'

'That's the one.' He covered her hand with his. 'Are you sure you're all right?'

Her fingers curled about his. 'D'you know how Mam took it?'

'You're best asking your Marty,' said Pete. 'I do know she went on holiday with a friend at Whit.'

'And Lil?'

'I heard she was getting married in September and they'll be living with your mother.'

Peggy's eyes glistened in the light from a street lamp. 'I'm glad. I-I suppose Dad being ... being dead is the reason why our Tommy's still around.'

'Seems likely, although I don't know much about it.'

'So where's he living? He's hardly spoken since the accident, so I've no idea how he came to be on a motorbike with Bernie.'

'According to Bernie's cousin, Tommy stole it,' said Pete.

'Oh, my goodness! I gave the policeman his real name.' Peggy giggled and then pressed her hand to her mouth. 'I don't know why I'm finding this funny,' she said in a muffled voice. 'It's been one shock after another today.'

'That's why,' said Pete, smiling. 'If you didn't laugh you'd cry.'

Peggy managed to pull herself together. 'I'd best be going,' she said, opening the door. 'I promised Mrs Henderson I'd be back as soon as I could.' There came the sound of waves hushing on the shore.

'Is she your boss?' he asked.

'Yes, I'm her general dogsbody.' She got out of the car.

'Why don't you give up the job?' said Pete, speaking rapidly. 'Come back to Liverpool!'

Peggy hesitated. 'Give me a little bit of time. I need to get my head around everything. Besides, I would have to serve my notice and anyway, Mrs Henderson needs time to find someone to replace me – what with it being high season. See you soon.'

'I hope so,' he said.

They continued to stare at each other for what felt like an age and then she closed the car door and walked away.

Twenty-Three

Marty gazed down at Bernie lying flat on her back. She had regained consciousness again a short while after he arrived but had not seemed to recognize him. A doctor had told him that she had a concussion and a spinal injury. When Marty had asked bluntly if she would survive, he had been told the prognosis for head injuries were not always easy to forecast but the fact that she had regained consciousness a couple of times already was a good sign. As for the spinal injury, it should knit with bed rest. Marty asked if a priest could be brought to his wife and, after having a word with him, Marty had slipped out of the room to tell Dougal what he had been told about Bernie's condition.

Marty found it hard to believe that this was happening. During the time since he had first been told about the accident, life had taken on a sense of unreality. He felt depressed, guilty and angry, not only with his brother and Bernie but also himself. But from the moment Irene's postcard had arrived from America, with its mention of the charming Harry driving her and Bobby all the way to San Jose, Marty had felt not only like smashing something, he had wished Bernie out of his life for good.

Perhaps Bernie had sensed his mood because she had started asking about Irene. She told him that one of the neighbours had harked back to the day Marty had arrived in his van with Irene on Whit Saturday. Apparently it had been the day of her mother's wedding and Irene had been dressed up to the nines and looked lovely. For some reason Bernie seemed to have expected him to have told her about Irene being *all dollied up* as she put it and had wanted to know exactly what they had done whilst in the house alone.

He had not answered her which had infuriated her. Then she had brought up the subject of the children's books that had belonged to Irene, saying they were rubbish and she was going to put them in the bin. Josie had been listening and shrieked that they were hers and they were not to be put in the bin. She had bitten Bernie's leg and then run out of the room.

Bernie would have gone after her and smacked her if Tommy had not arrived. Marty had no idea that he was expected but Bernie had wasted no time getting ready and whizzed out of the house, a headscarf trailing from a hand, saying that she was going into town and wouldn't be back until that evening. Marty had suggested that Tommy help him with the decorating but his brother said that he had a job to go to and had just dropped by to see how the family were getting on.

That was the moment when Marty should have smelled a rat but he had not even bothered seeing his brother to the door. Instead he had gone to see what the kids were up to and strip wallpaper from the last of the walls that needed decorating. Then Mrs Gianelli had called and, when she had seen what he was doing, offered to take the children from under his feet for the rest of the day. He had given his brother and wife little thought until Monica and a furious Dougal had turned up.

A nurse came into the room now to check his wife's blood pressure, take her temperature, lift her eyelids and flash a torch into her eyes. Then she left the room again. She was to continue to repeat these actions throughout the night until Sunday morning dawned. During that time Bernie stirred once or twice and opened her eyes and stared at Marty.

'Where's my husband?' she murmured.

'I'm here,' he answered.

'No!' She shook her head and winced. 'Tommy! Where's Tommy? He's not really dead, is he?'

'No, he's only broken his arm. Never mind Tommy. Rest now.'

She closed her eyes and drifted off again.

Marty sat back in the chair by the bed, thinking and wishing he was back home with the kids. Shortly after that, a different nurse came into the room and bid Marty a good morning.

'I believe you've been here all night, Mr Mc-Grath. Why don't you take a break and stretch your legs. You could even have a breath of fresh air. I'll stay with her,' she said, smiling at him.

It was a relief to leave the room. Whichever way things went for Bernie, life was going to be difficult. He decided not to think any further ahead than one day at a time.

Pete was sitting on a bench in the reception area of the hospital but there was no sign of Tommy or Dougal. Pete struggled to his feet and Marty wondered if he looked as weary and drawn as Pete did.

'How is she?' asked Pete.

Marty told him. 'She seemed muddled.'

'At least she's come round,' said Pete. 'That's a good sign.'

'So they keep telling me.' Marty changed the subject. 'Where are Tommy and Dougal?'

'Dougal left shortly after you told us what the doctor had said.' Pete rested a hand on the back of a bench. 'He said something about going to the police station. Your brother went off shortly after saying he was going to the toilet but he hasn't come back.'

'Thank God for that,' said Marty. 'He'll have it fixed in his head that Dougal's going to bring charges against him for taking his motorbike without permission and all the stuff from years ago will come to light and he could end up in prison. It wouldn't surprise me if our Tommy disappears for good this time.'

'He told Dougal the bike was scarcely damaged,' said Pete.

'Then maybe Dougal's hoping he can recover it from the police station and ride it back to Liverpool,' said Marty, thrusting his hands in his pockets. 'I'd better get back. You go home, Pete. I'll make my own way.'

Pete gave a tight little smile. 'I'll stick around for a while. My leg's a bit dicky and I don't feel up to driving yet. I must give Mam another ring and let her know I might be some time.'

'OK, if you prefer to do that, it's fine with me,' said Marty.

When he returned to Bernie's bedside, the nurse told him that his wife had spoken and asked where her husband was before going to sleep.

'You don't surprise me,' said Marty with a grimace. 'She looked at me earlier as if she didn't know who I was and told me I wasn't her husband.'

'I wouldn't worry about that. The memory can behave very oddly.' She told Marty that she would have a cup of tea brought to him. He asked if his friend waiting in reception could be given one as well. She nodded and left.

Being Sunday it was to be several hours before Marty saw a doctor again. By then Bernie was looking about her and had attempted to sit up but the nurse told her she had to lie flat. Several times Bernie's glance fell on Marty, but still there was no sign of recognition in her eyes and they did not linger on him. When he spoke to her, she did not answer.

During the two hours that passed before a neurologist arrived, Bernie attempted to sit up again but, knowing she had to lie flat, Marty prevented her from moving. She obviously did not like him doing so, if the expression in her eyes was anything to go by, but she made no further attempt and instead closed her eyes as if, suddenly, all the strength had gone out of her.

He was dismissed from the room on the arrival of the neurologist. Afterwards when Marty asked to speak to him, it was obvious the man was in a hurry. 'You're a Scouser, aren't you?' he said.

'What's that to do with anything?' asked Marty.

The neurologist smiled. 'I did some of my medical training in Liverpool. I suggest, Mr McGrath, that you go home and rest. I believe you've young children. There isn't anything you can do here and I'm sure they need you.'

'Yes, and I would like to get home to them but what about my wife?'

Without hesitation, the neurologist said briskly, 'Try not to worry about her. She's lucky to be alive considering she was not wearing a crash helmet. We'll have her transferred to Liverpool Royal Infirmary and you should be able to visit her there tomorrow evening.'

'She seems to be suffering from partial memory loss and doesn't believe I'm her husband.'

'Head injuries are tricky but hopefully all will be well. She is going to have to remain in hospital, flat on her back for several weeks to allow the spinal injury to heal. Good day, Mr McGrath.'

Marty watched the neurologist stride off down the corridor. Then he went back inside the side room to see Bernie before he left. Her eyes were open and she was staring into space.

'I'm going, Bernie. I'll see you tomorrow.' He hesitated before kissing her cheek. There was no response, except when he stepped back, she rubbed the spot where his lips had been as if to wipe away his touch. For a moment her gaze flicked over his face and then it moved away again.

He felt almost light-hearted when he left the room and hurried to where he had left Pete waiting. Would he still be there?

He was! Marty's relief intensified. 'Thanks, Pete.' He laid a hand on the other man's shoulder. 'I've been told to go home.'

'How is she?' asked Pete.

'Lucky to be alive. They're going to transfer her to the Royal in Liverpool. Her spinal injury means she'll have to stay there for several weeks.'

'Poor Bernie! I know what a long stay in a hospital bed is like. Still, it sounds promising that they consider her well enough to be moved to Liverpool,' said Pete.

'She still doesn't seem to recognize me but she mentioned Tommy. Anyway, there's nothing more I can do here and I need to get back to the kids. I'm going to have to get in touch with Bernie's mother. She'll want to know all the ins and outs and I don't want to tell her over the phone.' He began to walk towards the entrance.

'What about Peggy?' asked Pete, limping after him. 'Shouldn't you let her know how matters lie before we leave Blackpool?'

Marty had not forgotten about his sister. 'Do you remember where this hotel is?'

Pete nodded. 'She told me that she wouldn't be coming back to Liverpool with us.'

Marty was taken aback. 'Why not? You did tell her that Dad was dead? I just didn't think about it last night.'

'Of course I did!' Pete gritted his teeth as he followed Marty into the sunshine and leaned against a wall. 'She said that she would have to serve her notice and, as it was high season,' he gasped, 'she felt she would have to stay until her boss found someone to take her place.'

Marty frowned. 'Did she ask about Mam?'

'Yes. I told her that she'd had a holiday with a friend in Whit week; also that Lil was getting married in September and she and her husband would be living with your mother.'

'Did you tell her that I'd moved into Irene's old house because her mother had remarried?'

Pete shook his head. 'I thought she'd had enough news to contend with. Look, I'm in a great deal of pain, so can we get to the bloody car now and will you please drive?'

Marty cursed himself for his thoughtlessness after Pete had been of such help to him. He slipped an arm about the other man's waist. 'Lean on me and I'll get you there.'

They managed to reach the car without any mishaps. Marty suggested that Pete might be better in the back, sitting up with his legs stretched out. 'You'll be able to rest better.' Pete agreed.

As it was they did not have to seek out the hotel because just as they were about to leave the hospital grounds, Pete spotted Peggy crossing the road. 'Pull up just round the corner!' he cried. 'Here she is!'

Marty parked and Pete wound down the window and shouted to Peggy. She hurried over to them. 'How is Bernie? How's our Tommy?'

'Get in!' Marty ordered. 'I'm in the way here.'

She put a hand to her breast and gasped. 'Bernie's dead, isn't she? Oh hell!'

'Will you get in!' Marty ordered.

Peggy opened the front passenger door and climbed in. 'Did she have a priest?'

Marty nodded. 'He read the last rites, just in case, but she's not dead.'

'You mean she's still alive?'

'That's what not dead means,' said Marty, and drove off.

'There's no need to be sarcastic,' said Peggy. 'Anyway, where are we going?'

'Liverpool!'

'But ... but I can't go without letting Mrs Henderson know!' she cried. 'It's high season!'

'I need your help, Peg,' said Marty, glancing at her. 'I've got two kids who are going to need looking after and you owe us for going missing and worrying us sick.' A muscle twitched in his throat.

Tears welled in her eyes. 'I told Mam not to worry! I'm not such a child that I can't look after myself.' She fumbled for a handkerchief in her

298

jacket pocket. 'So what is going to happen to Bernie?'

'I don't know how the concussion and loss of memory is going to affect her in the long run,' he said. 'What I do know is that she's going to be in Liverpool's Royal Infirmary for weeks because of her spinal injury. She has to lie flat to give it a chance to heal.'

'But surely Bernie's mother and sister will be around to take care of the kids?' said Peggy.

'You've forgotten that we're not living with her mother any more,' said Marty. 'And besides, they're my responsibility! I'm not having Bernie's family taking them over.'

'OK, keep your hair on! Where are you living?' asked Peggy.

'We moved into Irene's mother's old house after she remarried.'

Peggy gasped. 'I had no idea.'

'You would if you'd bothered to write,' said Marty.

'I kept meaning to but never got round to it. I'm sorry! But I just didn't want anyone telling me what to do any more!' Peggy wiped away a tear. 'What happened to Jimmy and Irene?'

Pete spoke up from the back seat. 'Jimmy's gone back to sea and Irene's in America. The children's home closed down and she's gone to stay with Betty who's having a baby.'

'I suppose her doing that is no big surprise. Especially if she's out of a job.' She twisted in her seat and gazed down at Pete and asked in a trembling voice, 'Are you all right?'

'I've been better, thanks,' he said, tight-lipped.

299

'I'm sorry. This is all my fault.' She reached down a hand to him.

He clasped it. 'I'm not blaming you. I'm just glad you're safe.' Peggy swallowed the lump in her throat. 'I don't know what your mother must have thought of me.'

'Never mind that now, Peg,' Marty said. 'Turn round and sit in your seat properly. I don't want any more accidents.'

Pete and Peggy unclasped hands. She straightened up and stared ahead. 'So who's looking after the kids at the moment?' she asked.

'Monica, but she won't be able to carry on looking after them,' said Marty. 'Her Mam would never allow her to stay the night alone with me and the kids. You'll have to come and live with me, Peg, until I get things sorted out.'

Peggy was taken aback. Of course she was fond of her niece and nephew but she knew almost nothing about taking care of children. 'Won't Mam have something to say about that?' she asked. 'I mean, surely she'll expect you to ask her?'

'I've been going over and over in my head, trying to decide what's best to do. She'll never cope with them day in, day out. Bernie was forever complaining they were a handful and she's a lot younger than Mam.'

Peggy's mind was in a whirl. 'Irene would have been the perfect person to look after them,' she said abruptly. 'She wouldn't have had to stay the night because you'd be there for them.'

'But Irene's not here,' Marty muttered. 'I have to rely on you being there for me and the children. After all the worry you've caused it's the

300

least you can do!'

'All right,' said Peggy, wondering what Pete was making of this conversation. Obviously her brother had not given any consideration to the possibility that she and Pete might want to get together again. Suddenly she realized that she had forgotten completely about her other brother. 'Where's Tommy?'

'God only knows,' snapped Marty. 'He went off because Dougal decided to go to the police station and report him for taking his motorbike without permission.'

'How did he come to be with Bernie? I haven't got to the root of that.'

'He popped up at Dad's funeral,' said Marty. 'Not that he came and joined the family but later he turned up at the house in Litherland. You know what they say about Greeks?'

'What?' asked Peggy, puzzled.

'Beware of Greeks bringing gifts,' murmured Pete.

'Exactly. He brought presents for the kids and Bernie. She's always had a soft spot for him,' said Marty.

'Her mother never had a good word to say about him,' said Peggy. 'It makes you think, doesn't it?'

'She's got plenty of nous, has Bernie's mother,' said Marty.

'I'm sorry I wasn't there for you, Lil and Mam when Dad died,' said Peggy, imagining their mother's reaction to the news that Tommy had gone off again. Somehow Peggy knew that her own reappearance would not mean so much to her mother as Tommy's, the apple of Mary Mc-

Grath's eye. She asked no more questions and the rest of the journey passed in silence.

When they arrived at the house, Pete said that he would not come in but head off home.

'Are you all right to drive?' asked Peggy, watching him ease himself into the driving seat.

He nodded. 'I've rested all the way back.'

'Thanks for your help, Pete,' said Marty, shaking his hand. 'I'll never forget it.'

'That's all right! I'll be thinking of you all.'

Marty thanked him again and went to open the front door.

'See you, Peggy,' said Pete, gazing up at her. 'Don't be a stranger again.'

'I won't! But I don't know how things are going to go in the next few weeks.' Her bottom lip trembled.

'I can wait,' he said, driving off.

She waved, wondering when she would see him again. Only a couple of days ago she had believed she had managed to put Pete out of her life. And now here they were again, wondering what the future would hold for them. But for now she had to put such thoughts aside. The children had to come first and she had to face her mother. She was not going to think about what she might have to cope with when Bernie was able to leave hospital. What if the brain injury meant she wasn't safe to be left alone with her children?

Suddenly she remembered that she must telephone Mrs Henderson and apologize for going off the way she had done. She would also need to ask her to pack her belongings and send them to her and that meant sending a postal order to cover the cost.

Marty had left the front door open, so Peggy went right in. She could hear her brother's voice and then several others all talking at once, so there was a hell of a din. She took a deep breath as she paused in the kitchen doorway, her gaze sweeping over Bernie's mother's ravaged face, three of Bernie's sisters, as well as Peggy's own mother and sister. Monica was also there and she was nursing Jerry who was crying. As for Marty, who had his back to Peggy, he held his daughter in his arms.

Then he suddenly yelled, 'Be quiet!'

Jerry's sobs shuddered to a halt and the voices petered off.

Suddenly Mary McGrath caught sight of her daughter. 'It's our Peggy!' she cried.

'I told you so,' said Bernie's mother, glaring at Peggy. 'I told yer it was her who phoned.'

'I didn't know then that Marty wasn't living with you,' said Peggy.

'Never you mind that,' said Bernie's mother, shaking a finger at her. 'If you hadn't gone off, our Bernie would still be here. If yer Tommy weren't such a thief, she wouldn't have gone to Blackpool.'

'Don't you call my son a thief!' cried Mary, bridling.

'If there were any justice he'd go to prison for what he's done to my daughter!' Bernie's mother's voice cracked on the words.

Peggy said hesitantly, 'But it was an accident and she didn't have a crash helmet on. She's lucky to be alive!'

Bernie's mother took a deep, shuddering

303

breath. 'Y-y-you mean she's not dead?'

'Yes, she's regained consciousness and has spoken,' said Marty, wondering if Dougal had phoned ahead and told her that Bernie was at death's door. 'They're going to transfer her to the Royal Infirmary in Liverpool.'

'Hospital! I hate hospitals,' said Bernie's mother, shivering. 'They should send her home to her mother and I'll look after her.'

'Marty's her husband,' said Mary firmly. 'She belongs with him and the children.'

'They can all come back and live with me,' said Bernie's mother.

Marty turned to Monica. 'Will you go with Peggy and take the children to the park?'

Monica looked at Peggy and, nodding, lowered Jerry to the floor. For a moment Josie clung to her father and then he whispered to her and she slid down out of her arms and put one hand in Monica's and the other in Peggy's.

As soon as they were out of earshot, Marty turned and faced those remaining. 'Peggy's coming to live here and she'll help me look after the kids.'

Immediately one of her sisters said, 'Our Bernie's not going to like that.'

'No, she won't,' said her mother.

Marty stared at them. 'You haven't got it, have you? She's going to be flat on her back in hospital for several weeks until her spinal injury heals. And aside from that she is suffering memory loss; she had no idea who I was!'

'Holy Mary, mother of God!' gasped Bernie's mother, crossing herself. 'Oh, my poor daughter!

She needs me at a time like this! I have to go to her.'

'Take a hold of yourself, woman!' said Mary in a severe voice. 'I understand how you feel because I'm a mother, too, but there's nothing you can do but pray. Besides, Bernie's Marty's wife and my son has never been one to shirk his responsibilities. He'll take care of her when the time comes for her to leave hospital.'

Marty wished his mother had not spoken those words. He had to go out to work to provide for his family and unless Bernie was completely fit and well, he could not see himself managing without extra help. He could not put the whole load on Peggy but neither did he want Bernie's family taking over.

'How will he manage?' asked one of the sisters. 'Won't your Peggy need to get another job eventually?'

Marty said, 'Listen, what's happened has come as a shock to all of us. I feel we've discussed it enough for now. If you all don't mind going home, I'll be glad of some peace. I've been up all night and I've work in the morning and I can't afford to take time off. You'll be able to take turns to see Bernie in hospital during the week.'

'Yes, none of you are thinking of my poor son. It's not so long since we lost his father,' said Mary. 'This has all been a terrible shock to him.'

'He should have put his foot down and stopped his bloody brother taking our Bernie to Blackpool,' muttered one of the sisters. 'It seems odd to me that she went with Tommy.'

'Enough of that,' said Bernie's mother sharply.

305

She glanced at the partly redecorated walls. 'Anyway, I hope yer get this finished before yer bring her here, lad.'

Marty hung on to his patience. 'I'll see you out,' he said, expecting to have to hustle them out of the front door but they wasted no time leaving. He returned to the kitchen and was glad when Lil told him that she had put the kettle on.

'So where's our Tommy?' asked his mother, gripping her hands tightly together in her lap.

Marty sat down in an armchair and closed his eyes. 'He's done what he generally does, Mam, when he doesn't want to face up to things. He's run away.'

Mary took a deep breath. 'Good! And this time you don't go looking for him. I don't trust that family, saying he should be put in prison. As it was, if Peter's mother hadn't got in touch, I wouldn't have known Peggy was in Blackpool and you and Peter had gone haring off there! I think if Lil and I hadn't come here today, then Bernie's family would have taken the children. I must admit you surprised me by saying our Peggy is coming to live here with you. After all, what does she know about children? I brought up four of you.'

'Let him be, Mam,' said Lil. 'He knows what he's doing. Anyway, we've the wedding to think about and I might just have a baby straight off and I'll need your help to look after it. Besides it sounds to me like Bernie could be more of a problem.' She paused, tapping her brother on the shoulder. 'Marty, if you want something stronger than tea, I can always go to the off licence.'

'Tea would be fine,' he said, thinking he couldn't

afford to buy drink. He thought about Pete's mother not wasting time letting Marty's mother know that Peggy had been in touch and that he and Pete were on their way to Blackpool. Could it be that she still had hopes that Pete and Peggy might get together? His spirits plummeted even further, knowing that it would put him in a quandary if Bernie wasn't fit to look after the kids. How could he possibly stand in the way of Pete and Peggy's happiness if they did decide to marry?

Twenty-Four

Even before Pete could get his key in the lock, the front door opened and his mother stood there. 'About time, too,' said Gertie, her eyes bright. 'Did you find her?'

'Yes,' said Pete, stepping over the threshold as his mother moved out of the way.

'Good! So, how is Bernie?' asked Gertie, bustling back into the kitchen after putting on the kettle.

'She has memory loss and a spinal injury,' said Pete, lowering himself on to the sofa. 'She didn't recognize Marty.'

Gertie stuck her head around the door jamb. 'Not so good.'

'She's going to be in the Royal Infirmary for weeks, flat on her back.'

'Oh, my goodness,' said Gertie. 'Who's going to look after the children?'

Pete sighed. 'Peggy! She's going to be living with Marty.'

'Oh dear,' said Gertie, coming slowly back into the kitchen. 'That's a blow! I was preparing myself for a wedding. Were you glad to see each other?'

'Yes. She's been working in a hotel as a general dogsbody,' said Pete, beginning to unfasten his shoelaces and easing off his shoes with a sigh of relief. 'Anyway, she's back and I know she's safe. I'm thinking no further than that at the moment, Ma, so don't be going on about it. She'll have a lot on her plate with having a couple of little ones to look after. You know what that's like. As for Bernie, only God knows how Peggy will cope with her, or what'll happen if she never completely recovers. On top of that, her brother's injured and could soon have the police on his tail.'

'It doesn't rain but it pours,' said Gertie sadly, leaving her son alone.

Pete leaned back on the sofa, closed his eyes and was asleep in minutes.

Twenty-Five

Peggy pressed her lips tightly together as she lifted the dripping nappy from the enamel bucket and squeezed out the excess water before dropping the nappy into the steaming water in the washing machine. It was one of those that boiled water and had an agitator and a hinged lid with a mangle on the top. There was a knot of resentment and

308

rebellion inside her chest. She did not want to feel such emotions but she could not help it.

It was only three weeks since the accident, but she was already feeling the strain of taking care of the kids all day, doing the housework, shopping and cooking. She had only seen Bernie once as Marty, Bernie's mother and sisters had priority when it came to taking turns during visiting times. Even then, Peggy had been stumped when it came to talking to her sister-in-law. She appeared to be able to read magazines with the help of an overhead mirror that reflected the pages so she could see them whilst lying flat on her back. But she was unable to remember rightly whom she had married, getting the names of the brothers mixed up and asking for Tommy and apparently not recognizing Marty. This seemed very odd to Peggy, especially when she would have sworn that Bernie knew who she was and Monica had told her that Bernie's mother swore that she knew her all right, having talked about when Bernie was a little girl to her daughter.

Peggy sighed, deciding she did not want to think about when her sister-in-law came out of hospital, which wouldn't be long now. Instead she thought of her mother and all the other women who had kept house and reared children, admiring them for being so capable and seemingly enjoying the unpaid work.

She supposed it was different when the children were your own or you were getting paid for caring for them, as Irene did. At least she hoped so, because what joy would there be in it if it was just hard graft? There had been a postcard of San

309

Francisco which Irene praised to the skies as being really picturesque, agreeing with Betty that it was difficult to believe that so much of the city had been destroyed by fire during the earthquake of 1906. Marty had read the postcard and then gone and stood outside in the yard, gazing at nothing in particular. Peggy had realized then, if she had not done so earlier in the year, that her brother had strong feelings for Irene.

She dropped another nappy and four cot sheets into the machine and switched it to wash before washing her hands under the cold tap. She dried them on a tea towel and smoothed hand cream into her skin. Then she went into the kitchen where she had left her niece and nephew playing, relieved to remind herself that at least Josie was dry during the day, although she still wore a nappy at night, as did Jerry despite him being older.

It was now September and the weather had been cloudy and dull with the odd smattering of rain. For once the children were playing quietly and not squabbling. Jerry was making engine noises as he ran his Dinky cars over the linoleum. Josie was undressing her doll. Peggy decided it was time for a cup of tea and a biscuit and to listen to some music on the wireless. The children had been difficult with her at first, no doubt because she had been away for months and she was unfamiliar to them. Still, they were getting used to each other now, although they still asked for their mother, especially Jerry.

She wished she was still earning a wage. Marty handed over housekeeping money and said he'd like to give her more but that money was extremely tight at the moment. She could understand that and supposed she should be thankful for being housed and fed.

Before she settled herself in the armchair, she gave the children a dose of free cod liver oil in a spoonful of free National Health orange juice, followed by a Nice biscuit, then she switched on the wireless. She gazed out of the window on to the yard as she sipped her tea, thinking about Blackpool and how lively it had been once the holiday crowds began arriving. She'd made a friend of Gwen who had worked at the hotel and they'd gone out together a few times. How much her life had changed in the past year.

She was brought back to the present by the sound of Pat Boone singing *'Love Letters in the Sand'*, which had been way up there in the hit parade last year. She began to sing softly along with the music, thinking of Pete and the day when they had written *love you forever* in the sand. They had been completely oblivious to everyone else on the beach and the drama taking place in the sea. Irene had been fortunate but it was sad that her stepfather had died the way he did.

She thought of her own father, wishing she had happier memories of him and that he could have been honest with his children about his own youth. At least her mother seemed to be coping well without him and his death did mean that Peggy no longer had to worry about having his approval. She wondered, not for the first time, why Pete had not been in touch with her since her return. Perhaps he had realized that he no longer loved her after all. It would be her own fault if he didn't. She experienced an aching regret and wanted to weep.

She felt a tug at her skirt and looked down to see Josie holding the potty. 'Good girl,' she said.

Peggy could not help laughing. 'You are a good girl,' she said, taking the potty from her. 'And because you are, as soon as the washing stops and is on the drying rack, we'll go for a walk and you can have a treat.'

'Can I have a treat, too?' asked Jerry.

Peggy nodded and went to empty the potty.

She decided to take the pushchair and visit the shops on the other side of the canal. They could go to the post office and then to the park on Hatton Hill Road.

It was as she was waiting in the queue at the post office that someone tapped her on the shoulder. Peggy turned and her face lit up. 'Mrs Gianelli, I haven't seen you for ages.'

'I heard you were back and living with Marty,' said Nellie, smiling. 'My brother told me. He's seen your mother and been to visit your sister-in-law in hospital.'

Peggy hesitated. 'How did he find her?'

Nellie did not immediately answer but then said, 'He felt that he wasn't welcome. She seemed on edge as if she couldn't wait for him to leave.'

'Did she mention my brother, Tommy, to him?'

'No.' Nellie grimaced. 'Francis wondered where he is.'

'Bernie gets their names mixed up and thinks she's married to Tommy.'

The queue shifted up and they moved with it.

'It's very odd. If you feel you need someone to

312

talk to or a break from looking after the children, pop in and see me,' said Nellie. 'I'm around most of the time. Mine are at school now.'

Peggy felt a rush of gratitude. 'I am finding it hard work, so I might just do that. Mam's all wrapped up in the arrangements for my sister's wedding this month. To be honest, I'm missing having a job and mixing with people.'

'No doubt you're missing having a proper wage, too,' said Nellie.

'You can say that again,' sighed Peggy. 'I can hardly ask my brother to pay me when he's family and money's tight.'

Nellie stared at her. 'If you're not too busy, why don't you come back to the house with me now? The children can play in the garden if the rain holds off. We can have a bit of lunch and a chat.'

The idea of someone else making her something to eat really appealed, so Peggy accepted the offer. Soon she was settled comfortably in Nellie's kitchen. A pan of home-made soup simmered on the stove which smelled delicious. From a window she could keep a watch on the children playing in the garden with some of the Gianelli children's old toys.

'I don't suppose you've heard from Irene?' asked Nellie, refilling Peggy's teacup.

'Marty had a postcard from her as he's taken over her old house, but I doubt she knows I'm back in Liverpool. You'll have heard from her, of course.'

'Yes, me and our lodger, Deirdre. She worked with Irene but now has a job at Litherland Nursery. As it happens I wrote to Irene only yesterday.

313

I'd had a letter from her, telling me all her news. Betty's baby is due this month.' Nellie smiled. 'She's also been in touch with my widowed sister who's keeping Bobby, Lynette Walker's daughter, company on the voyage back to England.'

'Doesn't she have a brother, Nick?'

'Not her real brother. Sam and Lynne adopted him.'

'I remember now hearing the story from Jeanette,' said Peggy. 'His original adoptive father was murdered by his brother who disappeared to Canada and has yet to be found.' She sighed. 'It's surprising how easy it is to disappear but it's not fair on your family and friends.'

They were silent a moment.

'You do know that Jeanette and Davy have moved to New Brighton, don't you? Their baby's due around the same time as Betty's.'

Peggy almost dropped her cup. 'I'd forgotten that Jeanette was having a baby! And no, I didn't know she'd moved. We were such good friends when we worked in the Cunard building. We used to go the pictures together a lot until she was reunited with Davy. I remember I was talking to Pete when...' Her voice trailed off.

'I can get Jeanette's address for you if you like?'

'Thanks, I would like that.'

'I'm sure she'll be delighted to hear from you. You could drop her a line or even give her a ring,' suggested Nellie.

Twenty-Six

Pete glanced at the calendar on his desk as he shrugged on his jacket. September! It was almost a month since he had last seen Peggy and he had been asking himself how long he should wait before getting in touch with her. He sighed. She could have contacted him but what if she'd decided she didn't really want to see him again?

He said tarrah to the others in the office and left. Outside, it was a lovely evening, the sky washed a clear blue with light fluffy clouds tinged with peach and gold. He had not come in the car that morning because it was having a service and, on impulse, he decided not to catch the bus straight home but to visit the landing stage for a breath of fresh air and watch the ships coming and going.

He took his time, deciding that way he would miss the rush-hour crowds and it was much less strain on his lame leg. He had forgotten there would be plenty of commuters who worked in Liverpool, catching the ferry to their homes on the Wirral, and so he sat on a bench and rested. It was while he was there that he spotted Jeanette's husband, Davy, who worked on the Isle of Man boats, standing in the queue for the New Brighton ferry.

Pete called out to him. Davy turned his head and came over to him.

'How are you doing?' asked Pete. 'Haven't seen you for ages. How's Jeanette?'

They talked for several minutes until there was the bump and grinding noise of the ferry boat tying up alongside the landing stage. 'I'd better get going,' said Davy.

'Let me know when Jeanette has the baby,' said Pete.

Davy nodded, then said unexpectedly, 'Why don't you come and visit us before then? It'll be like a madhouse after the baby's born. Come to Sunday dinner this weekend! Most of the holiday crowds will be gone by then, so you shouldn't have any trouble getting a ferry. We have an old friend of Jeanette's coming too, whom you know.' He did not wait for Pete's answer but vanished into the crowd making their way to the ferry as the gangplank hit the ground.

Pete stared after him, wondering who Jeanette's old friend might be. Could it possibly be Peggy? After all, she and Jeanette had been friends when they had both worked in the Cunard building.

Twenty-Seven

Peggy banged down the casserole dish and stared across at Marty. 'I'm taking Sunday off,' she said. 'I've been in touch with Jeanette and I've been invited to dinner.'

He glanced across at her and said mildly, 'You don't have to make a song and dance of it, Peg. You do what you want. I'll take the kids to Mam's. Our Lil wants Josie to have a second fitting for her bridesmaid's frock. I'm not looking forward to this wedding. Aren't you lucky that you're not a bridesmaid because you went missing?'

His words took the wind out of her sail. 'Yes, but I'll still be glad when it's over. Our Lil is younger than me and I feel big sisters should get married first. I'm glad she's having her best friend for her chief bridesmaid. I take it the main reason you don't want to go is because Lil insists on you giving her away?' said Peggy, taking the lid off the casserole.

Steam weaved its way up from the stewing steak and carrots in onion gravy. 'Your cooking's improved,' said Marty, breathing deeply of the delicious smell. 'You'll make some man a good wife one day.'

'If I get the chance,' she said beneath her breath.

He stared at her. 'What's that supposed to mean?'

'I think you know,' said Peggy, beginning to dish out their supper. The children had already had theirs and were asleep. Marty had been working late on a job in West Derby, hence them only having theirs now.

'Guess who I saw today,' he said, seemingly changing the subject.

'I don't want to guess, so tell me,' she retorted.

'Pete's mother. I suppose she was visiting Irene's mother who lives in West Derby.'

Peggy sat down abruptly. 'Did she see you?'

'If she had, I would have spoken to her. She was coming out of a house and looked upset.'

'Why d'you think that is?'

He shrugged. 'How am I supposed to know?

317

Could be that she'd had bad news or was wishing that there was going to be a wedding in her family.'

'Very funny,' muttered Peggy, picking up her own plate of food and cutlery and leaving the kitchen.

Peggy rested her elbows on the side of the boat and gazed across the choppy surface of the Mersey towards the clock on the Liver building as the Princes landing stage and the line of Liverpool docks receded into the distance. The boat was going up and down and she thought there could be a storm brewing. She remained there for several minutes before turning and moving towards the other side of the boat as it forged its way towards New Brighton. She remembered many a happy day spent at the seaside resort when she was younger. Her mother would pack plenty of butties and home-made cake but she had always sent Marty to fetch a pot of tea from a café in the resort and they would picnic on the beach. They would build sandcastles or go crabbing amongst the rocks or paddle in the paddling pool. When they were a bit older they would swim in the open-air baths where the Miss New Brighton beauty contest was held or they might visit the fair. Sometimes they would walk along the promenade, watching what was happening on the beach. When their legs grew tired, they would sit on a bench and she would eye up the fellas.

'Hello, Peggy!'

The voice startled her and caused her to turn and stare at its owner in amazement. 'Jimmy Miller! What are you doing here?'

318

'I'm taking the ferry across the Mersey.' His teeth gleamed white in his tanned face. 'How are you?'

'I only went as far as Blackpool, unlike you. When did you get back?'

'About a week ago. I went to see my Mam in West Derby. I was surprised by my welcome.' A shadow crossed his face. 'She was dead pleased to see me but I wasn't asked to stay. I was shocked by her appearance to be honest. She's lost a heck of a lot of weight. I think she made a big mistake marrying again and taking on someone else's children. It's proving too much for her but she's not going to admit it.'

'My dad died while I was away,' Peggy blurted out. 'And Tommy has gone missing again.'

'So I heard.'

She frowned. 'I suppose Pete told you.'

'Haven't see Pete. It was Tony Gianelli.'

'I see.' She began to walk along the deck, pulling her tent coat tightly about her.

Jimmy fell into step beside her. 'I thought I might try for the Canada run in the spring.'

'That's a few months away.'

'Yeah. I thought I'd stay in Liverpool until then. The group have lost one of their guitarists and so I'm going to take his place. I've enough money to get by for a while.'

'So where are you staying?' asked Peggy.

'I'm lodging with the Gianellis.'

There was a pause. 'I thought they had a lodger and Mrs Gianelli's sister was coming to stay,' said Peggy, surprised.

'Her sister is staying but Deirdre decided that

319

working at the day nursery wasn't for her and applied for a position in the children's home in Formby when it came up. Apparently some of the children that she and our Irene used to care for were sent there and she missed them.' He paused. 'I thought I might drop in there when I give my stepbrother, Billy, a visit. At the moment I'm dossing down in Tony's room on a mattress and it could be that Billy and his wife will put me up for the odd couple of days.' He glanced at her. 'So what are you doing on the New Brighton ferry? You wouldn't be visiting Jeanette and Davy by any chance?'

'Is that where you're going?'

'I thought I'd surprise them.'

'D'you think it's right to surprise people on a Sunday? What if they've catered for only so many people? One extra could prove too much. You have to also think about Jeanette's baby being due soon.'

His face fell. 'I never thought of that.'

'Most men wouldn't,' she said drily.

'OK, you've made your point. I'll go and see them another time,' said Jimmy.

'You can always drop in at your old address and visit our Marty and me if you're at a loose end.'

He smiled. 'Thanks.'

They carried on walking around the deck, staggering slightly. Then suddenly Peggy saw Pete. She felt the blood rush to her cheeks. Jimmy had also noticed him. 'Hey, there's Pete,' he said.

'So it is,' said Peggy, knowing she would have to speak to him now. Was she ready for a serious conversation?

They walked towards him.

But it was Pete who spoke first. 'I was hoping it would be you.'

'What d'you mean?' asked Peggy.

'Davy said they had someone else coming to dinner – an old friend of Jeanette's that I knew.'

Peggy could not conceal her pleasure. It was obvious that Pete was pleased about that. 'So it was Davy who invited you to Sunday dinner?'

'I met him the other evening on the landing stage,' he said, smiling. 'How are things?'

'I'm managing. Bernie could be out of hospital in a week or so. It's our Lil's wedding next Saturday, so I don't know how things will go if the doctor decides she could come home that day said Peggy, grimacing. 'Marty's giving Lil away. I wish...'

'So do I,' said Pete, reaching out a hand.

Peggy took it.

Jimmy cleared his throat. 'Perhaps I should make myself scarce.'

Pete glanced at him. 'I'd heard you were back.'

'Who from?' asked Jimmy.

'Ma! She visits your mother.'

'How did she think Mam seemed?' asked Jimmy. 'I thought she didn't look well. Has she said anything to your Mam about him working her too hard?'

Pete hesitated.

Peggy looked at him and suddenly felt uneasy, remembering something her older brother had said the other evening. 'Marty saw your mother the other day, Pete. She was coming out of a house in West Derby. He thought she looked upset.'

'There you are then!' said Jimmy, almost triumphantly. 'Mam's having a lousy time with him.'

'Wake up, Jimmy,' said Pete, looking unhappy. 'Your ma's ill. If Irene was my sister, I'd be getting in touch with her and suggesting she came home.'

Jimmy stared at him wordlessly and then turned and walked away.

'Should we go after him?' Peggy asked huskily.

'No,' said Pete. 'He's best left alone. He saw that his mother didn't look well but he didn't want to believe that she could be seriously ill.'

'Jimmy's mother told your mother that?'

Pete nodded.

'Poor Jimmy! Poor Irene!'

Pete squeezed Peggy's hand. 'I know! There's always something to pull you down, isn't there? You just start believing things can get better, when someone you know has something lousy happening in their life.'

She agreed. 'But things can get better! I've just thought of something.'

'What?' asked Pete, gazing into her animated features. 'The best thing that can happen to me is that you and I get married.'

Peggy smiled. 'And you think that can't happen because I'm tied up with Marty's children?'

'Aren't you? Or is it that you think Bernie won't be able to cope with them when she comes out of hospital?'

Peggy frowned. 'I don't know if she can or not.' She paused and changed the subject, gazing towards where she could see the New Brighton landing stage. 'The boat will be tying up soon. I know that it looks a bit rough but are you up to a walk on the beach before we go looking for the house?'

He smiled. 'If that's what you want.'

White-capped waves were rolling way up on to the beach but there was still room for them to walk on the sand. Across the expanse of sea they could make out the Lancashire coastline.

'D'you remember that day when we wrote in the sand at Formby?' asked Pete.

She nodded. 'I was thinking about it only the other day. It was also the day Irene nearly drowned and we knew nothing about it at the time. We were so wrapped up in each other.'

'I meant every word I wrote,' said Pete, drawing her close.

'Me, too,' she whispered, her throat tight with emotion.

'So us getting married?' he said, brushing her lips with his. 'Is it on? And if so, when? Because to be honest, I feel we've waited long enough and we can have the ceremony wherever you want.'

'You're on,' said Peggy happily, putting her arms about his waist and pressing her lips against his. 'Just give me a little time to make some arrangements.'

After that they did not speak for a long time.

Monday morning came and, despite it being blowy again, Peggy was out with her niece and nephew shortly after nine o'clock. She was guessing Nellie would have seen her children across the main road to school and most likely would be having a second cup of tea or even coffee with

323

her sister from America now. Fingers crossed, she would not mind being disturbed. Peggy wanted Nellie's advice before she took a step that could bring her wedding day that little bit nearer.

There was no answer to Peggy's ring at the bell and she felt deeply disappointed. She so wanted to put her plan into operation. Then she heard female voices and at the same time could smell a bonfire burning. She pushed the pram around the side of the house.

There were three women. Two had their hands cupped around mugs while Nellie had a stick which she was using to poke at something in the fire.

'Hello!' called Peggy. 'I hope I'm not disturbing you.'

Nellie turned and smiled before saying, 'Girls, this is Peggy and she has her hands full taking care of her brother's children while their mother is in hospital.'

'Now that's what I call really heroic,' said the youngest and most fashionably dressed of the women. 'You must be Irene's friend who vanished; Marty's sister.'

Peggy was taken aback and did not know quite what to say. 'This is my sister, Babs,' said Nellie. 'She came to Liverpool on the liner with Bobby.'

'Bobby likes to talk,' said Babs, shaking hands with Peggy. 'There's nothing I don't know about you all.' Her eyes twinkled.

'She's teasing you,' said Nellie. 'Your secrets are safe.'

'I also have a book for a little girl called Josie,' said Babs.

Josie, who had been attempting to climb out of the pram, said, 'My name's Josie.'

'Why should you have a book for Josie?' asked Peggy, feeling slightly embarrassed as she forced her niece back into the pram.

'It's from Irene and a big hit in America,' said Babs. 'I'll go and fetch it.'

'Cup of tea, Peggy?' asked Nellie.

'I won't, thanks. I'd just like to ask your advice about something.'

Nellie handed her stick to the other woman who was dumpy and dressed plainly except for an ornate crucifix. 'This is my sister, Lottie, Lucia's mother.'

Peggy and Lottie said hello to each other.

'Keep your eye on the bonfire, Lottie,' said Nellie, linking her arm through Peggy's and drawing her aside. 'Now what is it?' she asked in a low voice.

'What chance do you think there is of Josie and Jerry being accepted for a free place at the day nursery?'

Nellie answered immediately. 'I think they have a fair chance. Are you asking this because you'd like to get a paid job once their mother leaves hospital?'

'Yes and no. Pete and I have decided to get married and I think some of the pressure would be off me when it comes to helping Bernie after I'm married. We'll be living with his mother in Bootle, so not too far away,' said Peggy.

Nellie hugged Peggy's arm. 'Well, I'm really pleased to hear you and Pete are together again. What does your mother have to say?'

Peggy pulled a face. 'She doesn't know and neither does Marty.'

'I see. But you'll have to tell him right away because it'll be him who'll have to apply for nursery places and there's bound to be a waiting list. How is Bernie by the way?'

'I haven't seen her for weeks. But Marty says she recognizes him now, with him visiting so much, but she still doesn't remember them getting married.'

Nellie frowned. 'What about the children?'

'Apparently she asks after them but he's wondering if that's only because Bernie's mother and sisters talk about them to her so much.'

'And Tommy?'

Peggy shrugged. 'Marty doesn't mention him.'

Nellie's frown deepened. 'What of her back injury?'

'They're getting her up this week and if she can walk, then she'll be allowed home. Possibly in time for my sister's wedding.'

'Well, the sooner you talk to Marty about your plans the better.'

'I'll do that this evening. There's something else I want your advice about. I know you've known Irene and Jimmy's mother a long time.'

'Yes, although we haven't been in touch for a while.'

'According to Pete's mother she's very ill. He's told Jimmy that he should get in touch with Irene and tell her to come home.'

'Oh, Lord,' murmured Nellie. 'That doesn't sound good but I think Pete's right and Irene should be told about her mother and the sooner

326

the better.'

Peggy said gloomily, 'I thought you'd say that. Her boyfriend's not going to like it.'

'What boyfriend?' asked Nellie.

'Marty mentioned her having one. I can't remember his name,' said Peggy. 'I wondered whether Pete's mother should write to her?'

'I'll give you Betty's address and you can see she gets it,' said Nellie.

At that moment Babs approached, carrying a book. 'Here it is.' She handed it to Peggy who looked at the cover and read the title. '*The Cat in the Hat* by Dr Seuss,' she murmured. 'What a peculiar looking cat! Although, I suppose it'll make a change from *Harry the Dirty Dog* and *Winnie the Pooh*. I'll give it to my brother. He's the one that reads the stories.' She glanced at Babs. 'Thanks.'

'It's not me you have to thank; it's Irene, and Bobby, of course,' said Babs.

Peggy smiled, placed the book in her shopping bag and took hold of the pram handle. 'I'd best be going. I've shopping to do.'

'I'll write down Irene's address for you,' said Nellie, and went into the house.

That evening, as they were eating their meal, Peggy told Marty that she and Pete were planning on getting married. He put down his knife and fork. 'I could see it coming,' he said. 'Although I'm not sure where it leaves me. Have you fixed a date? And where are you going to tie the knot?'

'We're going to get married as soon as I can make the arrangements. Pete said he'll fall in with whatever I want. And if you're wondering where we going to live, it'll be Pete's mother's.'

'I hope the pair of you'll be happy,' murmured Marty, picking up his knife and fork again. 'Your feelings for each other seemed to have stuck despite your ups and downs.'

'I'm glad you think so,' said Peggy happily. 'Anyway, I haven't finished. I've spoken to Mrs Gianelli about the chances of the children getting free places at Litherland Nursery. She thought you should apply. It'll take a load off Bernie's shoulders if she doesn't have to look after them day in, day out. I know what hard work that is. And I could still help out here if Bernie can't cope.'

Marty nodded. 'It sounds a good idea. Although when she comes home, you'll still be here for a while, won't you?'

Peggy nodded, pleased that he had taken her news so well. 'There's something else,' she said, getting up and going over to the sideboard and picking up the book there. 'Mrs Gianelli's sister asked me to give you this,' she said, handing the book to him.

'Why me?' asked Marty, surprised. 'I don't know her. And this is a children's book.'

'It's for Josie from Irene. Apparently it's very popular in America.'

Marty's spirits soared. He handled the book almost reverently, thinking *Her hands have held this book.* He flicked over the pages, looking at the illustrations and reading bits of text and smiling.

'Don't you think it's thoughtful of Irene?' asked Peggy.

'Very thoughtful,' he murmured, deeply touched by that thoughtfulness. 'Did Mrs Gianelli's sister have anything else to say about Irene?'

'No, although I spoke to Mrs Gianelli about Irene's mother being ill. She thought Irene should be told, so I'm going to ask Pete's mother to write to her, just in case Jimmy's letter goes missing.' Peggy glanced across at him. 'Perhaps you should write to her as well and thank her for the book.'

'Maybe I will. Mam would say it's only good manners,' said Marty.

Twenty-Eight

'Rock-a-bye baby on the treetops!' Irene sang softly as she bottle-fed baby Janet Elizabeth, who had arrived earlier than expected.

Betty sat on the window seat, gazing out over the garden, having refused to stay in bed any longer. 'I should be doing that! I feel a failure as it is, not being able to breast feed her.'

'Don't be daft!' said Irene. 'It's not your fault your milk failed to come in and anyway you're paying me to look after Janet.'

'A few dribbles, that's all I was able to give her,' mourned Betty, pushing back a handful of ginger hair.

'Just be glad that there are good dried milk powder substitutes these days,' said Irene. 'And those "few dribbles" as you call them will have done her good. You ate and drank healthily during your pregnancy, so you did your best for her and yourself. Your teeth are still all right, aren't they?'

'Yes.'

'Well, there you are then, all that milk you drank saved the baby from using up all your calcium to build her bones.'

'I never looked at it like that,' said Betty, her expression brightening. She rose from the window seat. 'I think I'll go and see if the morning paper and my magazine have come and if there's any mail.'

'Take it easy,' said Irene, hoping there would some letters for her. There were times when she really missed her mother, Jimmy and her friends, as well as the children from Fair Haven.

As for Marty, she often yearned for him, wondering if he still thought about her. Maybe when he had read the postcard she had sent with its mention of Harry, he had considered her fickle. Had she done the right thing giving *The Cat in the Hat* to Bobby for Josie? But as soon as she had seen it in the bookstore window, she had known both Marty and Josie would enjoy it. What would he think when Bobby handed it over to him? Although maybe she would give it to Bernie? Irene hoped not, convinced she wouldn't appreciate it.

She sighed, telling herself that she had been right to come to this house in the Willow Glen neighbourhood of San Jose. It was an interesting place to walk around, alive with individual, architecturally designed houses and tree-lined streets. So much to do and see and yet she couldn't forget Marty, especially as the attraction she felt for him could so easily have grown into something deep and satisfying. She thought about the way he haunted her dreams and she relived that kiss they had shared. Sometimes in that period between sleeping and waking, they weren't in the house in Litherland but on a beach, leaving messages in the sand. He would wrap his arms around her and kiss her passionately. When that happened, she longed for the dreaming to be reality but it was just an impossible dream, since he was a married man.

Irene eased the teat from the baby's mouth and gently winded her. She told herself that she would be better off, fixing her thoughts on Harry, who seemed to think nothing of driving thousands of miles across this vast state of California, living as he was over two thousand miles away in Hollywood. He was amusing and seemed to have taken a shine to her. He had driven her to the beach at Santa Cruz thirty miles away and had kissed her once or twice but those kisses did not have the power to stir her the way Marty's had done. Anyway, Harry was bound to meet someone much more exciting and attractive than her on a film set sooner or later, and deep down inside, she guessed that his first love was writing.

She placed the baby in her cradle, which was one of those fancy ones with rockers and a flower sprigged cotton and lace-edged canopy. She left her charge and went to deal with nappies and to wash and sterilize the bottle and teat in Milton solution.

A short while later, Betty came into the small washroom next to the nursery. 'There's mail for you.'

Irene dried her hands and picked up the airmail envelopes and looked at the first one with its Liverpool postmark. 'This is from our Jimmy! I recognize his handwriting. He must be back from New Zealand.'

'And the other two?' asked Betty, sitting on a chair, only to get up again. 'Let's go into the nursery. This chair's too hard for me.'

Betty smiled down at her daughter as she passed her cradle and then sat on the cushioned window seat. Irene sat beside her. 'I don't recognize the handwriting on the other two,' she murmured.

'So which one are you opening first?'

'I'll save our Jimmy's 'til last.'

Irene slit open one of the other envelopes and removed a single sheet of thin airmail paper. It did not take her long to read because it was short and to the point.

Dear Irene,

I just want to thank you for the book you sent for Josie. I've already read it twice to her and Jerry and we all enjoyed it. Maybe it won't be long before we see you back in Liverpool and we can thank you in person.

Yours, Marty

Her heart was beating fast as she read it again and then she folded it and returned it to its envelope and placed it in the pocket of her apron.

'Who's it from?' asked Betty, glancing sidelong at her.

'It's a thank you note from Marty, for the book I sent for his little girl.'

'Now that shows he has some good manners,' said Betty. 'Pity he's married.'

Irene opened the second envelope and this time it took her longer to read the letter. Her hands were trembling by the time she finished.

'Well?' asked Betty. 'What's it say? You look upset.'

Irene did not immediately reply but instead slit open her brother's letter and read it swiftly. Then she stood up and hurried from the room, went downstairs and outside. She sank on to the swing seat beneath the ripening fruit of the orange and lemon trees and gazed through her tears towards the vegetable patch where tomatoes and cour-gettes would soon be ready to pick. She did not want to believe what was written in the other two letters. Her mother had always seemed so strong and yet ... hadn't Irene always worried about that cough of hers? But how could she have become so ill so soon when she had been married such a short time? What was Alfred feeling right now, and his children? How could they possibly take care of her? Irene could guess why Maisie hadn't even hinted that she was seriously ill in her occasional short letters. No doubt she didn't want to worry Irene with her being so far away. What was she to do? Betty had only just had her baby and needed her help!

'What is it? What's wrong?' Betty stared down at Irene.

Irene kept her head lowered. 'It's nothing for you to worry about.'

'Don't lie to me!' said Betty firmly, lowering her-self carefully on to the swing seat. 'There's some-thing seriously wrong, isn't there?' She placed a hand on Irene's knee. 'Is it your mother?'

Irene's head shot up. 'How did you know?'

Betty sighed. 'Just a guess. I can't see there

being anything wrong with Jimmy and you were upset before you opened his letter. Whatever he wrote just made you worse.'

Irene's chin wobbled. 'Mam's very ill. Pete's mother has been visiting her and the first letter was from her.' Irene paused to gain control of herself and took a deep breath. 'Both say I should go home.'

'How long do they say she has?'

Tears rolled down Irene's cheeks. 'They say I shouldn't waste any time. I can't believe this should have happened so quickly.'

Betty squared her shoulders. 'You have to go.'

'But ... but what about Janet?'

'I'll just have to manage, won't I?' said Betty, smiling wryly. 'I'll phone Stuart at the office. Hopefully he's there and not on some building site.'

Irene was amazed at how quickly Stuart arranged everything. She was to fly from San Francisco airport to New York where she would get a flight to London. 'You'll have to make your own arrangements from there on,' said Betty.

Irene protested that she did not have the money to fly home but Betty only hugged her and said, 'What's money between friends?'

'I'll pay you back,' said Irene, resting her head on her friend's shoulder for a moment.

Betty patted her back and called her husband to take Irene to the airport.

Irene was exhausted by the time she stepped down from the train in Lime Street station. She had telephoned the Gianellis' house from London asking to speak to Jimmy. He had told her he would meet her under the clock in the station. She arrived there first and stood thinking about the other news that Pete's mother had told her in her letter. It was obvious that she was bubbling over with joy at the news that Pete and Peggy were going to get married and would be living with her.

She felt a tap on her shoulder and turned and saw her brother standing there. Not normally given to shows of physical affection, this time they hugged each other.

'What news is there?' she asked, as he picked up her suitcase. 'How's Mam?'

'Let's talk on the way. I thought we'd take a taxi,' said Jimmy, looking grim. 'You couldn't have come to Liverpool at a worse time. We've been experiencing gales and there's been piles of slates blown off roofs.'

'What about Mam?'

'I've some good news,' he said hastily. 'Jean-ette's had a baby boy. They're calling him George David.'

'Are they both all right?'

Jimmy nodded. 'And Pete and Peggy are get-ting married at last.' He came to a stop at the end of a taxi queue.

'I know that. His mother wrote to me. Now tell me – have you seen Mam since I phoned you from London?'

He nodded, but instead of telling her how Maisie was, he said, 'Peggy's sister's getting married today. Marty's giving his sister away and little Josie is a bridesmaid. I see something of him since he moved his family into our house. His wife won't be at the wedding because she only recently came out of hospital after the accident.'

The queue shifted up.

Irene just knew her brother wanted her to ask about the accident but she wasn't going to play his game. She was getting really impatient, scared and annoyed with him. 'Will you stop beating about the bush and tell me about Mam?' she said firmly.

He stared at her and moistened his lips. 'I'm sorry, our kid. She's dead.'

'Dead?' Irene felt as if everything was spinning around her and she staggered.

Jimmy steadied her. 'I was dreading telling you.'

'When?' asked Irene hoarsely.

'Shortly after you phoned. She was already in hospital. Alf had told the doctor he couldn't look after her.' Jimmy's voice broke. 'She ... she caught pneumonia an-and that was it!'

Irene fumbled in her handbag for a handkerchief. 'I can't believe it,' she whispered. 'I flew here thinking I could look after her. Why couldn't I have been told earlier that Mam was so ill?'

'She didn't tell me! If she had, I'd have let you know straight away,' said Jimmy earnestly.

'We should never have gone away,' said Irene, her voice shaking, scarcely aware that people were looking at them and they were now first in the queue.

Jimmy put an arm around her. 'Here's a taxi.'

She allowed him to help her into the back of the vehicle, tears rolling down her cheeks. She stared out of the window, a handkerchief clutched in her hand as the taxi drove out on to Lord Nelson

Street. Everything seemed brighter than usual, larger than life. A man and a woman and a child were standing on the edge of the pavement as the taxi turned the corner into one of the streets that led to London Road. With part of her mind, Irene noticed he was carrying a couple of suit-cases. Suddenly she realized the man was Peggy's brother, Tommy.

'Did you see who that was?' asked Irene.

Jimmy looked at her. 'Where?'

She waved a hand. 'Forget it. They've gone now.'

He leaned back and closed his eyes. 'I had a helluva night. It'll probably be best if we try and see Mam tomorrow. She could still be in the hospital morgue and you don't want to be going there.'

Irene agreed. She was still trying to come to terms with flying all the way to England, only to arrive too late to see her mother alive. 'Do ... do you think he'll have M-Mam taken back to his house?'

'I don't know. He said something that makes me wonder whether he'll have her taken straight to the funeral parlour and leave her there.'

'What was it?' she asked.

'It wasn't that long since his first wife died and he thinks it'll be traumatic for the children to have a coffin in the house. I can see his point.'

Irene took a deep breath and nodded. 'What can we do? We no longer have a home of our own.'

He sighed.

They both fell silent and did not speak for a while.

Then Irene glanced out of the window and

337

realized they were travelling along Stanley Road. 'Where are we going?'

'Nellie Gianelli told me to bring you back to her house.'

'I can't impose on her!' cried Irene, sitting bolt upright. 'She has enough people to look after without having me there, as well.'

'Don't worry about it. She'll find you somewhere to bunk down,' said Jimmy.

Irene groaned but she could not come up with an alternative. She did find herself wondering about Nellie's niece, Lucia, and what she thought of Jimmy staying at her aunt's house. As they were travelling through Bootle, she said, 'Does Pete's mother know Mam's gone?'

Jimmy glanced at her. 'I haven't told her.'

'Would Alf let her know?' asked Irene. Jimmy shrugged. 'Look, why don't we call there now?' she suggested. 'Gertie might be in.' Irene glanced at the taxi driver and said to her brother, 'We could walk from here.'

Jimmy hesitated. 'What about your suitcase?'

'Come on!' said Irene. 'You're not a seven-stone weakling, are you? If you can't carry it, I will. Besides, I could do with stretching my legs.'

Soon they were knocking at Gertie Marshall's door. There came hurrying footsteps along the lobby and the door opened and she stood there, gazing up at them.

'You came,' she said, reaching out for Irene.

Irene allowed herself to be almost smothered by Gertie's embrace and managed not to burst into tears. 'She's gone,' she croaked.

'I'm so sorry, love,' said Gertie, her eyes moist.

She patted Irene's back. 'Come in, both of you.'

An hour later, they were sitting in front of the fire, drinking tea and eating hot buttered toast. Irene could feel her spirits lifting. Once they had poured out their concerns about Alf and about their mother's funeral, Gertie told them to stop worrying. She would suggest to him that Maisie's body be brought back to her house and she and Irene could keep vigil the night before the funeral. After all, they had known her a lot longer than Alf had done. Irene felt a load fall from her shoulders. Gertie also soon had her and Jimmy laughing as she told them tales about what their mother had got up to in the sausage factory and on their outings together.

It was during one such story that they heard the front door open and voices in the lobby. Gertie stood up. 'That sounds like our Pete and Peggy back from her sister's wedding.'

The next moment, the couple came into the kitchen and everyone spoke at once until Pete brought about some semblance of order. Gertie went and made a fresh pot of tea, leaving the younger ones to talk. They soon broke into twos. Pete and Jimmy, and Peggy and Irene.

Commiserations and congratulations were given. Irene wiped away her tears and asked the question to which she had only Gertie's garbled account in her letter. How had Pete and Peggy got together again?

'Hasn't Jimmy told you about the accident?' said Peggy.

'He was going to tell me but—'

'I know,' said Peggy. 'You were distracted.'

339

'Tell me now,' Irene murmured.

Peggy nodded. 'But don't interrupt me with questions. Otherwise I'm bound to miss something out.' Irene agreed, and so Peggy told her all about the accident in Blackpool and everything that had happened in its aftermath.

Irene opened her mouth several times to butt in, only to remember what Peggy said, so kept quiet and waited until her friend had finished. Then Irene said with a hint of excitement, 'I saw Tommy earlier as the taxi was turning into that street at the back of the Empire. I recognized him from the photograph Marty gave me. He was with a woman and a little boy.'

Peggy's eyes widened. 'What did she look like?'

'I got the impression she was quite buxom but she was wearing a tent coat so that could have made her look fatter.'

'What colour was her hair?

'She was wearing a headscarf,' replied Irene. 'As for the little boy, I didn't have time to get a proper look at him. Tommy was carrying a couple of suitcases. They were probably going to catch a train.'

Peggy said, 'We haven't seen sight nor sound of Tommy since Blackpool. I can't wait to tell Marty what you've just told me.'

Soon after, Peter said he would give Jimmy and Irene a lift to the Gianellis' as he would be dropping Peggy back at Marty's.

On the way out, Gertie said, 'If it's a bit crowded at the Gianellis' house, Irene, you can always come and stay here until you decide what you're going to do.'

340

Irene was glad of the offer and accepted it, saying that she would see her in the morning. It was decided to leave her suitcase where it was after taking a few items of clothing from it. There was no way she was going to admit that she was hoping to catch a glimpse of Marty when they dropped off Peggy.

Marty was standing on the front step talking to his next-door neighbour when Pete's car drew up at the kerb. He instantly excused himself and hurried towards the car as Peggy climbed out.

'Bernie and Jerry aren't here,' he blurted out. 'The lad next door saw her leaving with him by the back way. She was carrying a suitcase. Father Francis—'

'Now there's a coincidence,' said Peggy, her eyes glinting. 'Irene was telling me something very interesting at Pete's mam's.' She turned back towards the car. 'Irene, come on out and tell Marty who you saw by Lime Street station!'

Irene's heart was thudding as she stepped out of the car. She gazed across the roof at Marty and wanted to reach out and take his hand and hold it tightly. 'I saw your brother. He was with a woman and a little boy and was carrying two suitcases.'

For several moments Marty could only stare at her and then he said, 'That figures. Do you mind coming inside, Irene?'

She glanced through the car window at Jimmy. 'You go with him,' he said, getting out. 'I'll walk to the Gianellis' from here.'

Irene looked at Marty. 'What does it all mean? When you said "it figures", you had something in mind. You mentioned Father Francis...'

'Let's get inside,' he said, leading the way.

She followed him and it wasn't until they sat down in the kitchen, opposite each other, that he said, 'I don't know how much you know.'

'Peggy told me about the accident.'

'Did she tell you that Bernie didn't recognize me as her husband and insisted that Tommy was the name of her husband?' he said, going straight to the point.

'Yes, I thought it ... odd to say the least. How could she appear not to recognize you as her husband but remember her husband's name was Tommy?' said Irene. 'What did the doctors and nurses think?'

'After being told memory is a strange thing and you can never tell with head injuries several times, I didn't bother them with any more questions,' said Marty. 'As it is I had a talk with Father Francis at Lil's wedding and...'

'I like Father Francis,' said Pete, who had followed them in.

'Me too" said Irene, having met the priest several times at the Gianellis' over the years. 'But what has he to do with this?'

'He saw a lot of head injuries during the Blitz and so Bernie's case interested him enough for him to question, like we did, her behaviour and why she was so insistent that Tommy was her husband.'

'And what conclusion did he come to?' asked Pete.

'That it needed looking into and I agreed,' said Marty. 'He offered to search through the diocesan marriage records just before Tommy vanished.'

342

'You mean... But surely if they...' Irene's mouth went suddenly dry, just thinking of the implications if Tommy and Bernie had married without letting their families know about it.

'If they'd married in the parish church, Father Francis would have known about it,' said Peggy swiftly. 'And if they married somewhere else they'd have had to live in a parish for three months beforehand.'

'Tommy was living with a mate outside Father Francis's parish after he left home, remember?' said Marty, his expression grim.

'Yes, but Bernie has never moved out of her mother's house, has she?' said Peggy.

'A registry office wedding?' suggested Pete.

The other three shook their heads.

Silence.

'I'll go and make some cocoa,' said Peggy, getting up and going into the back kitchen.

'I have another suggestion,' said Pete, staring at Marty, 'and don't immediately shoot me down this time.'

Marty smiled faintly. 'Go on, what is it?'

'My brother, the policeman, often says how dishonest people are. Such as someone saying they live at a certain address when they don't. Or at least they just stay there the odd night so if a neighbour was asked if they had seen them going in and out of the house, then they can honestly answer that they had.'

'Would the house be unoccupied otherwise?' asked Irene, thinking the evening had taken on an unreal quality.

'Not necessarily. Just like Tommy, they could be

staying with a friend,' said Pete. 'Surely Bernie had a best friend at the time?'

'Marie Gallagher,' said Peggy, who was standing in the doorway with a tin of cocoa in her hand. 'They worked together and if I'm not mistaken they were in the same class at school. They're still friends. She used to live in St Anthony's parish a few years ago. Then she moved to Crosby. Bernie could have gone along regularly to church with Marie so the priest got used to her going there and believed that's where she lived when she came to fill in the Application for Marriage form. She'd be over twenty-one, so she wouldn't need her mother's permission and there's no doubt about her being able to produce proof that she was baptized and confirmed in the Catholic church. Same with Tommy.'

'Maybe you should suggest to Father Francis that he starts there?' said Pete.

Irene could not resist staring at Marty to see what he made of that suggestion. Her heart was thudding inside her chest.

Marty nodded. 'Although, what I can't get my head around is if they cared for each other so much, why didn't he get in touch with her after he went missing? I can understand why they married in secret. Her mother would have had a blue fit. She says he's a criminal and can't stand him. But how did they manage to arrange to make a run for it today? Bernie was flat on her back for six weeks and he had a broken arm. And since she came home, Peggy has been here most of the time and I've been here the rest.' He made no mention of believing now that Jerry was his brother's son.

'Easy enough to remove a sling and conceal the plaster by wearing something with long sleeves and go and visit her,' said Pete.

'When?' asked Marty, exasperated. 'Either me or one of her family took up the visiting hours.'

'Maybe he disguised himself as a doctor?' suggested Irene.

'Or even a nurse,' put in Peggy. 'You know how crafty he is.' She vanished inside the back kitchen again.

'She put on some act,' said Marty, his eyes glinting, 'and I don't only mean after the accident. Deceitful, conniving!'

'At least if it can be proved that they did get married before he vanished, you'll be rid of her,' said Pete.

'If they were to find them, they might arrest them both,' said Peggy, making an appearance again. 'Bernie for bigamy and Tommy for theft. Your marriage will be declared null and void, Marty.'

'Aye,' said Marty, gazing at Irene. 'And what does that make Josie?' he said, running a hand through his hair.

'I'm sure the Archbishop of Liverpool will have an answer to that,' said Peggy. 'The church seems to have an answer to everything. Now, who's for cocoa?'

When Irene was ready to leave, Marty said that he would walk with her to the Gianellis'. She did not demur, glad to have this time with him alone. As they made their way up to the bridge, she told him that her mother had died a few hours after she had arrived in England.

He said how sorry he was and then paused before saying, 'Does that mean you'll be returning to America after the funeral?'

The question took her by surprise and for a moment she could not think how to answer. After all that had been said back at his house, she had been hoping they would have something more to discuss. She had thought that had been the reason for him suggesting he accompany her to Nellie's.

'It's too soon for me to make plans yet,' she said. 'I hardly know which way is up. I'd like to spend some time with Jimmy and be here to see Pete and Peggy married at last.'

Marty took a deep breath. 'What about Harry in America?'

They had reached the bridge and she paused. 'What about him?'

'You sounded as if you were enjoying yourself with him,' he murmured, gazing down at the water.

She realized what he must be thinking and smiled. 'Who wouldn't enjoy themself being in a different country and seeing so many new sights? I like Harry but my heart's back here in England,' she said softly.

He raised his head and their eyes met. 'You know I can't make you any promises?' he said roughly.

'Yes, but there's always hope,' she said, going into his arms.

Twenty-Nine

Maisie's funeral went off without a hitch and although it was a sad occasion, there was enough laughter to ease Irene's grief as memories were shared over the meal afterwards. She was also deeply touched by the sympathy that her younger step-siblings showed her as well as that of Terence's son, Billy. It came as something of a surprise to discover that Maisie had left both Irene and Jimmy two hundred pounds each. This meant a lot to her because she was able to pay back the money she owed Betty and Stuart for her air ticket.

She wrote to them, pouring out on paper all that had happened since she had arrived in Liverpool and was able to inform them that Pete and Peggy's wedding was set for the thirteenth of December. Irene had been asked if she would like to be chief bridesmaid as Lil suspected she could be pregnant and preferred to remain in the background. Also, as Norm would be at sea on that date, he wouldn't be able to be Pete's best man, so Jimmy was to take on that role. She wrote that she could not thank Betty and Stuart enough for their friendship and hospitality and prayed that one day, not too far away, she would see them again. She made no mention of the possibility that Marty's marriage might be annulled.

She applied for a vacancy that had come up at

Litherland Nursery and was accepted for the post. In the meantime, while she looked forward to the forthcoming wedding, and for news of Father Francis's investigations, she stayed at Gertie's house in Bootle.

This meant she was *au fait* with all the wedding arrangements and was ideally situated to visit her brother at the Gianellis' or Billy's house in Formby. She enjoyed listening to the music group rehearse and, of course, she was able to spend time in Marty and Josie's company, especially as the little girl was now attending the nursery and Irene volunteered daily to take her home.

Sometimes Peggy was not at the house but helping Pete decorate the parlour that was to be their living room and the bedroom that was to be theirs. Gertie had suggested that they exchange rooms with her, so that the married couple could have the bigger front room that she had once shared with her husband. Peggy confessed to Irene that some of her worries about living with her future mother-in-law were being laid to rest. Especially as she was often out in the evenings, although she never said where she was going.

Marty had not heard anything from Tommy or Bernie and neither had her mother or sisters. The news that Bernie had run away with Tommy, taking Jerry with them, had stunned his mother, and Bernie's family. And the news that Bernie might just be a bigamist was very hard for Bernie's mother to swallow as she regarded it as a worse sin than that of adultery. Even their Lord had called upon the Pharisees to have pity on the adulteress in the Gospels, she stated, although she still did not have a good word to say about Tommy.

As for Marty's mother, she called Bernie a whore and recalled her dear, dead husband, having the measure of Bernie when he had said that she had tricked Marty into marriage. At least she had Peggy's wedding to look forward to, despite her daughter marrying a Protestant. But at least her future son-in-law had promised, this time, that their children would be brought up in the Catholic faith.

As Peggy's wedding approached and Liverpool was blanketed in fog, Bernie's mother had still not got over the shock. When the news was broken to her that her daughter was indeed a bigamist, and that the matter was now in the hands of the Archbishop and the police, the old woman fainted. Father Francis explained to Marty that it could be months before the annulment went through, especially as there were children involved, but he knew that Marty had every intention of marrying Irene as soon as he was legally able to do so.

In the meantime there was Peggy and Pete's wedding to look forward to. Whilst there were peace talks in sunny Cyprus, where terrorists had been waging war on British soldiers, the snow began to fall in Liverpool and the surrounding countryside three days before the big day.

A dismayed Peggy watched the fat fluffy snowflakes settling on the ground. She and Pete had decided to spend a few days motoring in the Lake District for their honeymoon, stopping at Blackpool on the way for their wedding night. The weather forecast was more snow and ice and the advice given was not to travel unless absolutely necessary.

'What are we going to do?' she asked Pete that evening as they put the finishing touches to their bedroom.

He drew her down on to the bed. 'I phoned the bed and breakfast in Ambleside as soon as it started snowing. Mrs Dwyer said there's no snow up there. Although if it did snow she told me it looks really magical.'

Peggy liked the idea of spending their honeymoon somewhere magical but getting there could be difficult. 'I don't know what to decide,' she said.

'Mam has given me my grandfather's camera. It's a Leica, one of the best cameras around. She said I'd be able to take some lovely photographs of the Lake District,' he said persuasively.

He glanced around the bedroom. 'The only other option is that we spend our honeymoon as well as our wedding night here.'

'With your mother and Irene in the house!' Peggy's mouth firmed. 'It's not what I'd call romantic.'

'Then let's play it by ear and see what happens. At least we're not like Irene and Marty, who could still have a long wait before they can be together.'

Peggy spent the next three days in a flurry of activity, having a final fitting for her wedding dress created by Lynne Walker. With the arrival of the snow, Lynne had offered her the loan of a white fur jacket from a box of old clothes in the attic that had belonged to her theatrical dresser grandmother.

Peggy accepted the offer but continued to pray as she listened to the forecast on the wireless which spoke of the snow moving south. She read in the *Echo* of cars crashing on icy roads in Liverpool and commuters having to leave buses stranded in the snow and walking home. On the Friday, a freezing fog blanketed Merseyside but, thank God, that evening, the wind blew lifting the fog, and the rain came down in torrents.

There might have only been a watery pale sun in the clouded sky the morning of her wedding day but Peggy's heart was singing as Marty cooked the breakfast and she roused Josie from her slumbers. As they both sat at the breakfast table with Marty, Peggy said, 'Isn't it a lovely morning.'

He smiled. 'There speaks a woman who's besotted. All the snow hasn't gone yet, you know?'

'But there isn't so much of it and you have to admit that it's slightly warmer,' said Peggy.

'When can I put on my new frock?' asked Josie.

Peggy looked at her niece, who no longer asked when Jerry and Mam were coming back. 'Soon.'

Within the hour, the florist had delivered the flowers and Irene had arrived. She hugged Marty because in her eyes he was already an unmarried man and then asked aunt and niece if they were ready to go to the hairdresser's.

Two hours later, Marty's mother and younger sister and her husband turned up. Then a trickle of other guests began to arrive. Marty dealt with them with the help of his mother and sister. While upstairs Irene dressed Josie in her peach bridesmaid frock before changing herself. Then she helped Peggy on with her bridal gown made of satin and lace, decorated here and there with sparkling crystals. Josie watched with shining

351

eyes as her Auntie Lil set a chaplet of artificial orange blossom and diamantés on Peggy's light brown hair, holding the veil in place.

Irene handed a bouquet of white and peach carnations and trailing maidenhead fern to Peggy. 'You look beautiful,' she said sincerely. 'All set to go and meet your Prince Charming?'

There came a knock at the bedroom door. 'The cars are here,' called Marty. 'Irene, you and Josie will have to come down.'

Irene opened the door and they smiled at each other. 'You look stunning,' he said. 'You suit peach.'

She laughed and kissed him. 'Wait until you see your sister.'

'Will I get another shock?' he said, returning her kiss and whispering in her ear, 'Our day will come.'

'Daddy, look at me! Am I stunning, too?' asked Josie.

He swung his daughter up into his arms. 'You're fantastic! Come on, Princess, time for everyone to see how lovely you look.'

Twenty minutes later there came another knock on the bedroom door. 'Are you ready, Peg?' asked Marty.

Peggy opened the door. 'Am I ever!' she said, smiling up at him. She linked her arm through her brother's. 'This is the day I've been waiting for!'

The publishers hope that this book has given you enjoyable reading. Large Print Books are especially designed to be as easy to see and hold as possible. If you wish a complete list of our books please ask at your local library or write directly to:

Magna Large Print Books
Magna House, Long Preston,
Skipton, North Yorkshire.
BD23 4ND

This Large Print Book for the partially sighted, who cannot read normal print, is published under the auspices of

THE ULVERSCROFT FOUNDATION